# ⌐CELLiES

## JOE FLOOD | DAVID STEWARD II

# CELLiES

**Created by**
**DAVID STEWARD II**

**Story and Art by**
**JOE FLOOD**

**Editor**
**AMANDA MEADOWS**

**Assistant Editor**
**AMANDA VERNON**

## ROAR

ISBN: 978-1-941302-95-8
LCCN: 2018954310

Cellies Vol. 2, published 2019, by The
Lion Forge, LLC. Copyright 2019 The
Lion Forge, LLC. Portions of this book
were previously published in Cellies Vol.
2, Issues 6-10. LIONFORGE™, ROAR™
and their associated distinctive designs,
as well as all characters featured in this
book and the distinctive names and
likenesses thereof, and all related indicia,
are trademarks of The Lion Forge, LLC. All
Rights Reserved. No similarity between
any of the names, characters, persons,
or institutions in this book with those of
any living or dead person or institution is
intended, and any such similarity which
may exist is purely coincidental. Printed
in China.

10 9 8 7 6 5 4 3 2 1

# CHAPTER 1

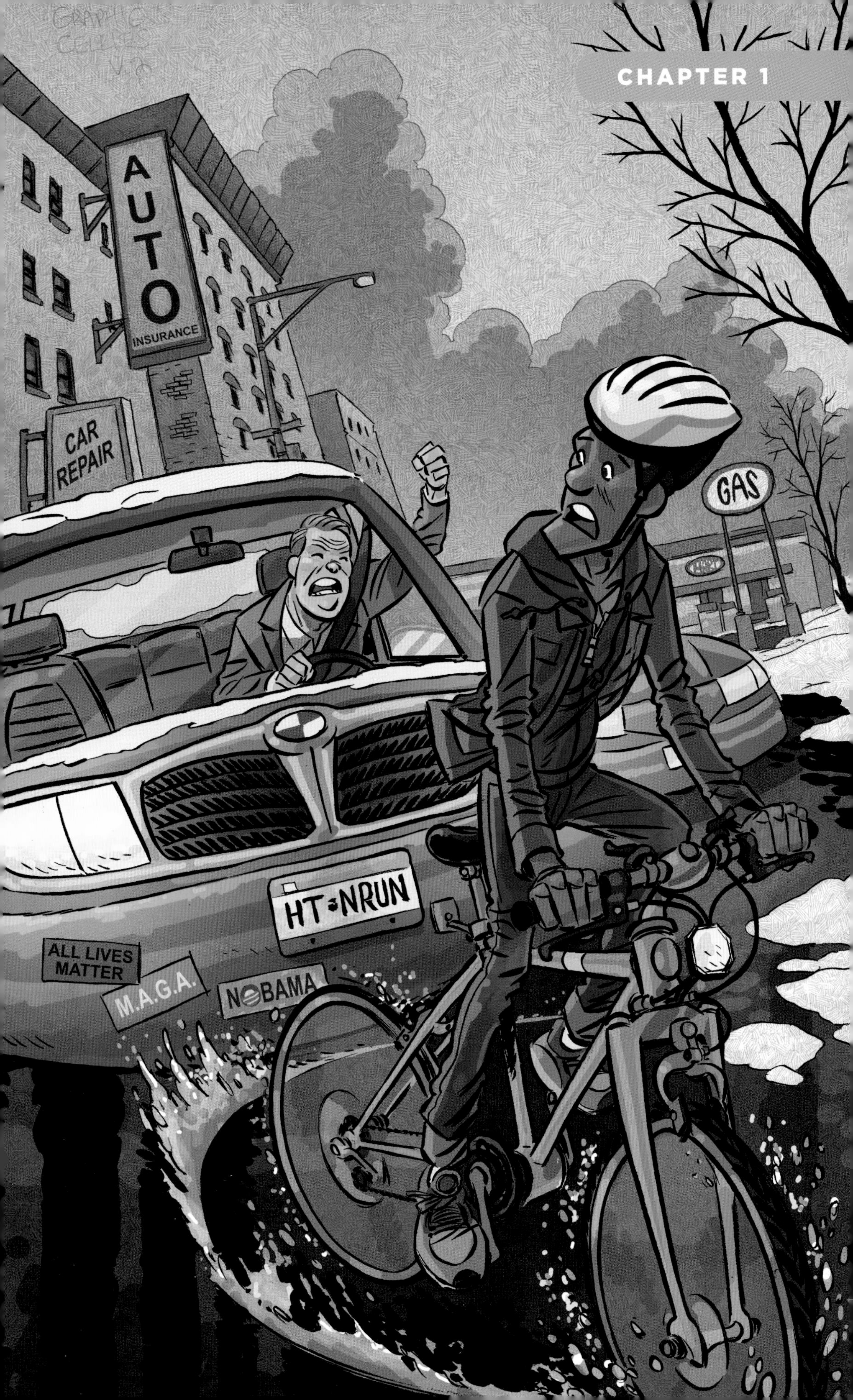
AUTO
INSURANCE
CAR REPAIR
GAS
HT NRUN
ALL LIVES MATTER
M.A.G.A.
NOBAMA

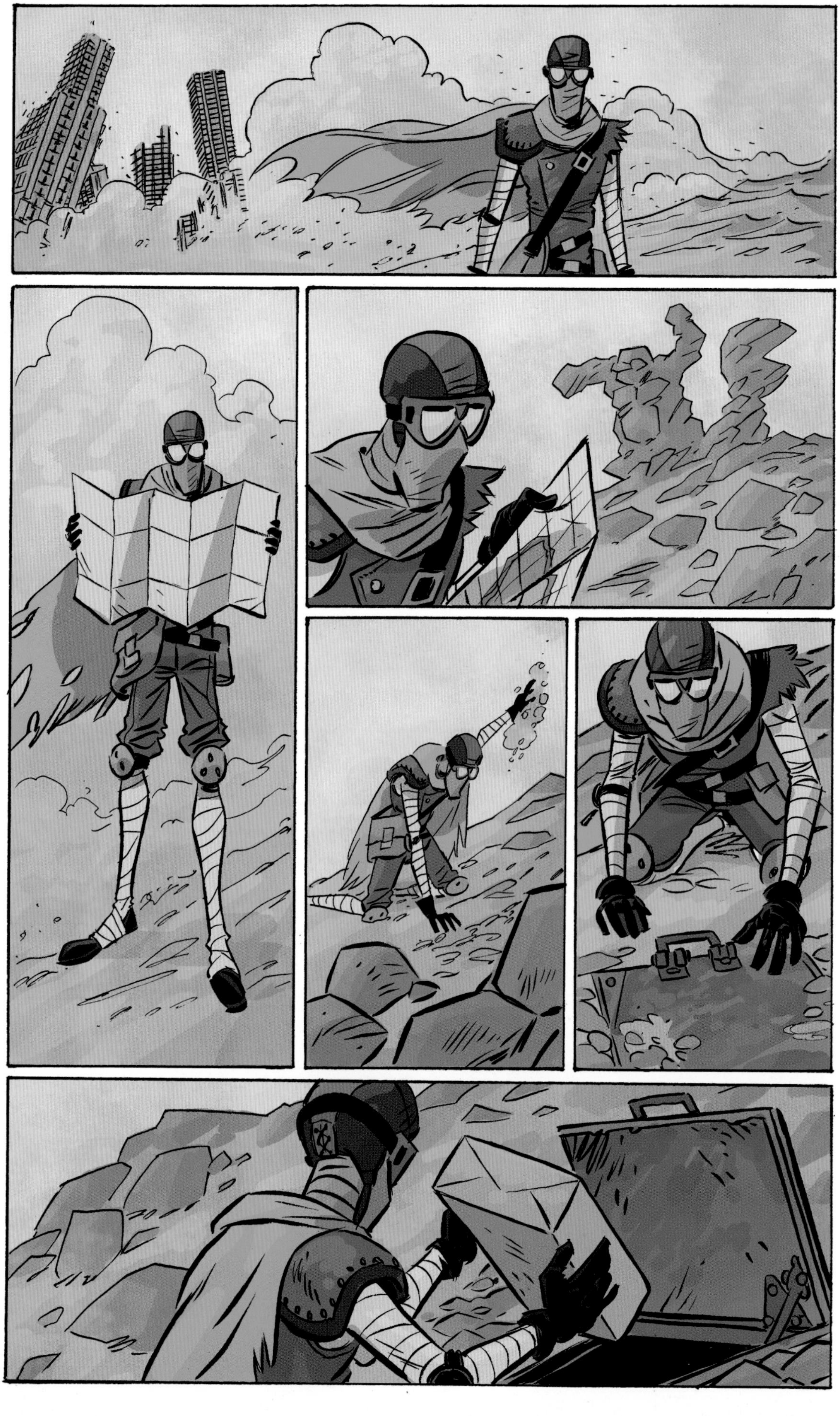

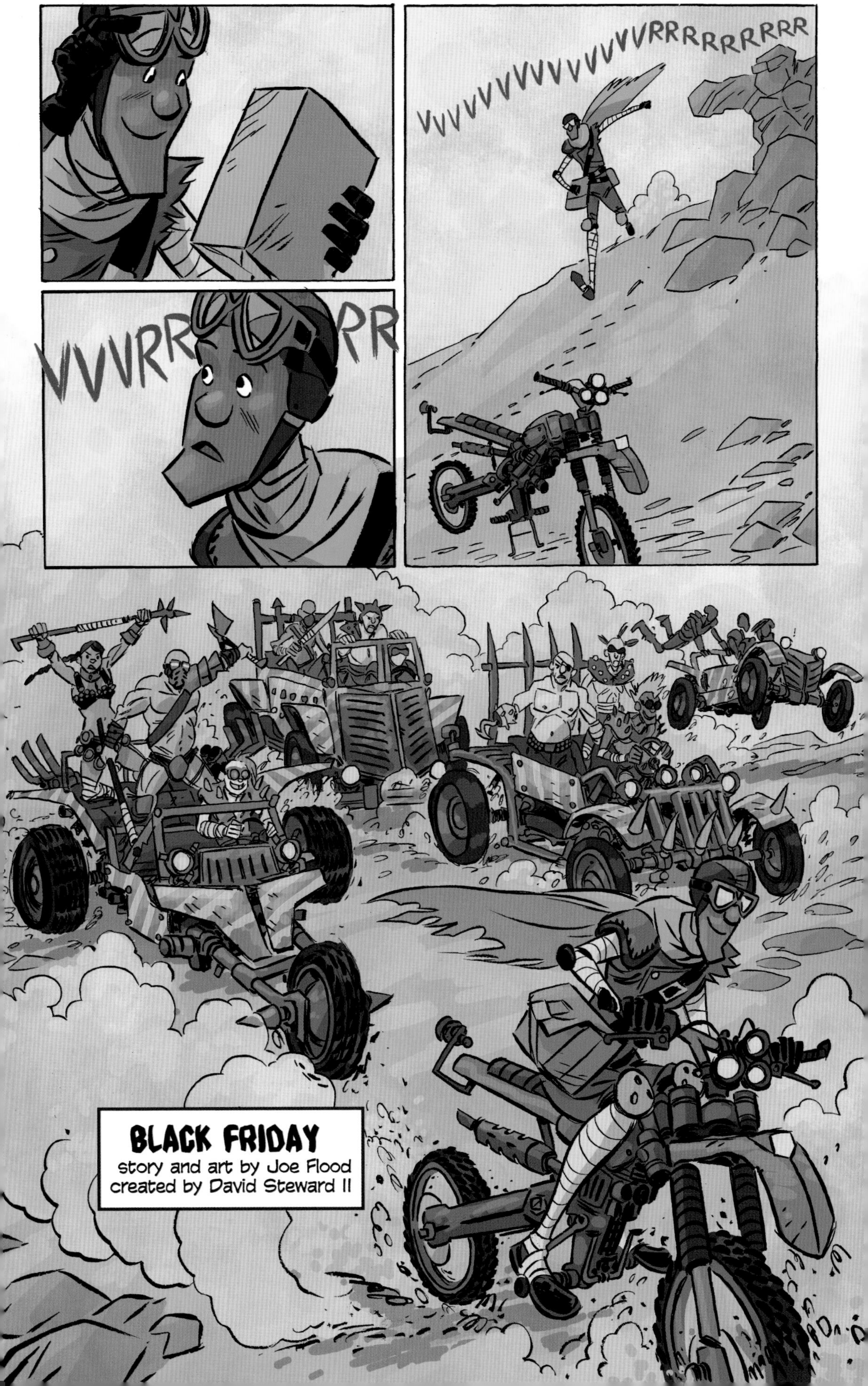
VVVRR RR
VVVVVVVVVVVVVVVVVRRRRRRRRRR
BLACK FRIDAY
story and art by Joe Flood
created by David Steward II

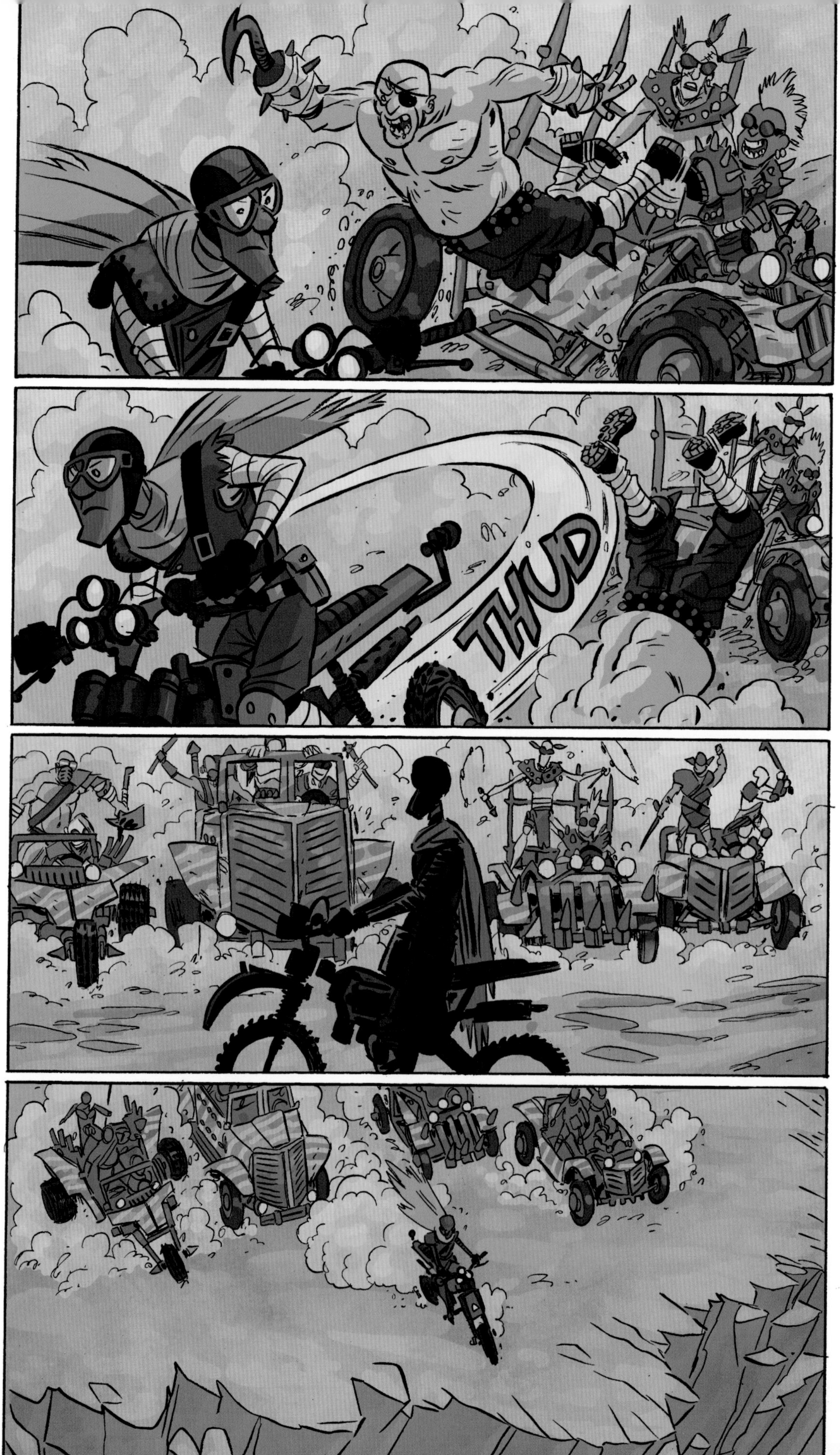
THUD

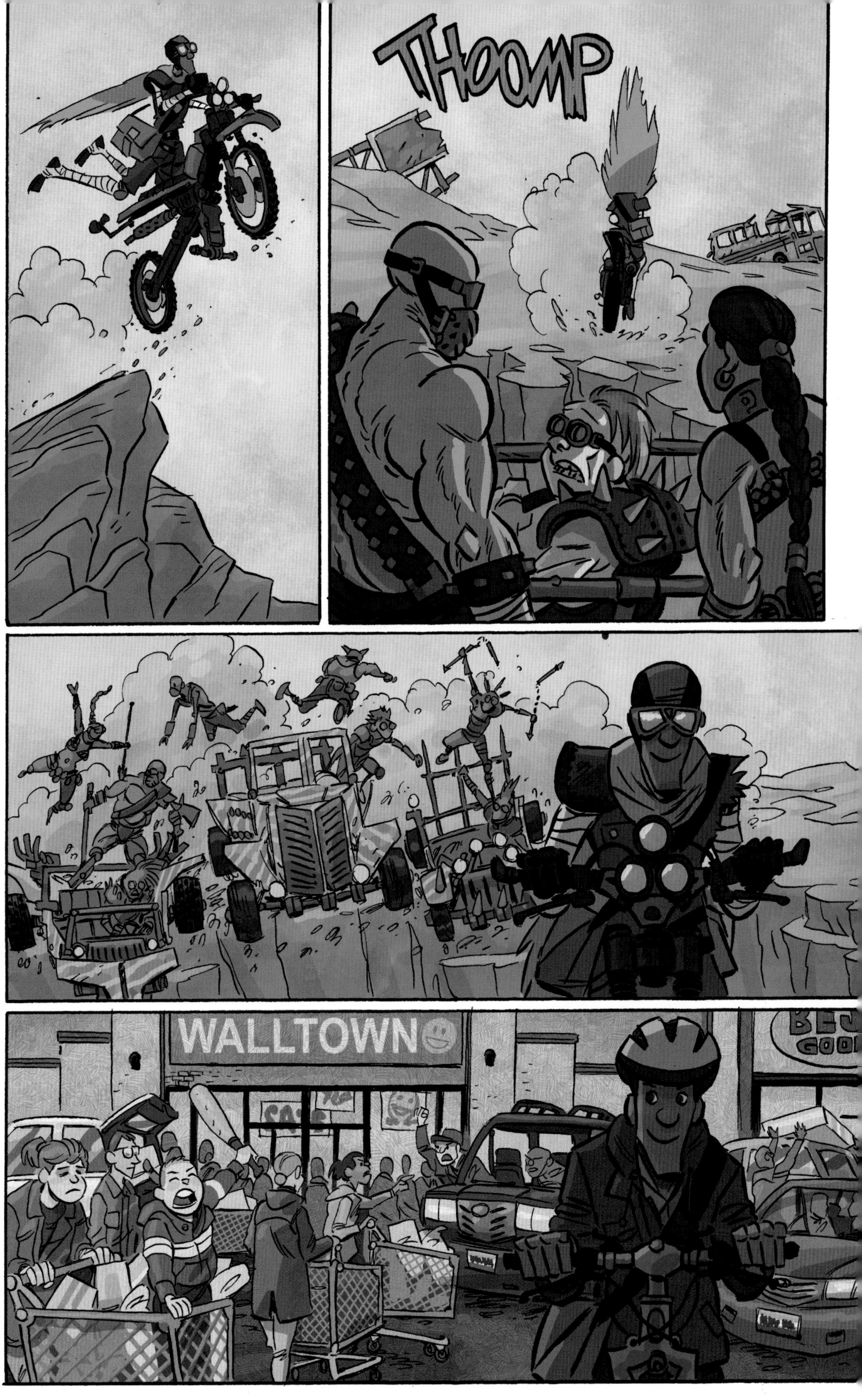
THOOMP
WALLTOWN

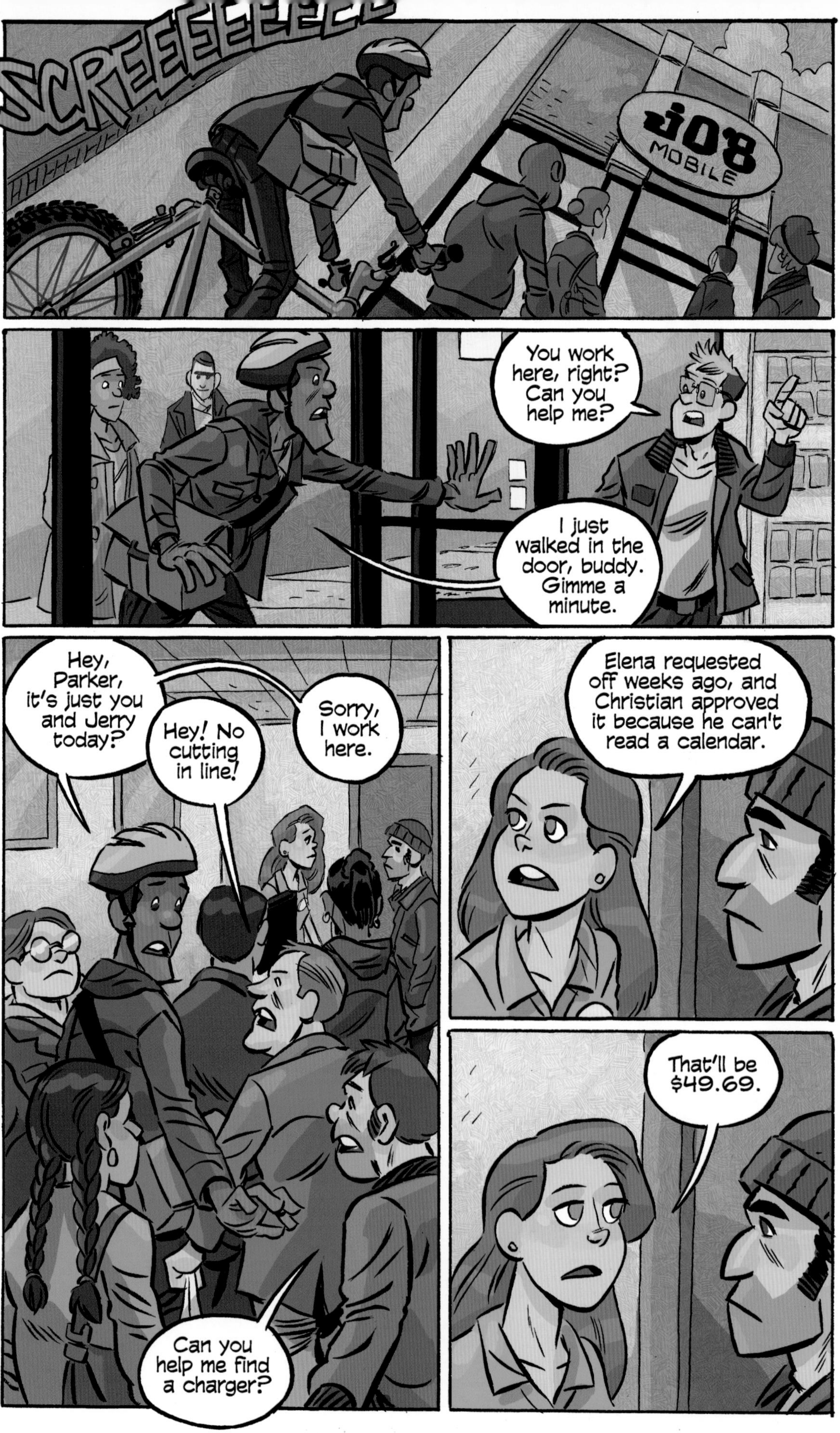
SCREEEEEEEE
JOB MOBILE
You work here, right? Can you help me?
I just walked in the door, buddy. Gimme a minute.
Hey, Parker, it's just you and Jerry today?
Hey! No cutting in line!
Sorry, I work here.
Can you help me find a charger?
Elena requested off weeks ago, and Christian approved it because he can't read a calendar.
That'll be $49.69.

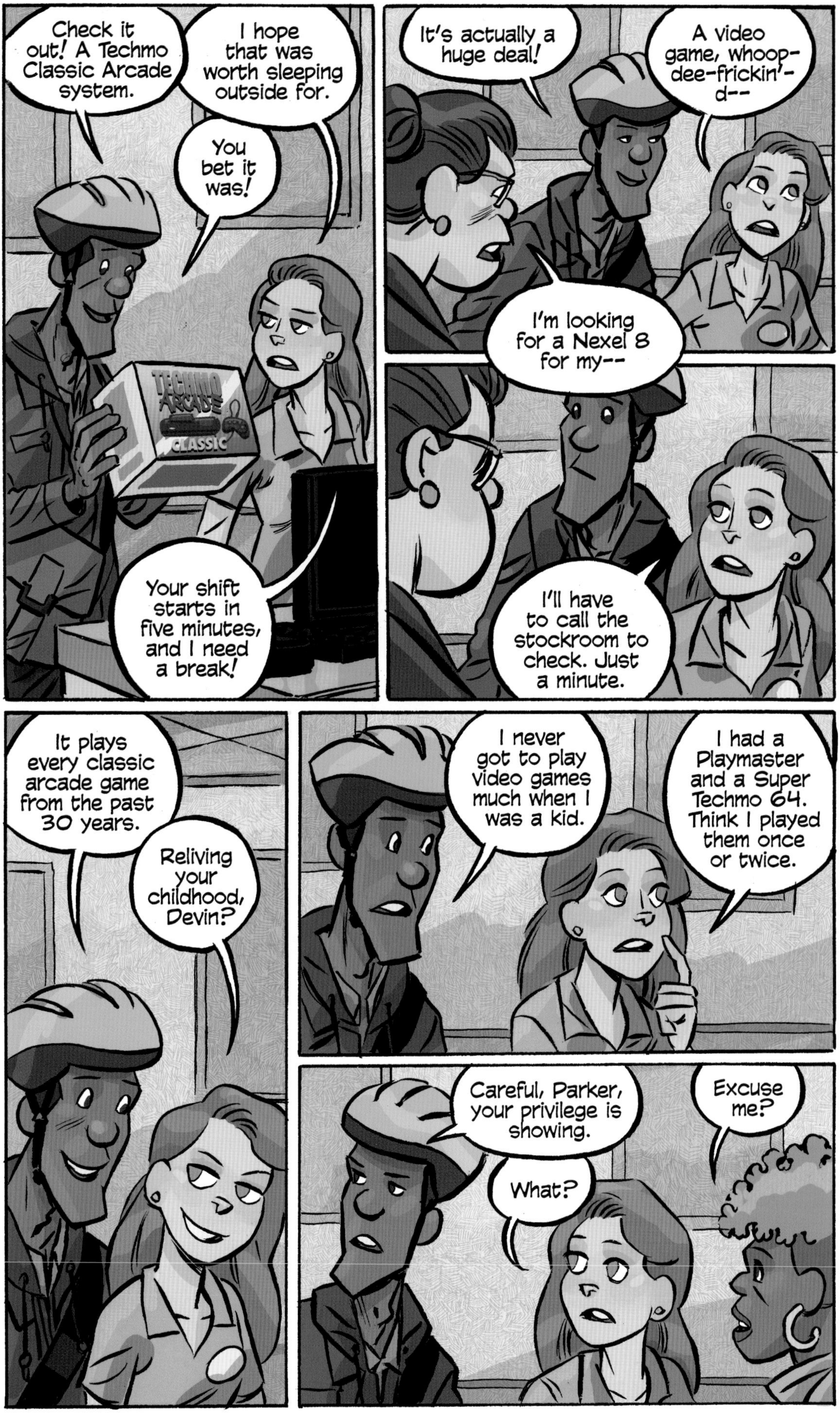
Check it out! A Techmo Classic Arcade system.
I hope that was worth sleeping outside for.
You bet it was!
TECHMO ARCADE CLASSIC
Your shift starts in five minutes, and I need a break!
It's actually a huge deal!
A video game, whoop-dee-frickin'-d--
I'm looking for a Nexel 8 for my--
I'll have to call the stockroom to check. Just a minute.
It plays every classic arcade game from the past 30 years.
Reliving your childhood, Devin?
I never got to play video games much when I was a kid.
I had a Playmaster and a Super Techmo 64. Think I played them once or twice.
Careful, Parker, your privilege is showing.
Excuse me?
What?

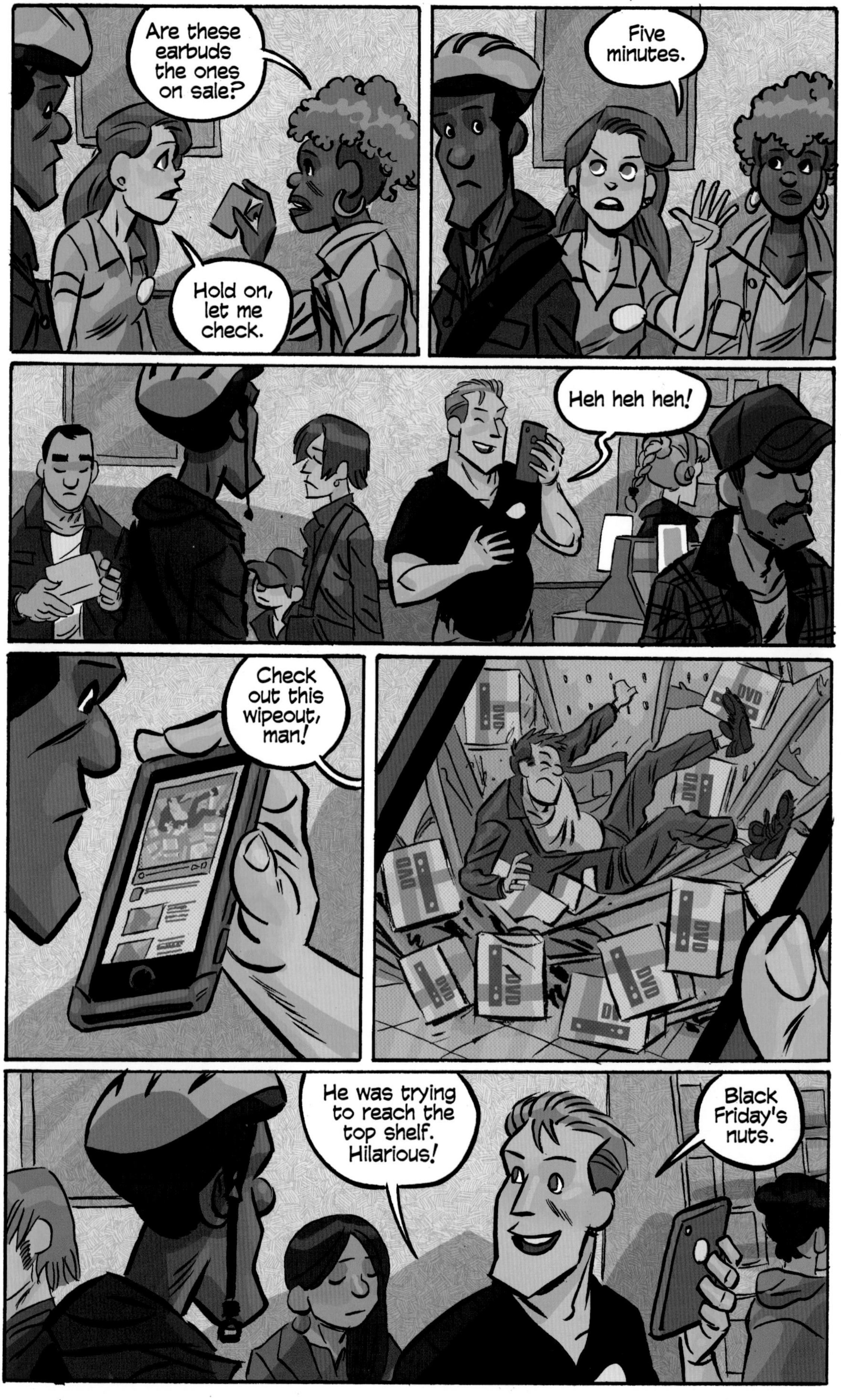

Are these earbuds the ones on sale?
Hold on, let me check.
Five minutes.
Heh heh heh!
Check out this wipeout, man!
DVD
He was trying to reach the top shelf. Hilarious!
Black Friday's nuts.

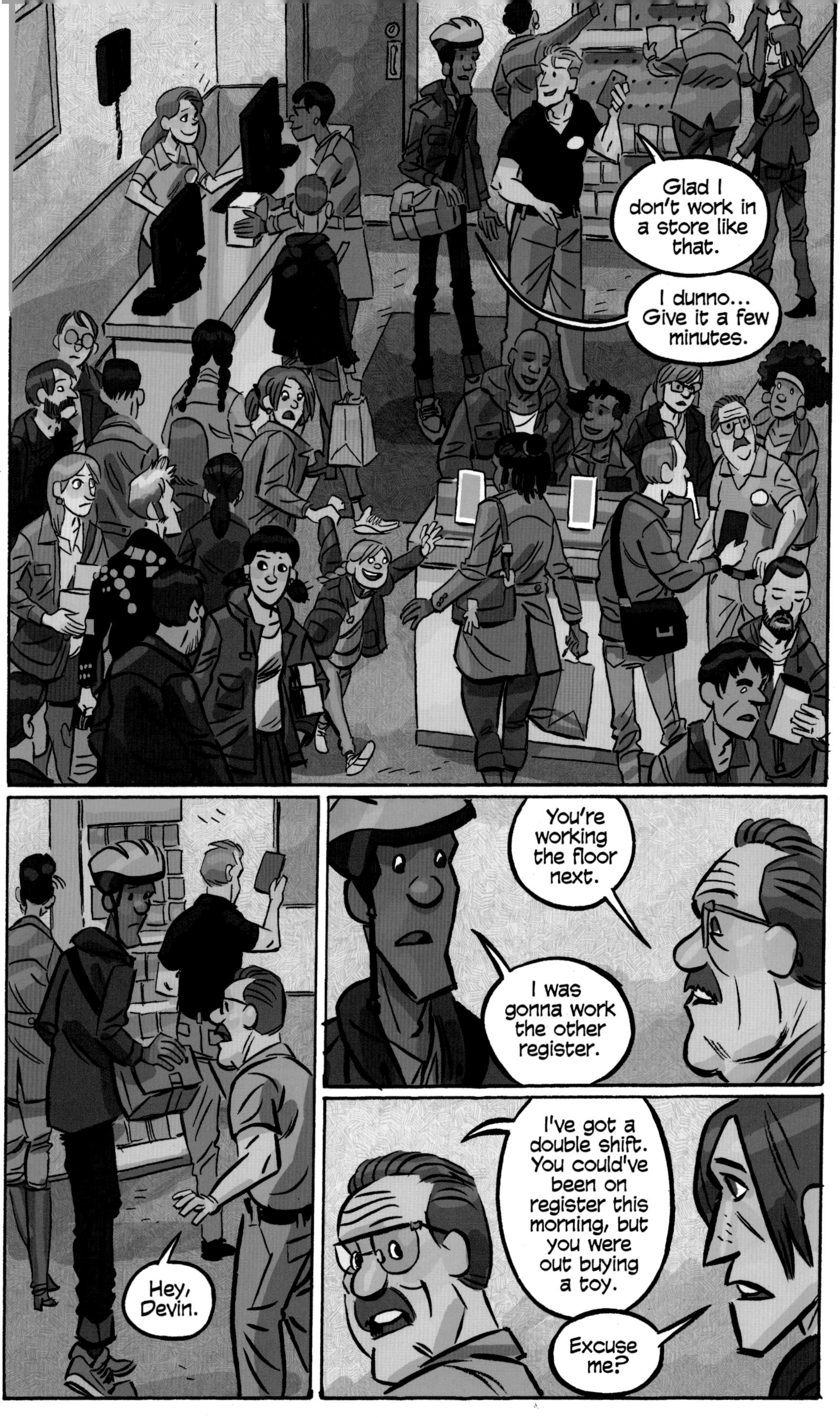
Glad I don't work in a store like that.
I dunno... Give it a few minutes.
Hey, Devin.
You're working the floor next.
I was gonna work the other register.
I've got a double shift. You could've been on register this morning, but you were out buying a toy.
Excuse me?

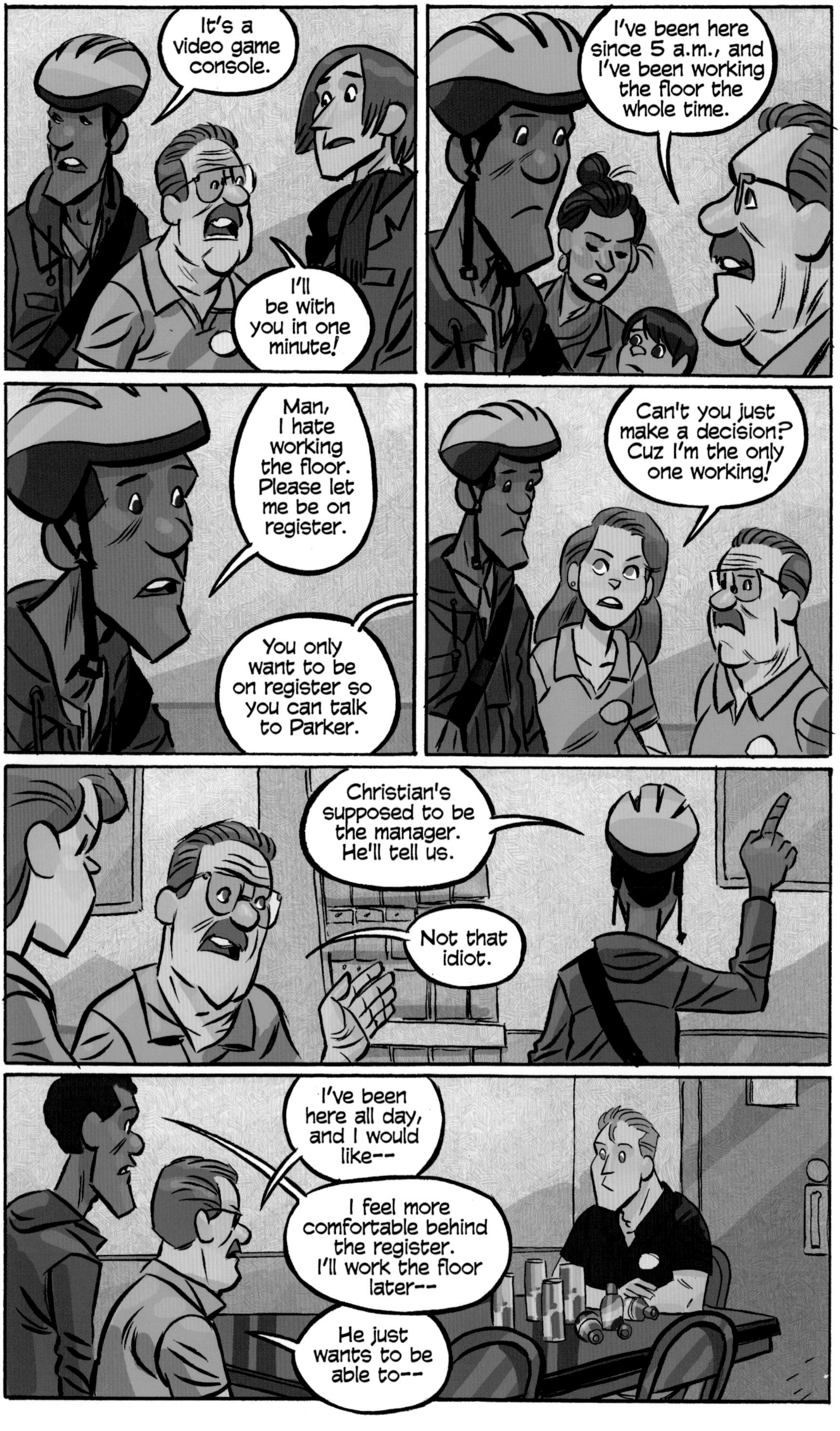
It's a video game console.
I'll be with you in one minute!
I've been here since 5 a.m., and I've been working the floor the whole time.
Man, I hate working the floor. Please let me be on register.
You only want to be on register so you can talk to Parker.
Can't you just make a decision? Cuz I'm the only one working!
Christian's supposed to be the manager. He'll tell us.
Not that idiot.
I've been here all day, and I would like--
I feel more comfortable behind the register. I'll work the floor later--
He just wants to be able to--

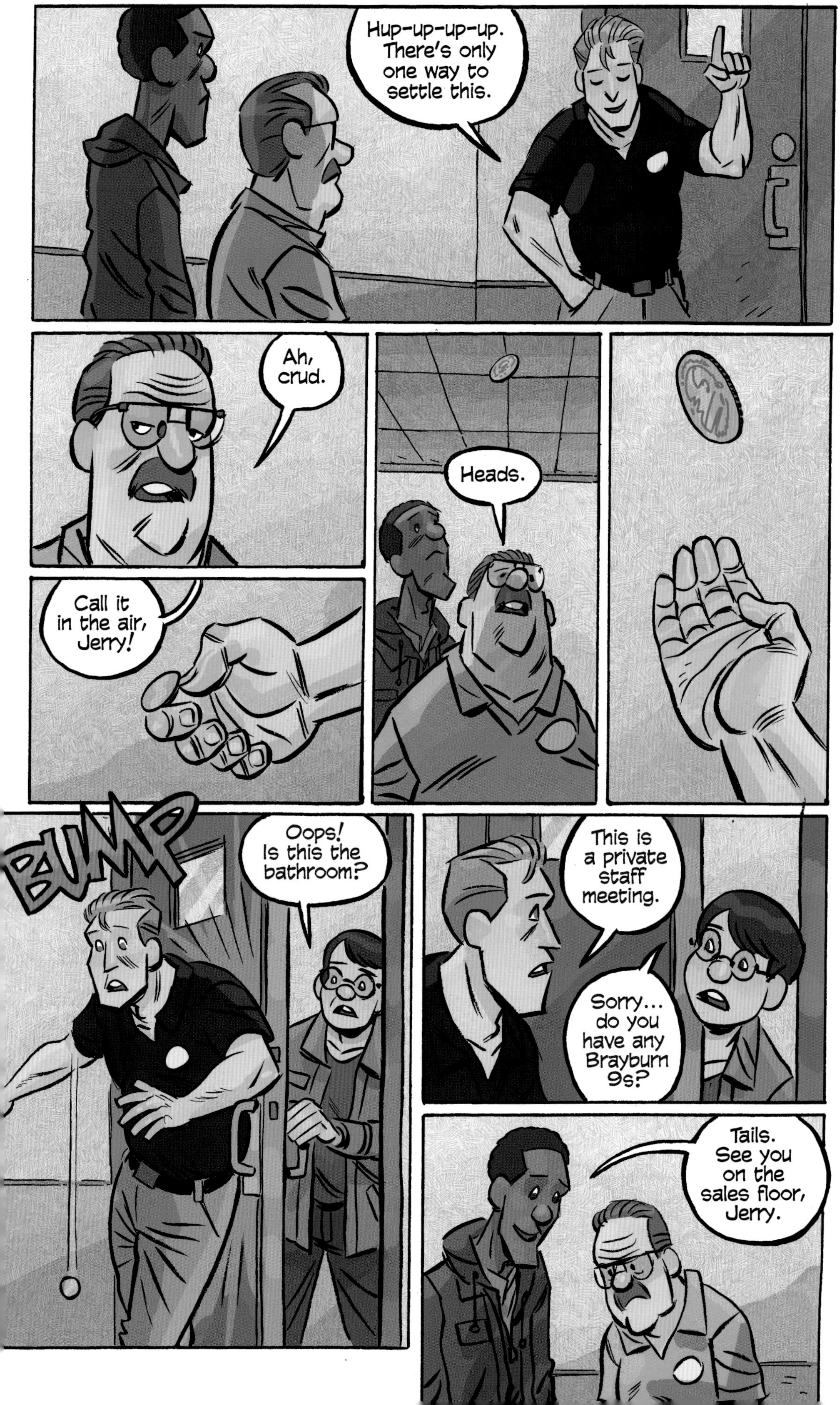
Hup-up-up-up. There's only one way to settle this.
Ah, crud.
Call it in the air, Jerry!
Heads.
BUMP
Oops! Is this the bathroom?
This is a private staff meeting.
Sorry... do you have any Brayburn 9s?
Tails. See you on the sales floor, Jerry.

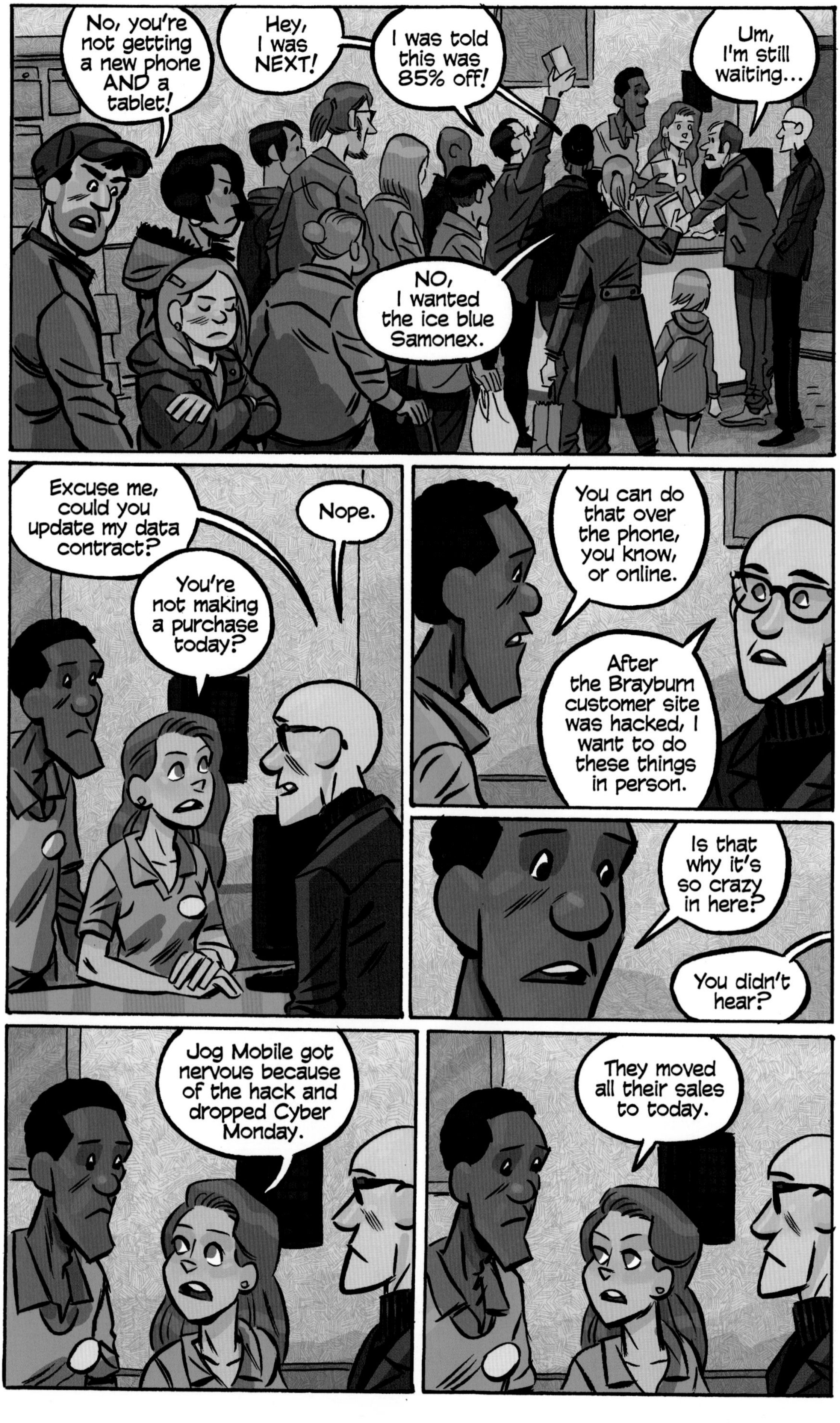
No, you're not getting a new phone AND a tablet!
Hey, I was NEXT!
I was told this was 85% off!
Um, I'm still waiting...
NO, I wanted the ice blue Samonex.
Excuse me, could you update my data contract?
Nope.
You're not making a purchase today?
You can do that over the phone, you know, or online.
After the Brayburn customer site was hacked, I want to do these things in person.
Is that why it's so crazy in here?
You didn't hear?
Jog Mobile got nervous because of the hack and dropped Cyber Monday.
They moved all their sales to today.

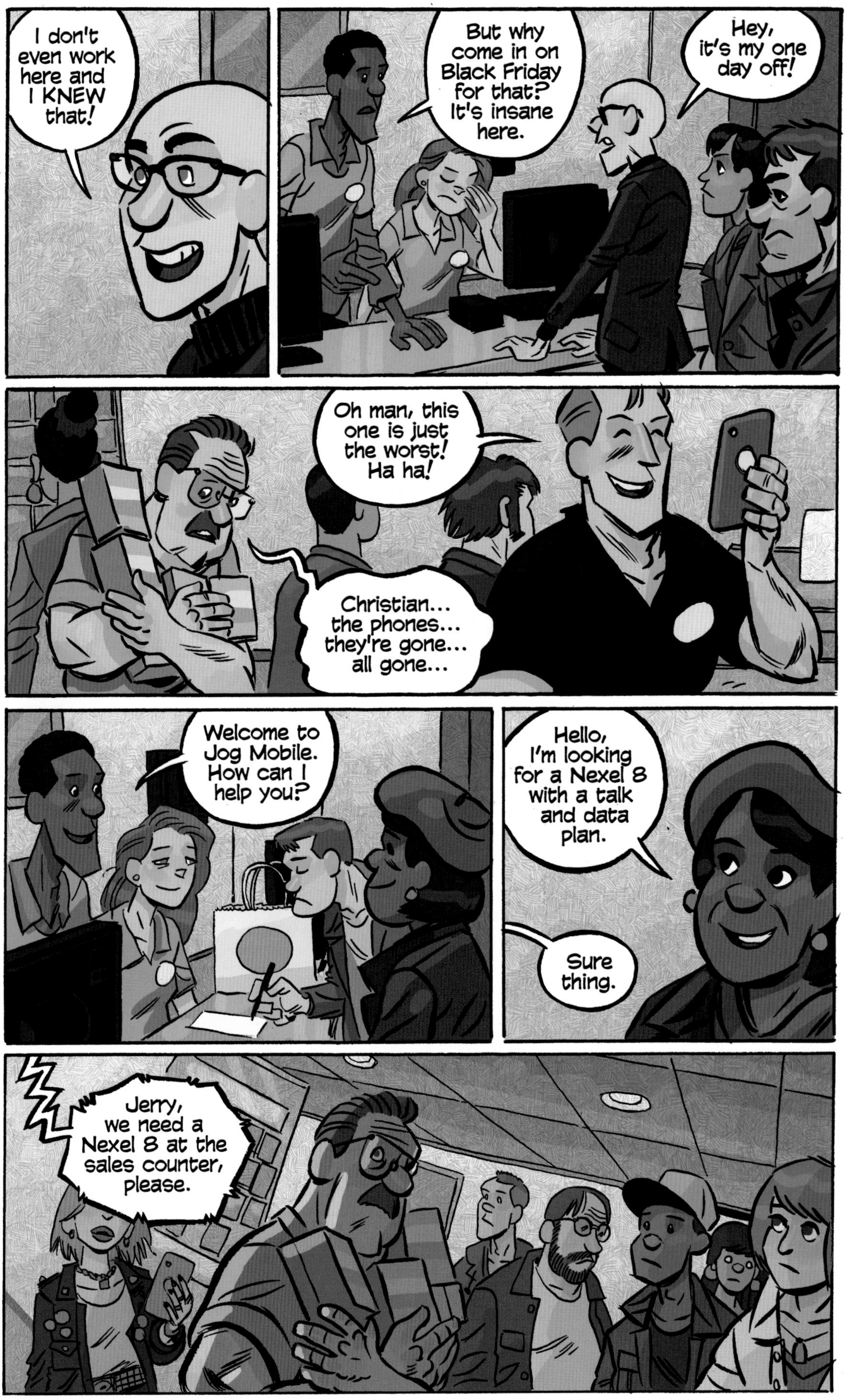
I don't even work here and I KNEW that!
But why come in on Black Friday for that? It's insane here.
Hey, it's my one day off!
Oh man, this one is just the worst! Ha ha!
Christian... the phones... they're gone... all gone...
Welcome to Jog Mobile. How can I help you?
Hello, I'm looking for a Nexel 8 with a talk and data plan.
Sure thing.
Jerry, we need a Nexel 8 at the sales counter, please.

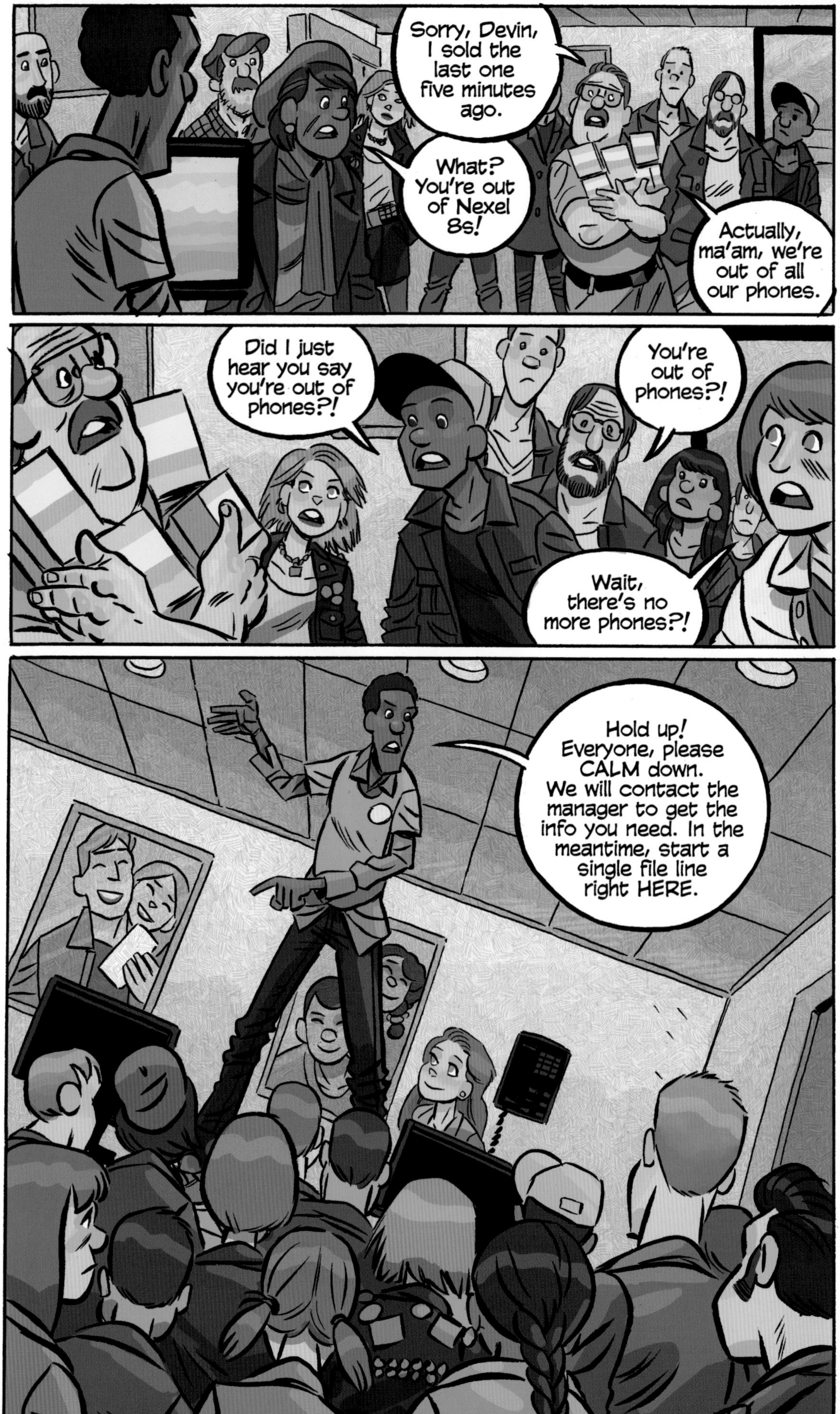
Sorry, Devin, I sold the last one five minutes ago.
What? You're out of Nexel 8s!
Actually, ma'am, we're out of all our phones.
Did I just hear you say you're out of phones?!
You're out of phones?!
Wait, there's no more phones?!
Hold up! Everyone, please CALM down. We will contact the manager to get the info you need. In the meantime, start a single file line right HERE.

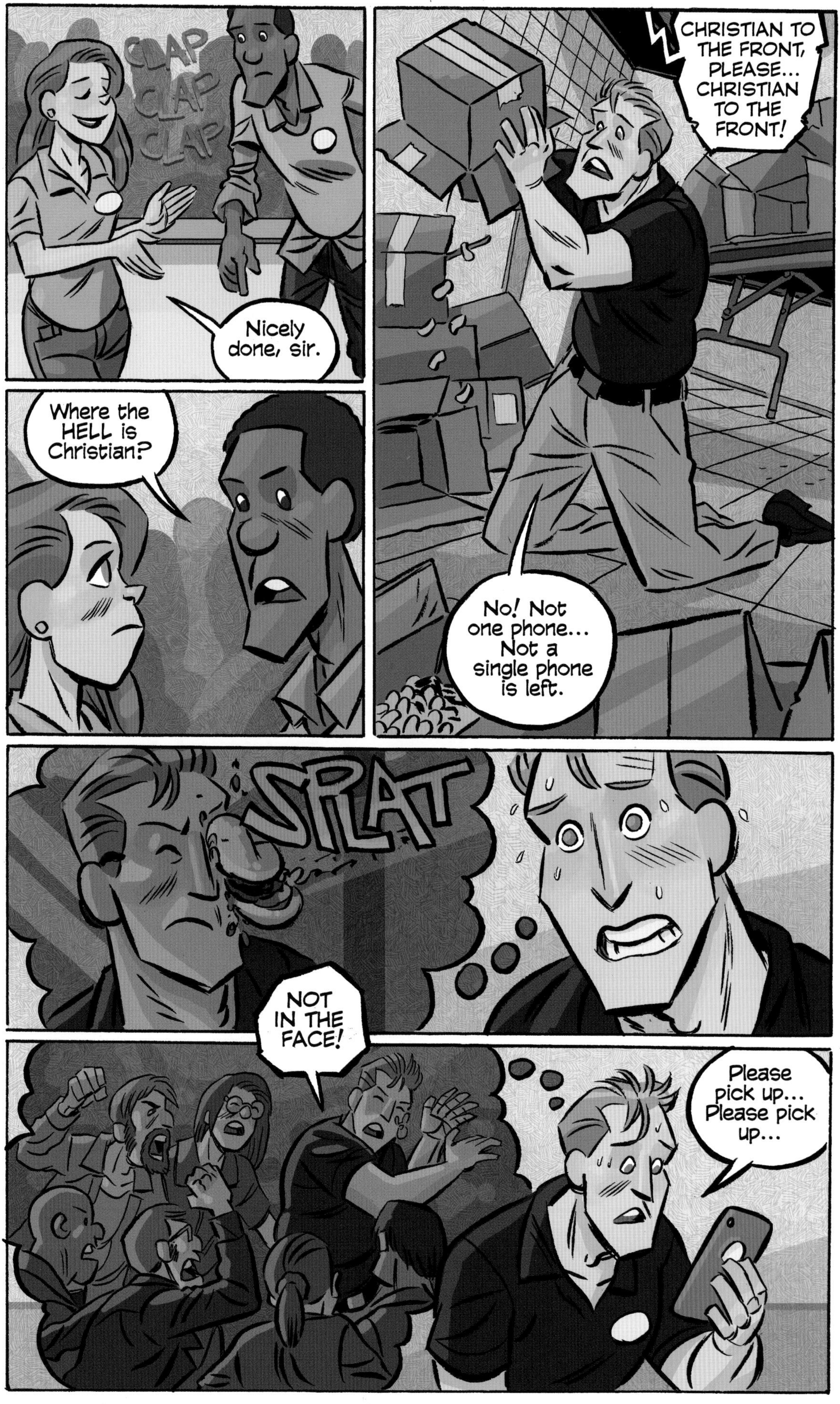
CLAP CLAP CLAP
Nicely done, sir.
CHRISTIAN TO THE FRONT, PLEASE... CHRISTIAN TO THE FRONT!
Where the HELL is Christian?
No! Not one phone... Not a single phone is left.
SPLAT
NOT IN THE FACE!
Please pick up... Please pick up...

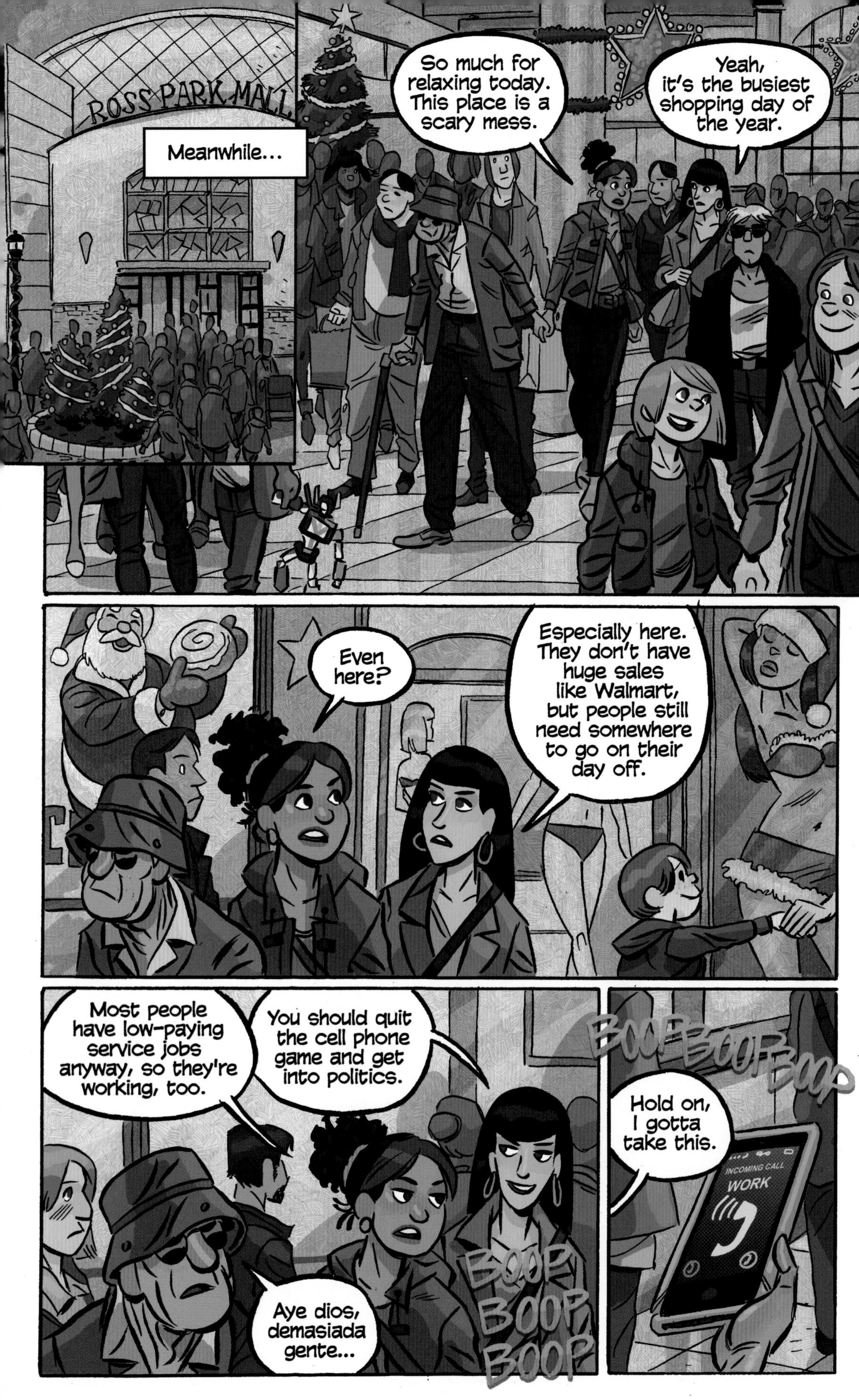
ROSS PARK MALL
Meanwhile...
So much for relaxing today. This place is a scary mess.
Yeah, it's the busiest shopping day of the year.
Even here?
Especially here. They don't have huge sales like Walmart, but people still need somewhere to go on their day off.
Most people have low-paying service jobs anyway, so they're working, too.
You should quit the cell phone game and get into politics.
Aye dios, demasiada gente...
BOOP BOOP BOOP
BOOP BOOP BOOP
Hold on, I gotta take this.
INCOMING CALL
WORK

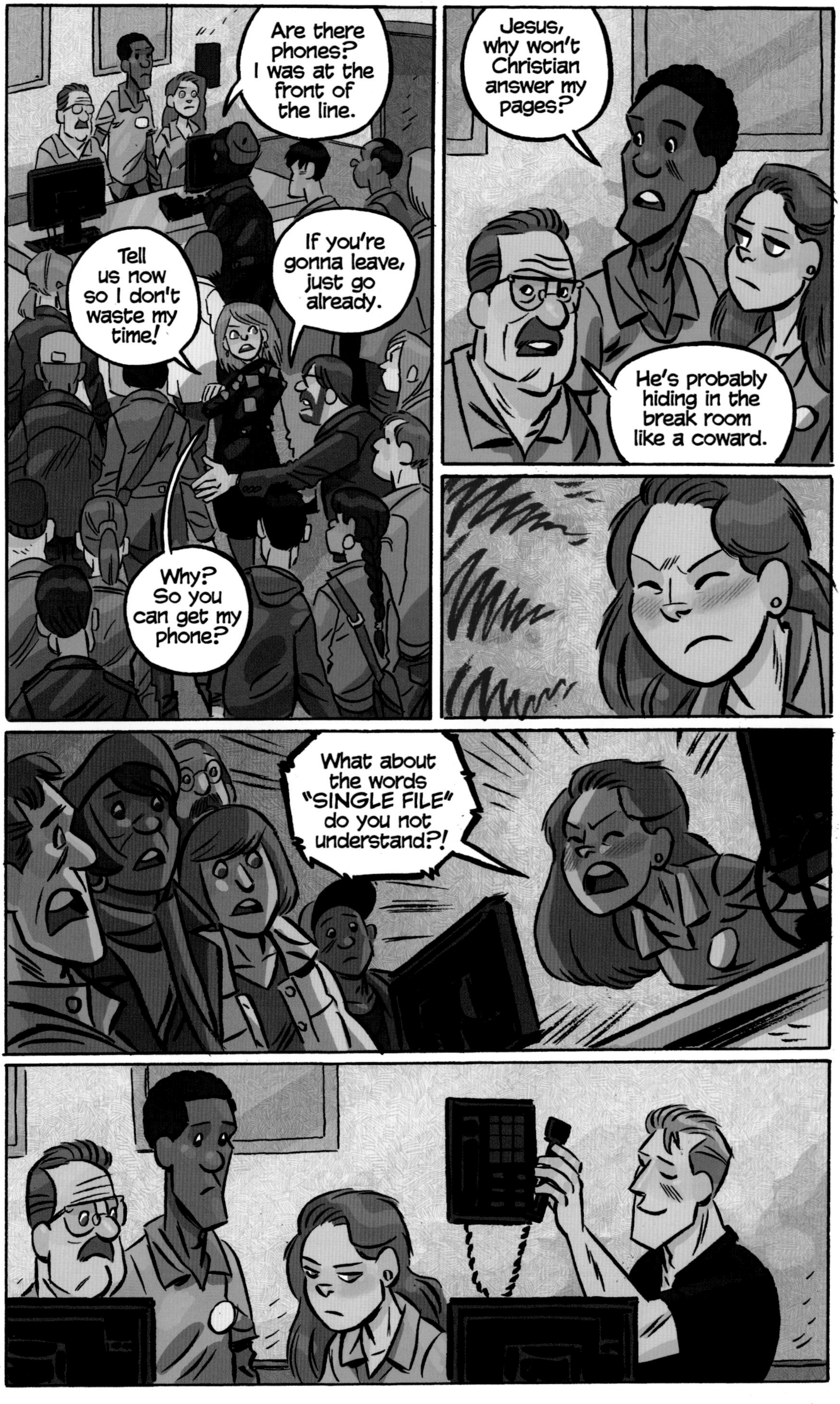

Are there phones? I was at the front of the line.
Tell us now so I don't waste my time!
If you're gonna leave, just go already.
Why? So you can get my phone?
Jesus, why won't Christian answer my pages?
He's probably hiding in the break room like a coward.
What about the words "SINGLE FILE" do you not understand?!

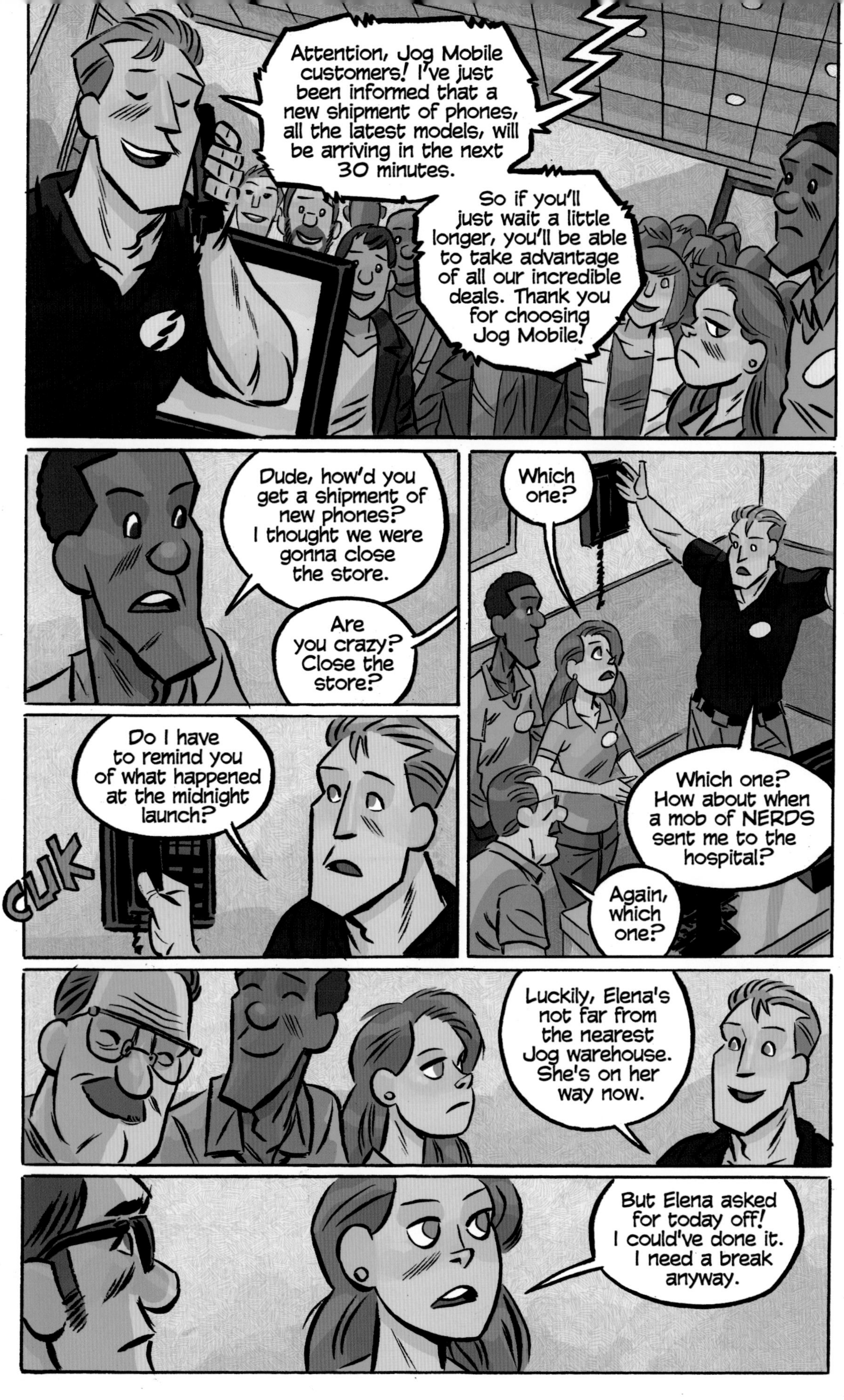
Attention, Jog Mobile customers! I've just been informed that a new shipment of phones, all the latest models, will be arriving in the next 30 minutes.
So if you'll just wait a little longer, you'll be able to take advantage of all our incredible deals. Thank you for choosing Jog Mobile!
Dude, how'd you get a shipment of new phones? I thought we were gonna close the store.
Are you crazy? Close the store?
Do I have to remind you of what happened at the midnight launch?
CLIK
Which one?
Which one? How about when a mob of NERDS sent me to the hospital?
Again, which one?
Luckily, Elena's not far from the nearest Jog warehouse. She's on her way now.
But Elena asked for today off! I could've done it. I need a break anyway.

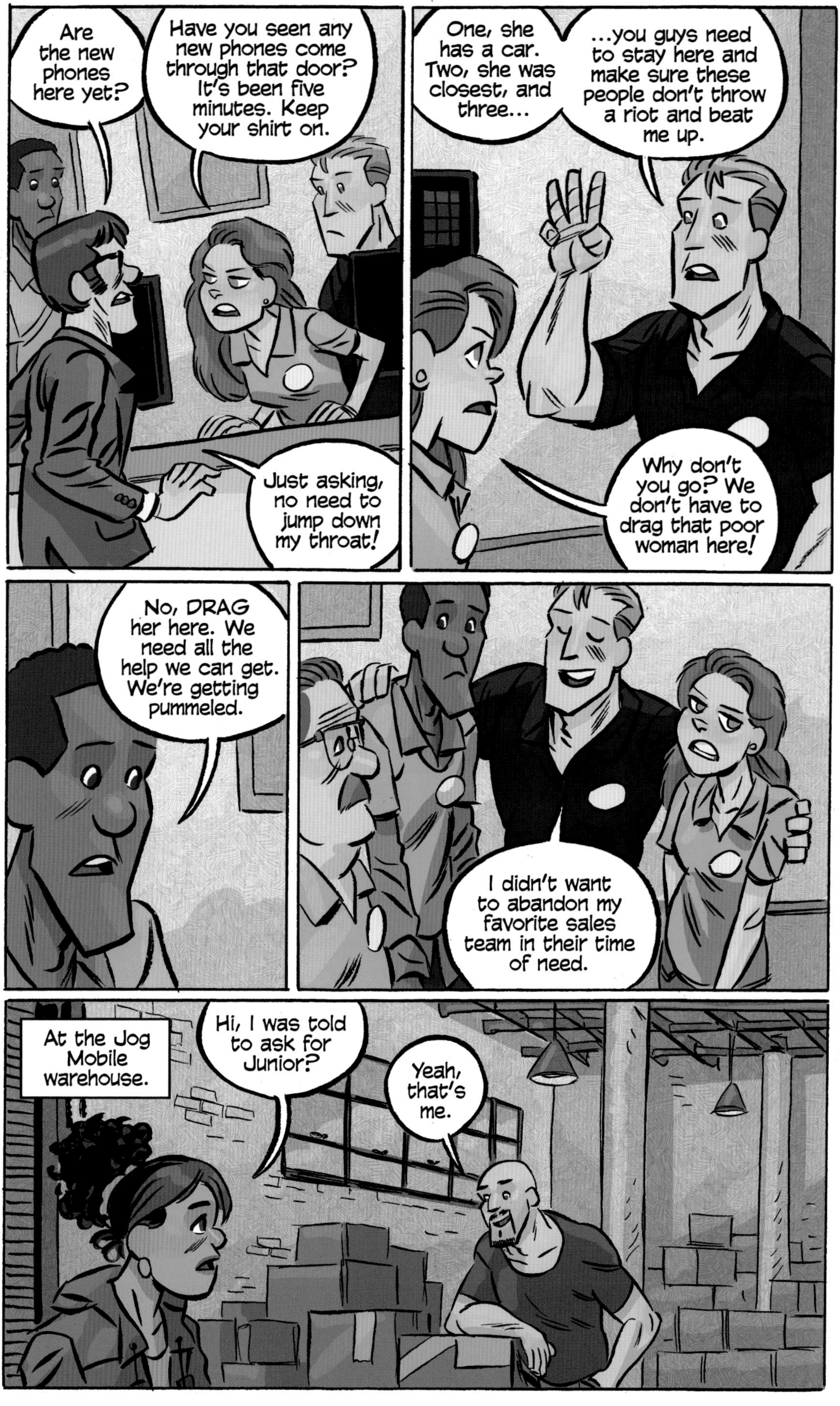
Are the new phones here yet?
Have you seen any new phones come through that door? It's been five minutes. Keep your shirt on.
Just asking, no need to jump down my throat!
One, she has a car. Two, she was closest, and three...
...you guys need to stay here and make sure these people don't throw a riot and beat me up.
Why don't you go? We don't have to drag that poor woman here!
No, DRAG her here. We need all the help we can get. We're getting pummeled.
I didn't want to abandon my favorite sales team in their time of need.
At the Jog Mobile warehouse.
Hi, I was told to ask for Junior?
Yeah, that's me.

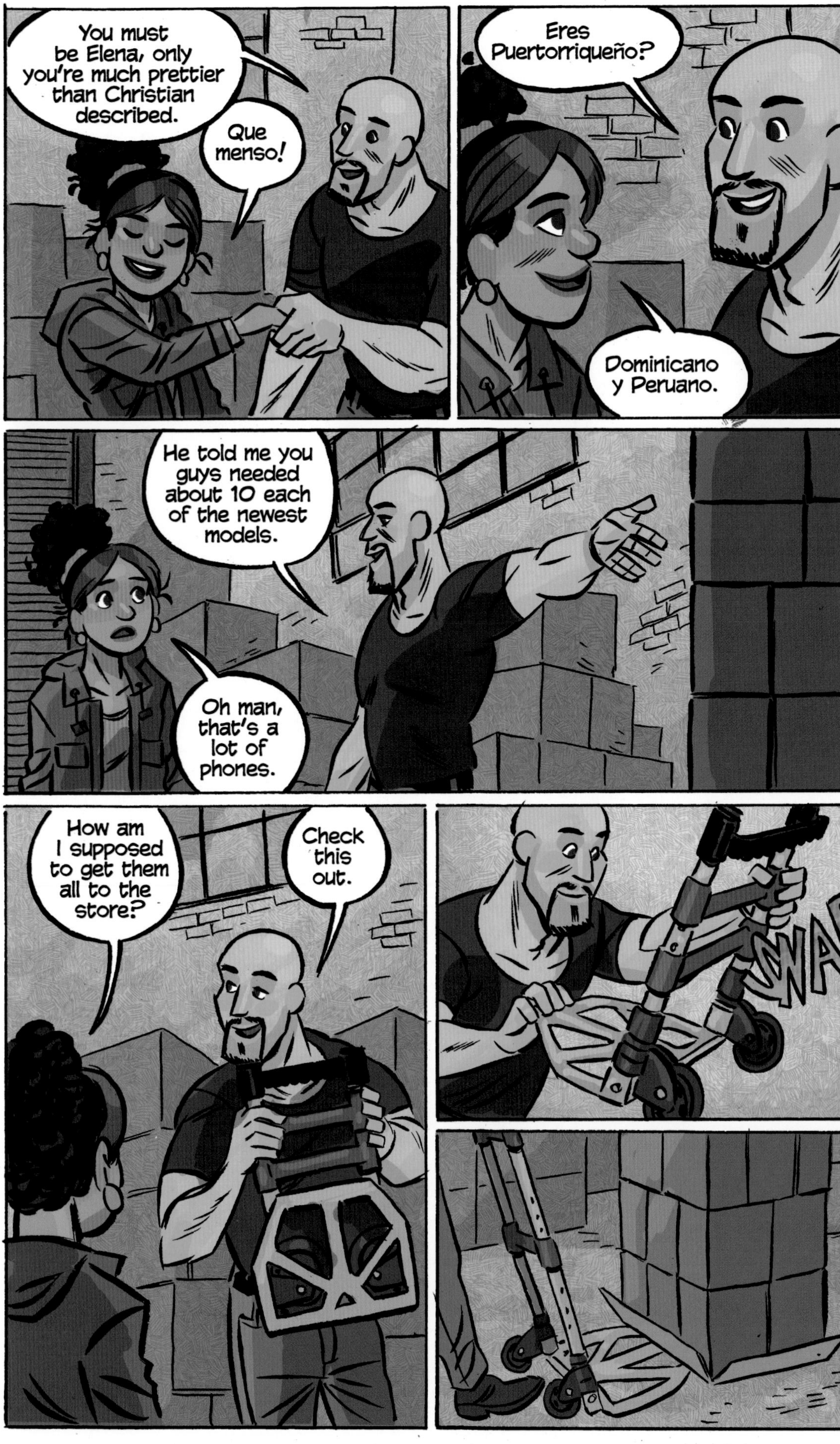
You must be Elena, only you're much prettier than Christian described.
Que menso!
Eres Puertorriqueño?
Dominicano y Peruano.
He told me you guys needed about 10 each of the newest models.
Oh man, that's a lot of phones.
How am I supposed to get them all to the store?
Check this out.
SNAP

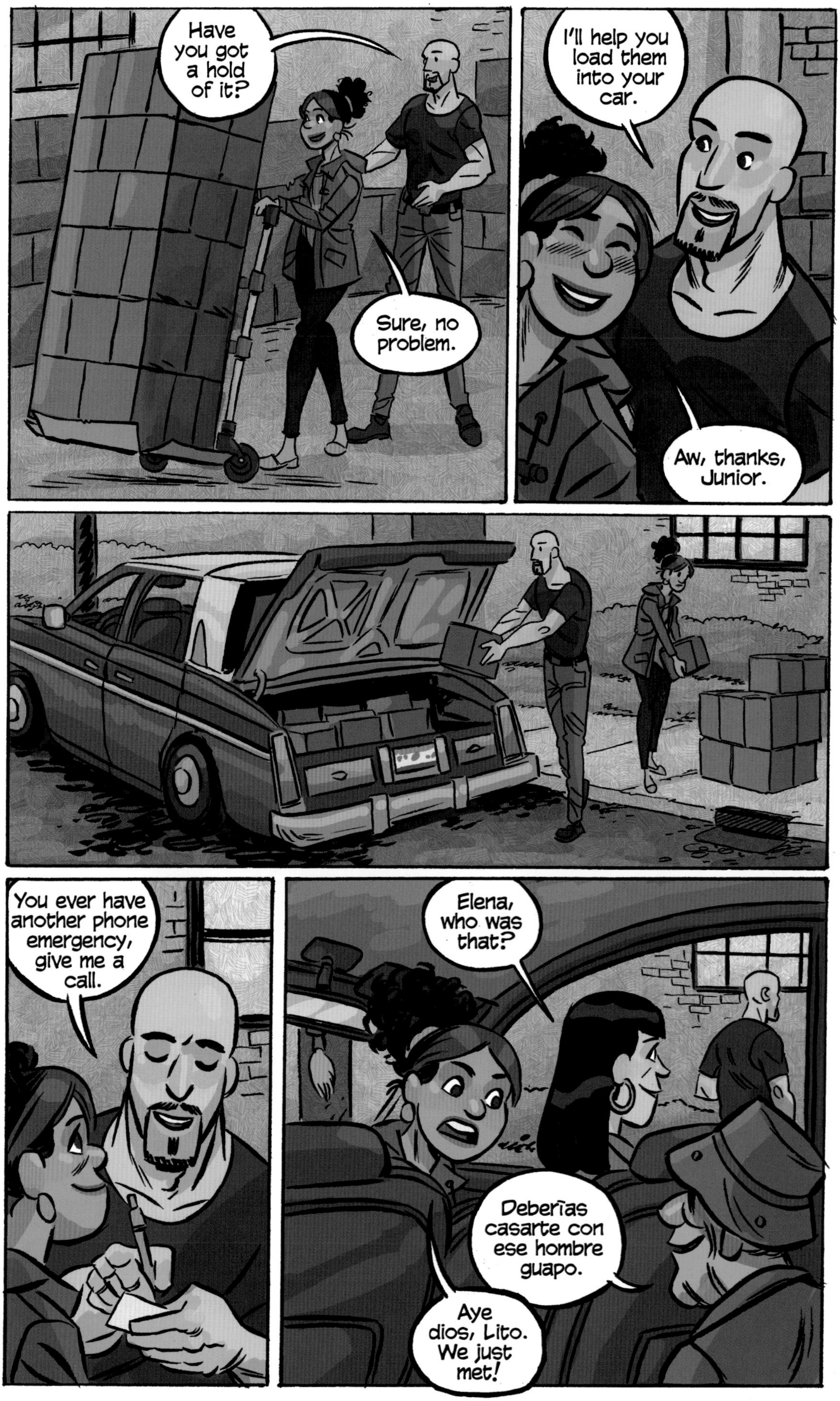
Have you got a hold of it?
Sure, no problem.
I'll help you load them into your car.
Aw, thanks, Junior.
You ever have another phone emergency, give me a call.
Elena, who was that?
Deberías casarte con ese hombre guapo.
Aye dios, Lito. We just met!

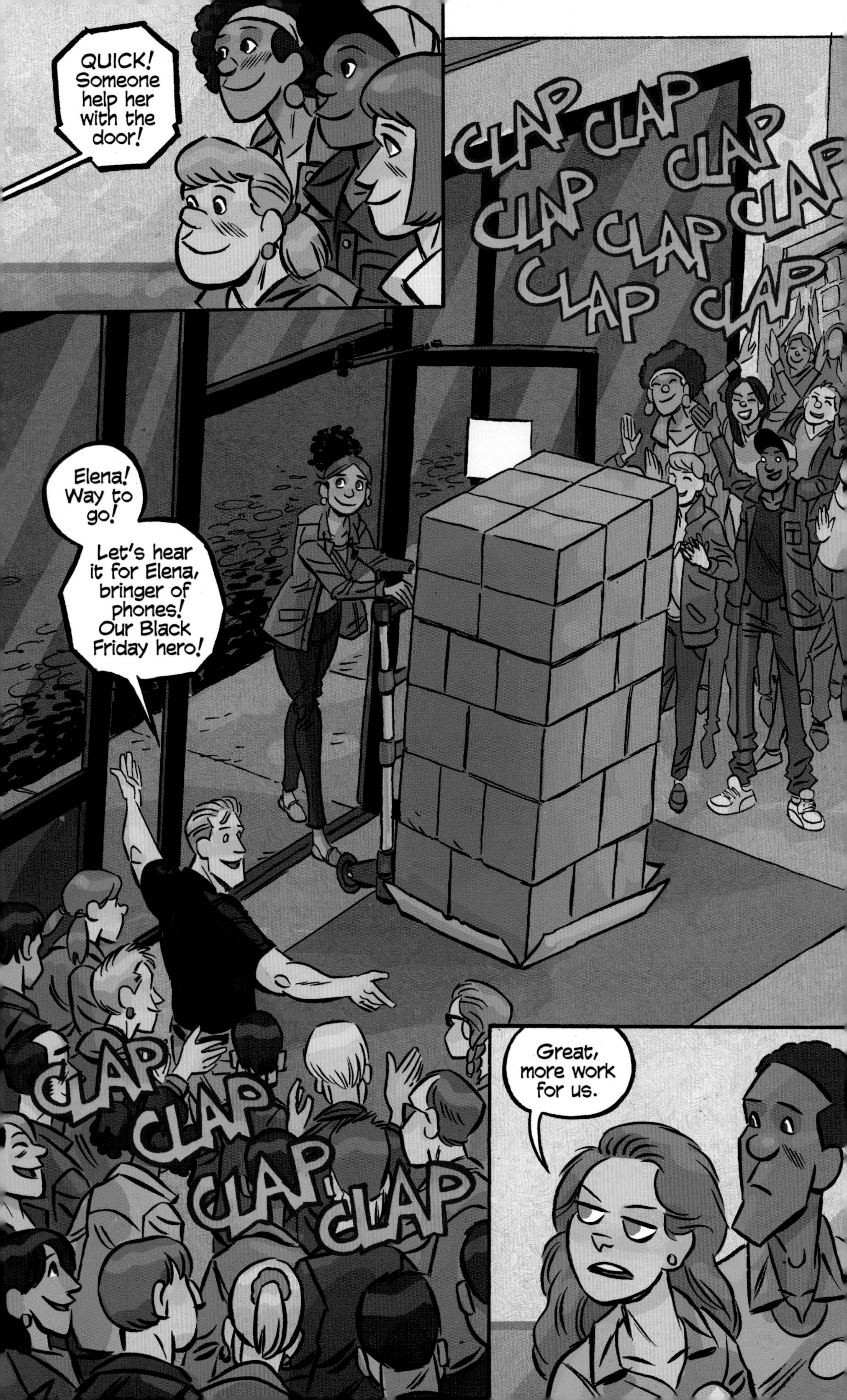
QUICK! Someone help her with the door!
CLAP CLAP CLAP CLAP CLAP CLAP CLAP CLAP CLAP
Elena! Way to go!
Let's hear it for Elena, bringer of phones! Our Black Friday hero!
CLAP CLAP CLAP CLAP
Great, more work for us.

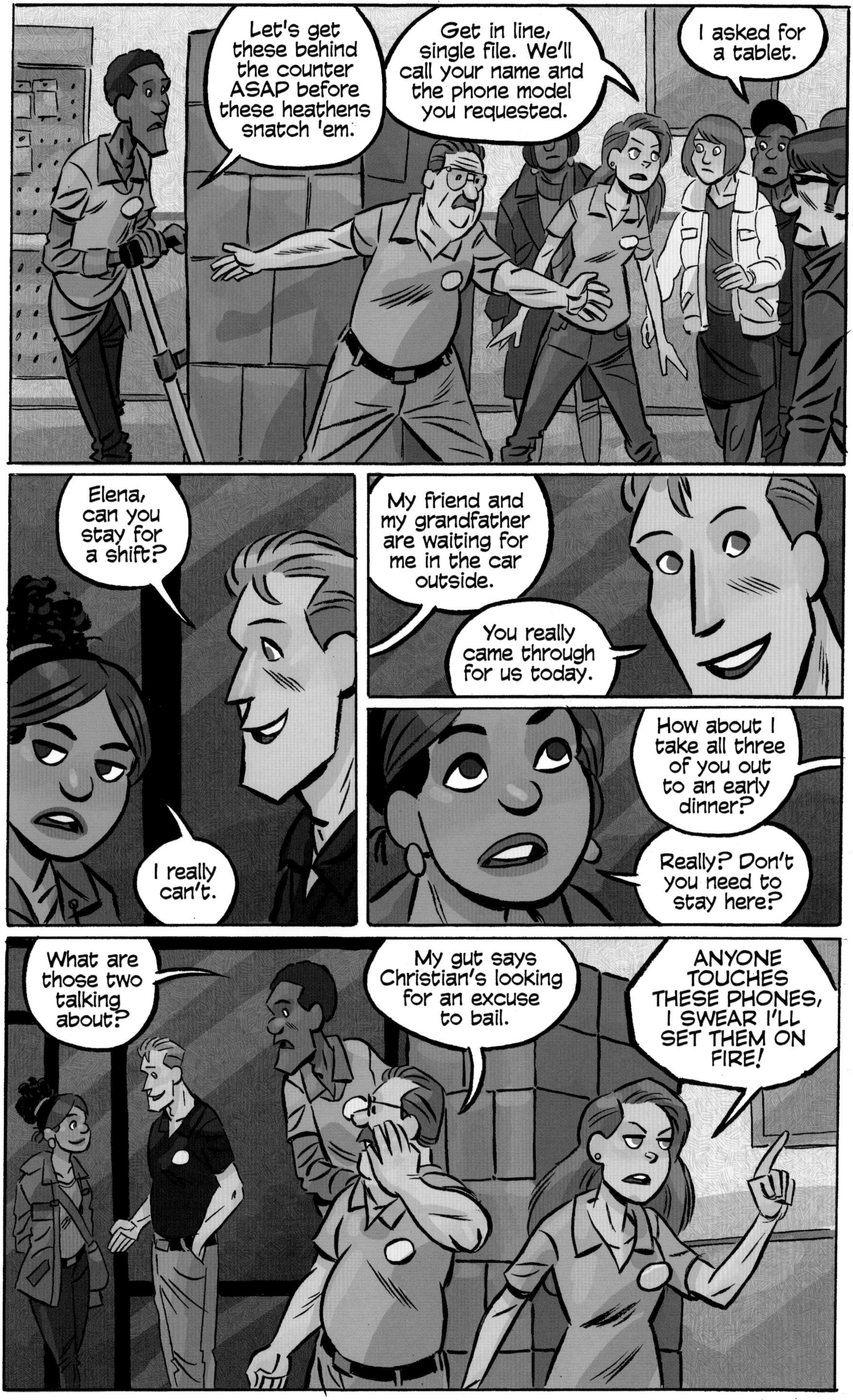
Let's get these behind the counter ASAP before these heathens snatch 'em.
Get in line, single file. We'll call your name and the phone model you requested.
I asked for a tablet.
Elena, can you stay for a shift?
I really can't.
My friend and my grandfather are waiting for me in the car outside.
You really came through for us today.
How about I take all three of you out to an early dinner?
Really? Don't you need to stay here?
What are those two talking about?
My gut says Christian's looking for an excuse to bail.
ANYONE TOUCHES THESE PHONES, I SWEAR I'LL SET THEM ON FIRE!

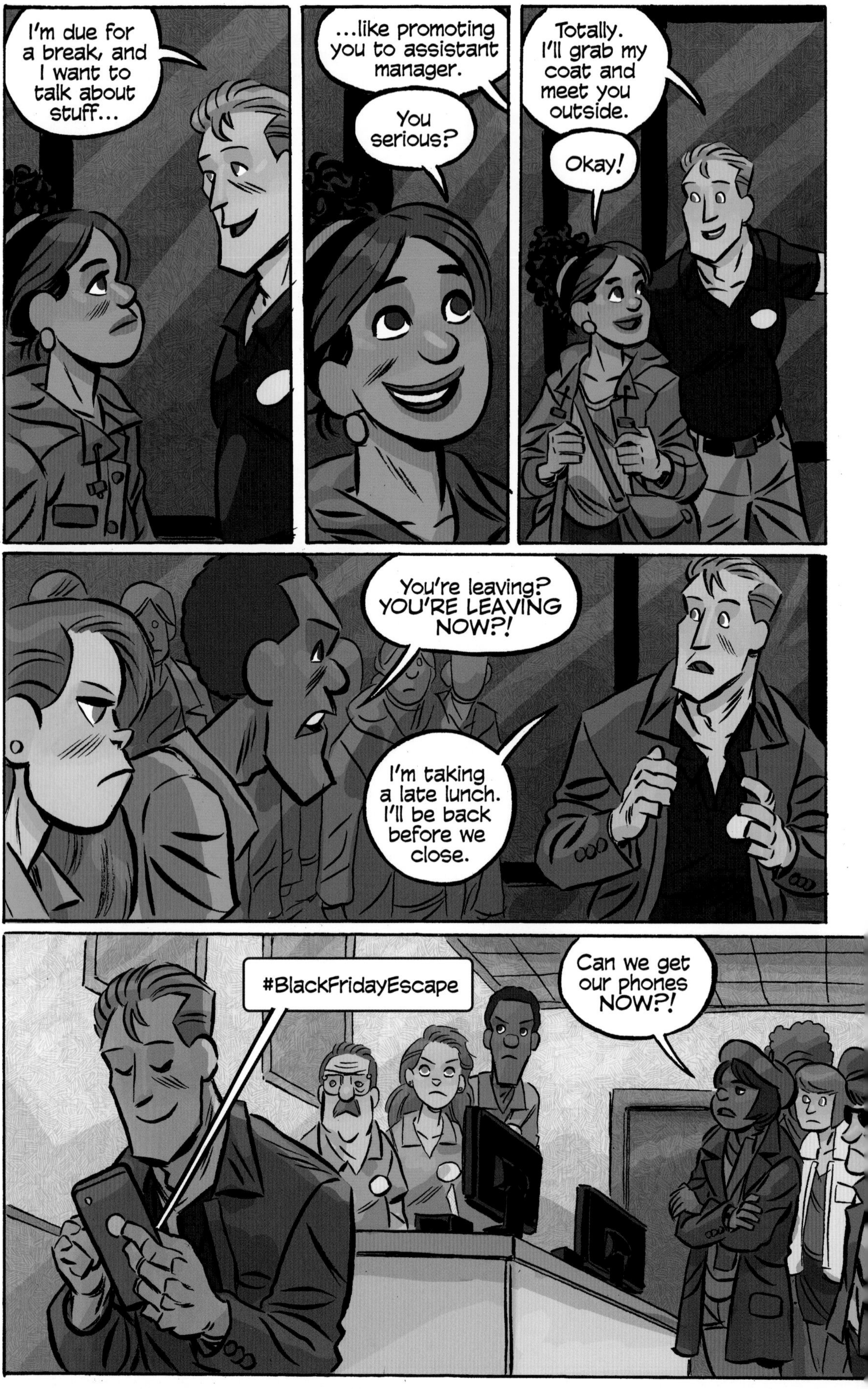
I'm due for a break, and I want to talk about stuff...
...like promoting you to assistant manager.
You serious?
Totally. I'll grab my coat and meet you outside.
Okay!
You're leaving? YOU'RE LEAVING NOW?!
I'm taking a late lunch. I'll be back before we close.
#BlackFridayEscape
Can we get our phones NOW?!

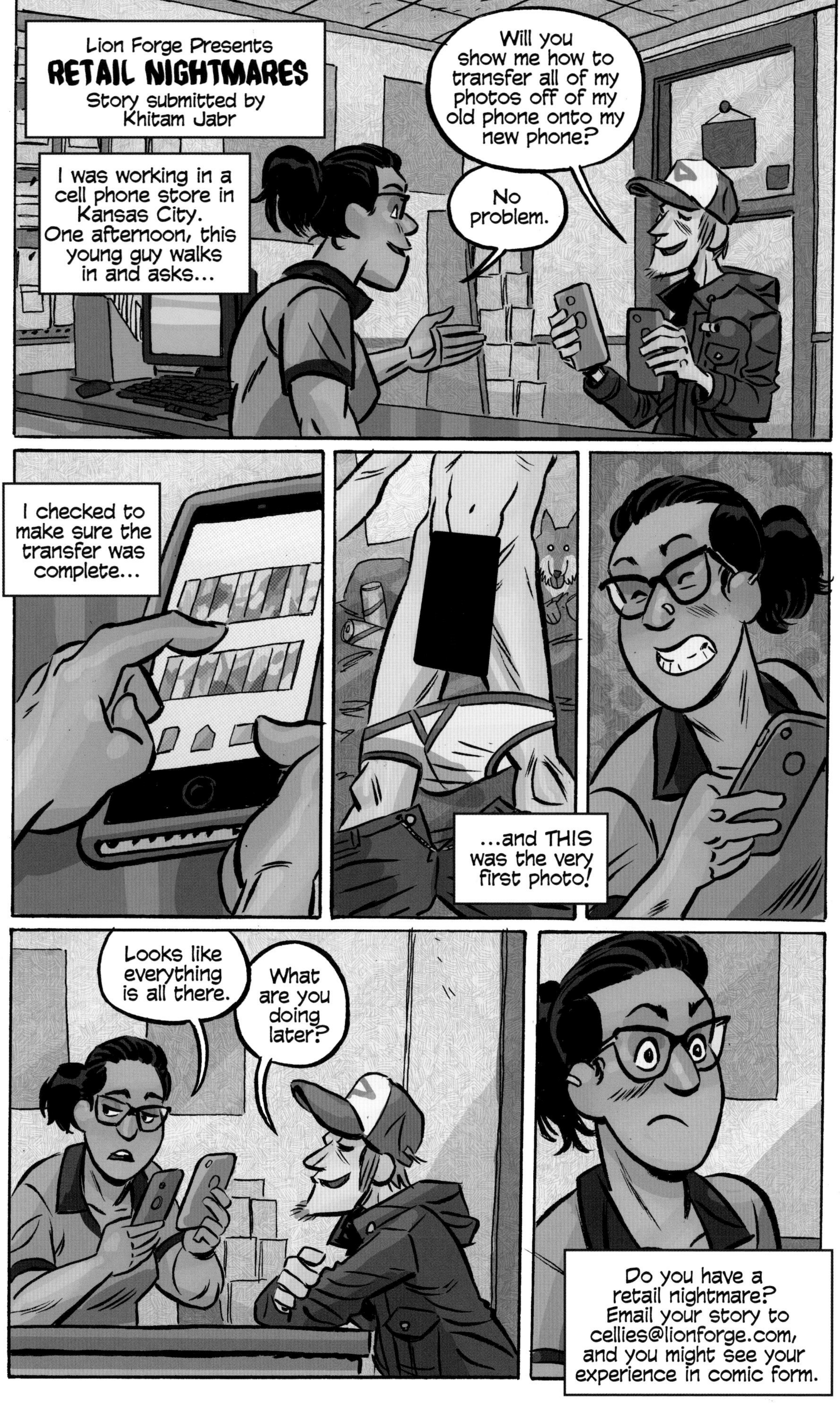
Lion Forge Presents
RETAIL NIGHTMARES
Story submitted by Khitam Jabr
I was working in a cell phone store in Kansas City. One afternoon, this young guy walks in and asks...
Will you show me how to transfer all of my photos off of my old phone onto my new phone?
No problem.
I checked to make sure the transfer was complete...
...and THIS was the very first photo!
Looks like everything is all there.
What are you doing later?
Do you have a retail nightmare? Email your story to cellies@lionforge.com, and you might see your experience in comic form.

## CHAPTER 2

Sorry WE'RE CLOSED
HE'S HERE TO RUIN CLOSING TIME! HE'S...
THE LAST-MINUTE CUSTOMER!

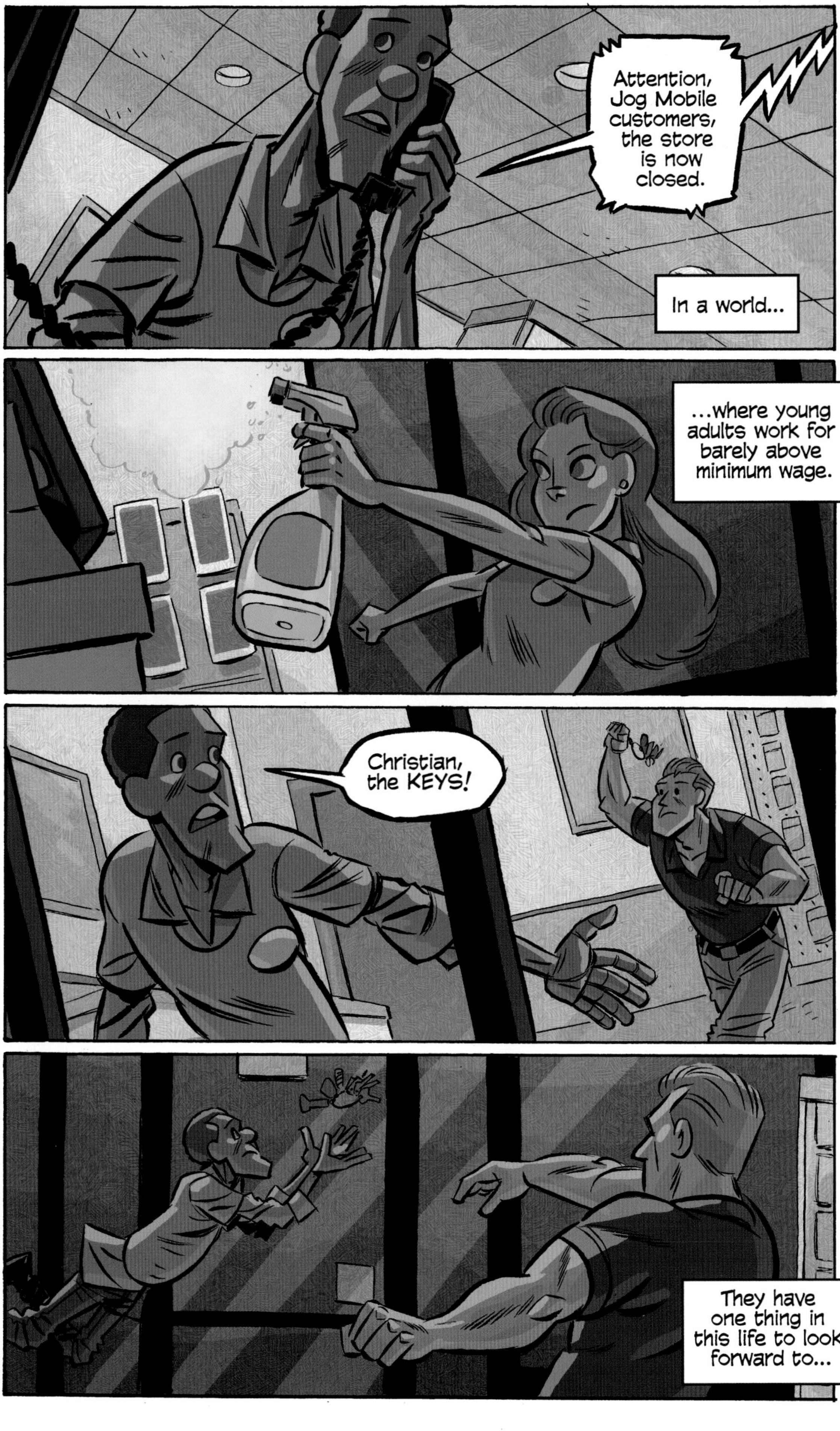
Attention, Jog Mobile customers, the store is now closed.
In a world...
...where young adults work for barely above minimum wage.
Christian, the KEYS!
They have one thing in this life to look forward to...

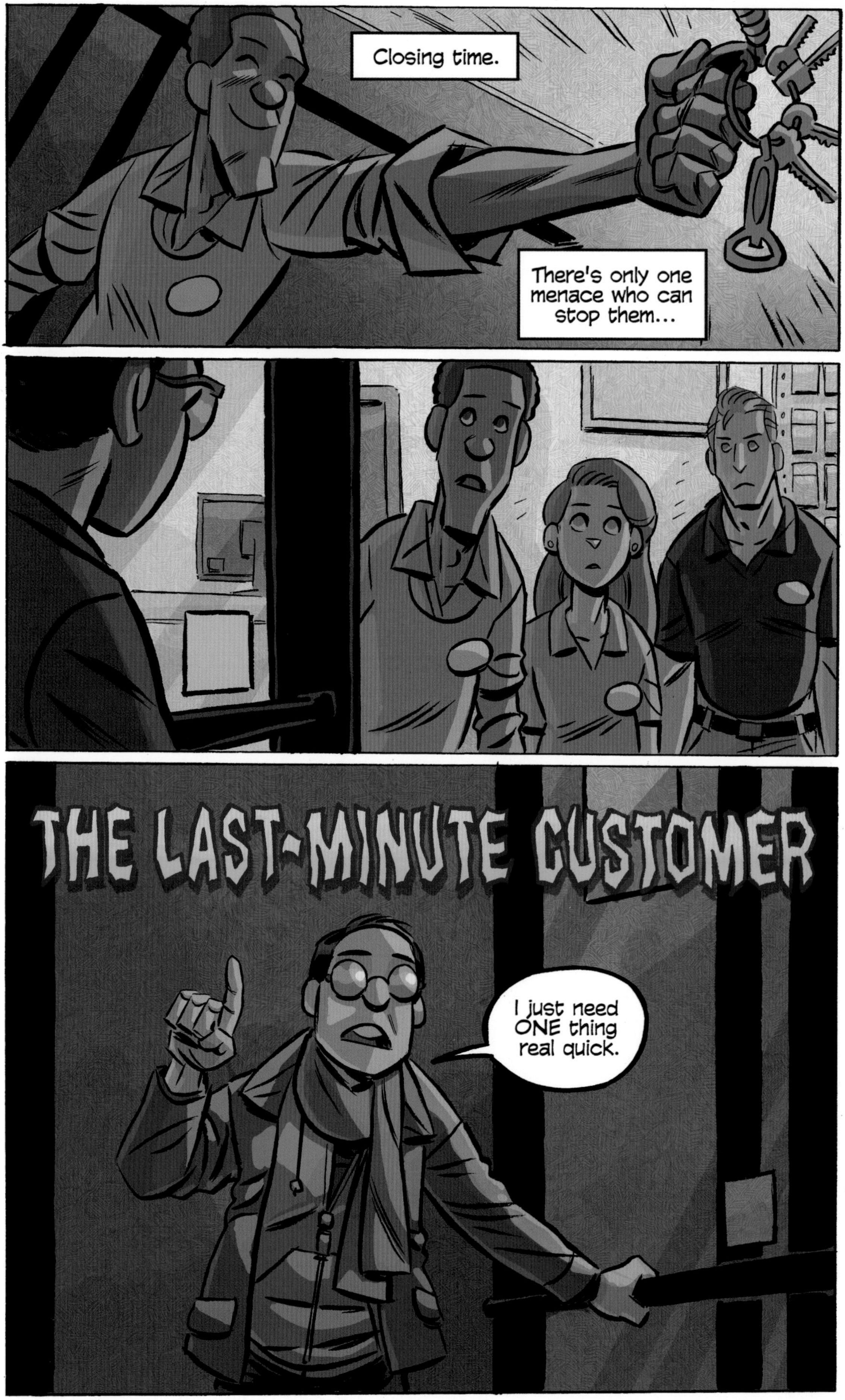
Closing time.
There's only one menace who can stop them...
THE LAST-MINUTE CUSTOMER
I just need ONE thing real quick.

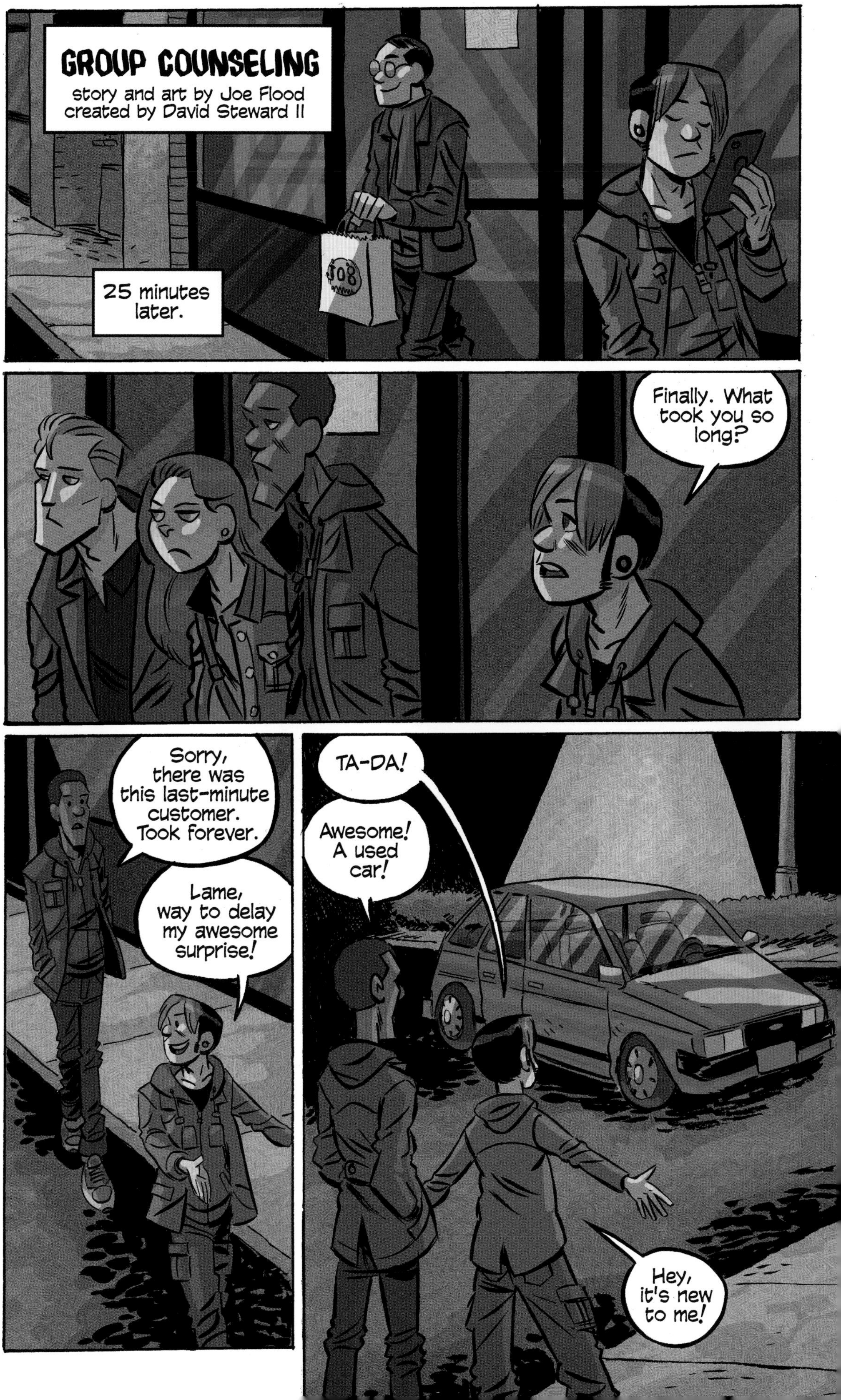
GROUP COUNSELING
story and art by Joe Flood
created by David Steward II
25 minutes later.
Finally. What took you so long?
Sorry, there was this last-minute customer. Took forever.
Lame, way to delay my awesome surprise!
TA-DA!
Awesome! A used car!
Hey, it's new to me!

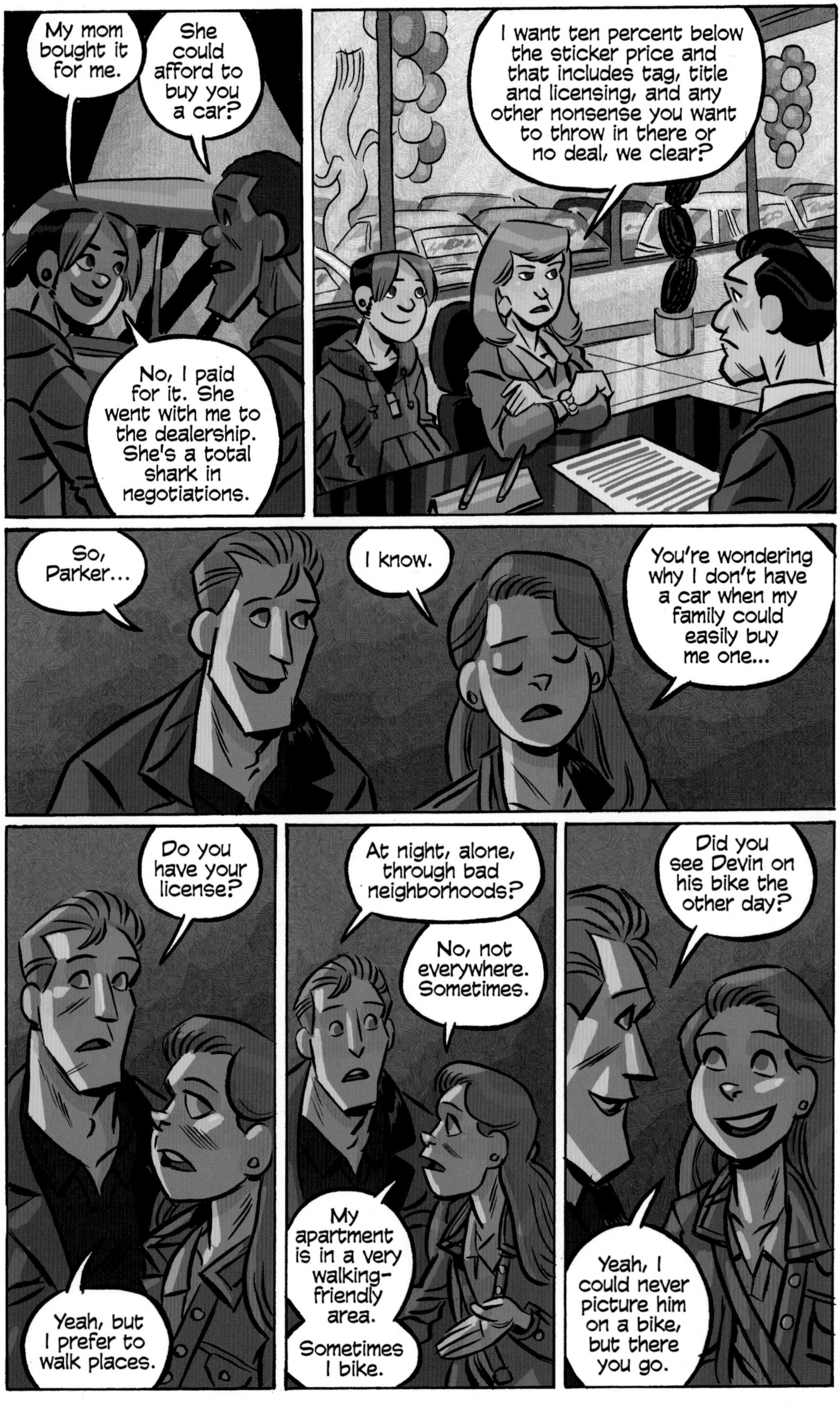
My mom bought it for me.
She could afford to buy you a car?
No, I paid for it. She went with me to the dealership. She's a total shark in negotiations.
I want ten percent below the sticker price and that includes tag, title and licensing, and any other nonsense you want to throw in there or no deal, we clear?
So, Parker...
I know.
You're wondering why I don't have a car when my family could easily buy me one...
Do you have your license?
Yeah, but I prefer to walk places.
At night, alone, through bad neighborhoods?
No, not everywhere. Sometimes.
My apartment is in a very walking-friendly area.
Sometimes I bike.
Did you see Devin on his bike the other day?
Yeah, I could never picture him on a bike, but there you go.

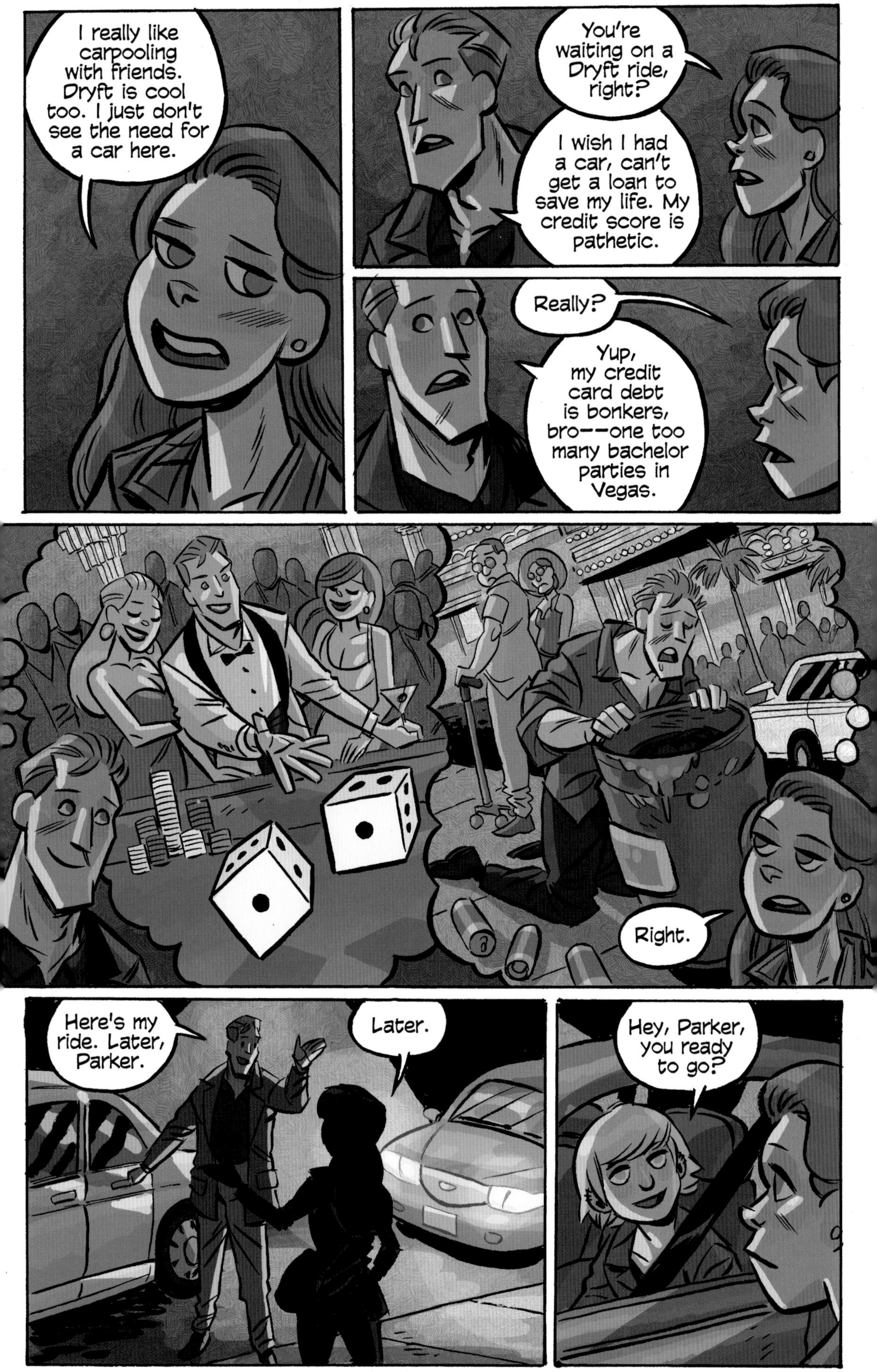
I really like carpooling with friends. Dryft is cool too. I just don't see the need for a car here.
You're waiting on a Dryft ride, right?
I wish I had a car, can't get a loan to save my life. My credit score is pathetic.
Really?
Yup, my credit card debt is bonkers, bro--one too many bachelor parties in Vegas.
Right.
Here's my ride. Later, Parker.
Later.
Hey, Parker, you ready to go?

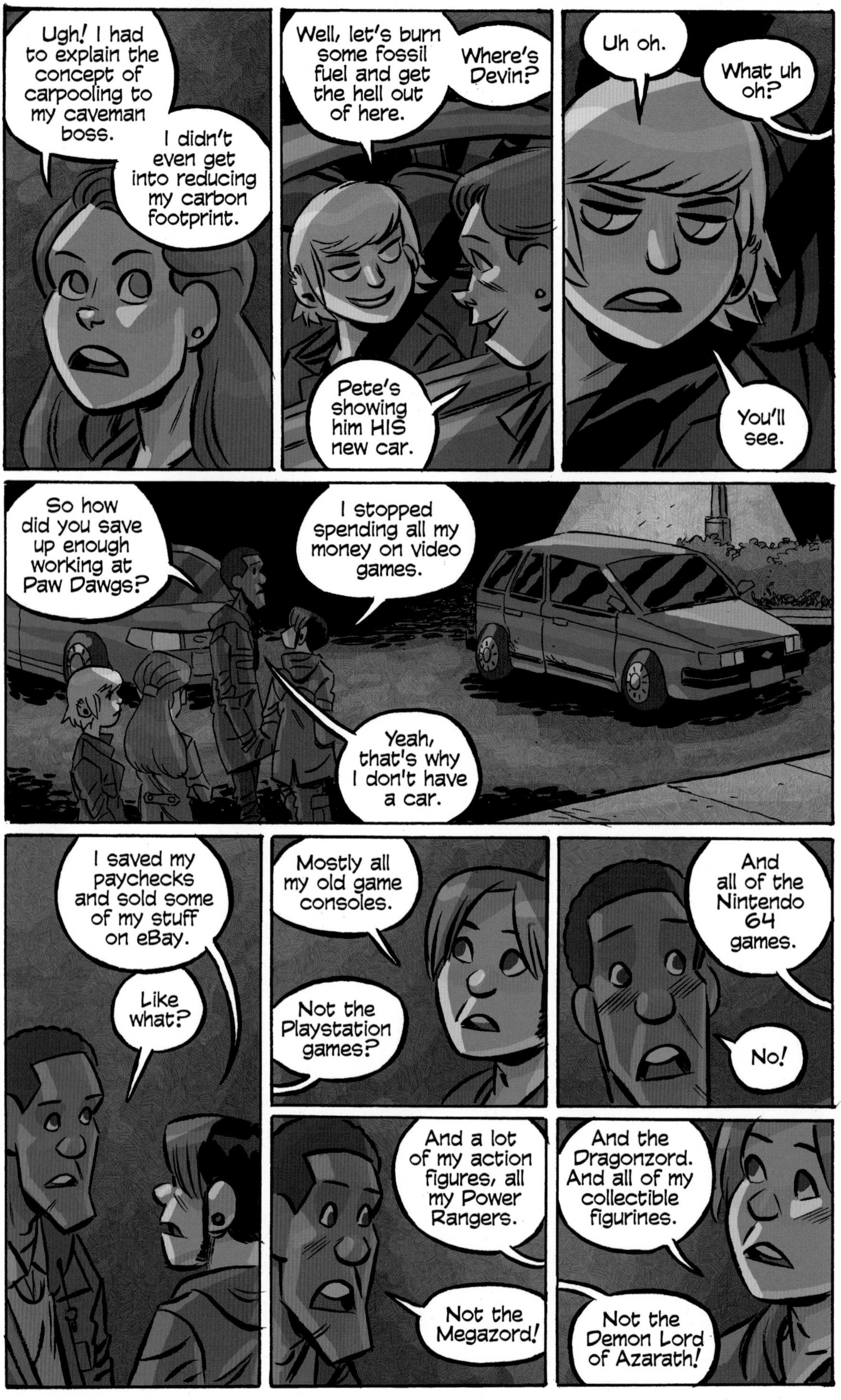
Ugh! I had to explain the concept of carpooling to my caveman boss.
I didn't even get into reducing my carbon footprint.
Well, let's burn some fossil fuel and get the hell out of here.
Where's Devin?
Pete's showing him HIS new car.
Uh oh.
What uh oh?
You'll see.
So how did you save up enough working at Paw Dawgs?
I stopped spending all my money on video games.
Yeah, that's why I don't have a car.
I saved my paychecks and sold some of my stuff on eBay.
Like what?
Mostly all my old game consoles.
Not the Playstation games?
And all of the Nintendo 64 games.
No!
And a lot of my action figures, all my Power Rangers.
Not the Megazord!
And the Dragonzord. And all of my collectible figurines.
Not the Demon Lord of Azarath!

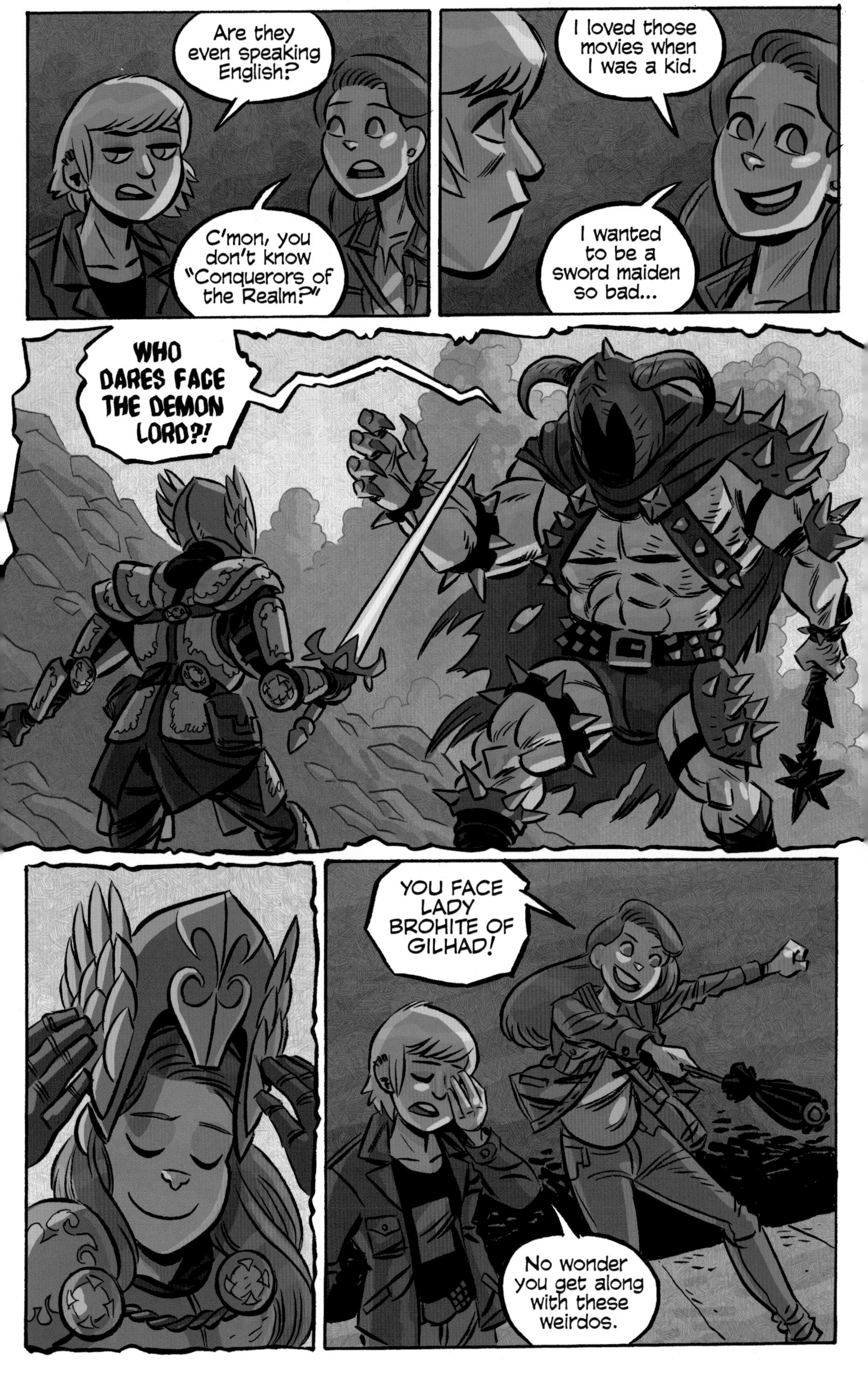
Are they even speaking English?
C'mon, you don't know "Conquerors of the Realm?"
I loved those movies when I was a kid.
I wanted to be a sword maiden so bad...
WHO DARES FACE THE DEMON LORD?!
YOU FACE LADY BROHITE OF GILHAD!
No wonder you get along with these weirdos.

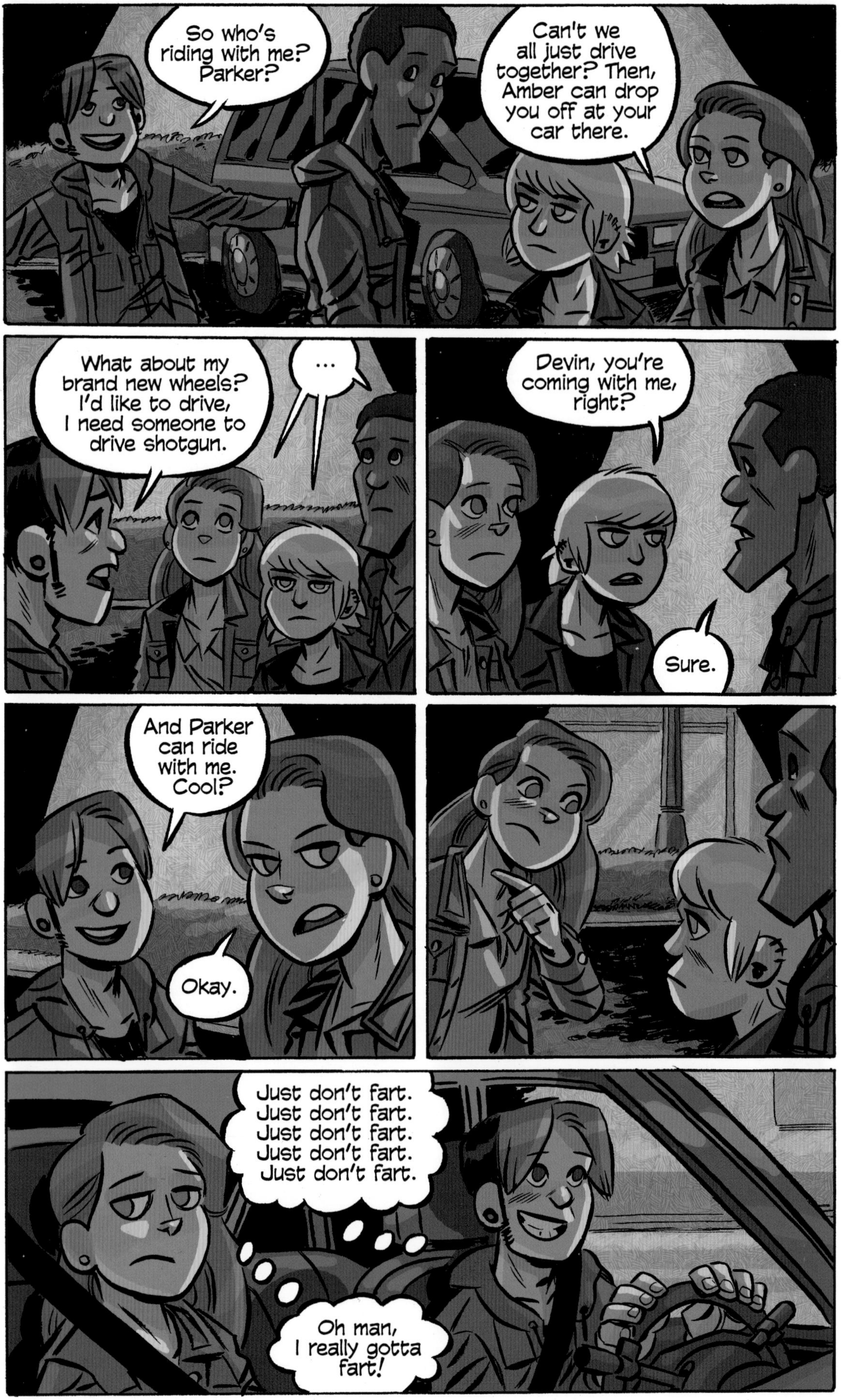
So who's riding with me? Parker?
Can't we all just drive together? Then, Amber can drop you off at your car there.
What about my brand new wheels? I'd like to drive, I need someone to drive shotgun.
...
Devin, you're coming with me, right?
Sure.
And Parker can ride with me. Cool?
Okay.
Just don't fart. Just don't fart. Just don't fart. Just don't fart. Just don't fart.
Oh man, I really gotta fart!

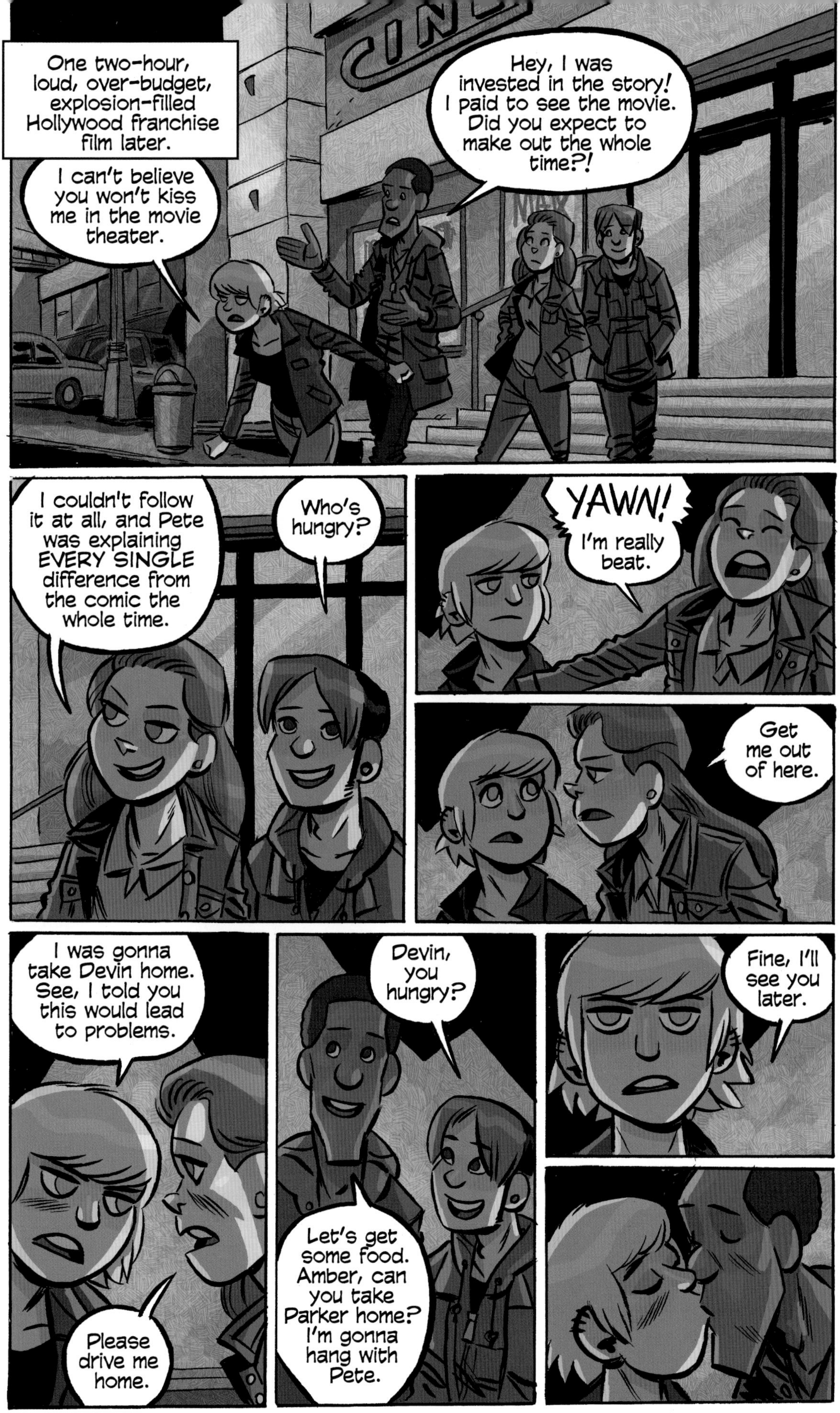
One two-hour, loud, over-budget, explosion-filled Hollywood franchise film later.
I can't believe you won't kiss me in the movie theater.
Hey, I was invested in the story! I paid to see the movie. Did you expect to make out the whole time?!
I couldn't follow it at all, and Pete was explaining EVERY SINGLE difference from the comic the whole time.
Who's hungry?
YAWN!
I'm really beat.
Get me out of here.
I was gonna take Devin home. See, I told you this would lead to problems.
Please drive me home.
Devin, you hungry?
Let's get some food. Amber, can you take Parker home? I'm gonna hang with Pete.
Fine, I'll see you later.

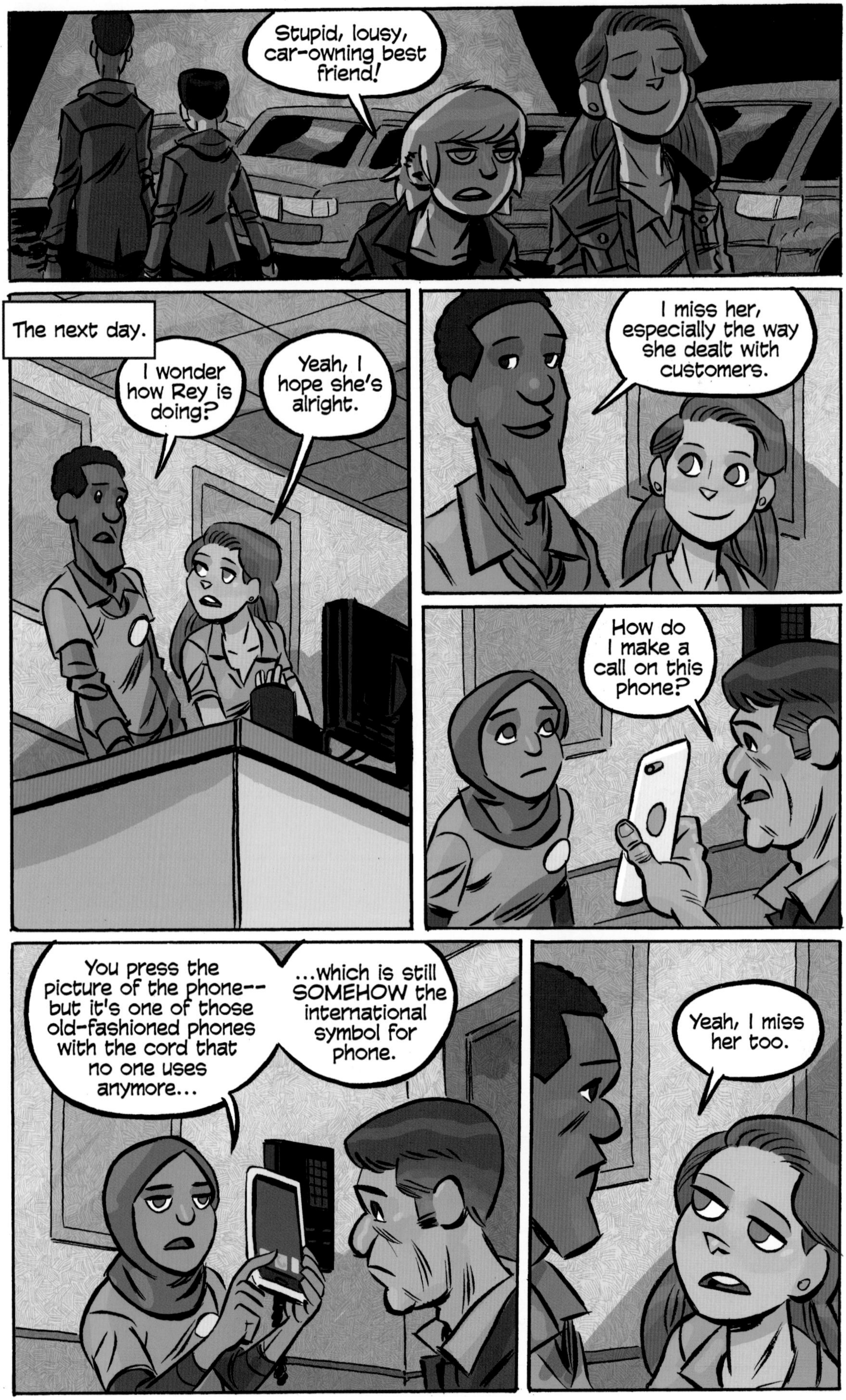
Stupid, lousy, car-owning best friend!
The next day.
I wonder how Rey is doing?
Yeah, I hope she's alright.
I miss her, especially the way she dealt with customers.
How do I make a call on this phone?
You press the picture of the phone-- but it's one of those old-fashioned phones with the cord that no one uses anymore...
...which is still SOMEHOW the international symbol for phone.
Yeah, I miss her too.

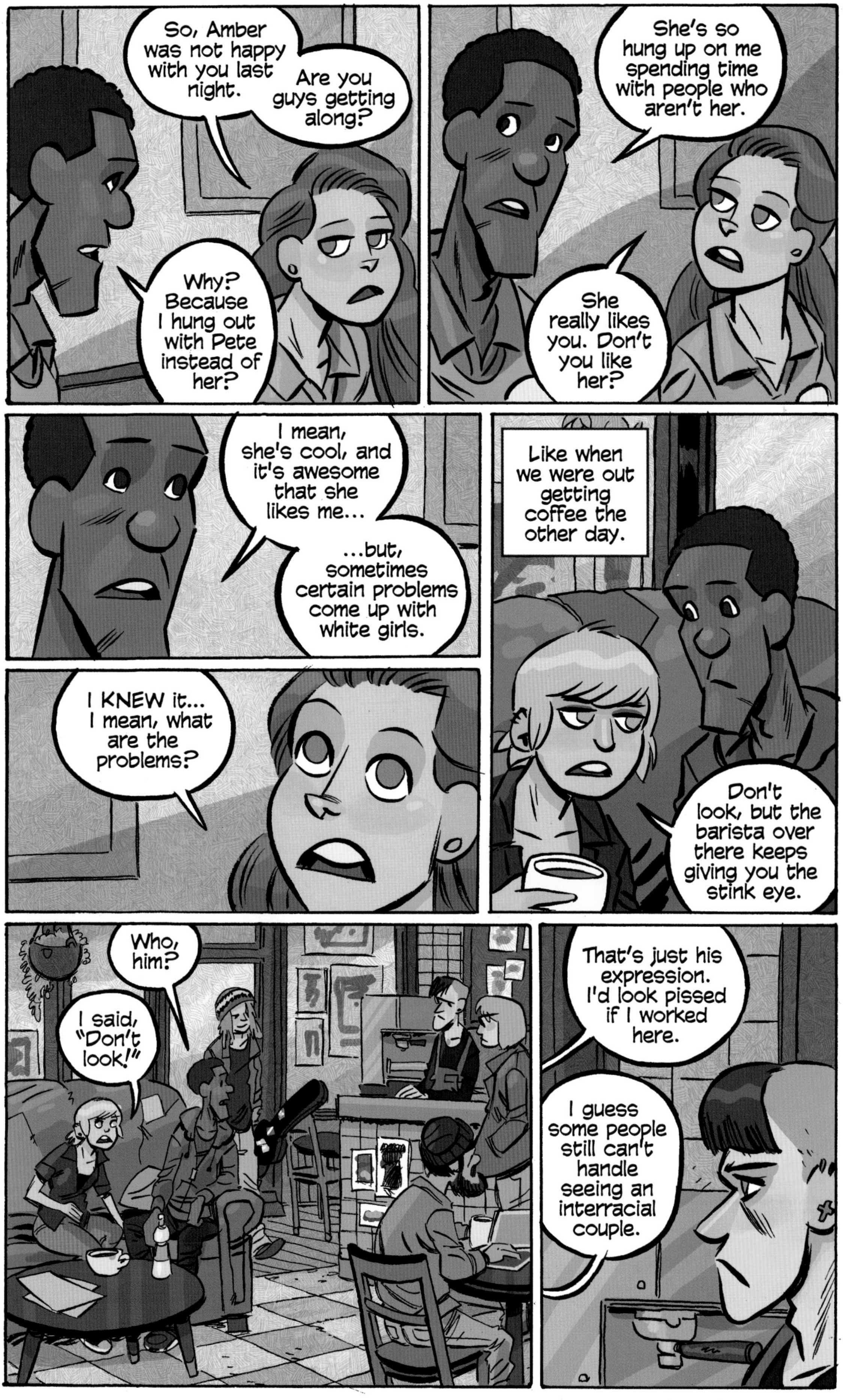
So, Amber was not happy with you last night.
Are you guys getting along?
Why? Because I hung out with Pete instead of her?
She's so hung up on me spending time with people who aren't her.
She really likes you. Don't you like her?
I mean, she's cool, and it's awesome that she likes me...
...but, sometimes certain problems come up with white girls.
I KNEW it... I mean, what are the problems?
Like when we were out getting coffee the other day.
Don't look, but the barista over there keeps giving you the stink eye.
Who, him?
I said, "Don't look!"
That's just his expression. I'd look pissed if I worked here.
I guess some people still can't handle seeing an interracial couple.

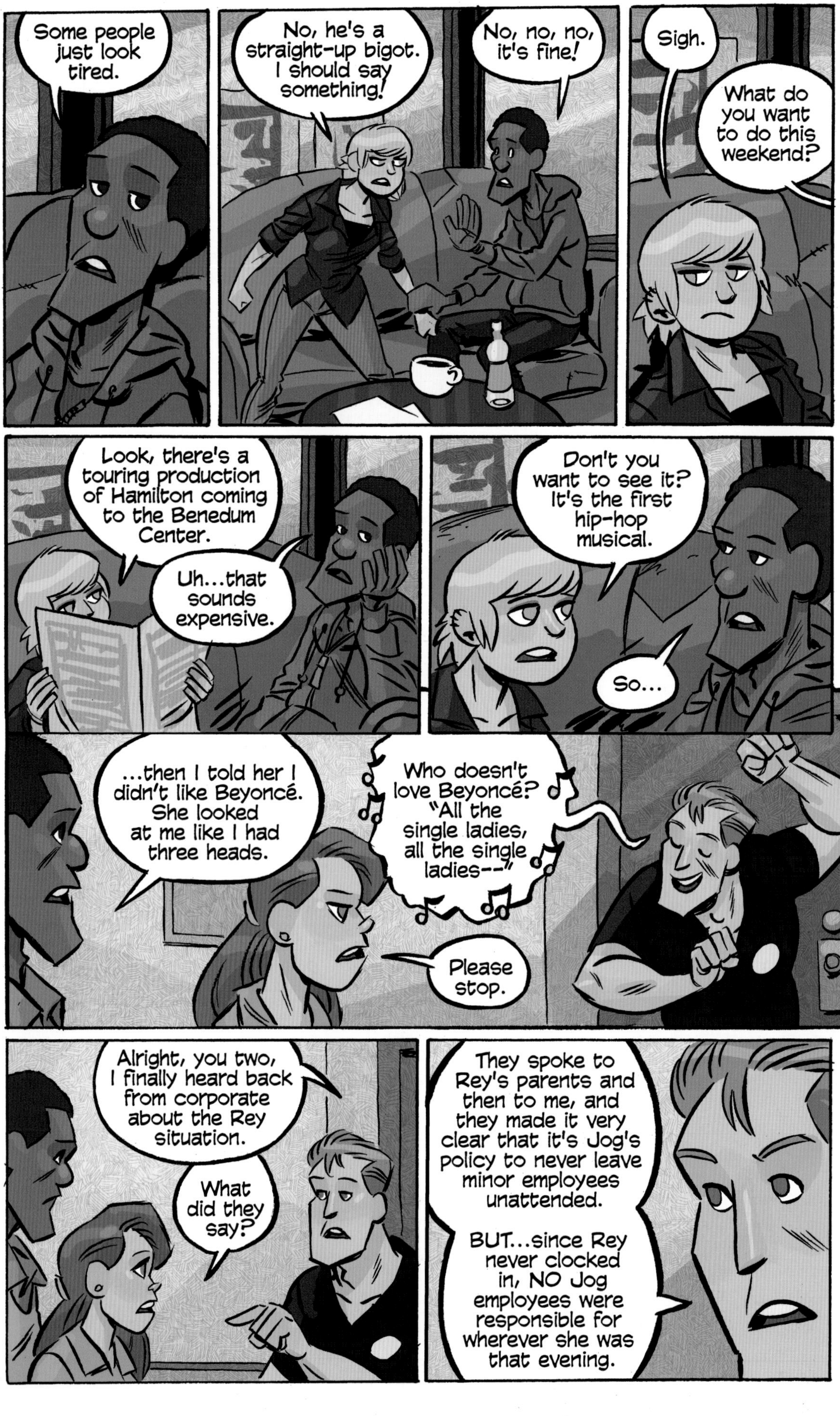
Some people just look tired.
No, he's a straight-up bigot. I should say something!
No, no, no, it's fine!
Sigh.
What do you want to do this weekend?
Look, there's a touring production of Hamilton coming to the Benedum Center.
Uh...that sounds expensive.
Don't you want to see it? It's the first hip-hop musical.
So...
...then I told her I didn't like Beyoncé. She looked at me like I had three heads.
Who doesn't love Beyoncé? "All the single ladies, all the single ladies--"
Please stop.
Alright, you two, I finally heard back from corporate about the Rey situation.
What did they say?
They spoke to Rey's parents and then to me, and they made it very clear that it's Jog's policy to never leave minor employees unattended.
BUT...since Rey never clocked in, NO Jog employees were responsible for wherever she was that evening.

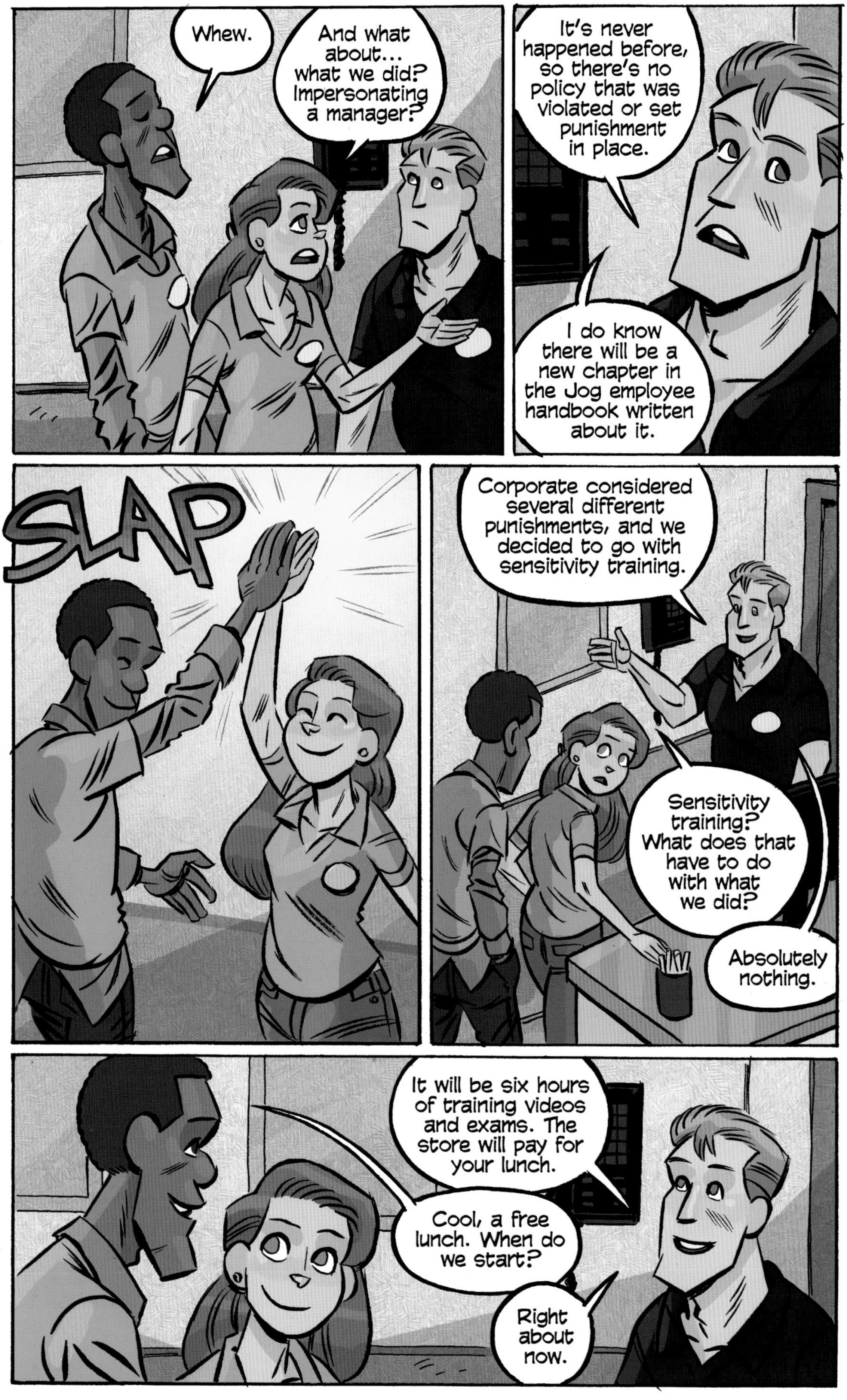
Whew.
And what about... what we did? Impersonating a manager?
It's never happened before, so there's no policy that was violated or set punishment in place.
I do know there will be a new chapter in the Jog employee handbook written about it.
SLAP
Corporate considered several different punishments, and we decided to go with sensitivity training.
Sensitivity training? What does that have to do with what we did?
Absolutely nothing.
It will be six hours of training videos and exams. The store will pay for your lunch.
Cool, a free lunch. When do we start?
Right about now.

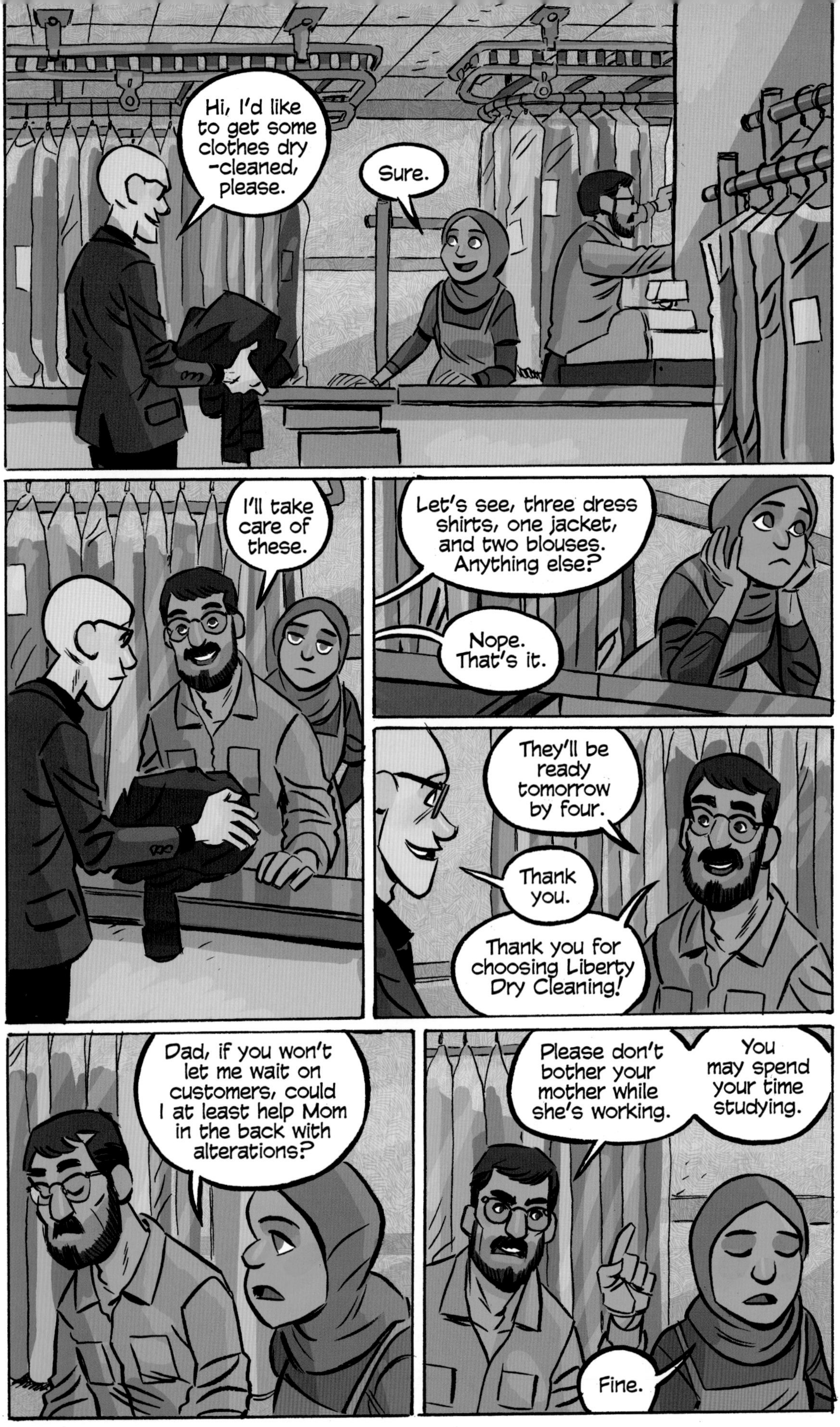
Hi, I'd like to get some clothes dry -cleaned, please.
Sure.
I'll take care of these.
Let's see, three dress shirts, one jacket, and two blouses. Anything else?
Nope. That's it.
They'll be ready tomorrow by four.
Thank you.
Thank you for choosing Liberty Dry Cleaning!
Dad, if you won't let me wait on customers, could I at least help Mom in the back with alterations?
Please don't bother your mother while she's working.
You may spend your time studying.
Fine.

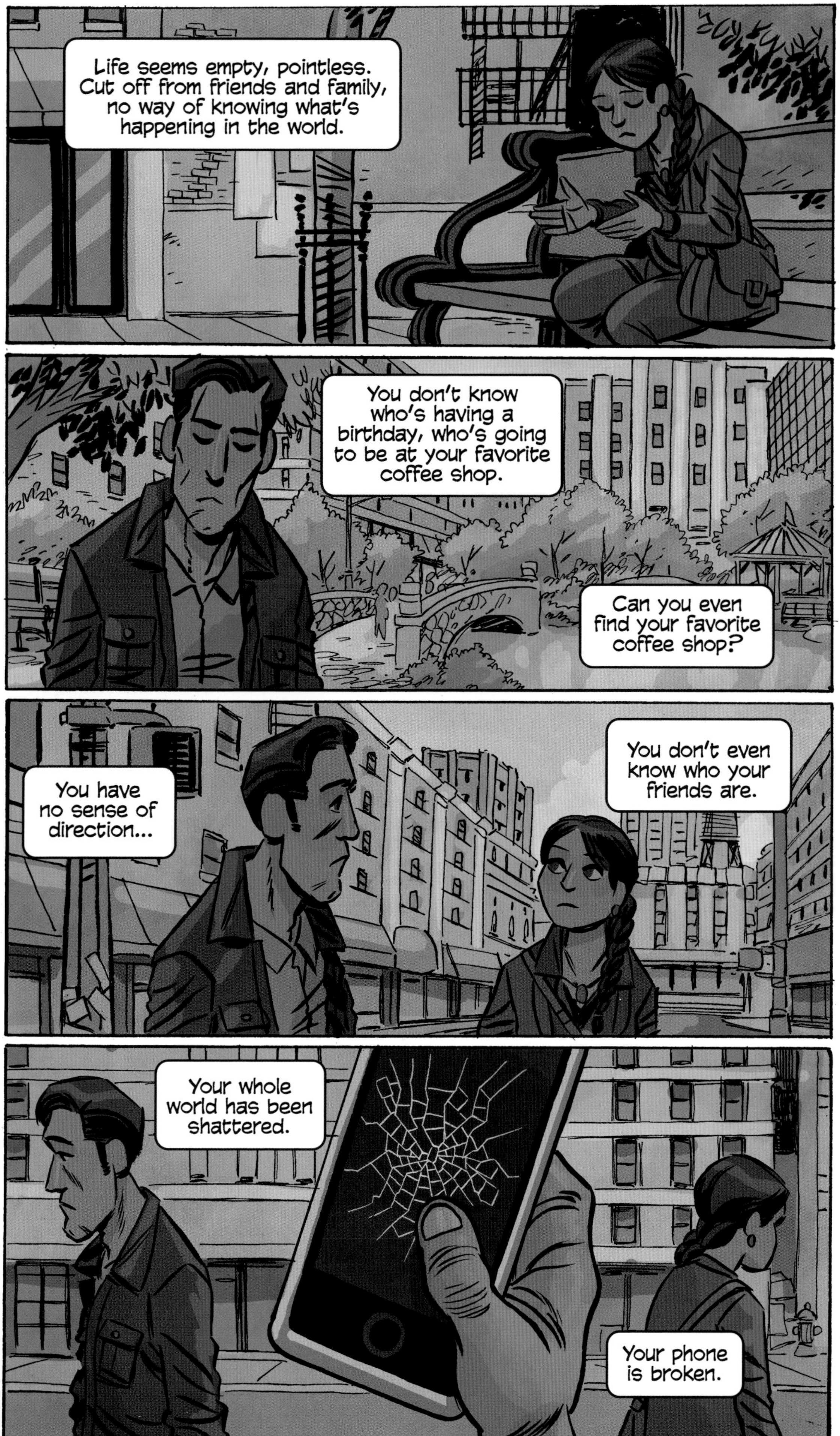
Life seems empty, pointless. Cut off from friends and family, no way of knowing what's happening in the world.
You don't know who's having a birthday, who's going to be at your favorite coffee shop.
Can you even find your favorite coffee shop?
You have no sense of direction...
You don't even know who your friends are.
Your whole world has been shattered.
Your phone is broken.

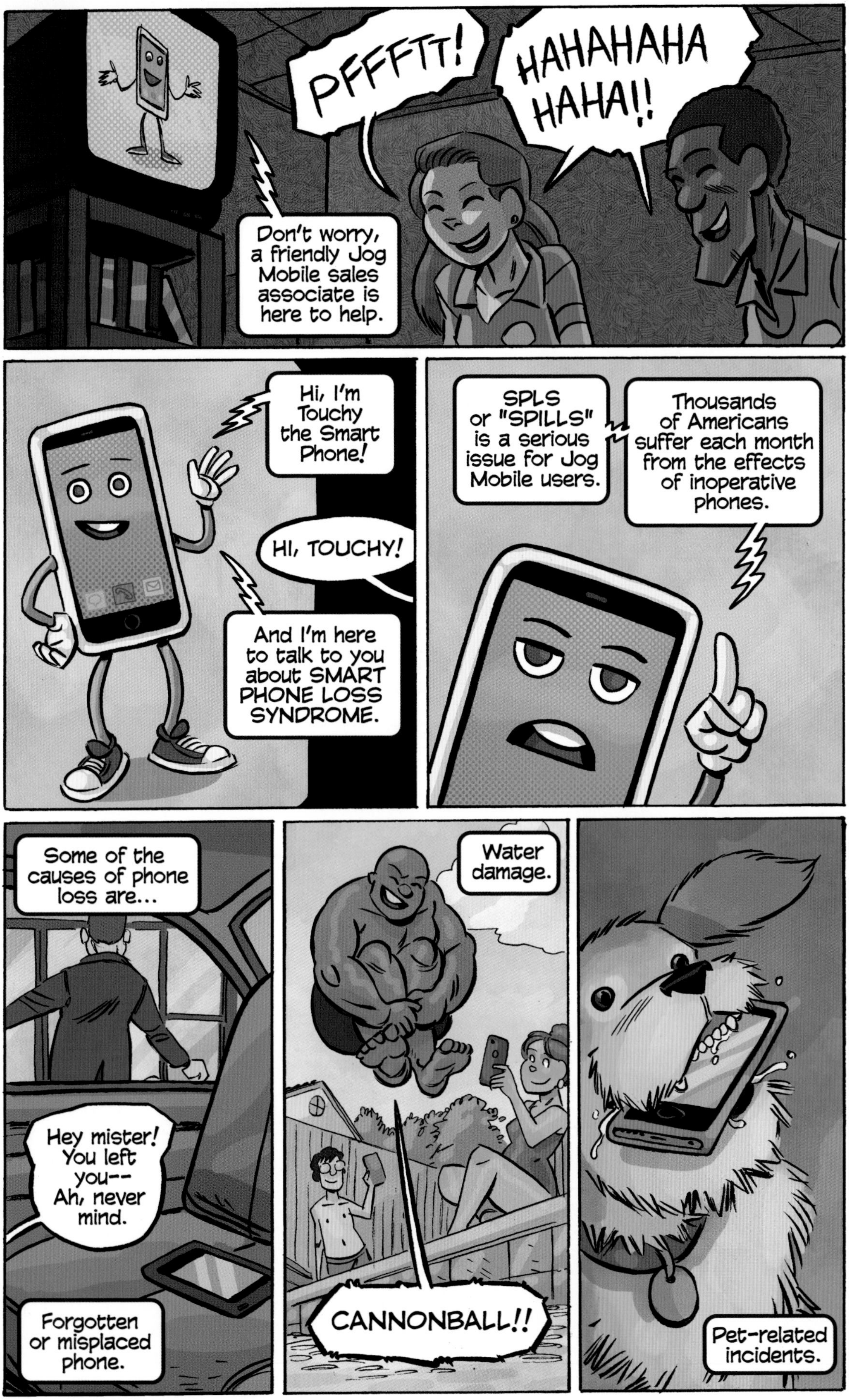
PFFFTT!
HAHAHAHA HAHA!!
Don't worry, a friendly Jog Mobile sales associate is here to help.
Hi, I'm Touchy the Smart Phone!
HI, TOUCHY!
And I'm here to talk to you about SMART PHONE LOSS SYNDROME.
SPLS or "SPILLS" is a serious issue for Jog Mobile users.
Thousands of Americans suffer each month from the effects of inoperative phones.
Some of the causes of phone loss are...
Hey mister! You left you-- Ah, never mind.
Forgotten or misplaced phone.
Water damage.
CANNONBALL!!
Pet-related incidents.

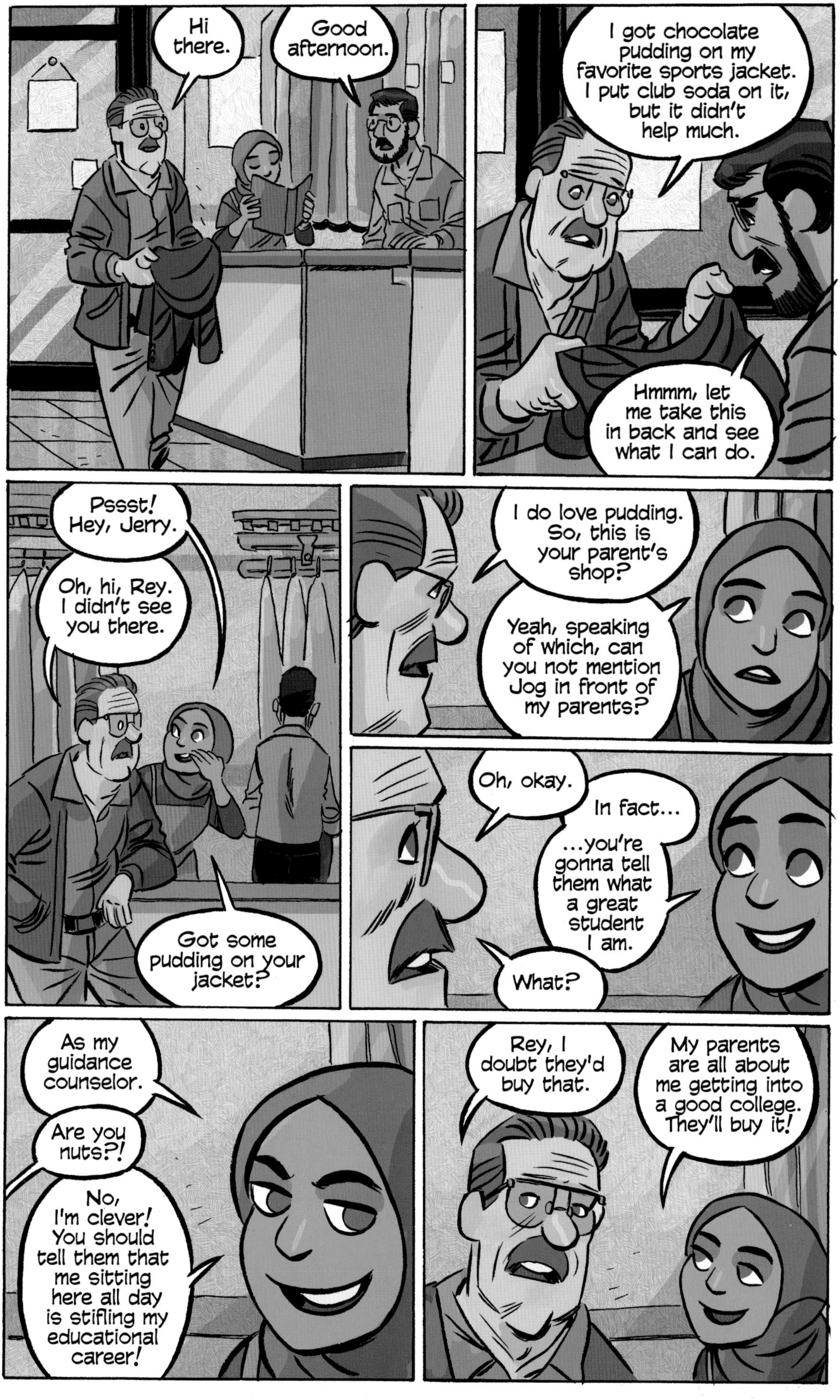
Hi there.
Good afternoon.
I got chocolate pudding on my favorite sports jacket. I put club soda on it, but it didn't help much.
Hmmm, let me take this in back and see what I can do.
Pssst! Hey, Jerry.
Oh, hi, Rey. I didn't see you there.
Got some pudding on your jacket?
I do love pudding. So, this is your parent's shop?
Yeah, speaking of which, can you not mention Jog in front of my parents?
Oh, okay.
In fact...
...you're gonna tell them what a great student I am.
What?
As my guidance counselor.
Are you nuts?!
No, I'm clever! You should tell them that me sitting here all day is stifling my educational career!
Rey, I doubt they'd buy that.
My parents are all about me getting into a good college. They'll buy it!

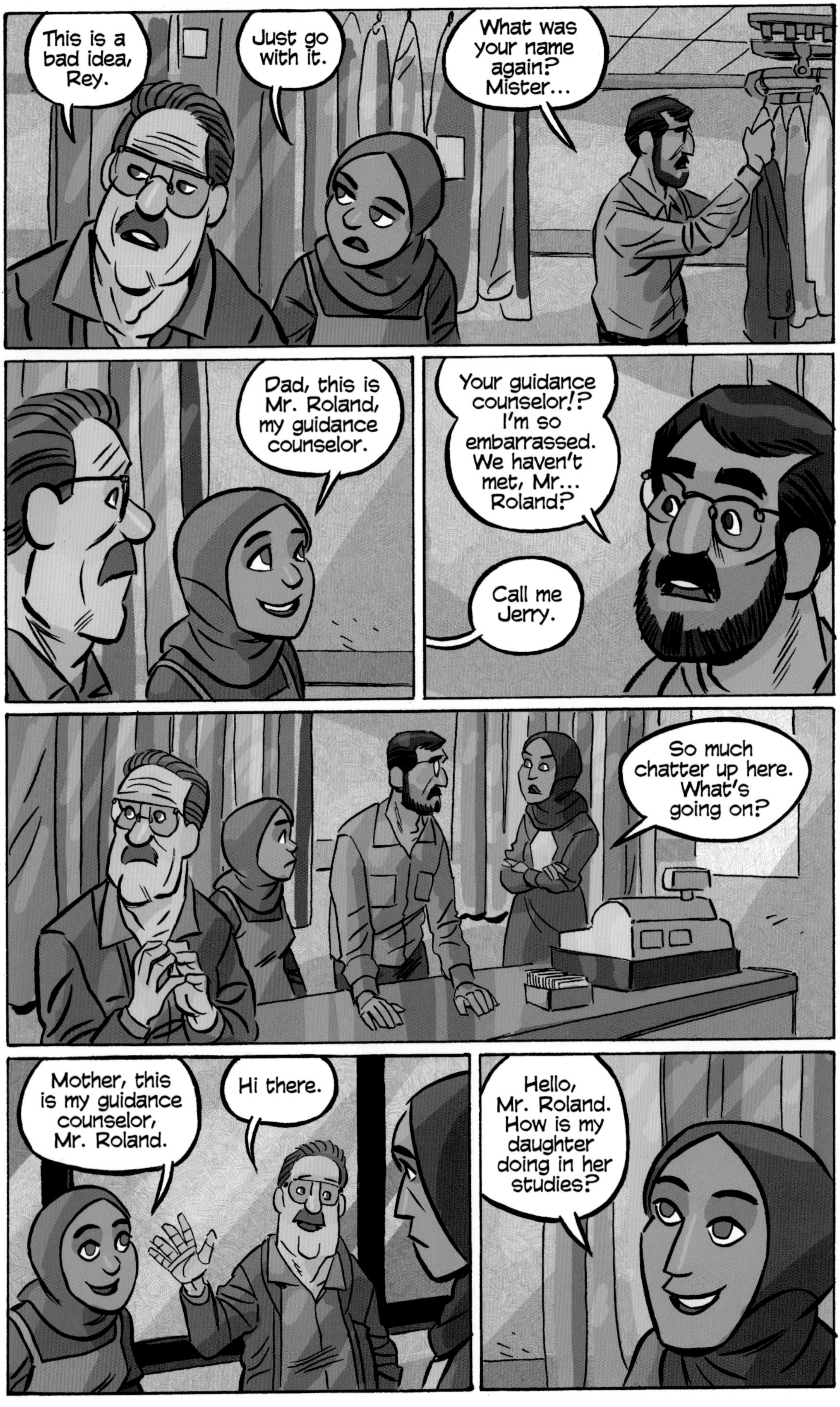
This is a bad idea, Rey.
Just go with it.
What was your name again? Mister...
Dad, this is Mr. Roland, my guidance counselor.
Your guidance counselor!? I'm so embarrassed. We haven't met, Mr... Roland?
Call me Jerry.
So much chatter up here. What's going on?
Mother, this is my guidance counselor, Mr. Roland.
Hi there.
Hello, Mr. Roland. How is my daughter doing in her studies?

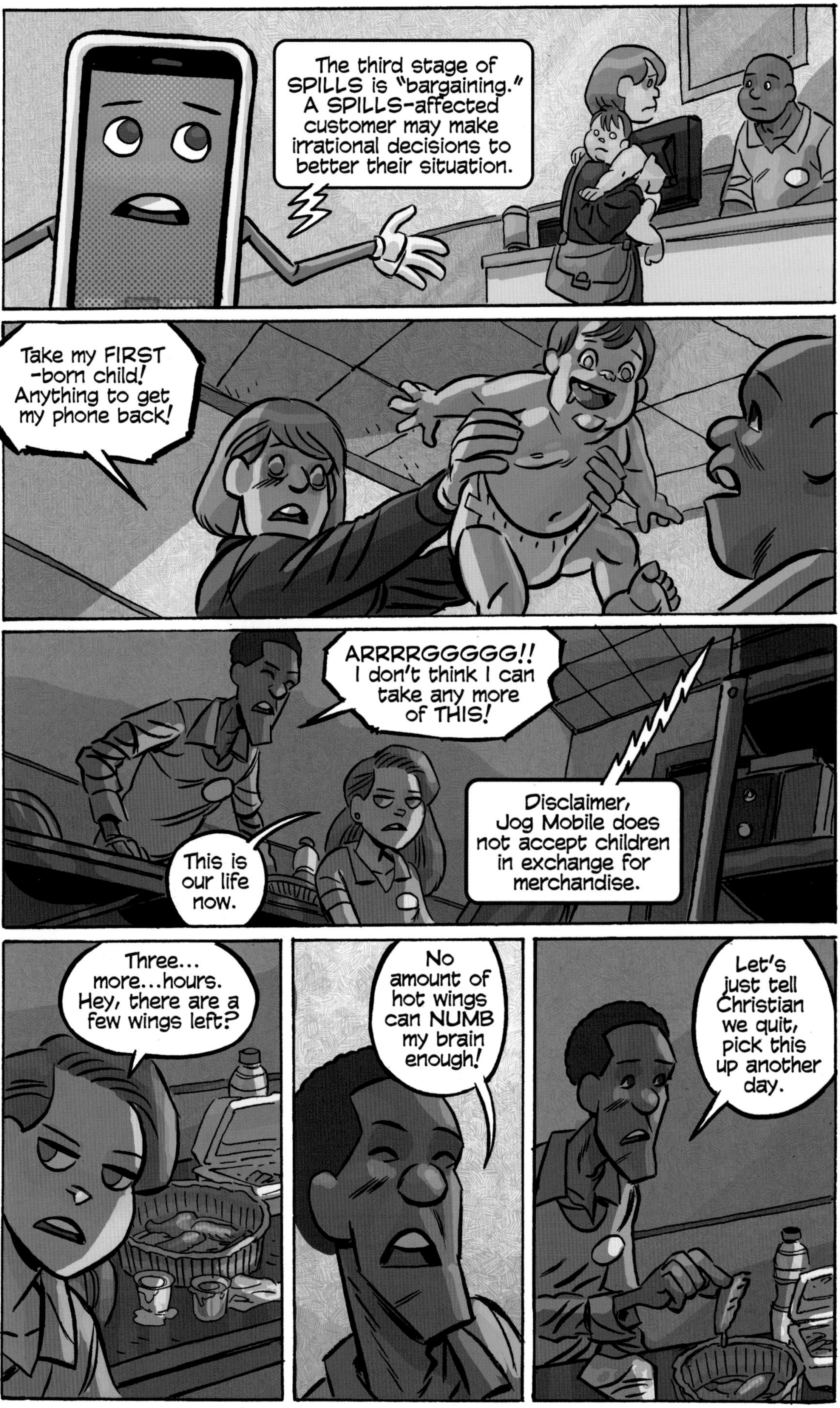
The third stage of SPILLS is "bargaining." A SPILLS-affected customer may make irrational decisions to better their situation.
Take my FIRST-born child! Anything to get my phone back!
ARRRRGGGGG!! I don't think I can take any more of THIS!
This is our life now.
Disclaimer, Jog Mobile does not accept children in exchange for merchandise.
Three... more...hours. Hey, there are a few wings left?
No amount of hot wings can NUMB my brain enough!
Let's just tell Christian we quit, pick this up another day.

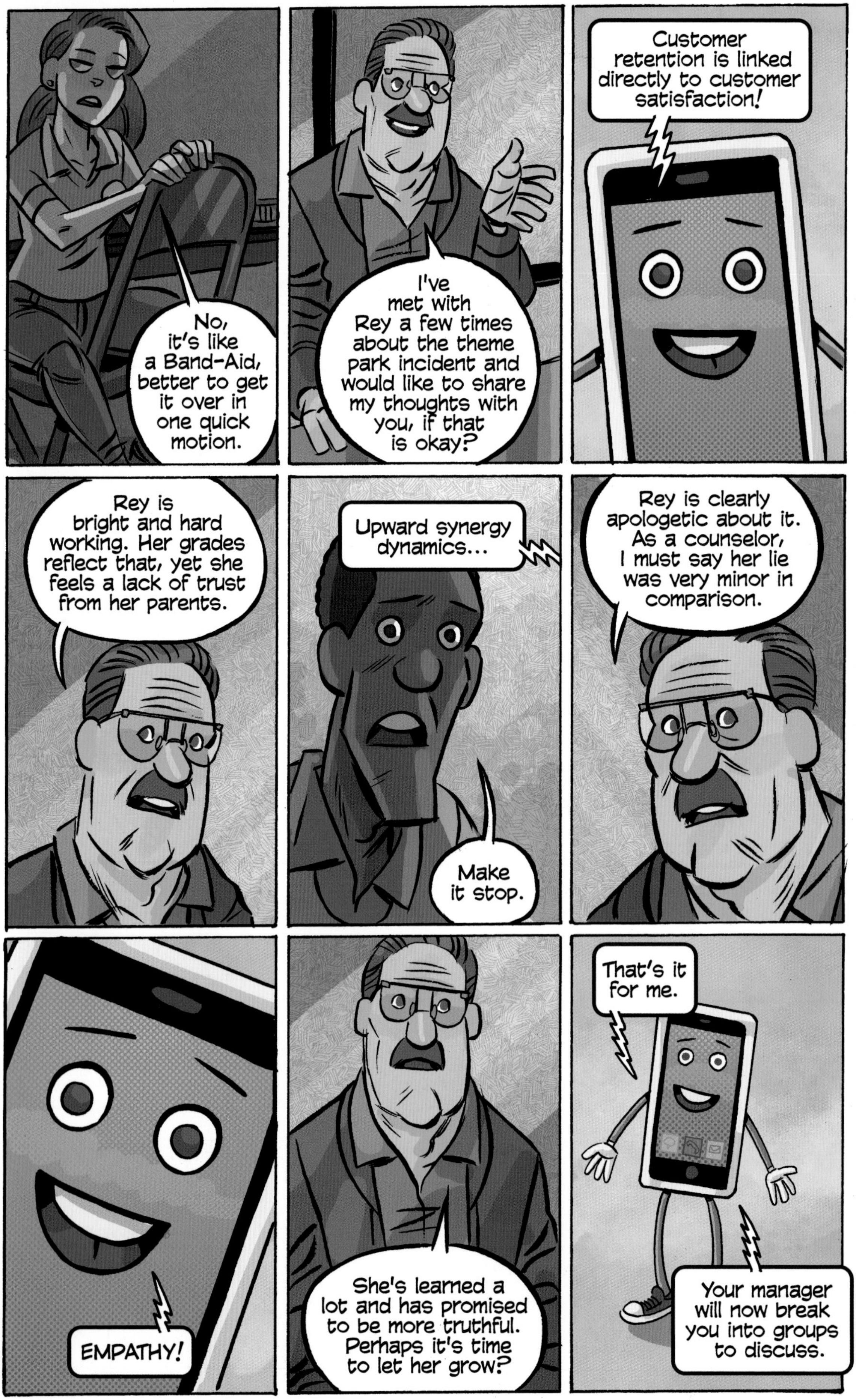
No, it's like a Band-Aid, better to get it over in one quick motion.
I've met with Rey a few times about the theme park incident and would like to share my thoughts with you, if that is okay?
Customer retention is linked directly to customer satisfaction!
Rey is bright and hard working. Her grades reflect that, yet she feels a lack of trust from her parents.
Upward synergy dynamics...
Make it stop.
Rey is clearly apologetic about it. As a counselor, I must say her lie was very minor in comparison.
EMPATHY!
She's learned a lot and has promised to be more truthful. Perhaps it's time to let her grow?
That's it for me.
Your manager will now break you into groups to discuss.

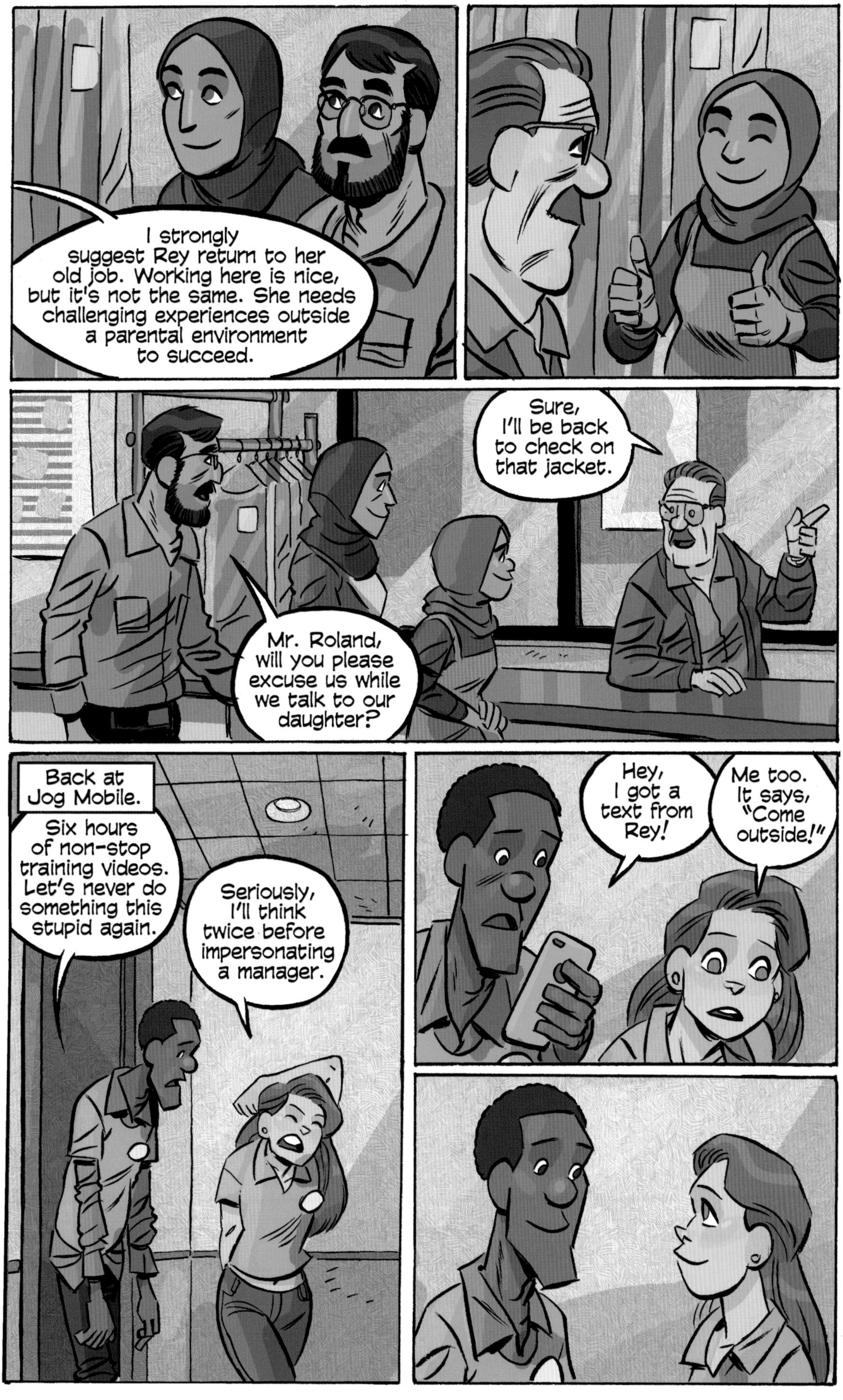
I strongly suggest Rey return to her old job. Working here is nice, but it's not the same. She needs challenging experiences outside a parental environment to succeed.
Sure, I'll be back to check on that jacket.
Mr. Roland, will you please excuse us while we talk to our daughter?
Back at Jog Mobile.
Six hours of non-stop training videos. Let's never do something this stupid again.
Seriously, I'll think twice before impersonating a manager.
Hey, I got a text from Rey!
Me too. It says, "Come outside!"

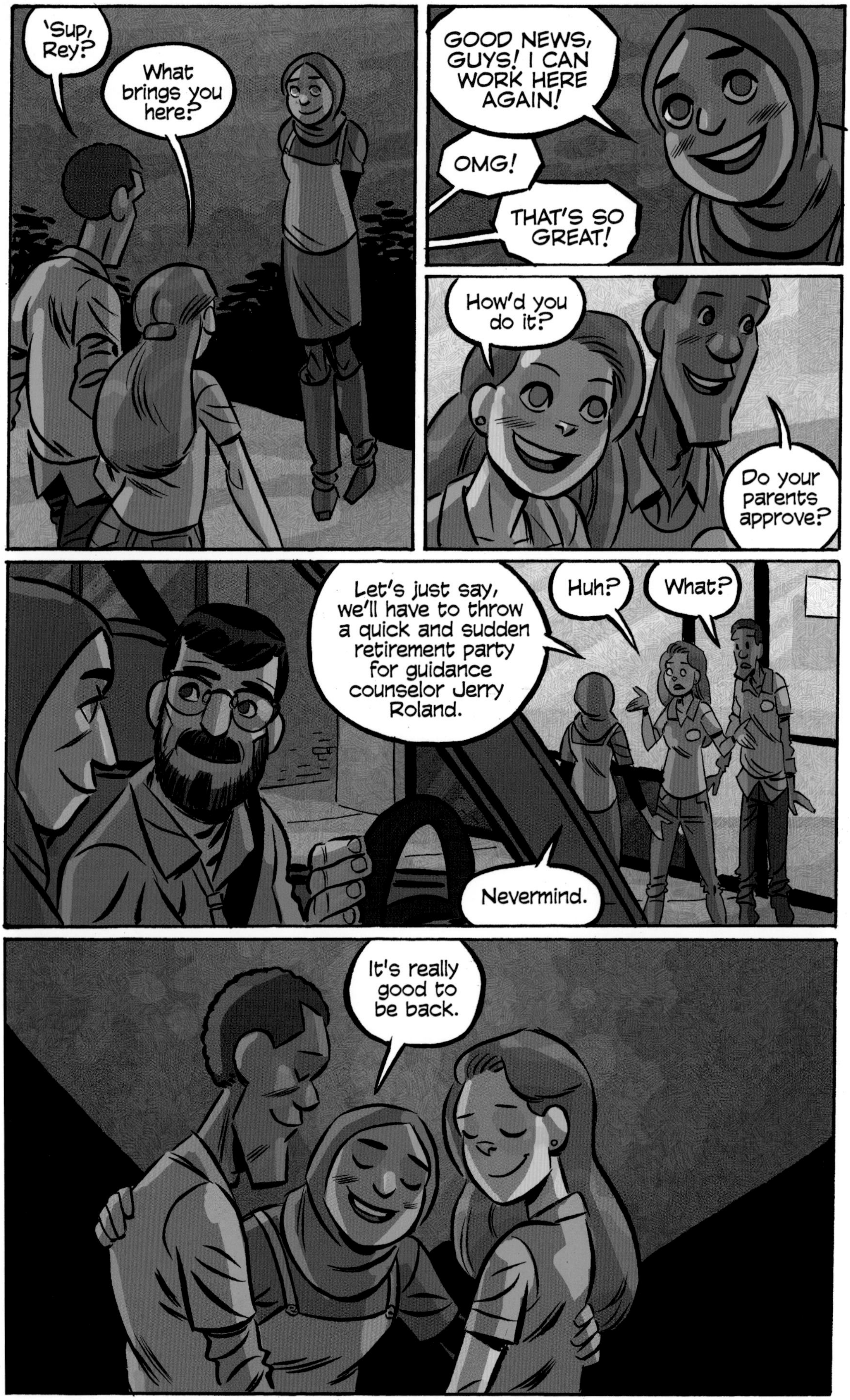
'Sup, Rey?
What brings you here?
GOOD NEWS, GUYS! I CAN WORK HERE AGAIN!
OMG!
THAT'S SO GREAT!
How'd you do it?
Do your parents approve?
Let's just say, we'll have to throw a quick and sudden retirement party for guidance counselor Jerry Roland.
Huh?
What?
Nevermind.
It's really good to be back.

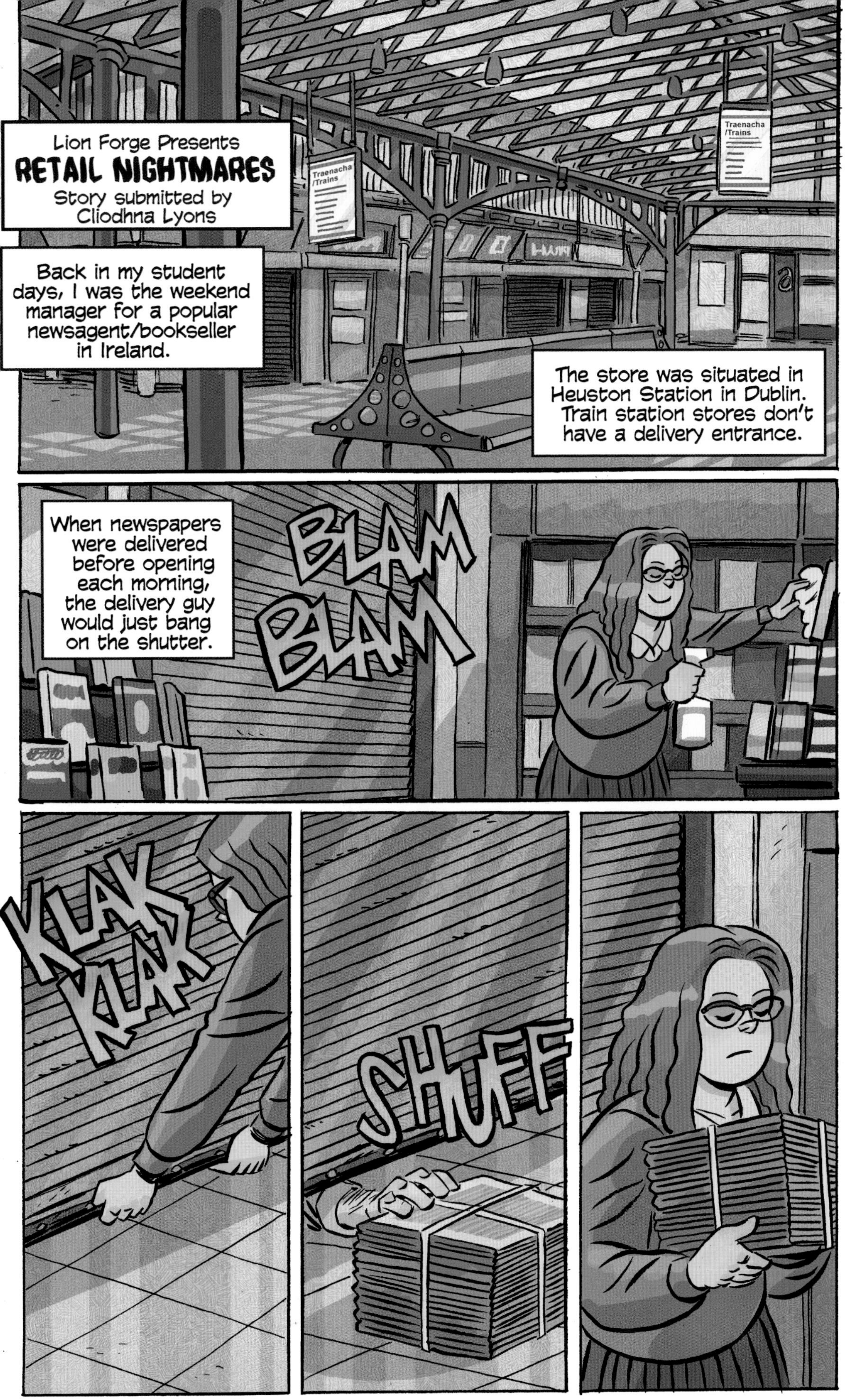
Lion Forge Presents
RETAIL NIGHTMARES
Story submitted by
Cliodhna Lyons
Traenacha
/Trains
Traenacha
/Trains
Back in my student days, I was the weekend manager for a popular newsagent/bookseller in Ireland.
The store was situated in Heuston Station in Dublin. Train station stores don't have a delivery entrance.
When newspapers were delivered before opening each morning, the delivery guy would just bang on the shutter.
BLAM
BLAM
KLAK
KLAK
SHUFF

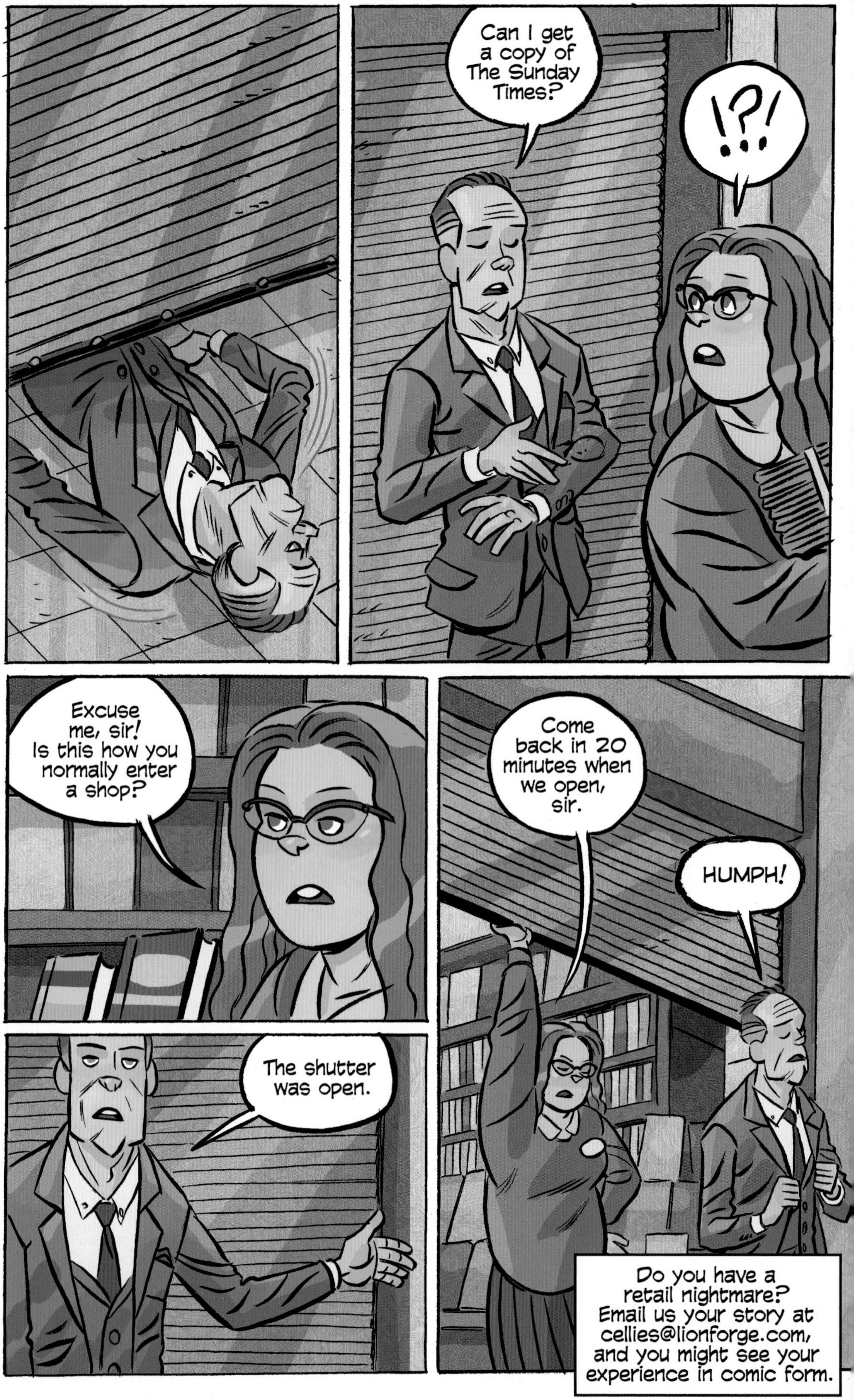
Can I get a copy of The Sunday Times?
!?!
Excuse me, sir! Is this how you normally enter a shop?
The shutter was open.
Come back in 20 minutes when we open, sir.
HUMPH!
Do you have a retail nightmare? Email us your story at cellies@lionforge.com, and you might see your experience in comic form.

# CHAPTER 3

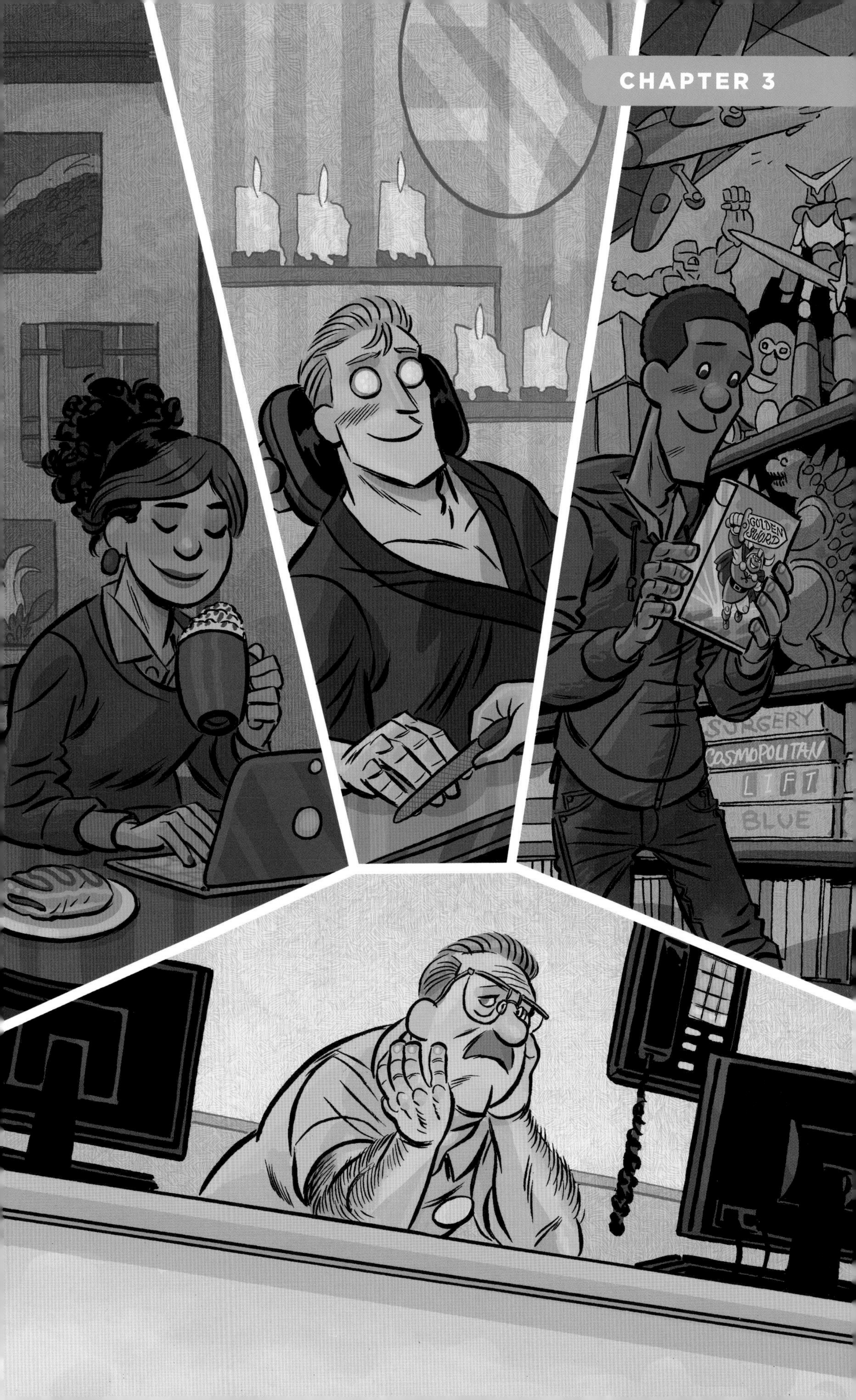
GOLDEN SWORD
SURGERY
COSMOPOLITAN
LIFT
BLUE

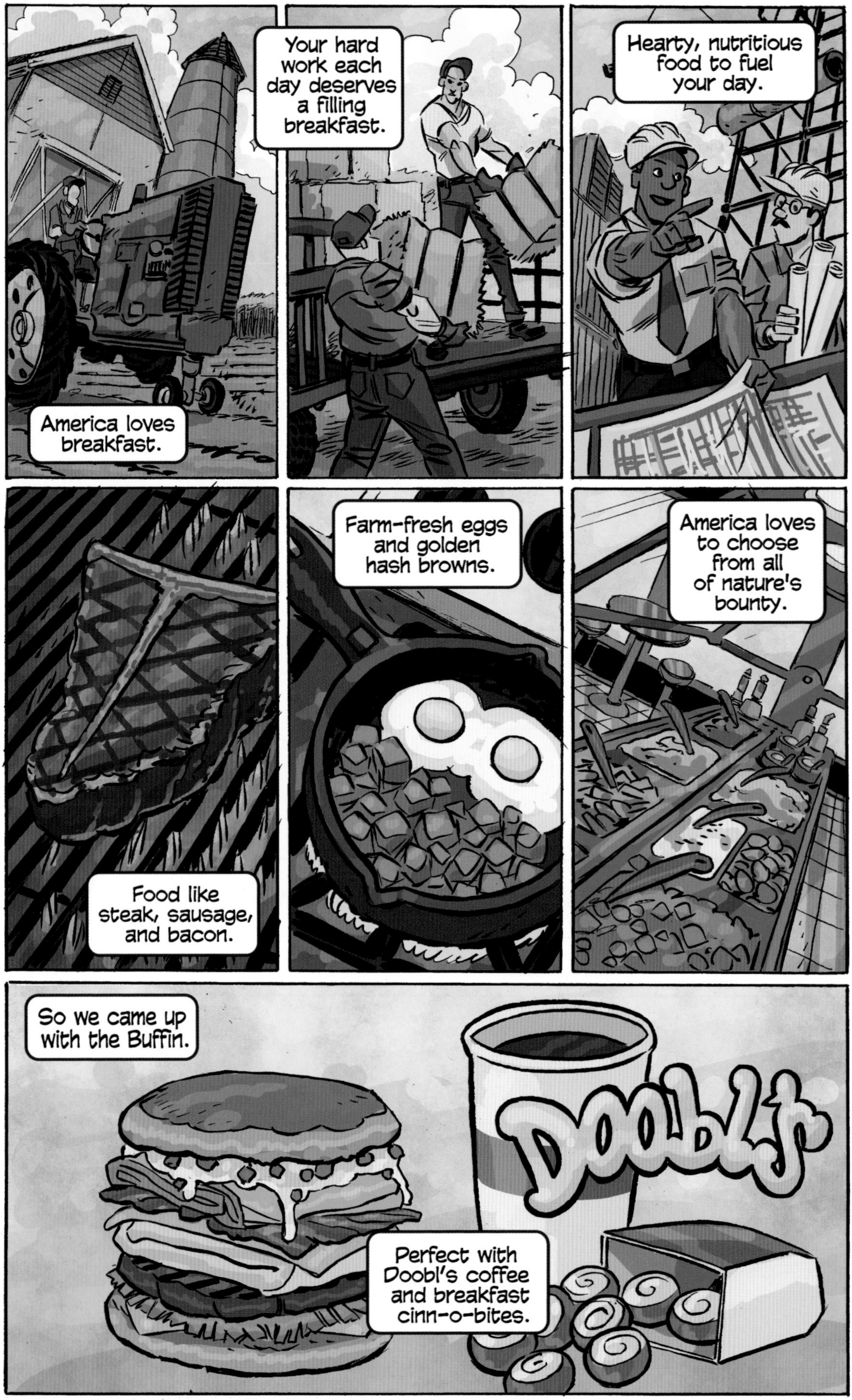
America loves breakfast.
Your hard work each day deserves a filling breakfast.
Hearty, nutritious food to fuel your day.
Food like steak, sausage, and bacon.
Farm-fresh eggs and golden hash browns.
America loves to choose from all of nature's bounty.
So we came up with the Buffin.
Doobl's
Perfect with Doobl's coffee and breakfast cinn-o-bites.

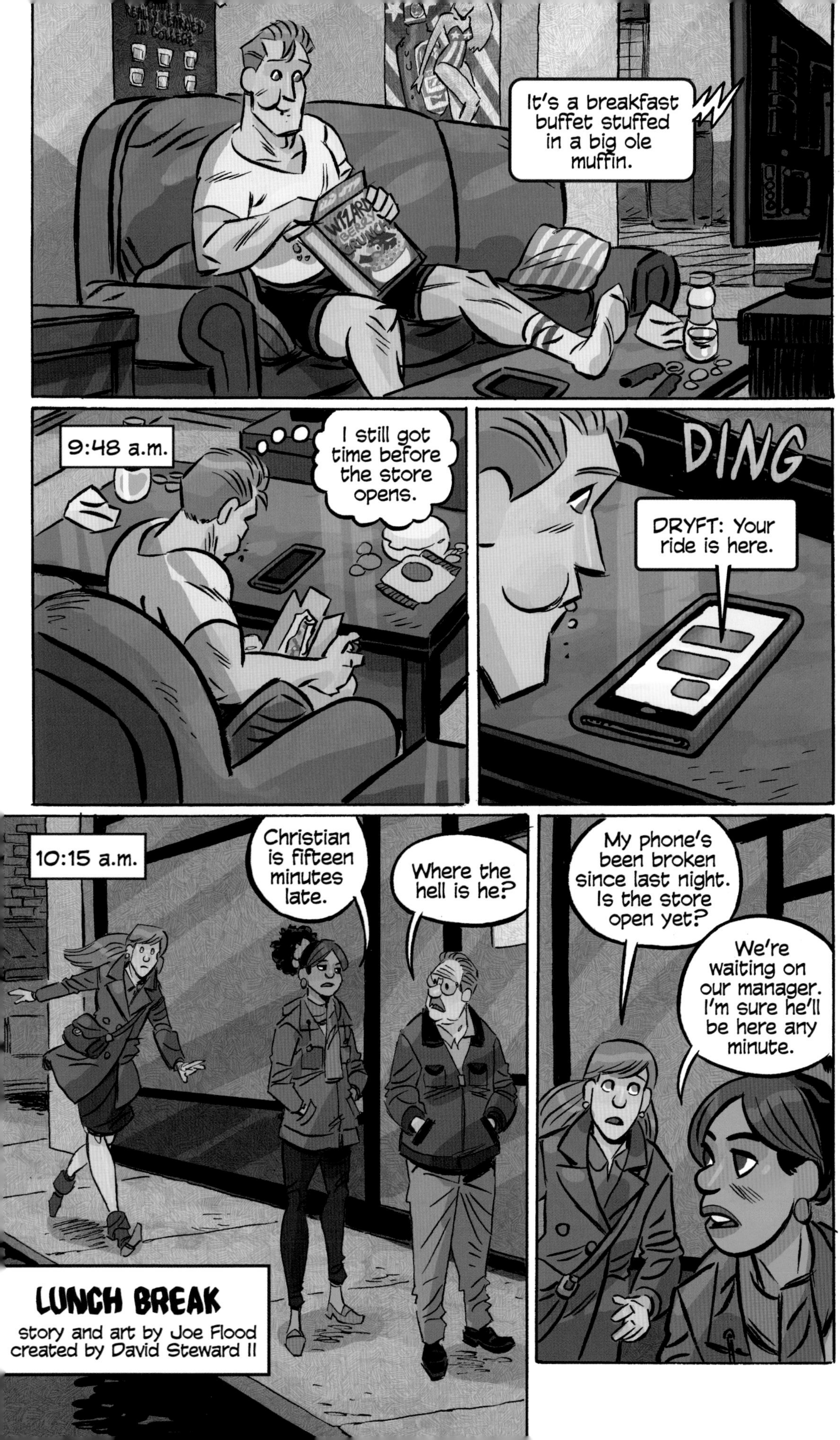
It's a breakfast buffet stuffed in a big ole muffin.
WIZARD BERRY CRUNCH
9:48 a.m.
I still got time before the store opens.
DING
DRYFT: Your ride is here.
10:15 a.m.
Christian is fifteen minutes late.
Where the hell is he?
My phone's been broken since last night. Is the store open yet?
We're waiting on our manager. I'm sure he'll be here any minute.
LUNCH BREAK
story and art by Joe Flood
created by David Steward II

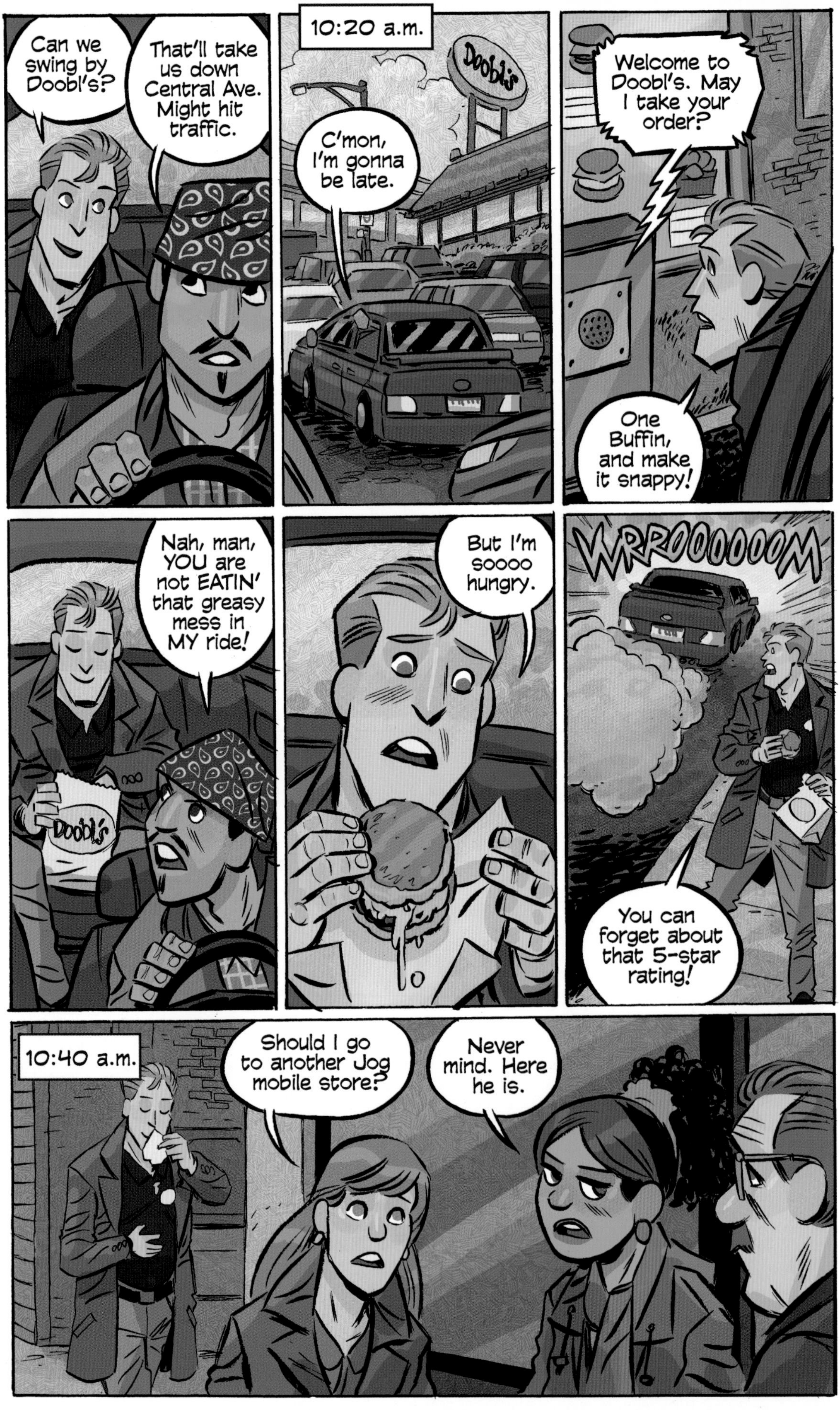

Can we swing by Doobl's?
That'll take us down Central Ave. Might hit traffic.
10:20 a.m.
Doobl's
C'mon, I'm gonna be late.
Welcome to Doobl's. May I take your order?
One Buffin, and make it snappy!
Nah, man, YOU are not EATIN' that greasy mess in MY ride!
Doobl's
But I'm soooo hungry.
WRROOOOOOM
You can forget about that 5-star rating!
10:40 a.m.
Should I go to another Jog mobile store?
Never mind. Here he is.

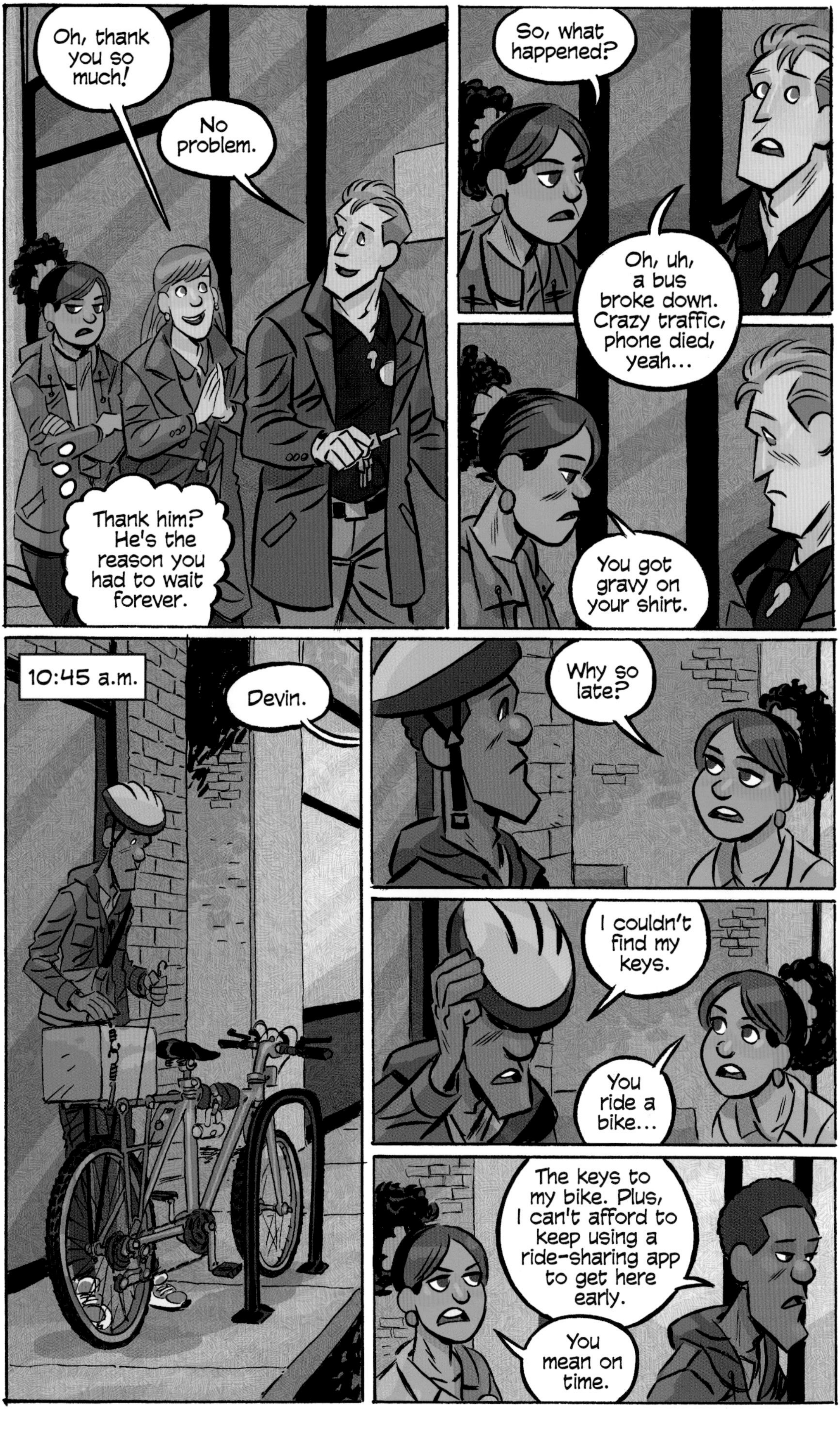
Oh, thank you so much!
No problem.
Thank him? He's the reason you had to wait forever.
So, what happened?
Oh, uh, a bus broke down. Crazy traffic, phone died, yeah...
You got gravy on your shirt.
10:45 a.m.
Devin.
Why so late?
I couldn't find my keys.
You ride a bike...
The keys to my bike. Plus, I can't afford to keep using a ride-sharing app to get here early.
You mean on time.

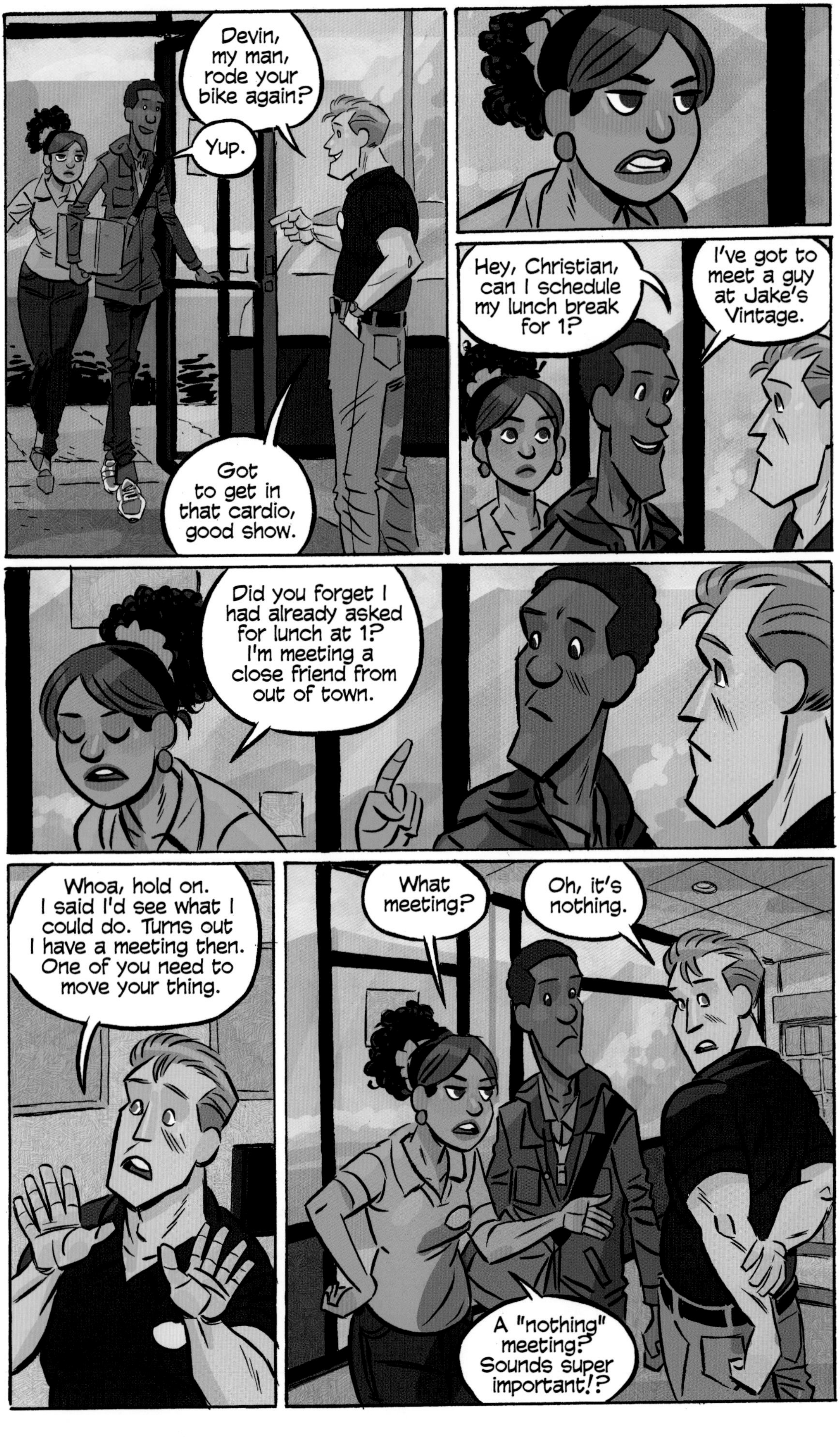
Devin, my man, rode your bike again?
Yup.
Got to get in that cardio, good show.
Hey, Christian, can I schedule my lunch break for 1?
I've got to meet a guy at Jake's Vintage.
Did you forget I had already asked for lunch at 1? I'm meeting a close friend from out of town.
Whoa, hold on. I said I'd see what I could do. Turns out I have a meeting then. One of you need to move your thing.
What meeting?
Oh, it's nothing.
A "nothing" meeting? Sounds super important!?

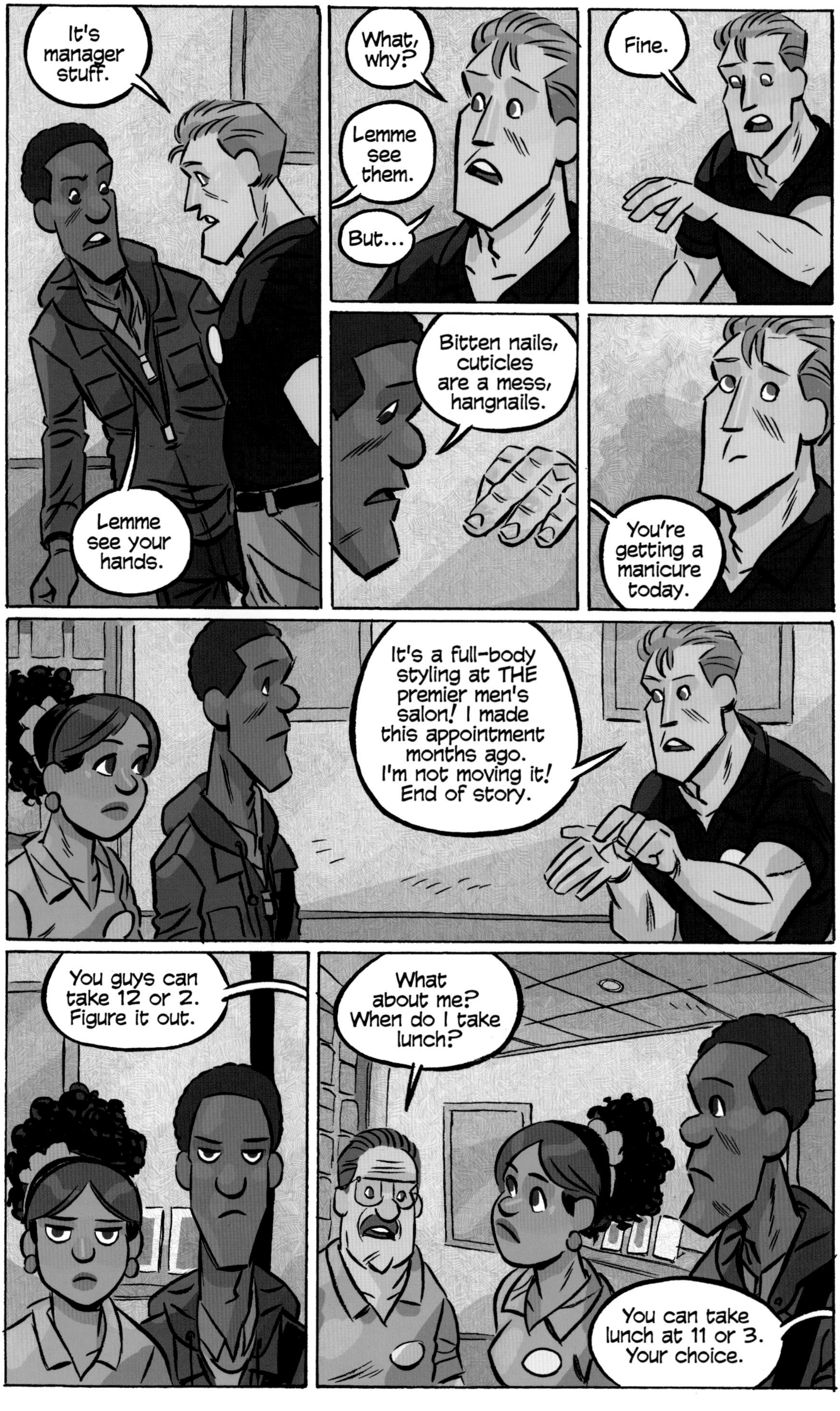
It's manager stuff.
Lemme see your hands.
What, why?
Lemme see them.
But...
Fine.
Bitten nails, cuticles are a mess, hangnails.
You're getting a manicure today.
It's a full-body styling at THE premier men's salon! I made this appointment months ago. I'm not moving it! End of story.
You guys can take 12 or 2. Figure it out.
What about me? When do I take lunch?
You can take lunch at 11 or 3. Your choice.

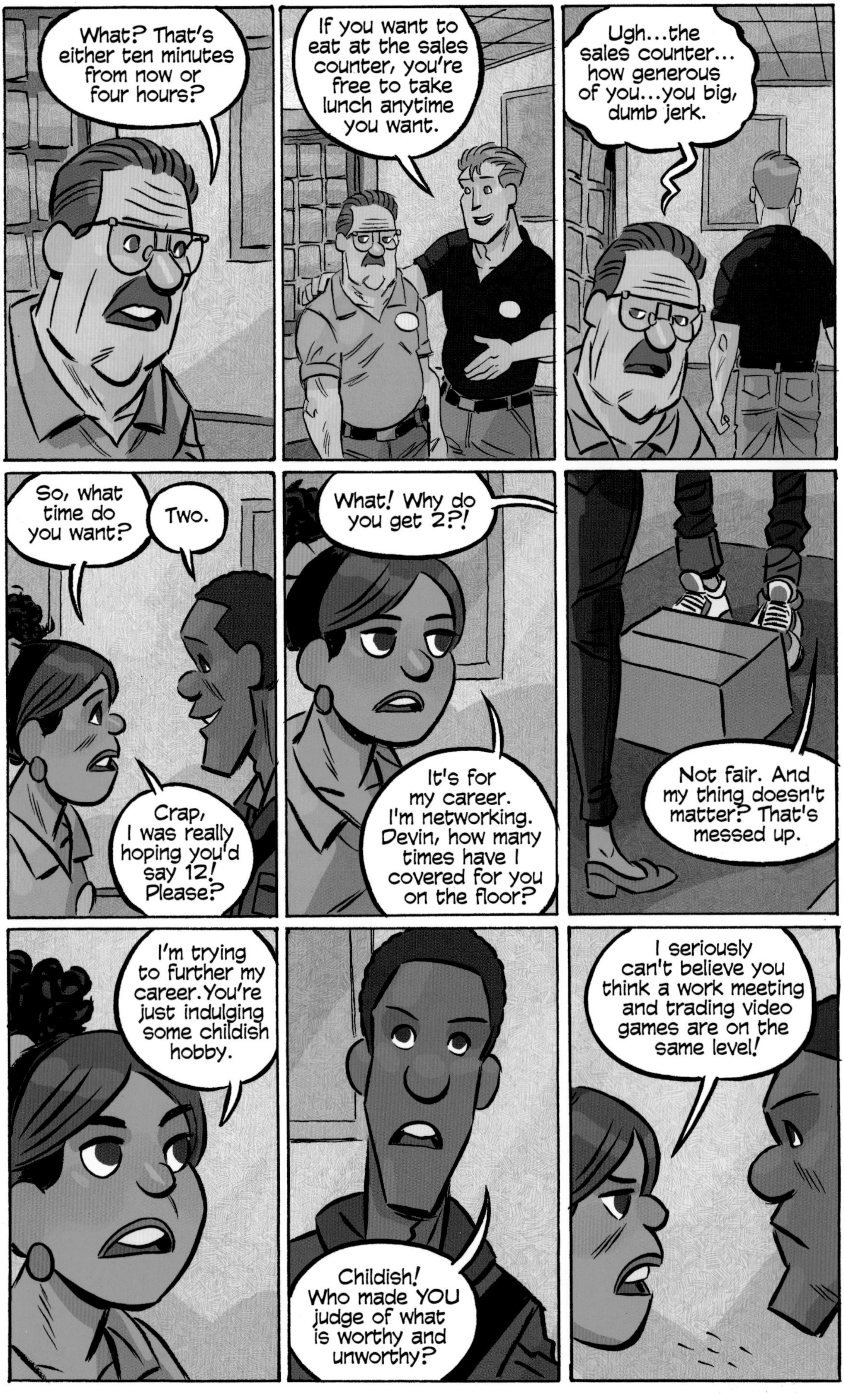
What? That's either ten minutes from now or four hours?
If you want to eat at the sales counter, you're free to take lunch anytime you want.
Ugh...the sales counter... how generous of you...you big, dumb jerk.
So, what time do you want?
Two.
Crap, I was really hoping you'd say 12! Please?
What! Why do you get 2?!
It's for my career. I'm networking. Devin, how many times have I covered for you on the floor?
Not fair. And my thing doesn't matter? That's messed up.
I'm trying to further my career. You're just indulging some childish hobby.
Childish! Who made YOU judge of what is worthy and unworthy?
I seriously can't believe you think a work meeting and trading video games are on the same level!

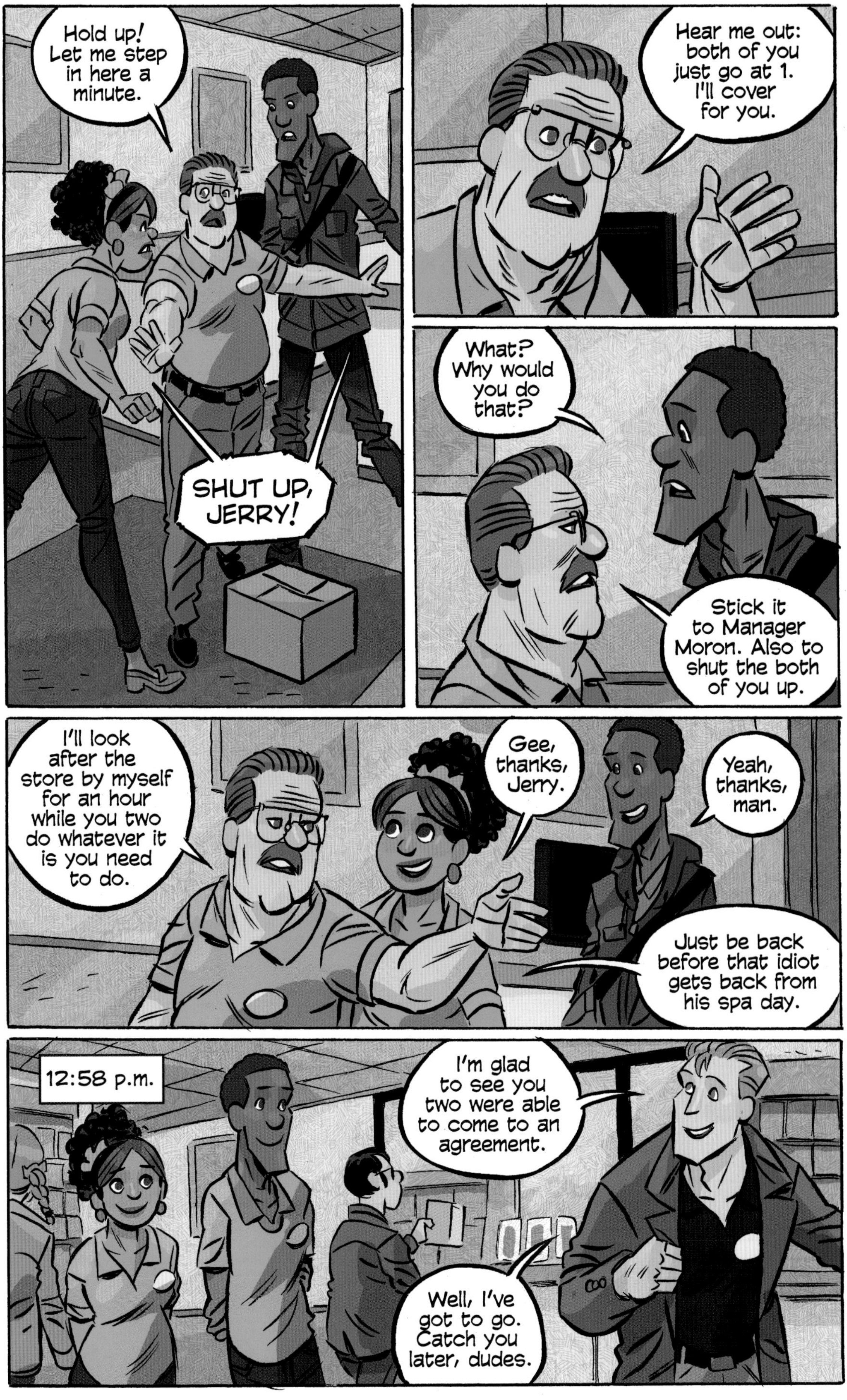
Hold up! Let me step in here a minute.
SHUT UP, JERRY!
Hear me out: both of you just go at 1. I'll cover for you.
What? Why would you do that?
Stick it to Manager Moron. Also to shut the both of you up.
I'll look after the store by myself for an hour while you two do whatever it is you need to do.
Gee, thanks, Jerry.
Yeah, thanks, man.
Just be back before that idiot gets back from his spa day.
12:58 p.m.
I'm glad to see you two were able to come to an agreement.
Well, I've got to go. Catch you later, dudes.

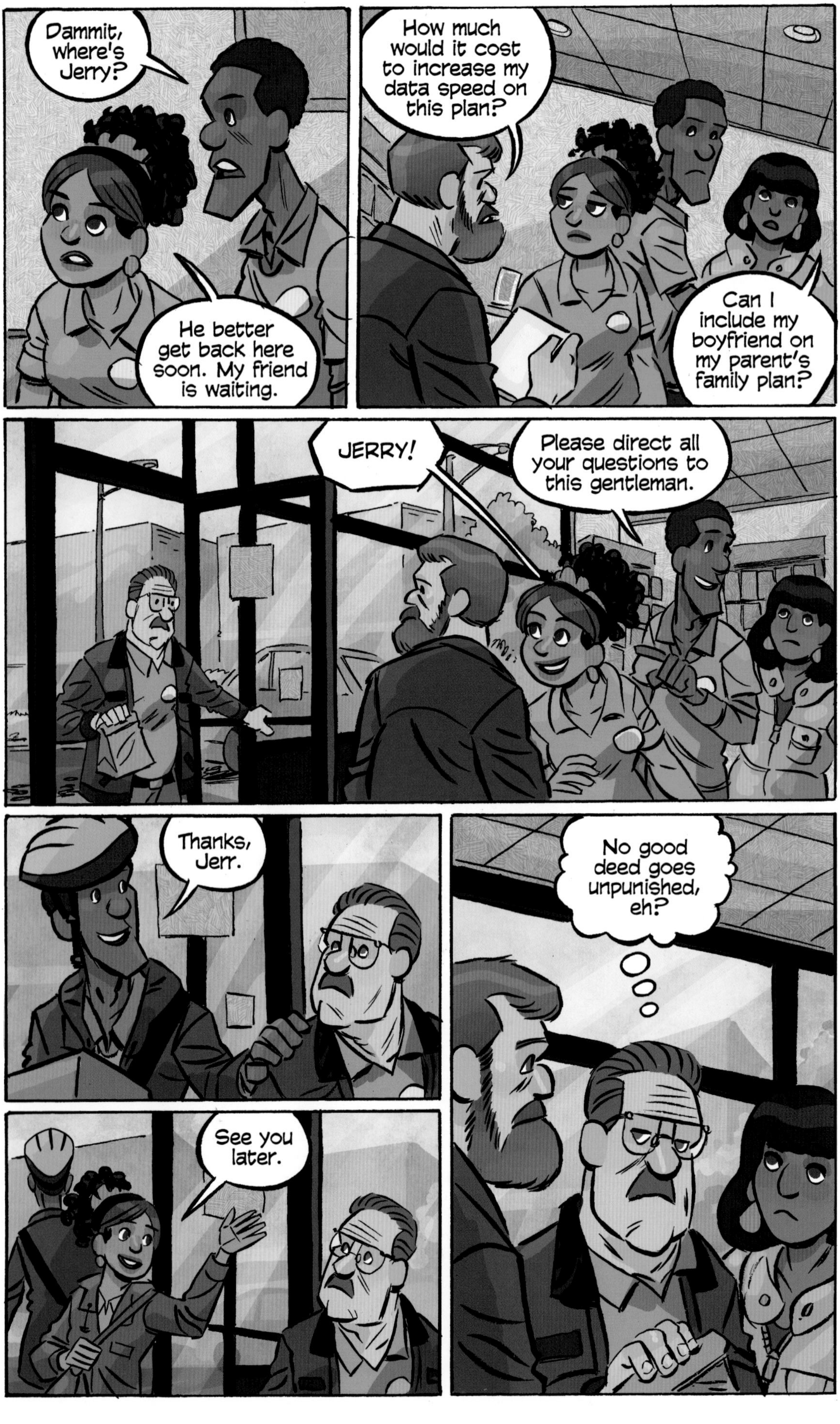
Dammit, where's Jerry?
He better get back here soon. My friend is waiting.
How much would it cost to increase my data speed on this plan?
Can I include my boyfriend on my parent's family plan?
JERRY!
Please direct all your questions to this gentleman.
Thanks, Jerr.
See you later.
No good deed goes unpunished, eh?

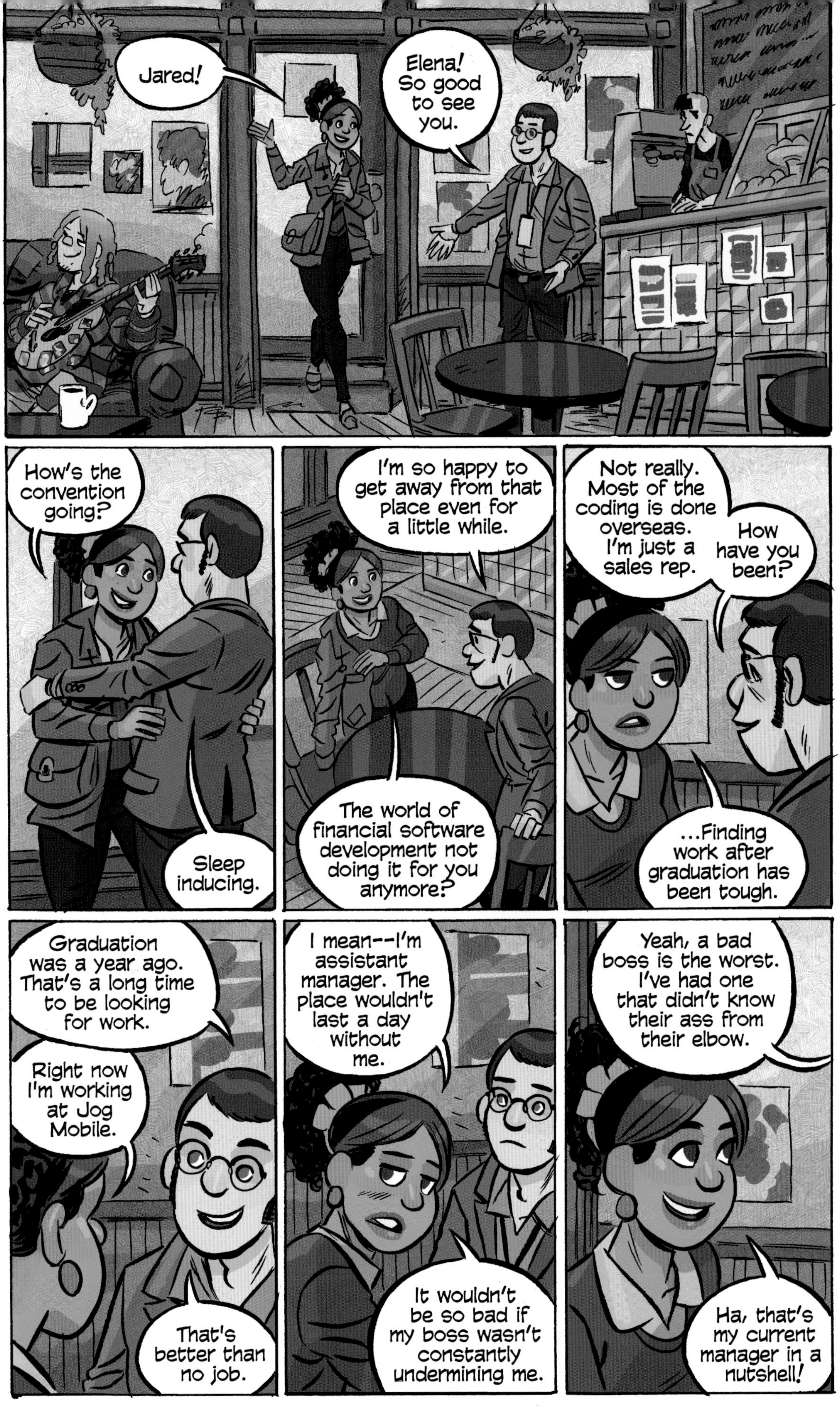
Jared!
Elena! So good to see you.
How's the convention going?
Sleep inducing.
I'm so happy to get away from that place even for a little while.
The world of financial software development not doing it for you anymore?
Not really. Most of the coding is done overseas. I'm just a sales rep.
How have you been?
...Finding work after graduation has been tough.
Graduation was a year ago. That's a long time to be looking for work.
Right now I'm working at Jog Mobile.
That's better than no job.
I mean--I'm assistant manager. The place wouldn't last a day without me.
It wouldn't be so bad if my boss wasn't constantly undermining me.
Yeah, a bad boss is the worst. I've had one that didn't know their ass from their elbow.
Ha, that's my current manager in a nutshell!

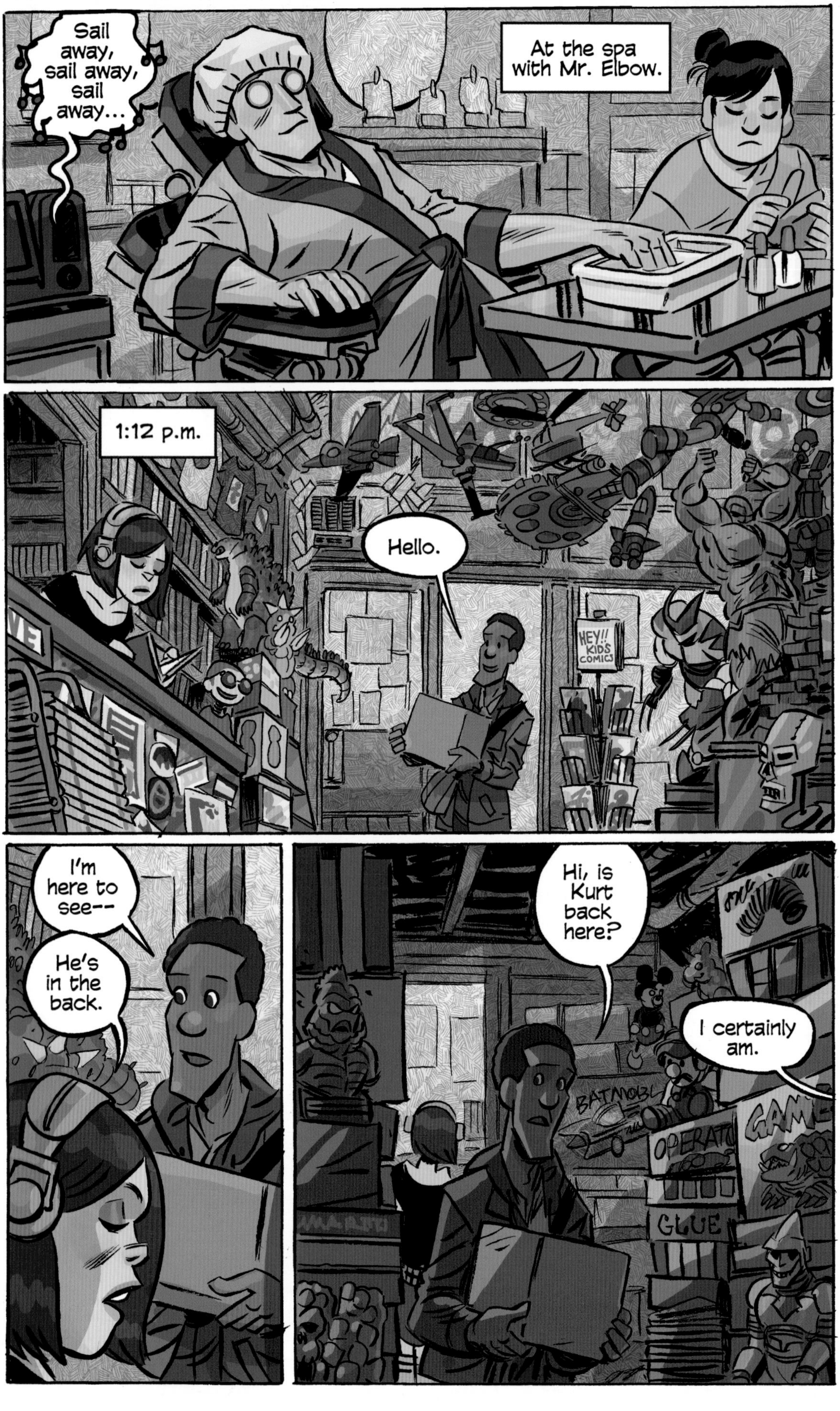

Sail away, sail away, sail away...
At the spa with Mr. Elbow.
1:12 p.m.
Hello.
HEY!! KIDS COMICS
I'm here to see--
He's in the back.
Hi, is Kurt back here?
I certainly am.
GLUE

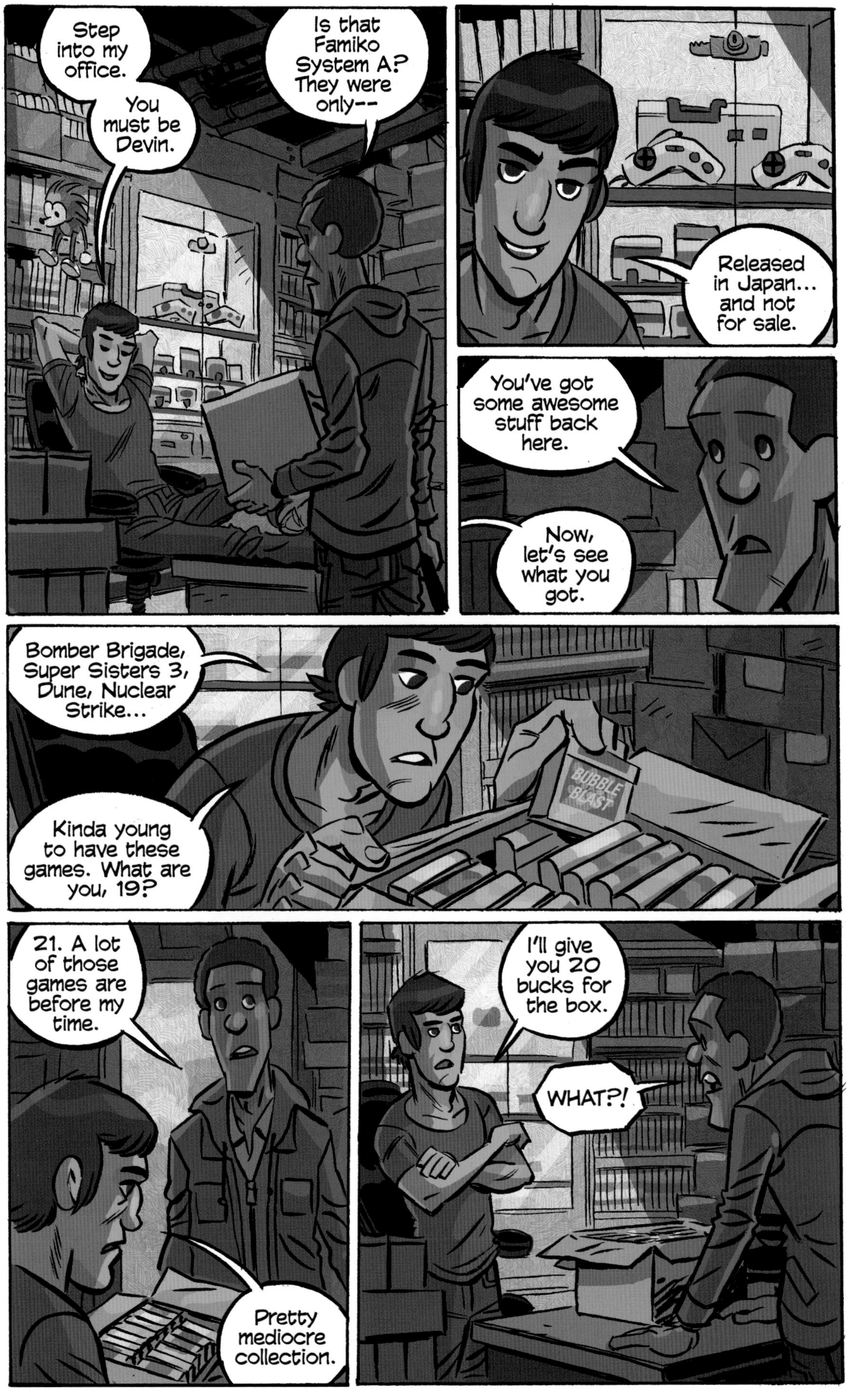
Step into my office.
You must be Devin.
Is that Famiko System A? They were only--
Released in Japan... and not for sale.
You've got some awesome stuff back here.
Now, let's see what you got.
Bomber Brigade, Super Sisters 3, Dune, Nuclear Strike...
BUBBLE BLAST
Kinda young to have these games. What are you, 19?
21. A lot of those games are before my time.
Pretty mediocre collection.
I'll give you 20 bucks for the box.
WHAT?!

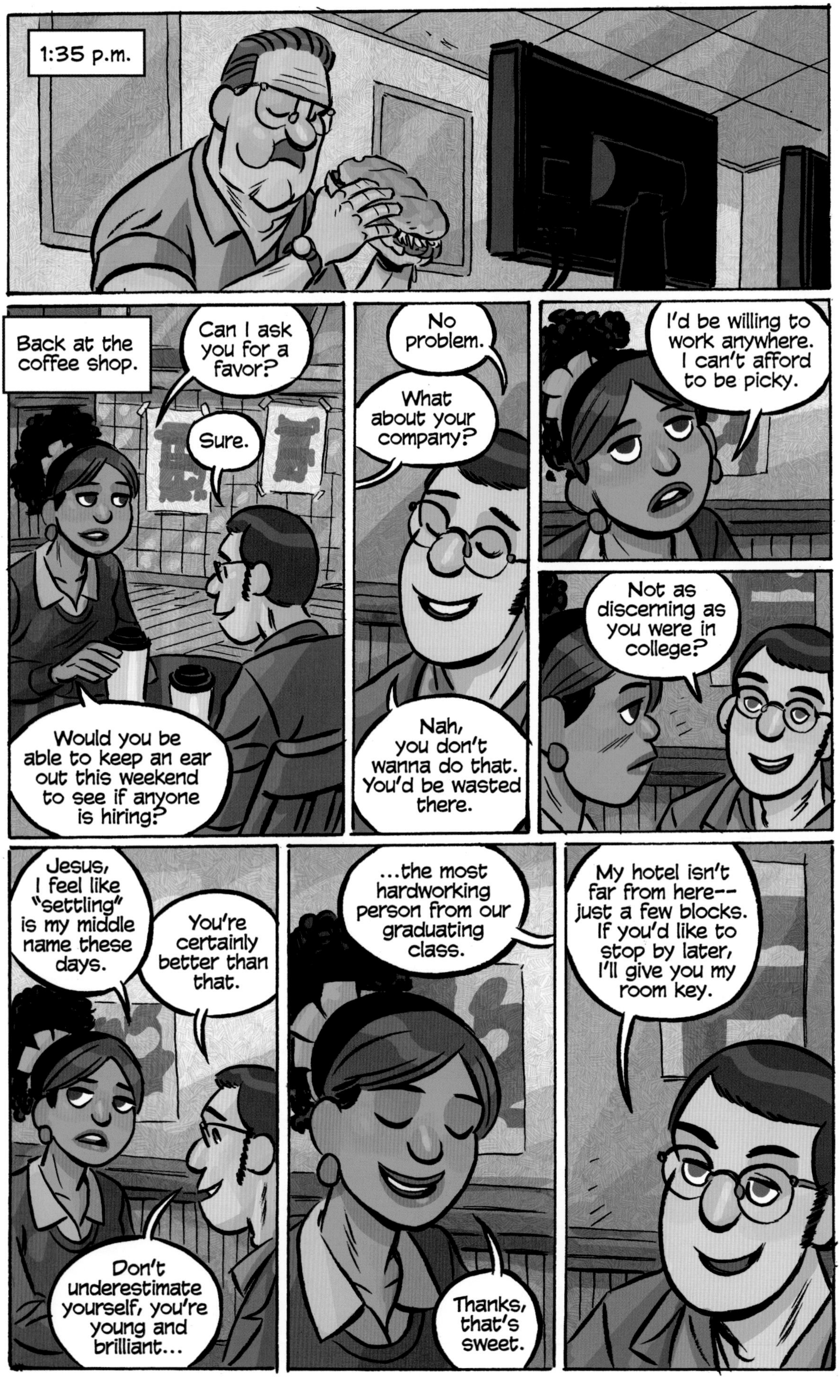
1:35 p.m.
Back at the coffee shop.
Can I ask you for a favor?
Sure.
Would you be able to keep an ear out this weekend to see if anyone is hiring?
No problem.
What about your company?
Nah, you don't wanna do that. You'd be wasted there.
I'd be willing to work anywhere. I can't afford to be picky.
Not as discerning as you were in college?
Jesus, I feel like "settling" is my middle name these days.
You're certainly better than that.
Don't underestimate yourself, you're young and brilliant...
...the most hardworking person from our graduating class.
Thanks, that's sweet.
My hotel isn't far from here--just a few blocks. If you'd like to stop by later, I'll give you my room key.

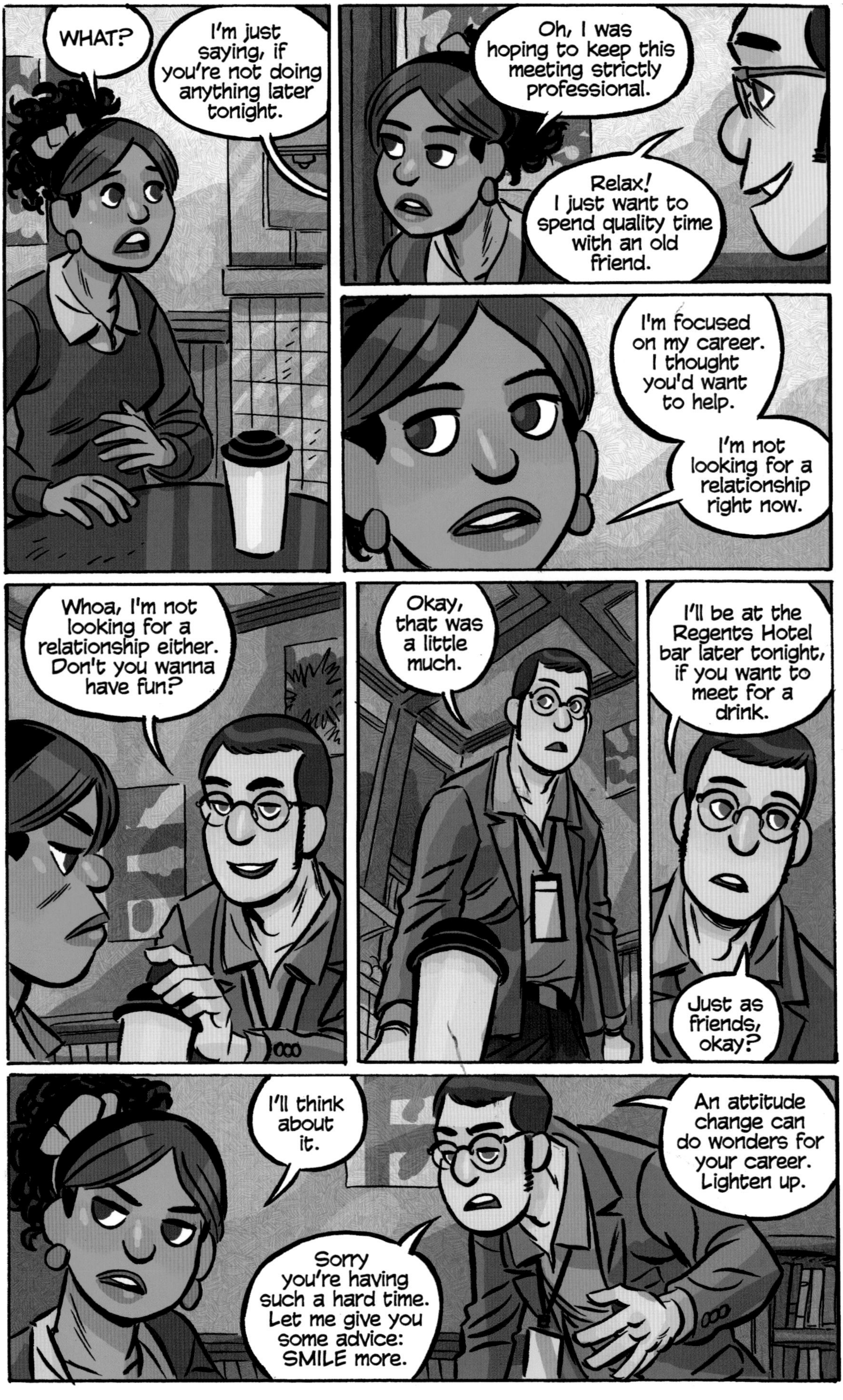
WHAT?
I'm just saying, if you're not doing anything later tonight.
Oh, I was hoping to keep this meeting strictly professional.
Relax! I just want to spend quality time with an old friend.
I'm focused on my career. I thought you'd want to help.
I'm not looking for a relationship right now.
Whoa, I'm not looking for a relationship either. Don't you wanna have fun?
Okay, that was a little much.
I'll be at the Regents Hotel bar later tonight, if you want to meet for a drink.
Just as friends, okay?
I'll think about it.
An attitude change can do wonders for your career. Lighten up.
Sorry you're having such a hard time. Let me give you some advice: SMILE more.

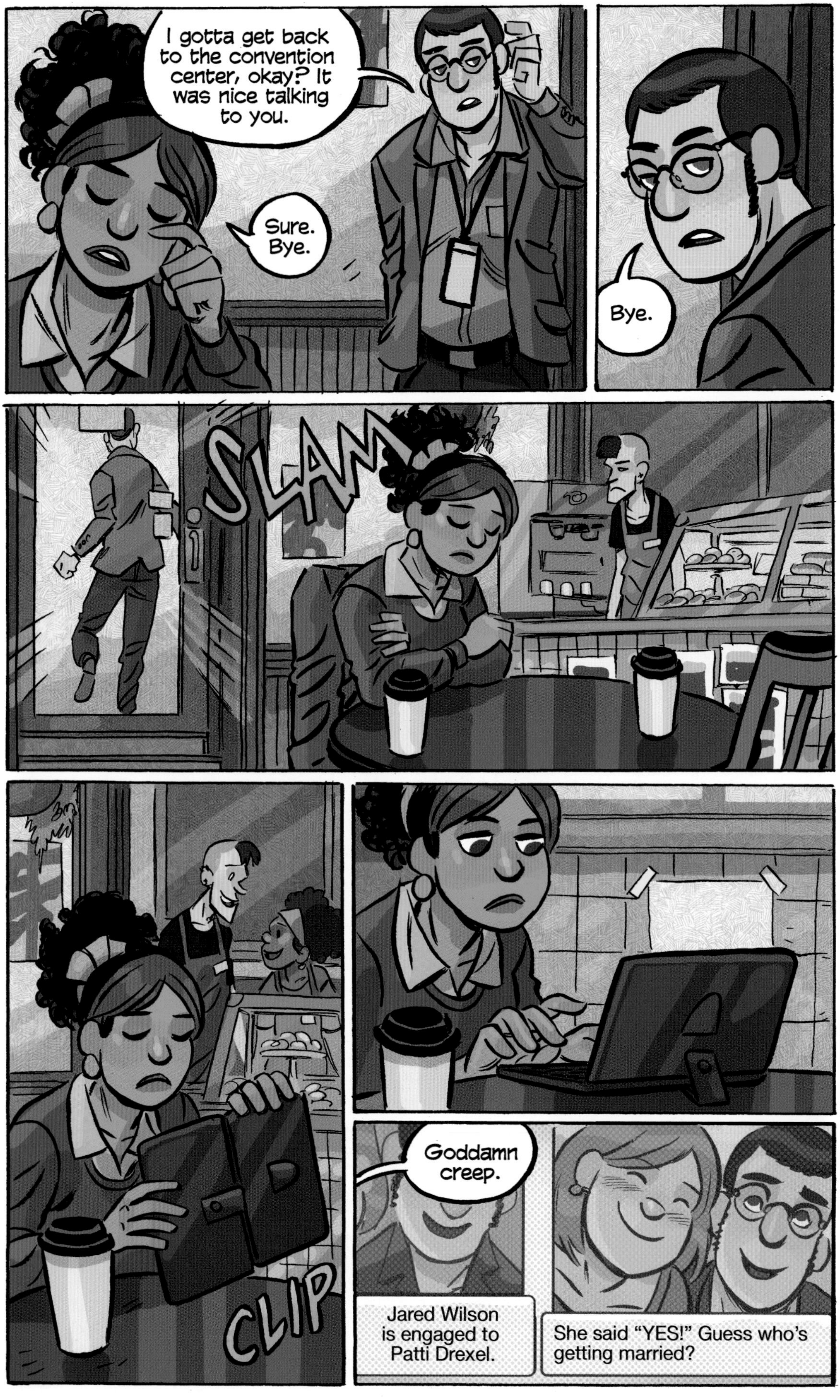
I gotta get back to the convention center, okay? It was nice talking to you.
Sure. Bye.
Bye.
SLAM
CLIP
Goddamn creep.
Jared Wilson is engaged to Patti Drexel.
She said "YES!" Guess who's getting married?

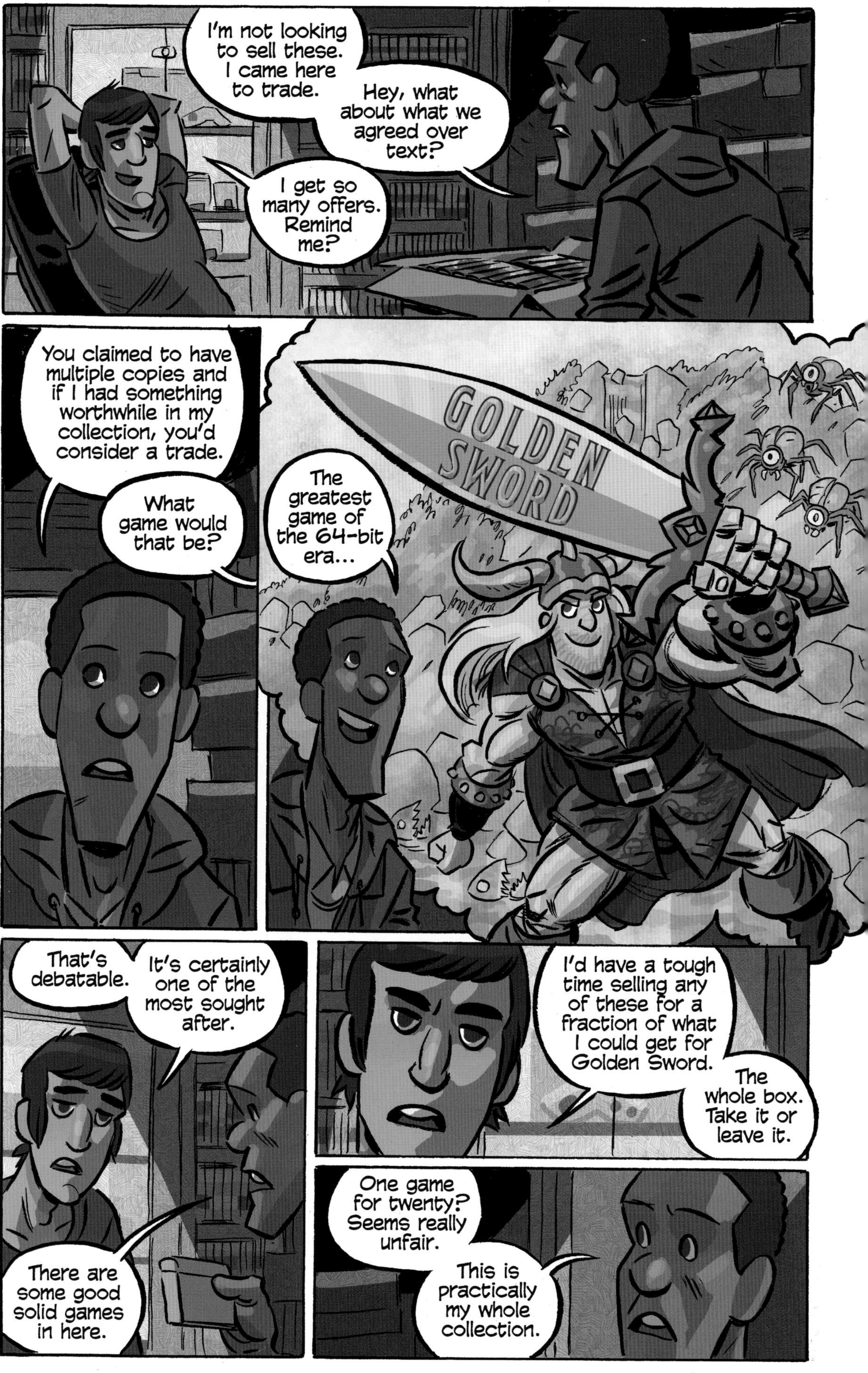

I'm not looking to sell these. I came here to trade.
Hey, what about what we agreed over text?
I get so many offers. Remind me?
You claimed to have multiple copies and if I had something worthwhile in my collection, you'd consider a trade.
What game would that be?
The greatest game of the 64-bit era...
GOLDEN SWORD
That's debatable.
It's certainly one of the most sought after.
There are some good solid games in here.
I'd have a tough time selling any of these for a fraction of what I could get for Golden Sword.
The whole box. Take it or leave it.
One game for twenty? Seems really unfair.
This is practically my whole collection.

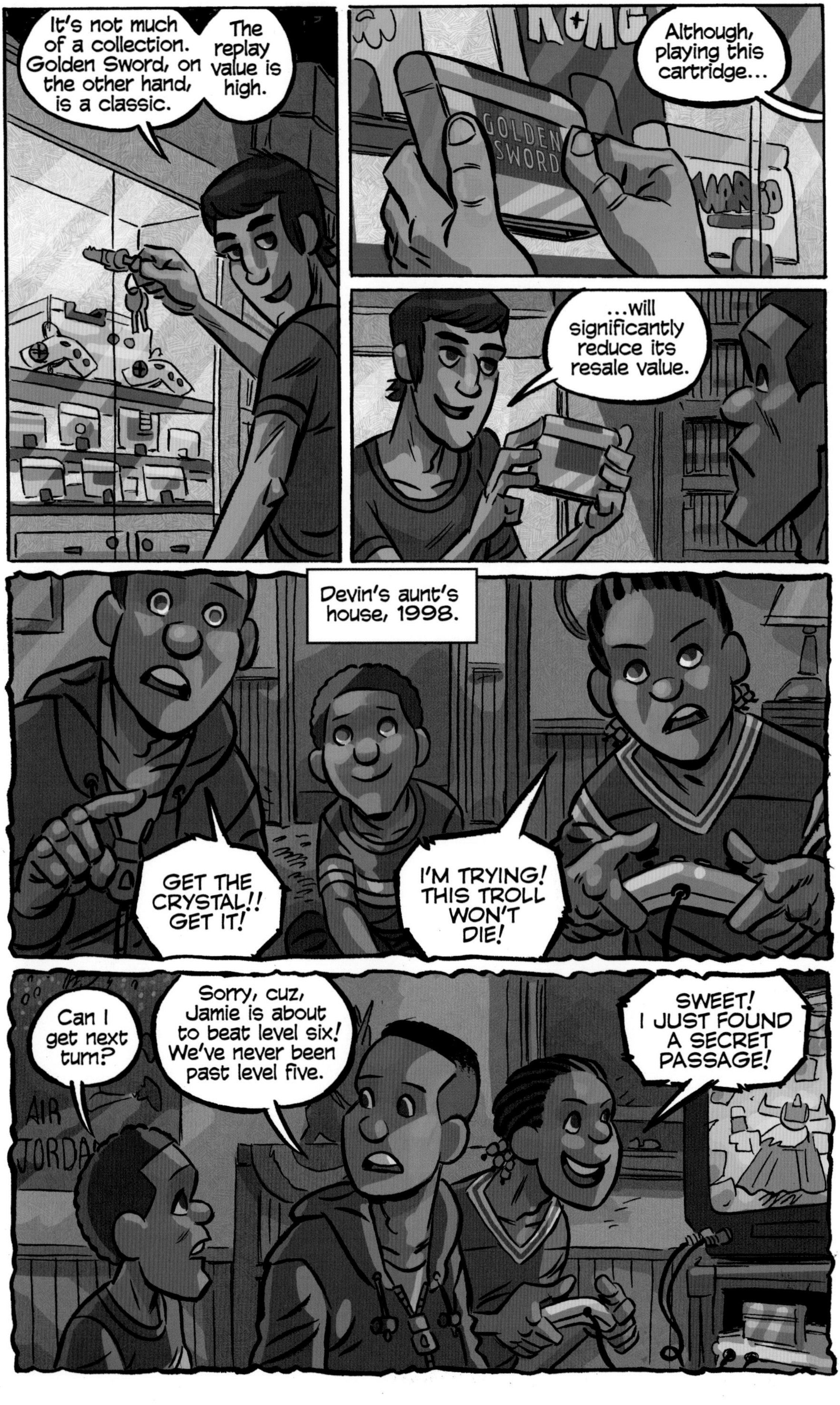
It's not much of a collection. Golden Sword, on the other hand, is a classic.
The replay value is high.
Although, playing this cartridge...
GOLDEN SWORD
...will significantly reduce its resale value.
Devin's aunt's house, 1998.
GET THE CRYSTAL!! GET IT!
I'M TRYING! THIS TROLL WON'T DIE!
Can I get next turn?
Sorry, cuz, Jamie is about to beat level six! We've never been past level five.
SWEET! I JUST FOUND A SECRET PASSAGE!

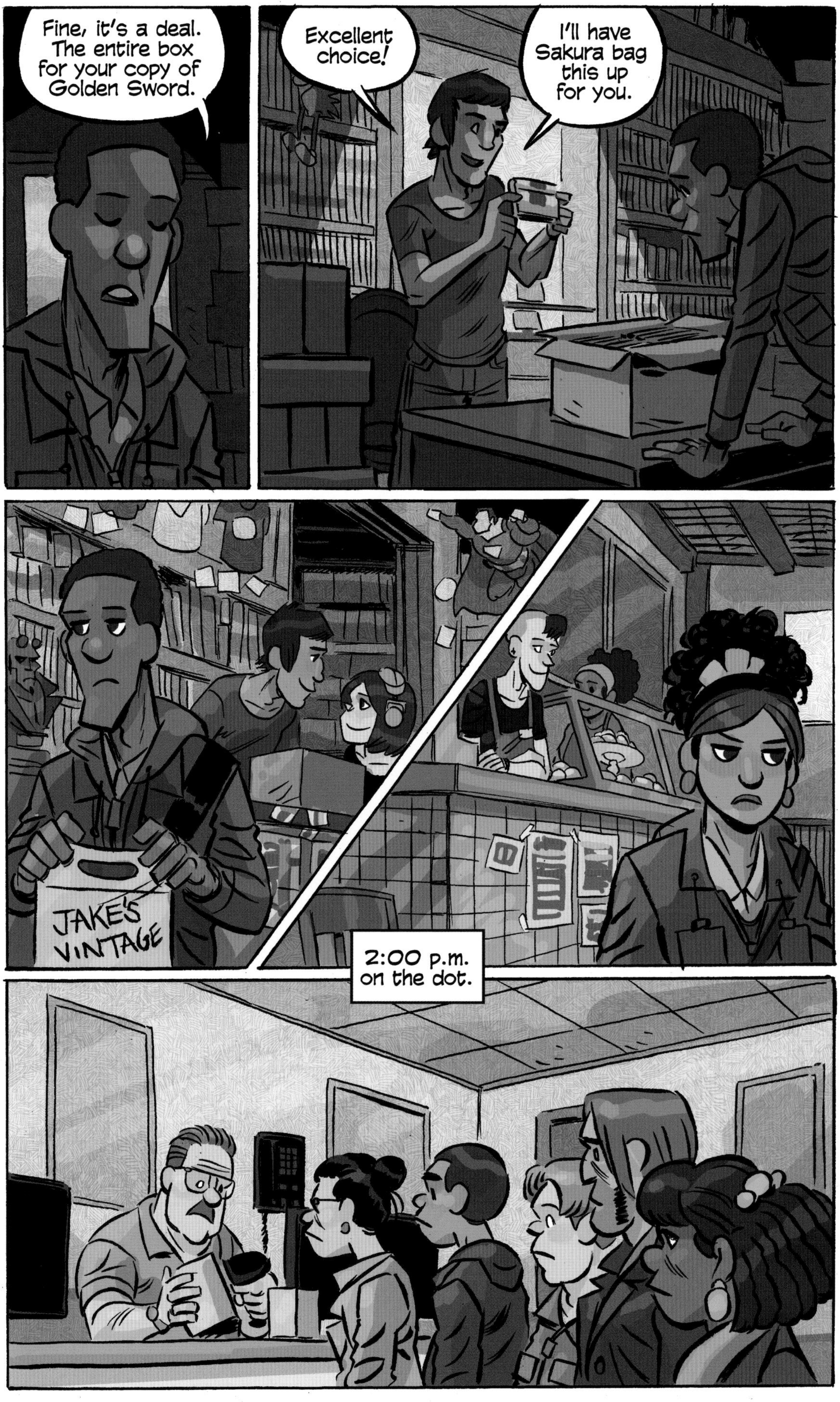
Fine, it's a deal. The entire box for your copy of Golden Sword.
Excellent choice!
I'll have Sakura bag this up for you.
JAKE'S VINTAGE
2:00 p.m. on the dot.

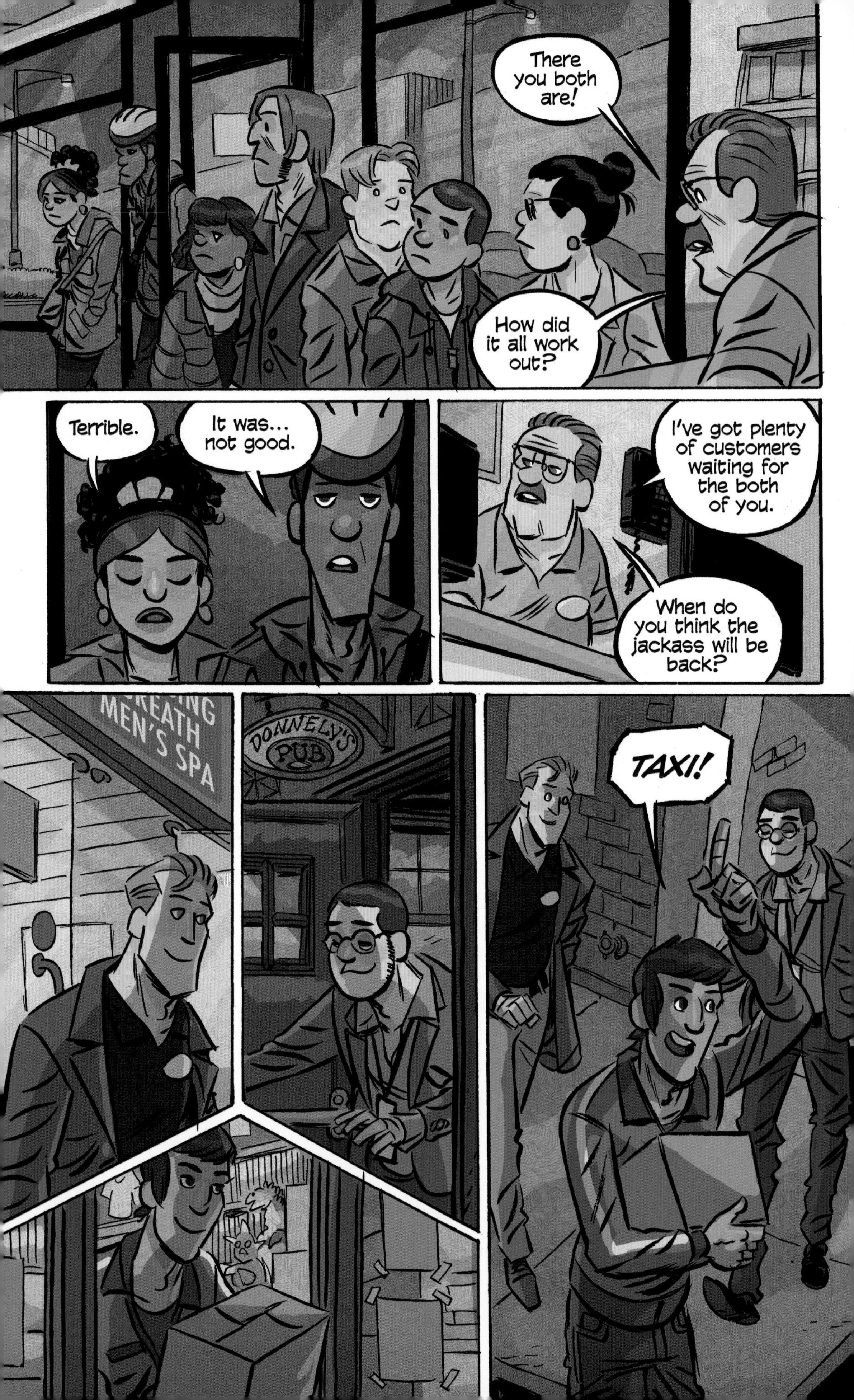
There you both are!
How did it all work out?
Terrible.
It was... not good.
I've got plenty of customers waiting for the both of you.
When do you think the jackass will be back?
MEN'S SPA
DONNELY'S PUB
TAXI!

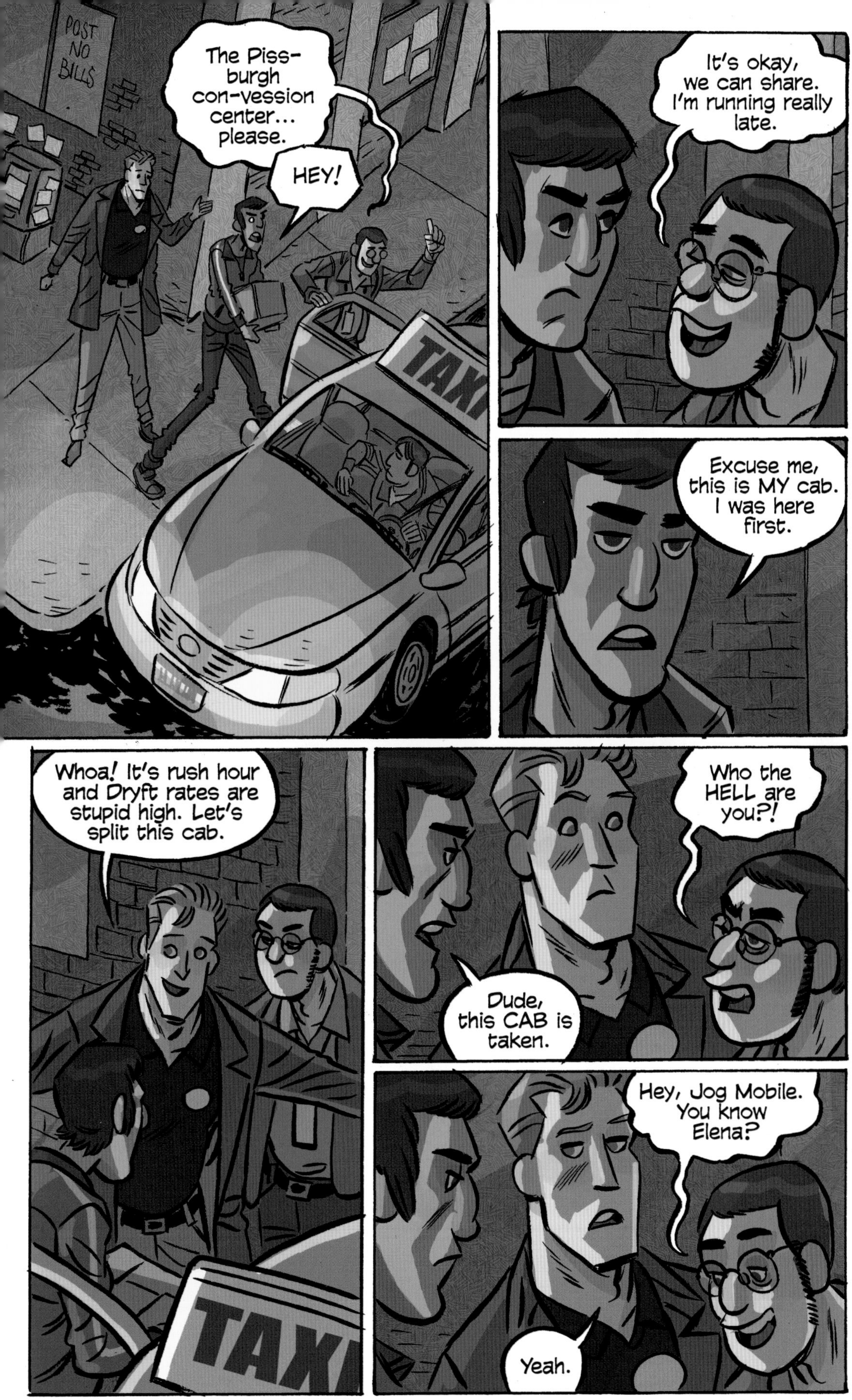

The Piss-burgh con-vession center... please.
HEY!
POST NO BILLS
TAXI
It's okay, we can share. I'm running really late.
Excuse me, this is MY cab. I was here first.
Whoa! It's rush hour and Dryft rates are stupid high. Let's split this cab.
TAXI
Who the HELL are you?!
Dude, this CAB is taken.
Hey, Jog Mobile. You know Elena?
Yeah.

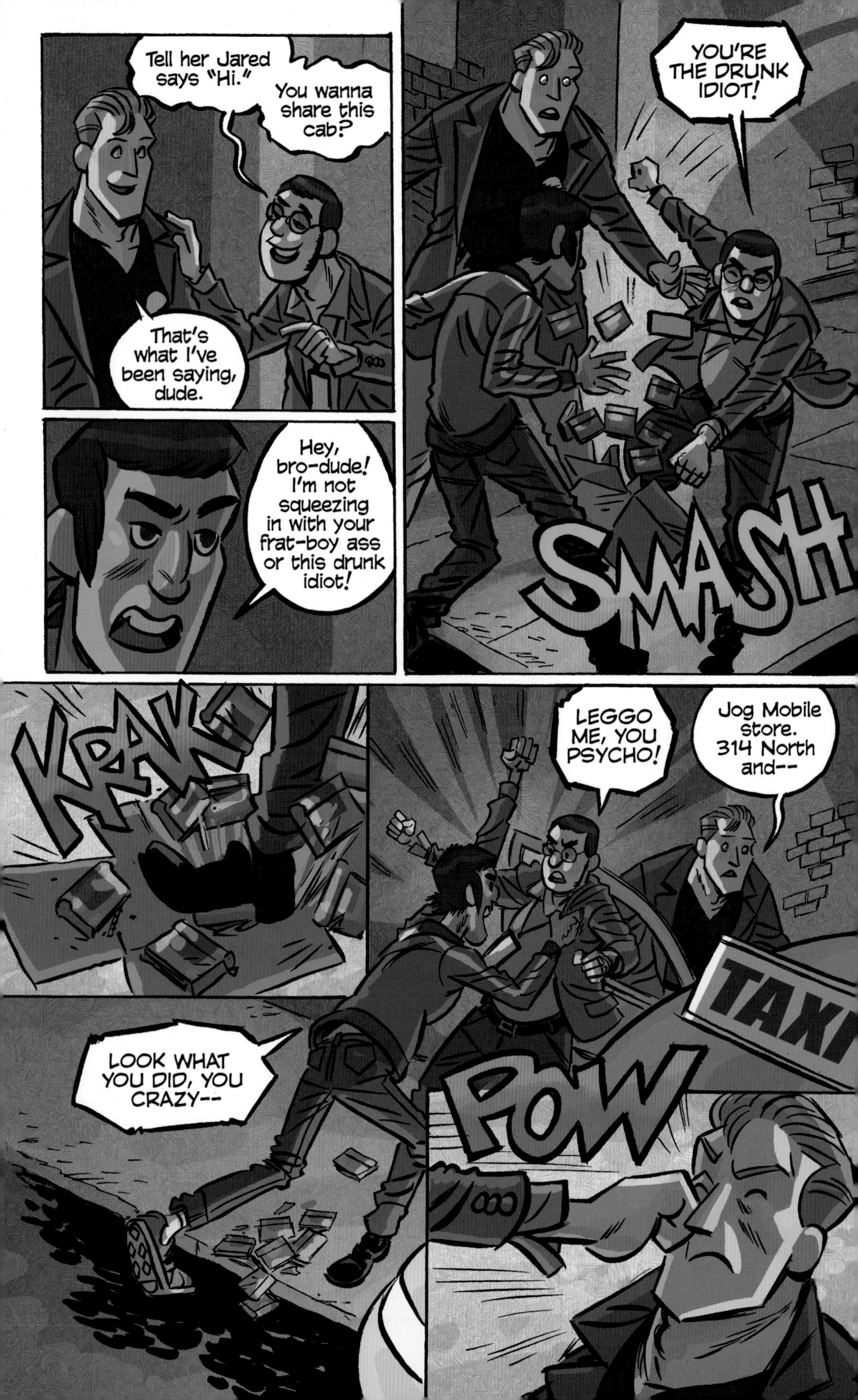
Tell her Jared says "Hi."
You wanna share this cab?
That's what I've been saying, dude.
Hey, bro-dude! I'm not squeezing in with your frat-boy ass or this drunk idiot!
YOU'RE THE DRUNK IDIOT!
SMASH
KRAK
LEGGO ME, YOU PSYCHO!
Jog Mobile store. 314 North and--
TAXI
LOOK WHAT YOU DID, YOU CRAZY--
POW

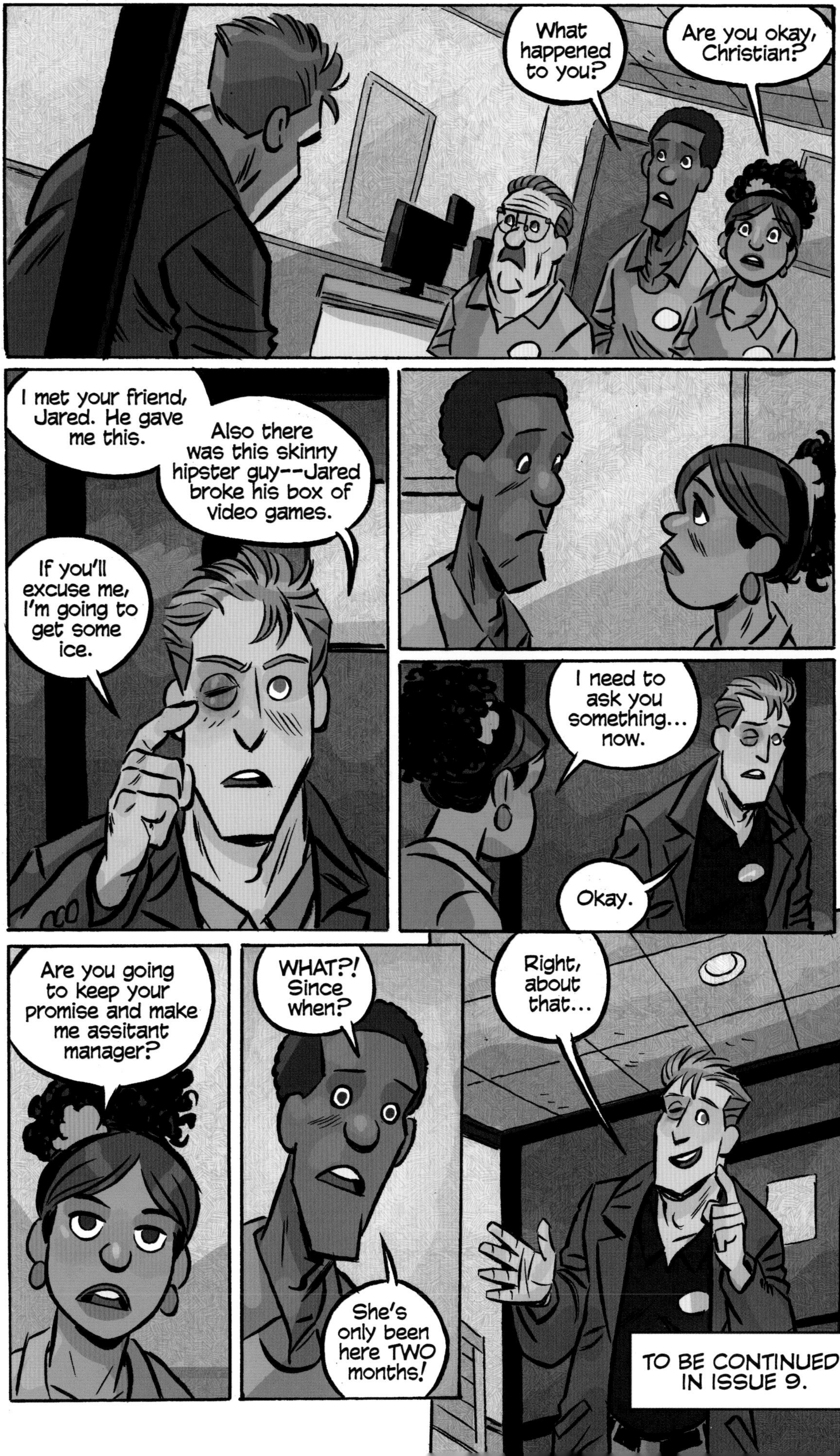
What happened to you?
Are you okay, Christian?
I met your friend, Jared. He gave me this.
Also there was this skinny hipster guy--Jared broke his box of video games.
If you'll excuse me, I'm going to get some ice.
I need to ask you something... now.
Okay.
Are you going to keep your promise and make me assitant manager?
WHAT?! Since when?
She's only been here TWO months!
Right, about that...
TO BE CONTINUED IN ISSUE 9.

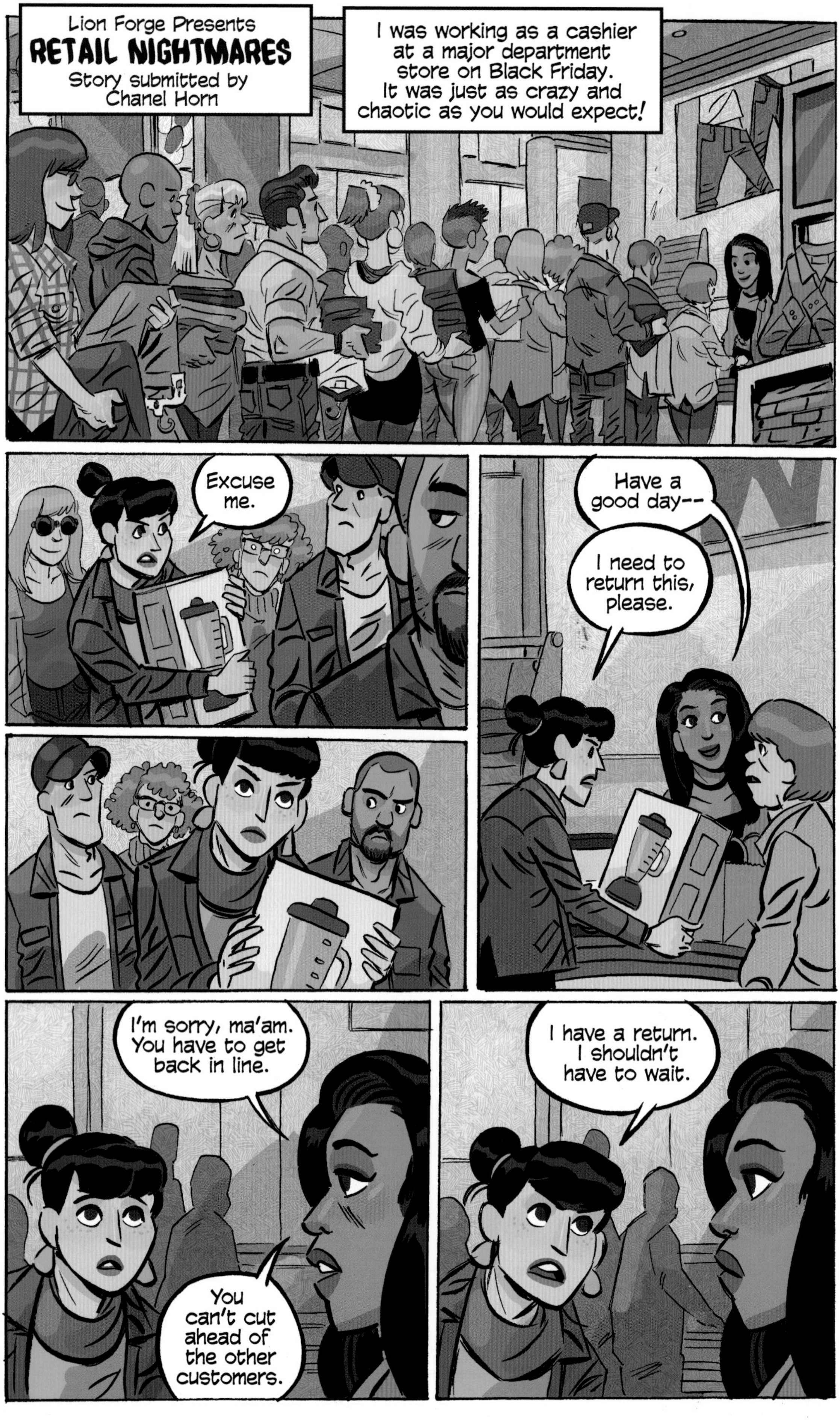
Lion Forge Presents
RETAIL NIGHTMARES
Story submitted by
Chanel Horn
I was working as a cashier at a major department store on Black Friday. It was just as crazy and chaotic as you would expect!
Excuse me.
Have a good day--
I need to return this, please.
I'm sorry, ma'am. You have to get back in line.
You can't cut ahead of the other customers.
I have a return. I shouldn't have to wait.

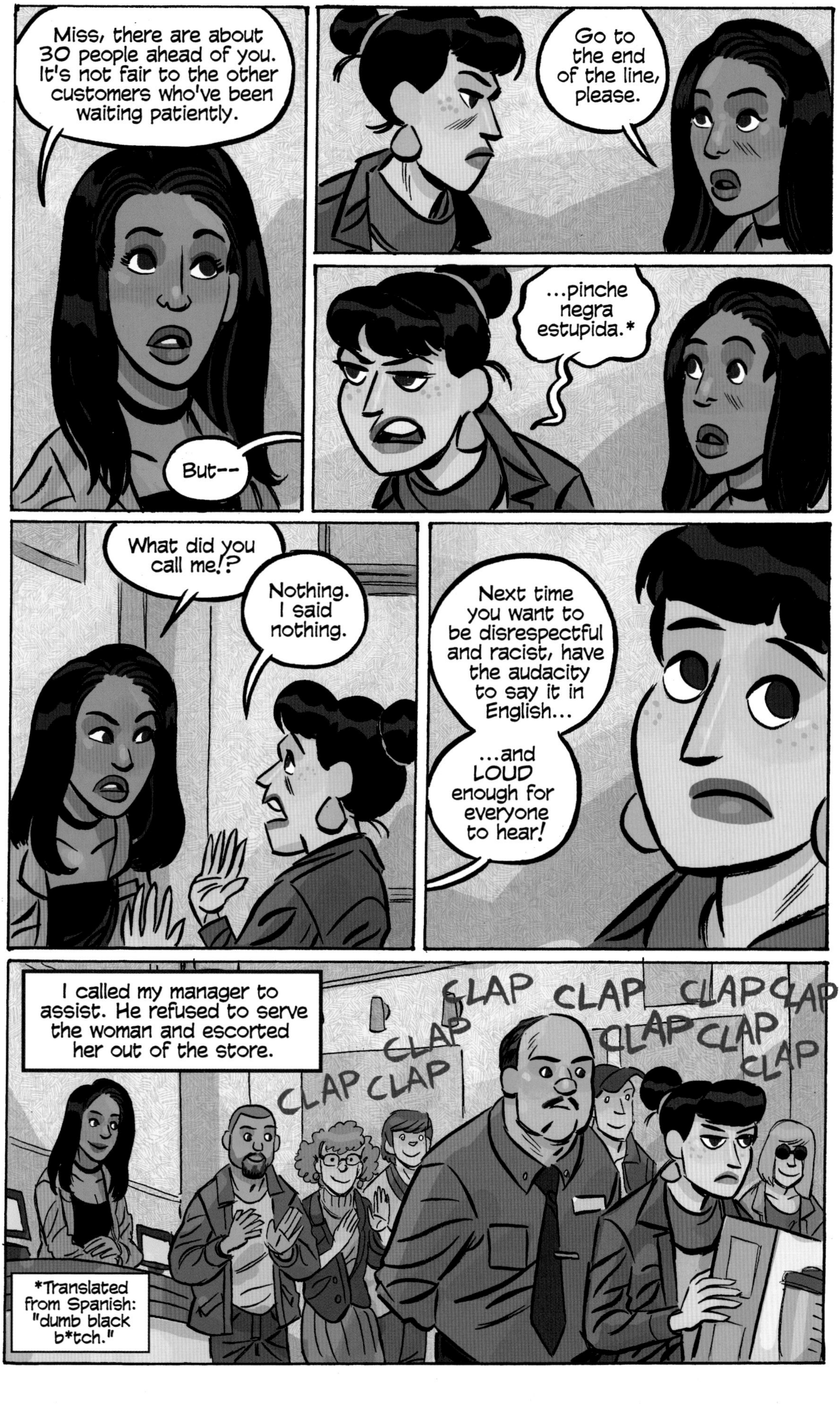

Miss, there are about 30 people ahead of you. It's not fair to the other customers who've been waiting patiently.
But--
Go to the end of the line, please.
...pinche negra estupida.*
What did you call me!?
Nothing. I said nothing.
Next time you want to be disrespectful and racist, have the audacity to say it in English...
...and LOUD enough for everyone to hear!
I called my manager to assist. He refused to serve the woman and escorted her out of the store.
CLAP CLAP CLAP CLAP CLAP CLAP CLAP CLAP CLAP CLAP CLAP CLAP
*Translated from Spanish: "dumb black b*tch."

# CHAPTER 4

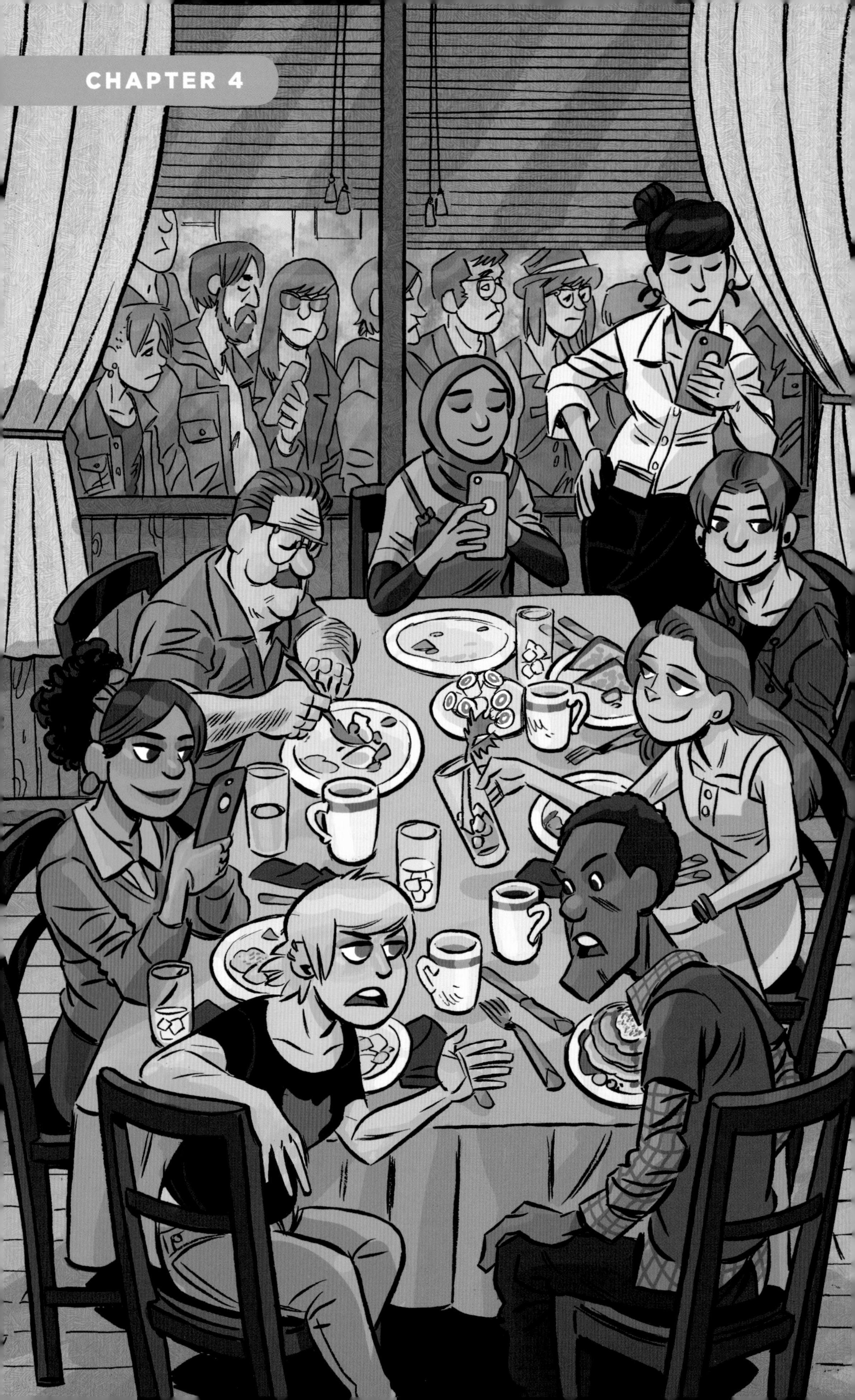

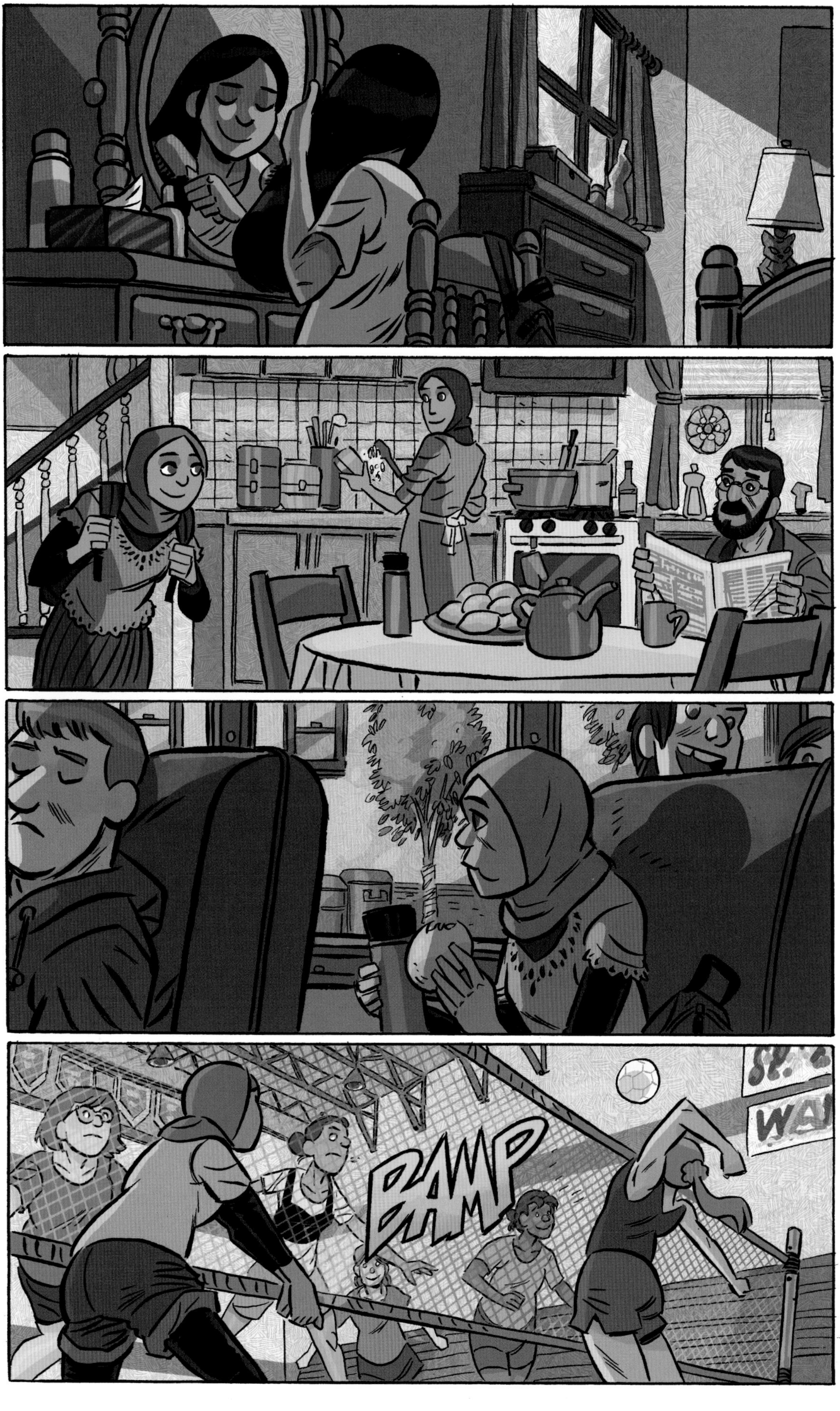
BAMP

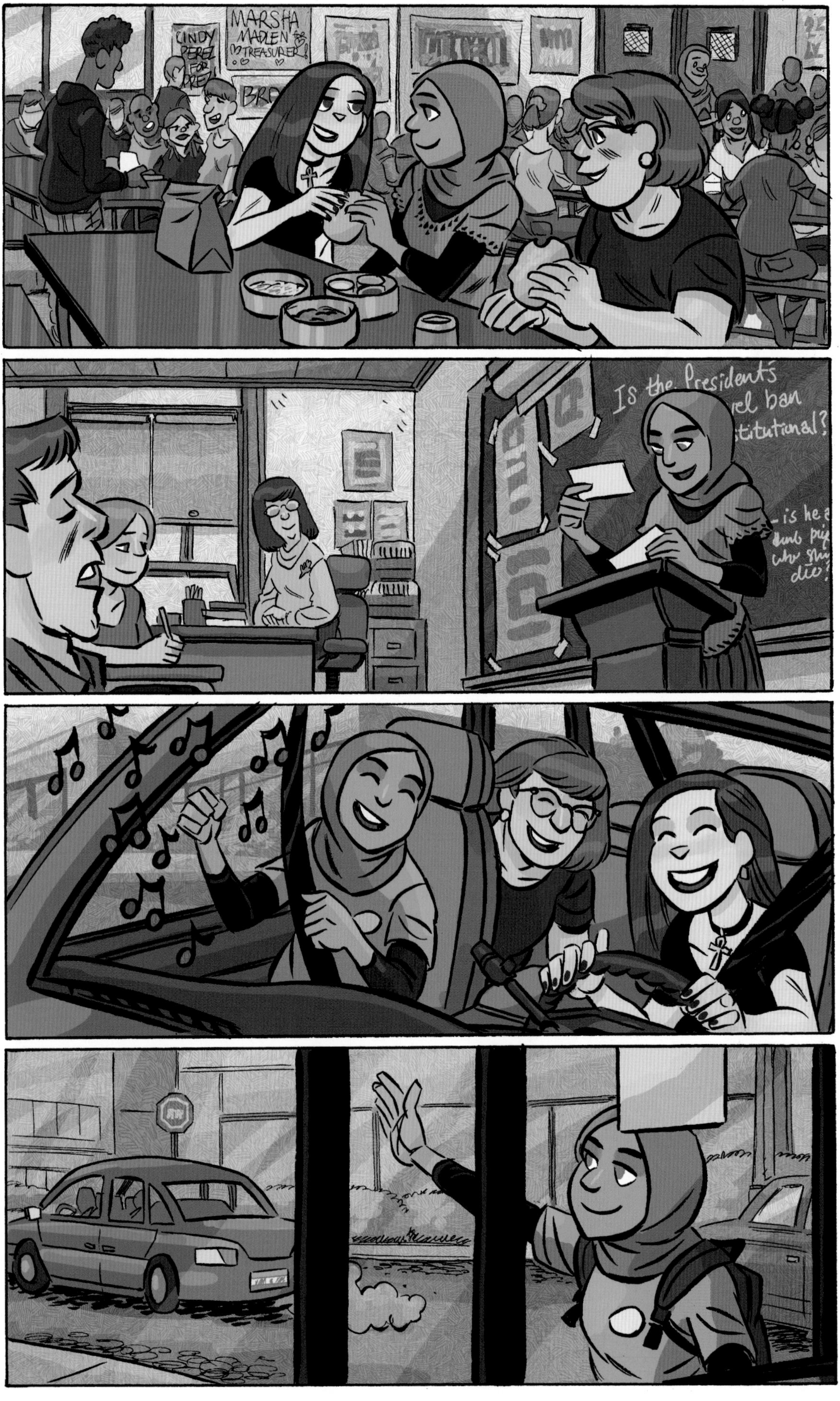
CINDY PEREZ FOR PRE
MARSHA MADLEN for TREASURER
Is the President's
vel ban
stitutional?

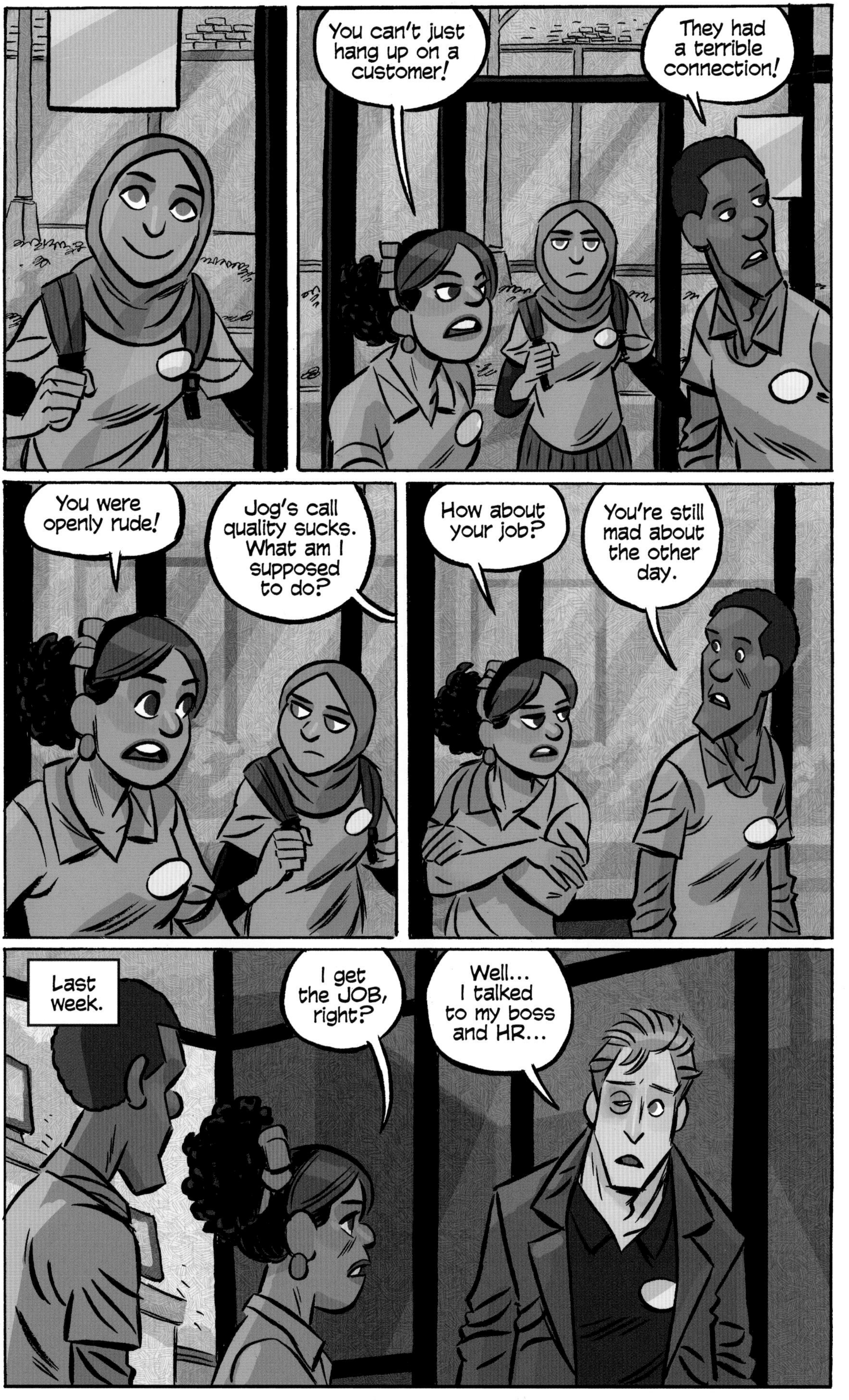
You can't just hang up on a customer!
They had a terrible connection!
You were openly rude!
Jog's call quality sucks. What am I supposed to do?
How about your job?
You're still mad about the other day.
Last week.
I get the JOB, right?
Well... I talked to my boss and HR...

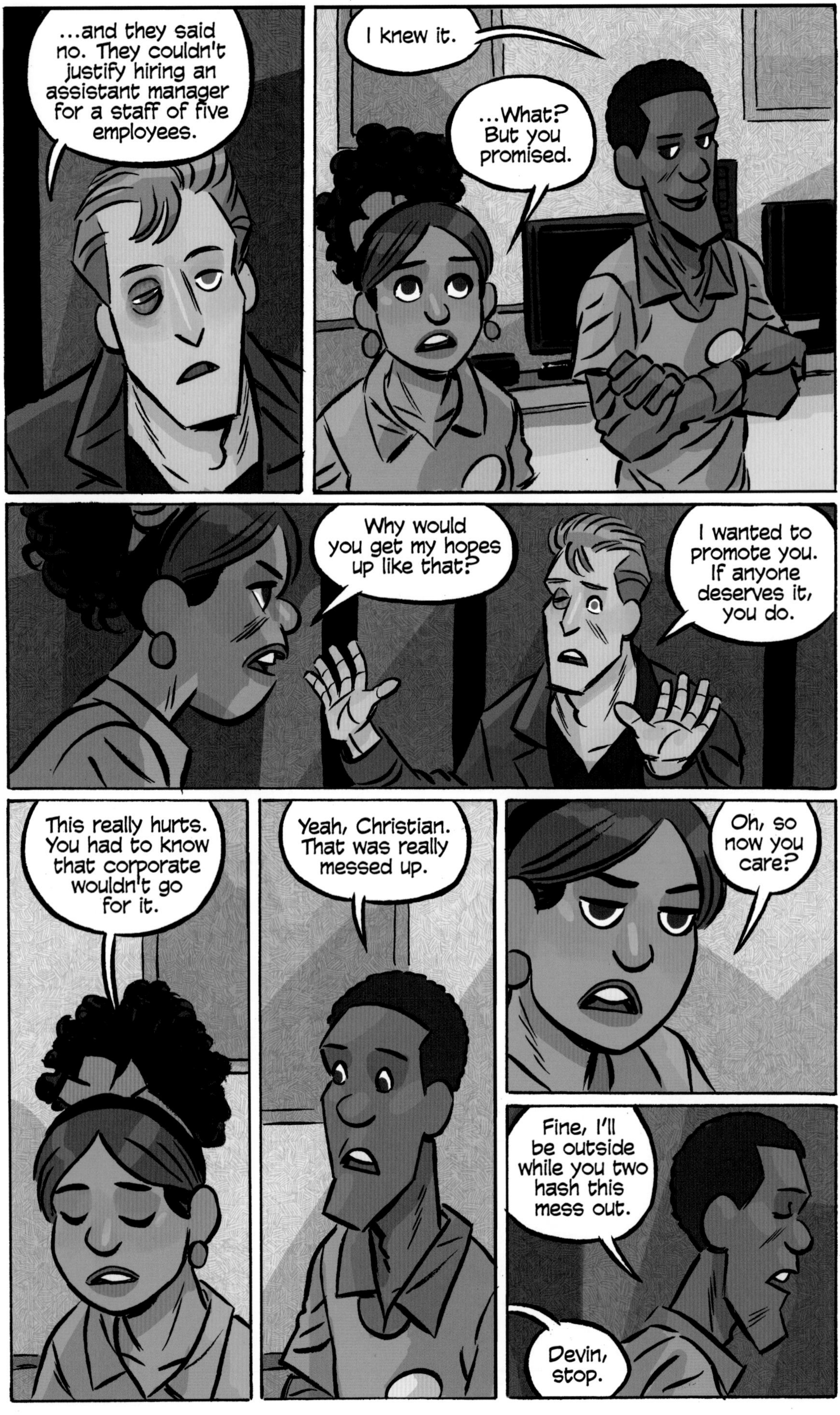
...and they said no. They couldn't justify hiring an assistant manager for a staff of five employees.
I knew it.
...What? But you promised.
Why would you get my hopes up like that?
I wanted to promote you. If anyone deserves it, you do.
This really hurts. You had to know that corporate wouldn't go for it.
Yeah, Christian. That was really messed up.
Oh, so now you care?
Fine, I'll be outside while you two hash this mess out.
Devin, stop.

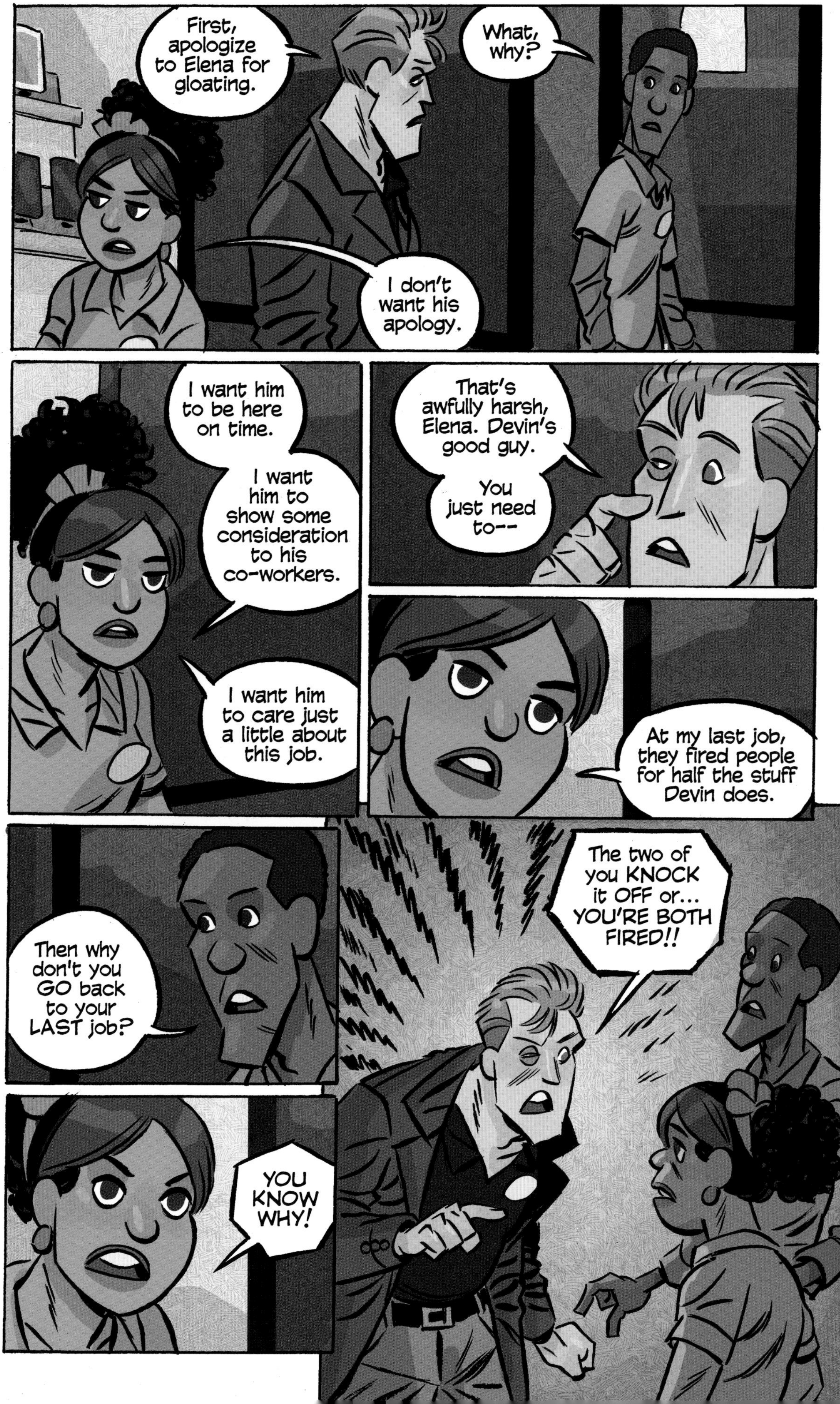
First, apologize to Elena for gloating.
What, why?
I don't want his apology.
I want him to be here on time.
I want him to show some consideration to his co-workers.
I want him to care just a little about this job.
That's awfully harsh, Elena. Devin's good guy.
You just need to--
At my last job, they fired people for half the stuff Devin does.
Then why don't you GO back to your LAST job?
YOU KNOW WHY!
The two of you KNOCK it OFF or... YOU'RE BOTH FIRED!!

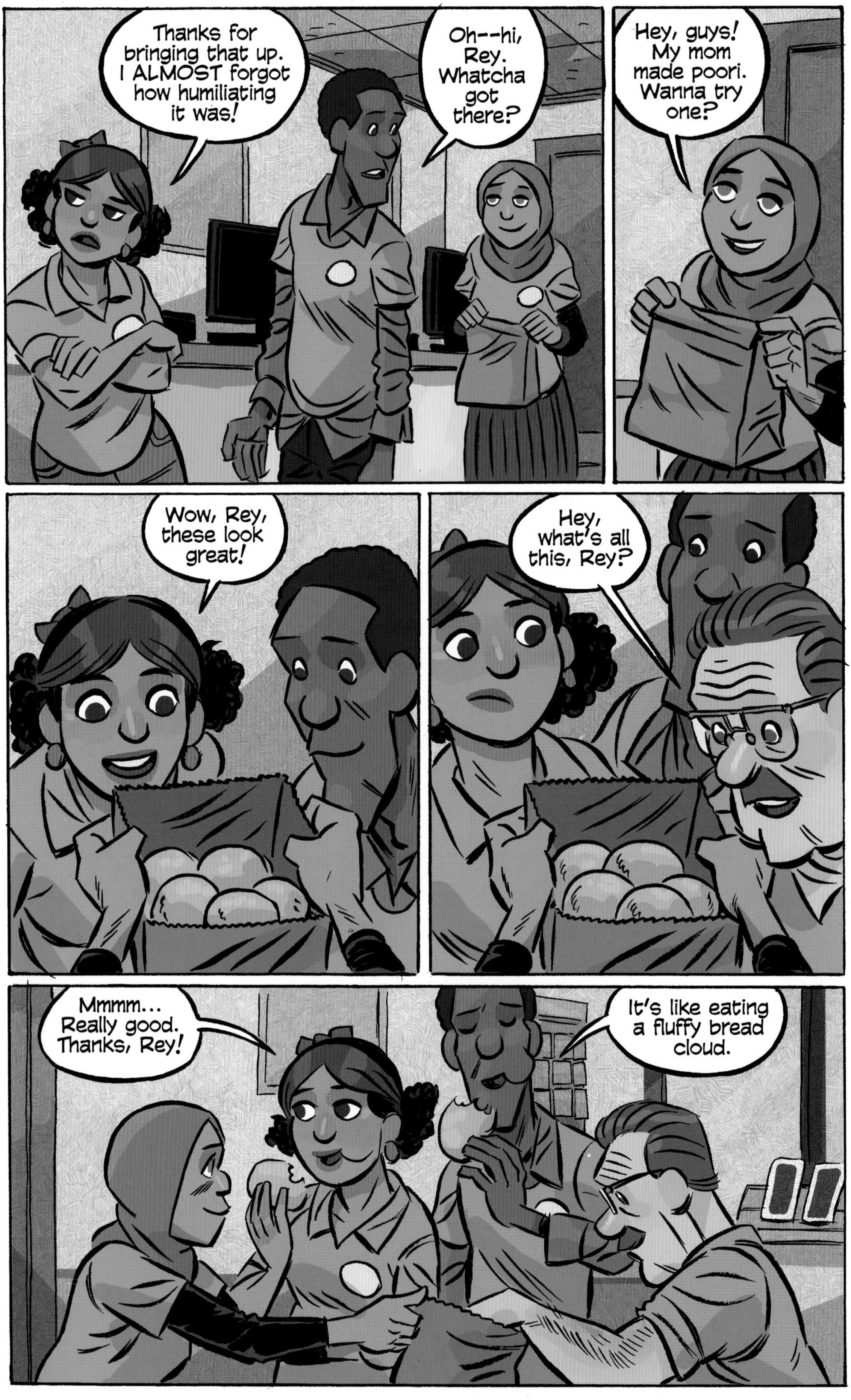
Thanks for bringing that up. I ALMOST forgot how humiliating it was!
Oh--hi, Rey. Whatcha got there?
Hey, guys! My mom made poori. Wanna try one?
Wow, Rey, these look great!
Hey, what's all this, Rey?
Mmmm... Really good. Thanks, Rey!
It's like eating a fluffy bread cloud.

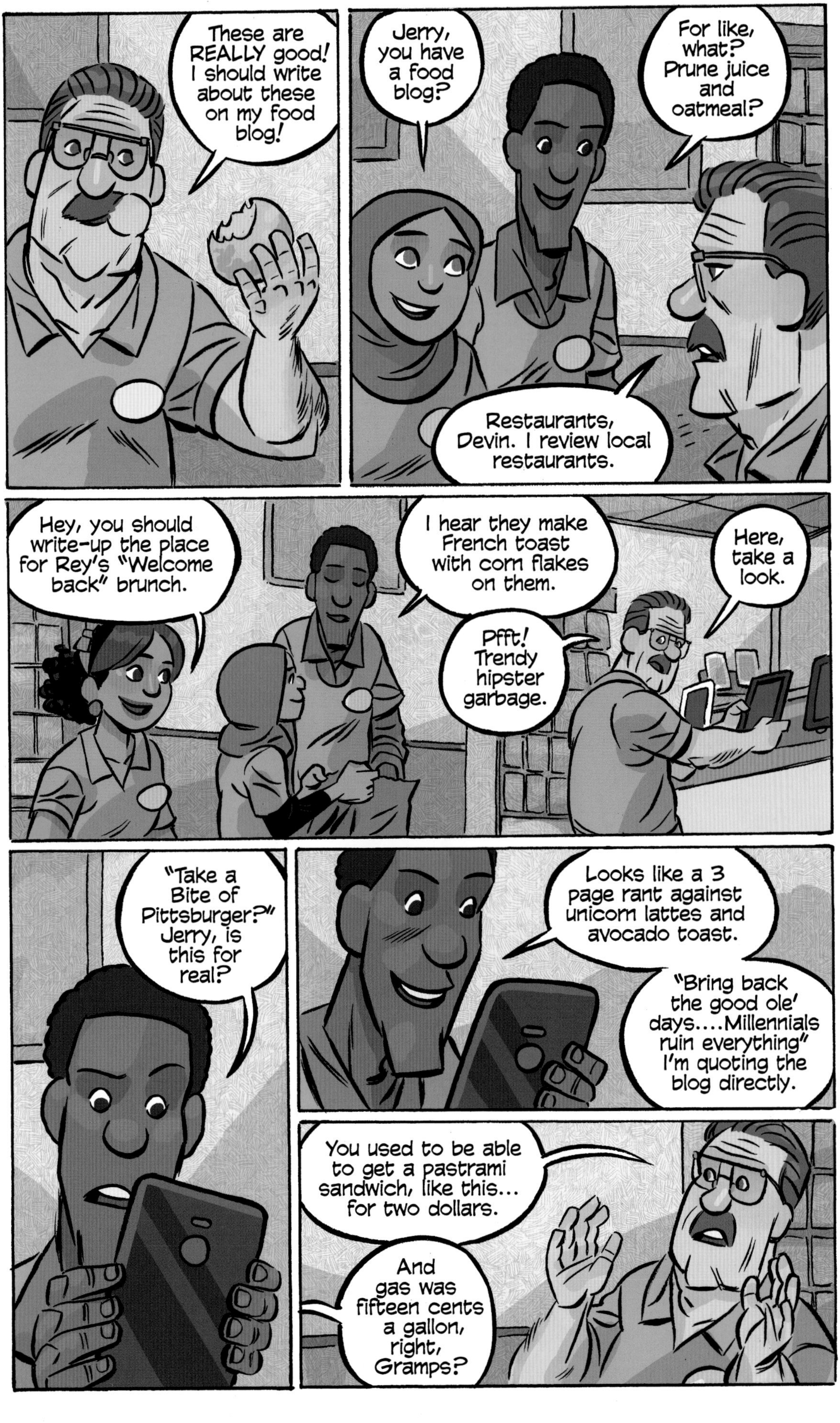
These are REALLY good! I should write about these on my food blog!
Jerry, you have a food blog?
For like, what? Prune juice and oatmeal?
Restaurants, Devin. I review local restaurants.
Hey, you should write-up the place for Rey's "Welcome back" brunch.
I hear they make French toast with corn flakes on them.
Pfft! Trendy hipster garbage.
Here, take a look.
"Take a Bite of Pittsburger?" Jerry, is this for real?
Looks like a 3 page rant against unicorn lattes and avocado toast.
"Bring back the good ole' days....Millennials ruin everything" I'm quoting the blog directly.
You used to be able to get a pastrami sandwich, like this... for two dollars.
And gas was fifteen cents a gallon, right, Gramps?

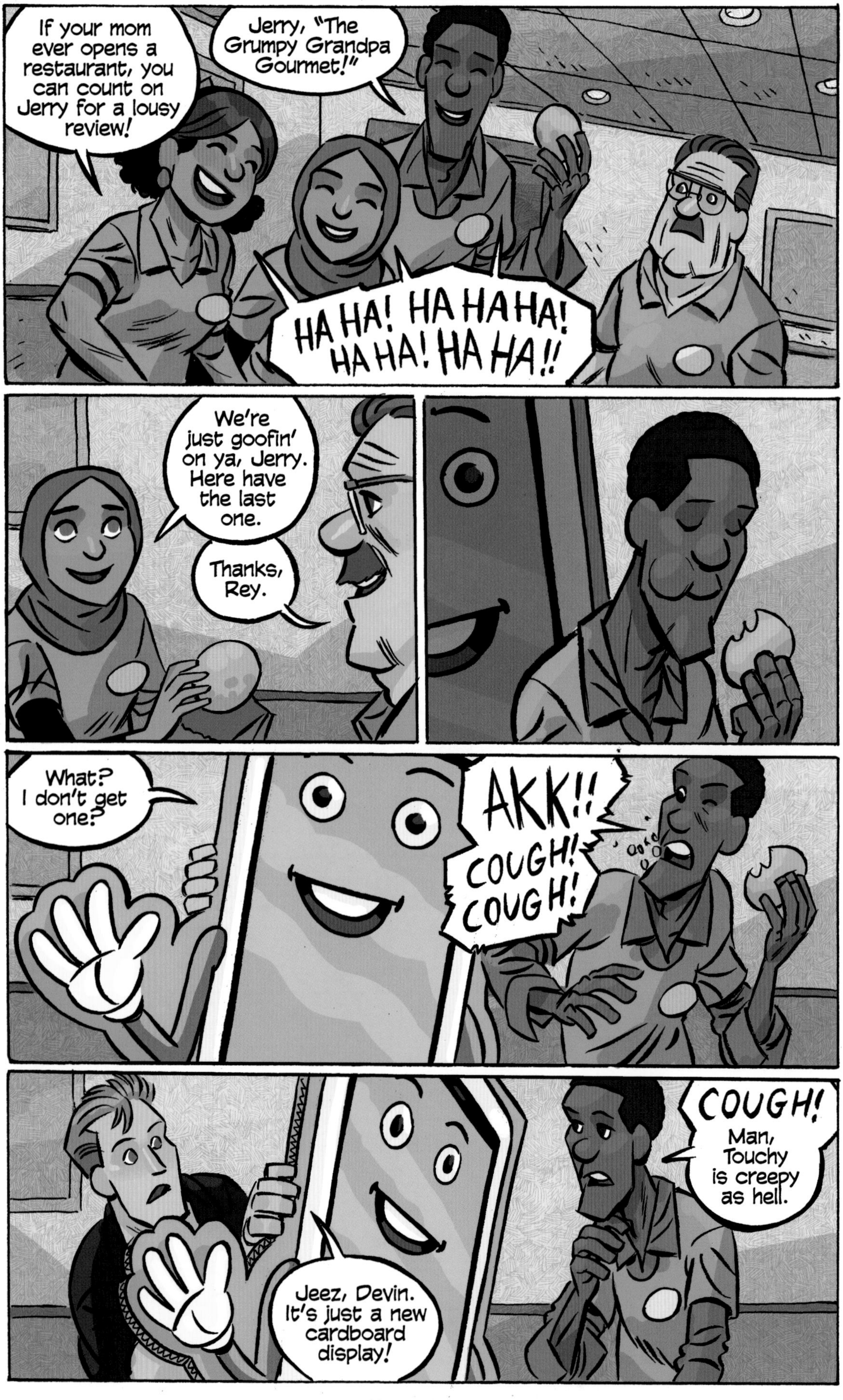
If your mom ever opens a restaurant, you can count on Jerry for a lousy review!
Jerry, "The Grumpy Grandpa Gourmet!"
HA HA! HA HA HA! HA HA! HA HA!!
We're just goofin' on ya, Jerry. Here have the last one.
Thanks, Rey.
What? I don't get one?
AKK!!
COUGH! COUGH!
COUGH!
Man, Touchy is creepy as hell.
Jeez, Devin. It's just a new cardboard display!

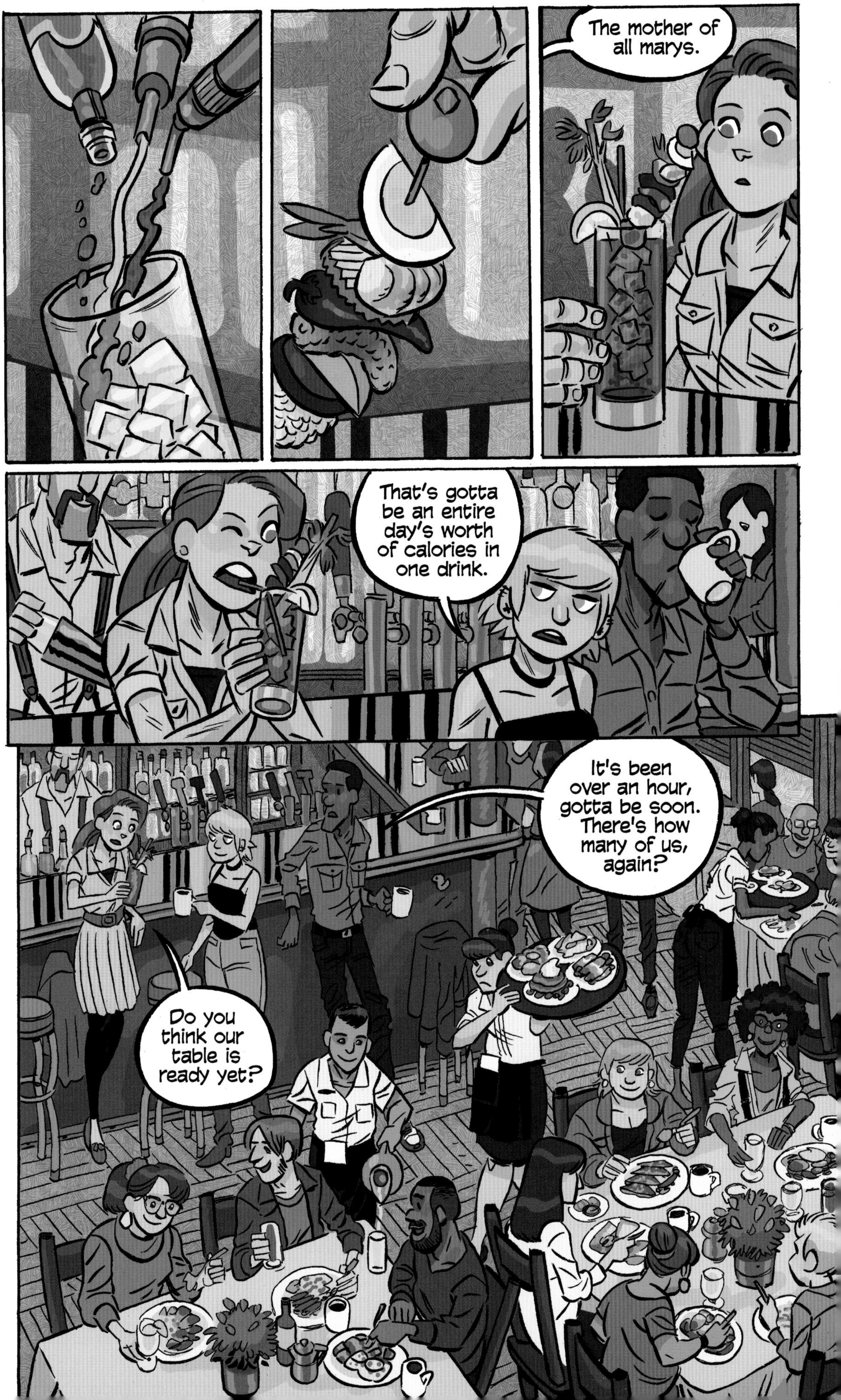
The mother of all marys.
That's gotta be an entire day's worth of calories in one drink.
Do you think our table is ready yet?
It's been over an hour, gotta be soon. There's how many of us, again?

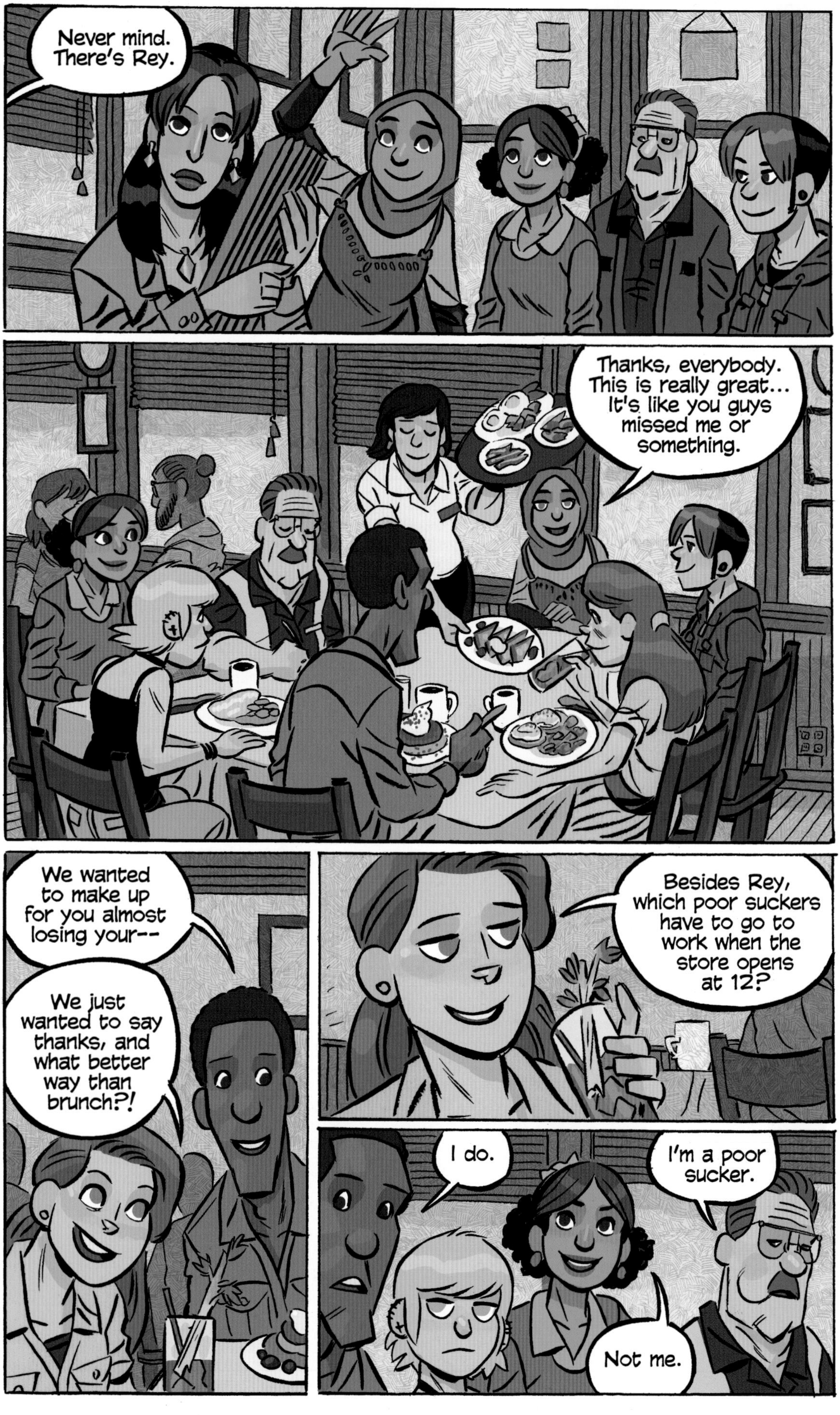
Never mind. There's Rey.
Thanks, everybody. This is really great... It's like you guys missed me or something.
We wanted to make up for you almost losing your--
We just wanted to say thanks, and what better way than brunch?!
Besides Rey, which poor suckers have to go to work when the store opens at 12?
I do.
I'm a poor sucker.
Not me.

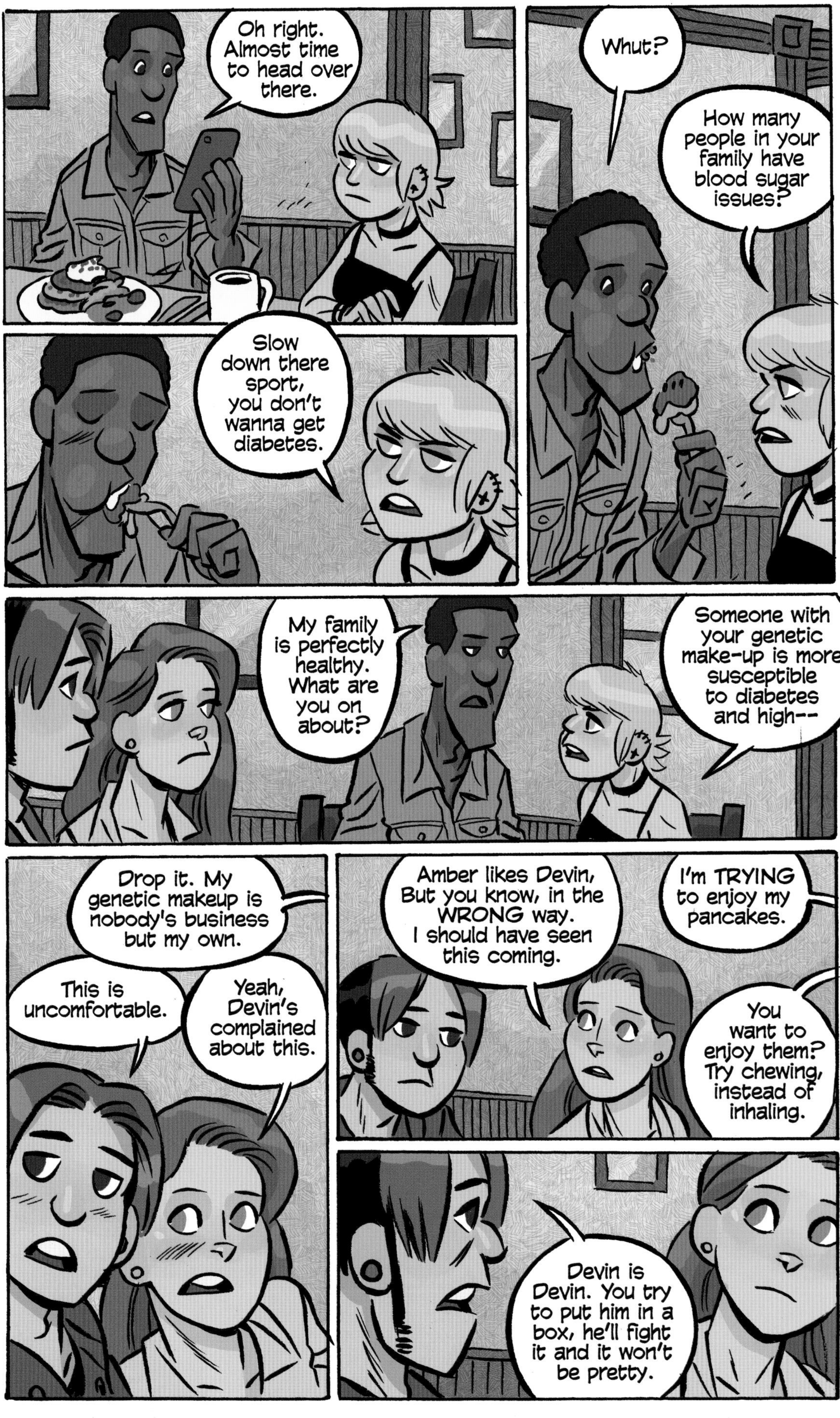
Oh right. Almost time to head over there.
Whut?
How many people in your family have blood sugar issues?
Slow down there sport, you don't wanna get diabetes.
My family is perfectly healthy. What are you on about?
Someone with your genetic make-up is more susceptible to diabetes and high--
Drop it. My genetic makeup is nobody's business but my own.
This is uncomfortable.
Yeah, Devin's complained about this.
Amber likes Devin, But you know, in the WRONG way. I should have seen this coming.
I'm TRYING to enjoy my pancakes.
You want to enjoy them? Try chewing, instead of inhaling.
Devin is Devin. You try to put him in a box, he'll fight it and it won't be pretty.

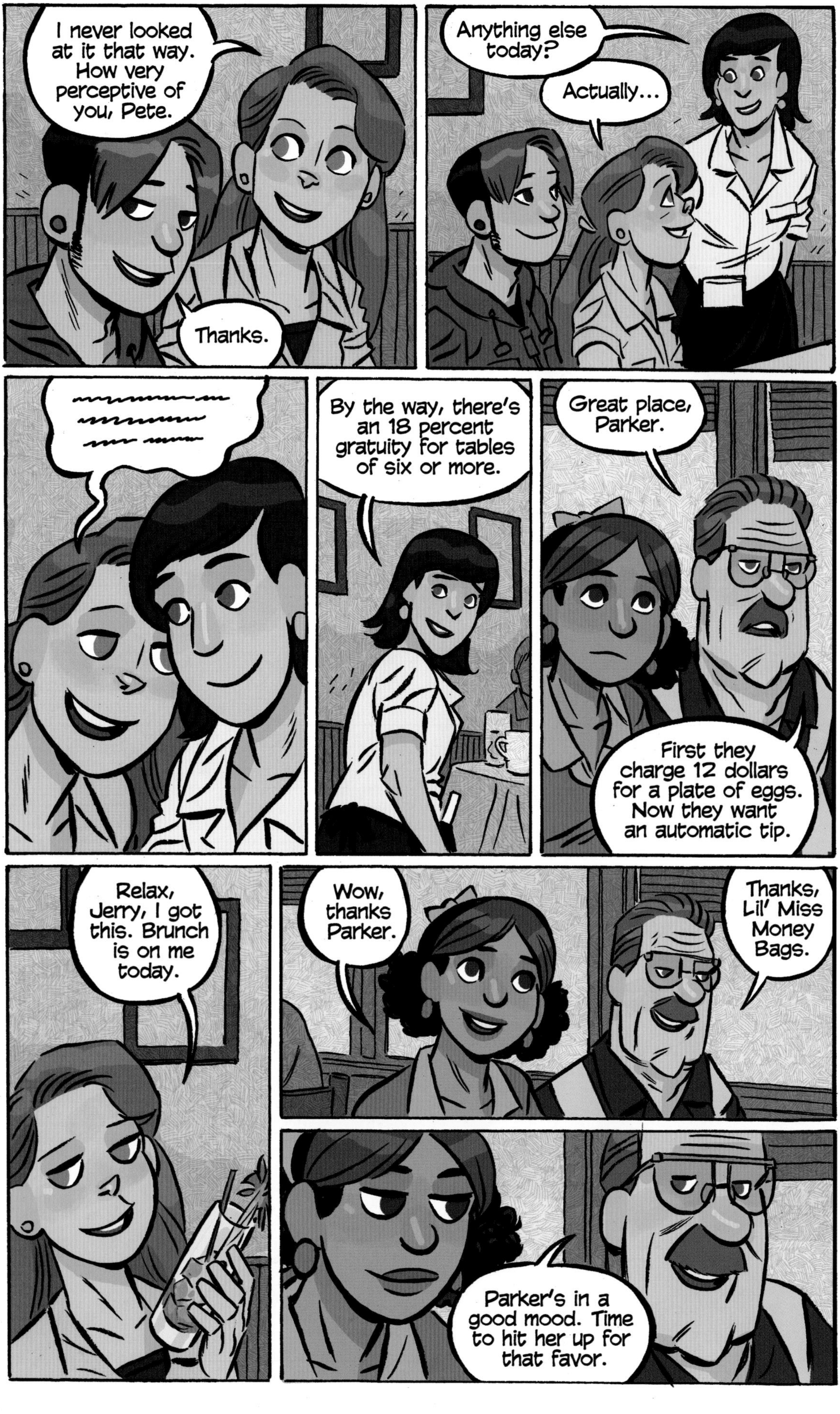
I never looked at it that way. How very perceptive of you, Pete.
Thanks.
Anything else today?
Actually...
By the way, there's an 18 percent gratuity for tables of six or more.
Great place, Parker.
First they charge 12 dollars for a plate of eggs. Now they want an automatic tip.
Relax, Jerry, I got this. Brunch is on me today.
Wow, thanks Parker.
Thanks, Lil' Miss Money Bags.
Parker's in a good mood. Time to hit her up for that favor.

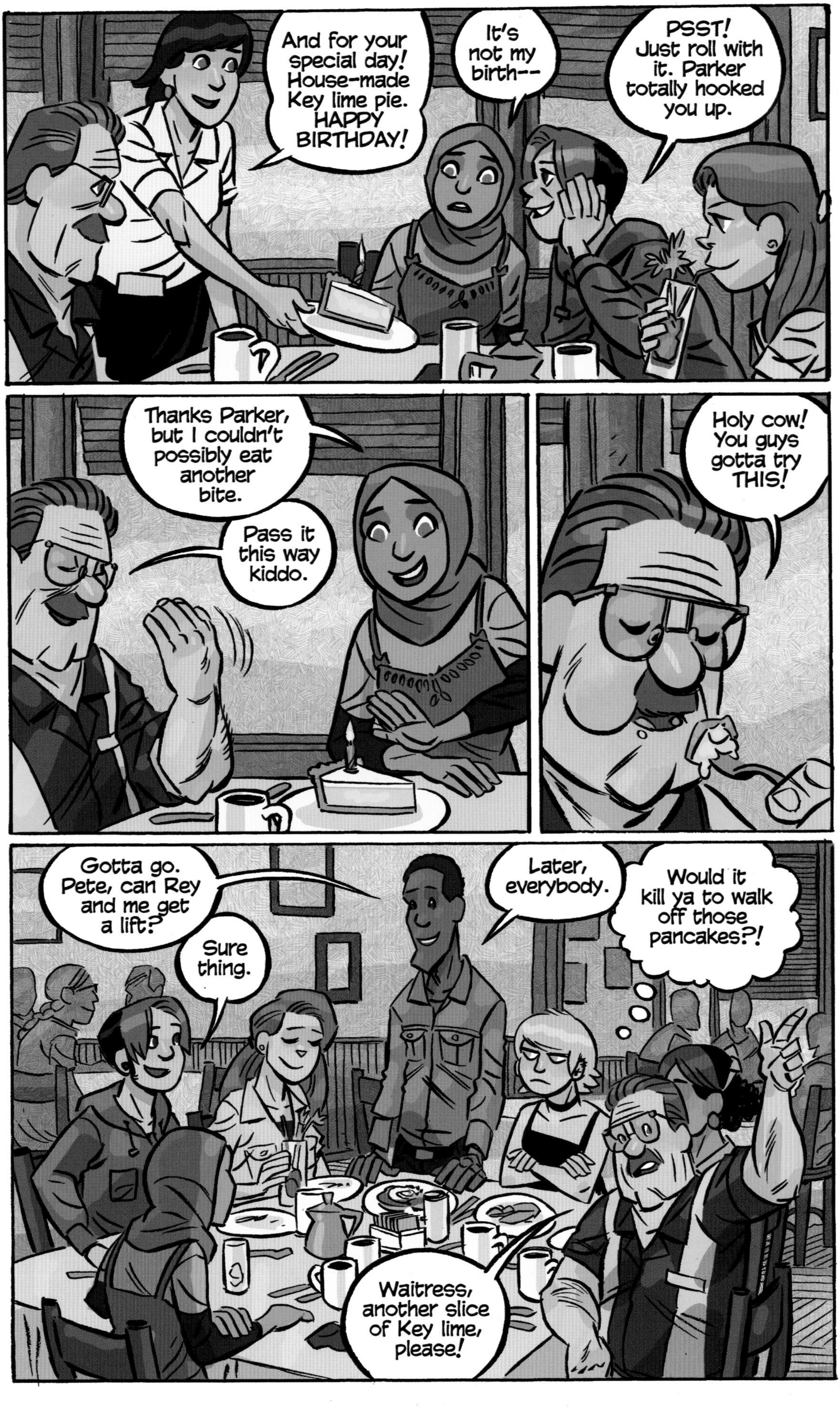
And for your special day! House-made Key lime pie. HAPPY BIRTHDAY!
It's not my birth--
PSST! Just roll with it. Parker totally hooked you up.
Thanks Parker, but I couldn't possibly eat another bite.
Pass it this way kiddo.
Holy cow! You guys gotta try THIS!
Gotta go. Pete, can Rey and me get a lift?
Sure thing.
Later, everybody.
Would it kill ya to walk off those pancakes?!
Waitress, another slice of Key lime, please!

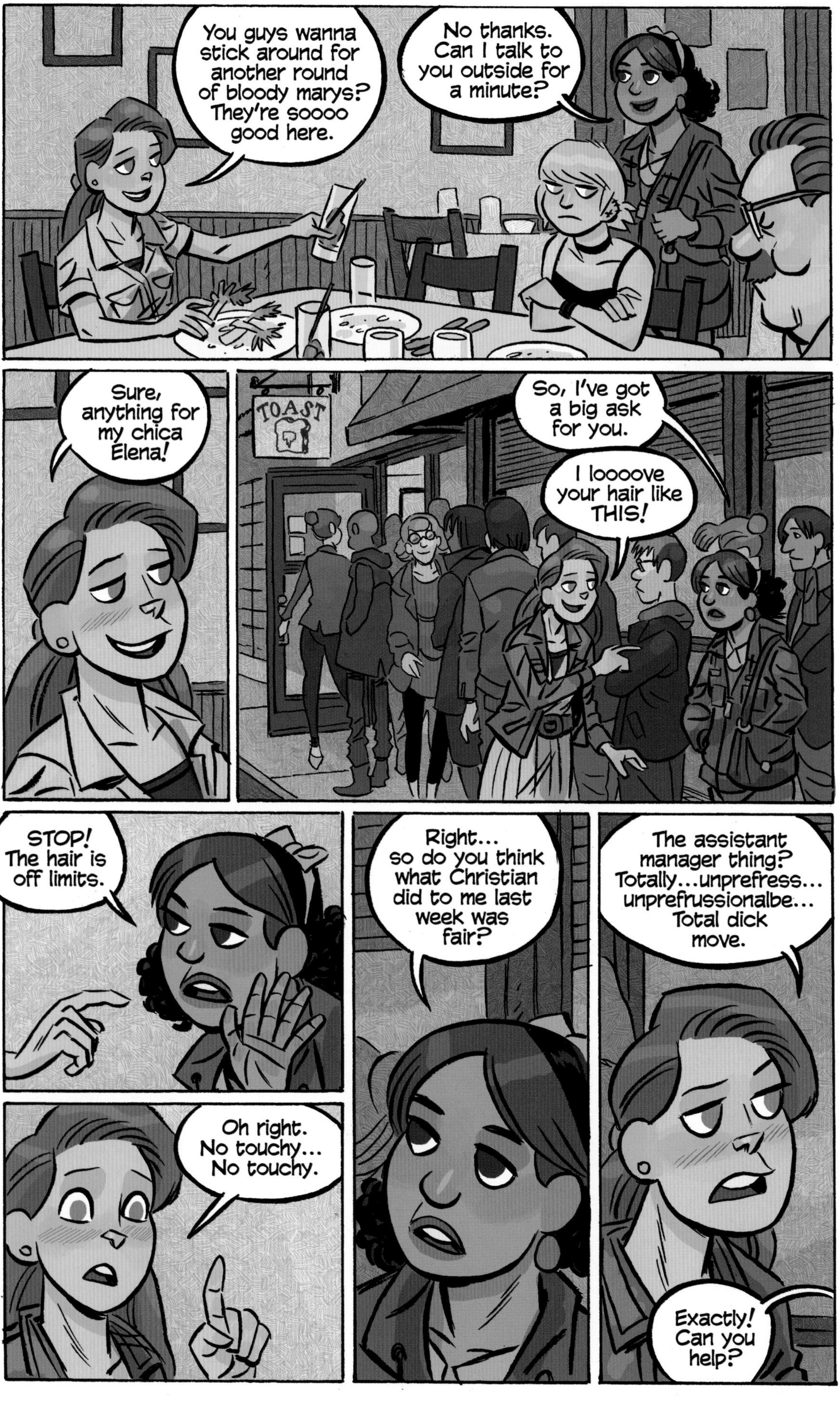
You guys wanna stick around for another round of bloody marys? They're soooo good here.
No thanks. Can I talk to you outside for a minute?
Sure, anything for my chica Elena!
TOAST
So, I've got a big ask for you.
I loooove your hair like THIS!
STOP! The hair is off limits.
Oh right. No touchy... No touchy.
Right... so do you think what Christian did to me last week was fair?
The assistant manager thing? Totally...unprefress... unprefrussionalbe... Total dick move.
Exactly! Can you help?

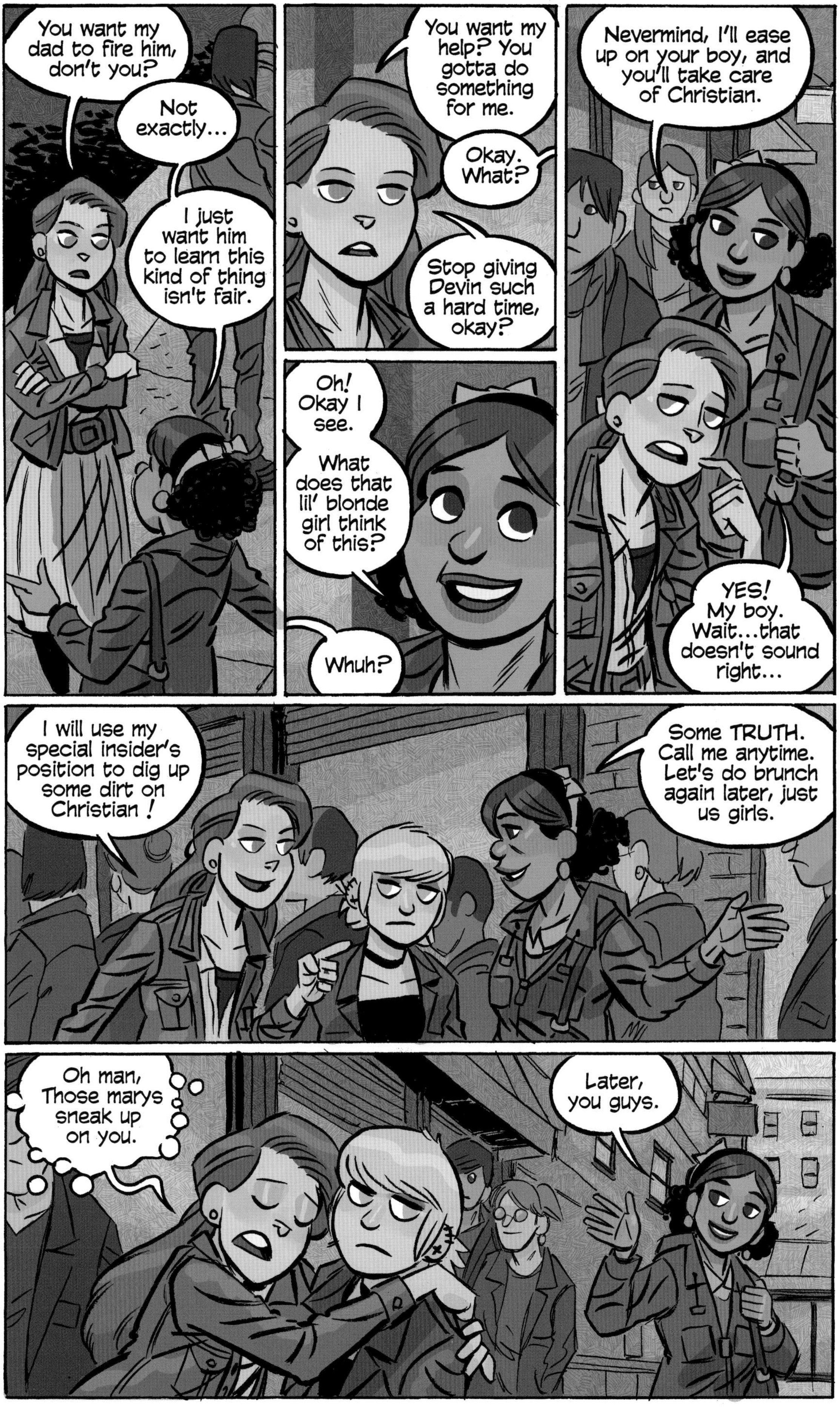
You want my dad to fire him, don't you?
Not exactly...
I just want him to learn this kind of thing isn't fair.
You want my help? You gotta do something for me.
Okay. What?
Stop giving Devin such a hard time, okay?
Oh! Okay I see.
What does that lil' blonde girl think of this?
Whuh?
Nevermind, I'll ease up on your boy, and you'll take care of Christian.
YES! My boy. Wait...that doesn't sound right...
I will use my special insider's position to dig up some dirt on Christian!
Some TRUTH. Call me anytime. Let's do brunch again later, just us girls.
Oh man, Those marys sneak up on you.
Later, you guys.

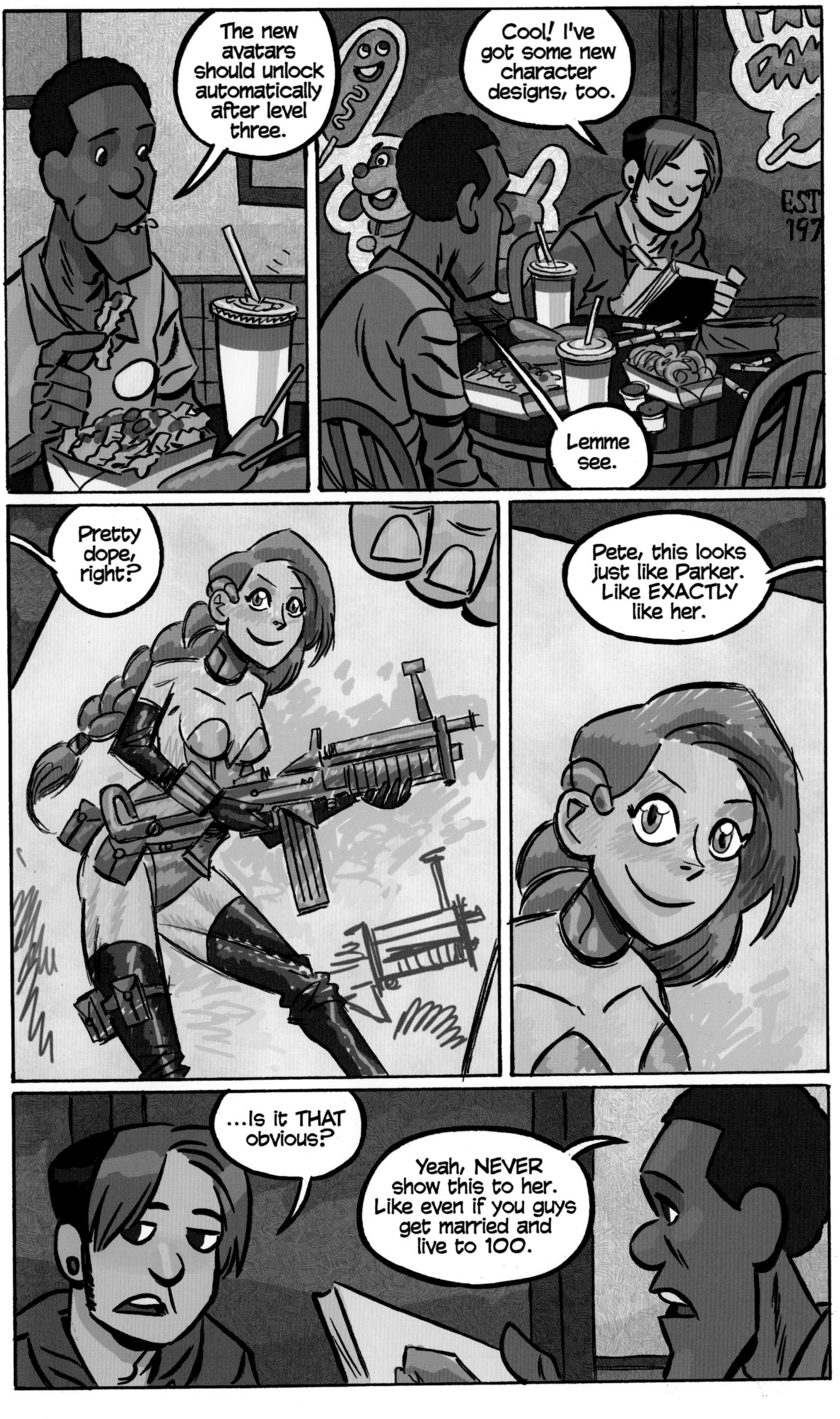
The new avatars should unlock automatically after level three.
Cool! I've got some new character designs, too.
Lemme see.
Pretty dope, right?
Pete, this looks just like Parker. Like EXACTLY like her.
...Is it THAT obvious?
Yeah, NEVER show this to her. Like even if you guys get married and live to 100.

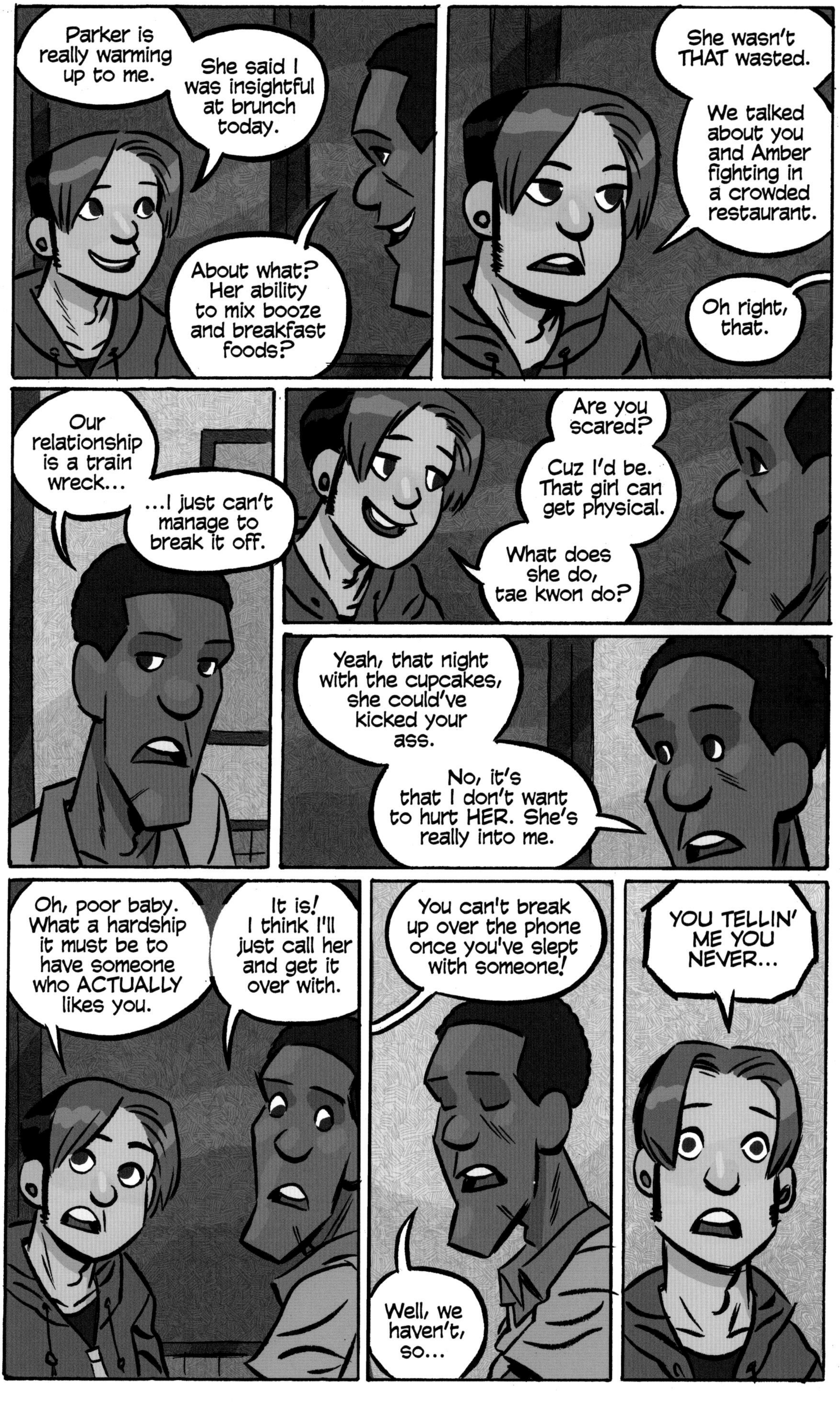
Parker is really warming up to me.
She said I was insightful at brunch today.
About what? Her ability to mix booze and breakfast foods?
She wasn't THAT wasted.
We talked about you and Amber fighting in a crowded restaurant.
Oh right, that.
Our relationship is a train wreck...
...I just can't manage to break it off.
Are you scared?
Cuz I'd be. That girl can get physical.
What does she do, tae kwon do?
Yeah, that night with the cupcakes, she could've kicked your ass.
No, it's that I don't want to hurt HER. She's really into me.
Oh, poor baby. What a hardship it must be to have someone who ACTUALLY likes you.
It is! I think I'll just call her and get it over with.
You can't break up over the phone once you've slept with someone!
Well, we haven't, so...
YOU TELLIN' ME YOU NEVER...

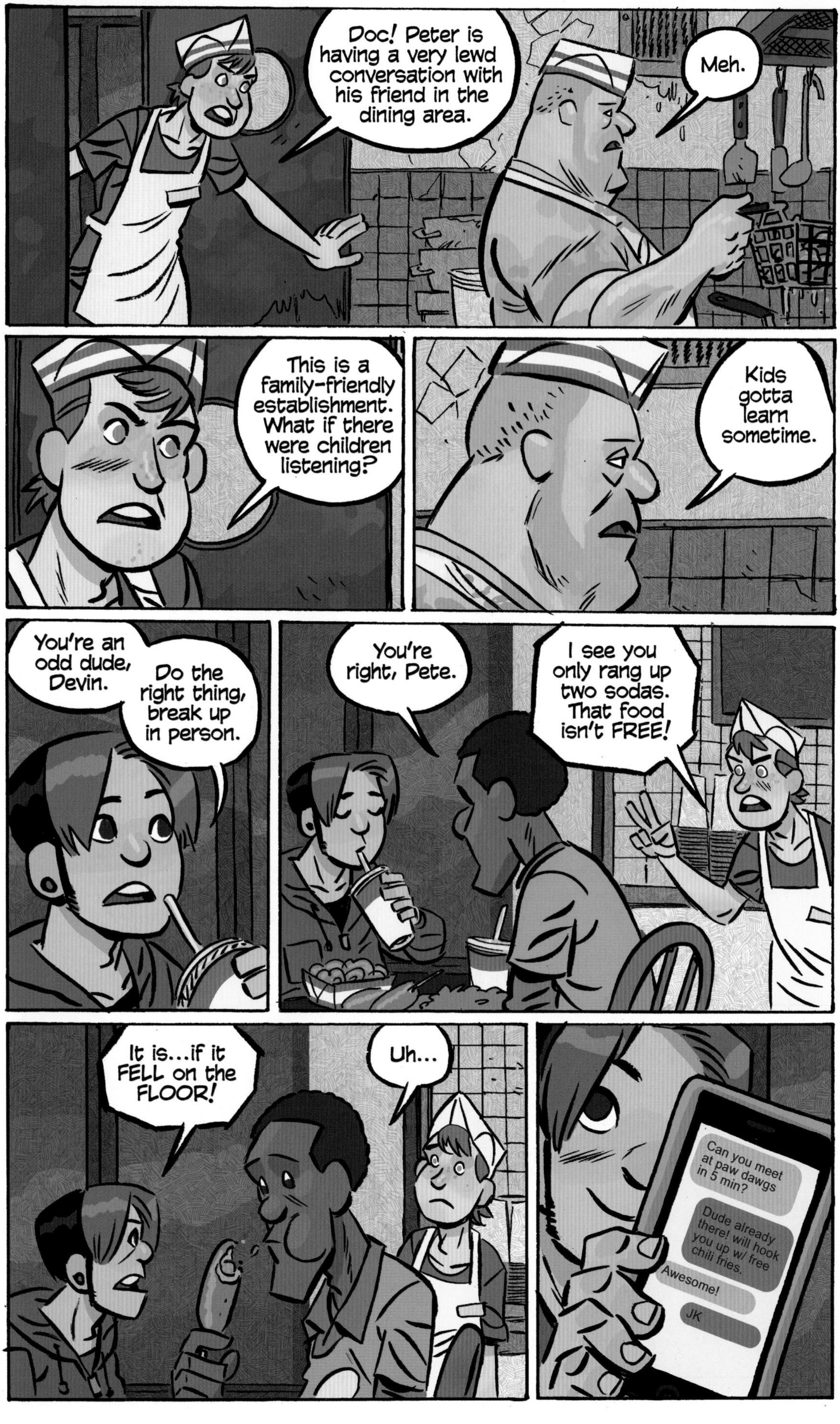
Doc! Peter is having a very lewd conversation with his friend in the dining area.
Meh.
This is a family-friendly establishment. What if there were children listening?
Kids gotta learn sometime.
You're an odd dude, Devin.
Do the right thing, break up in person.
You're right, Pete.
I see you only rang up two sodas. That food isn't FREE!
It is...if it FELL on the FLOOR!
Uh...
Can you meet at paw dawgs in 5 min?
Dude already there! will hook you up w/ free chili fries.
Awesome!
JK

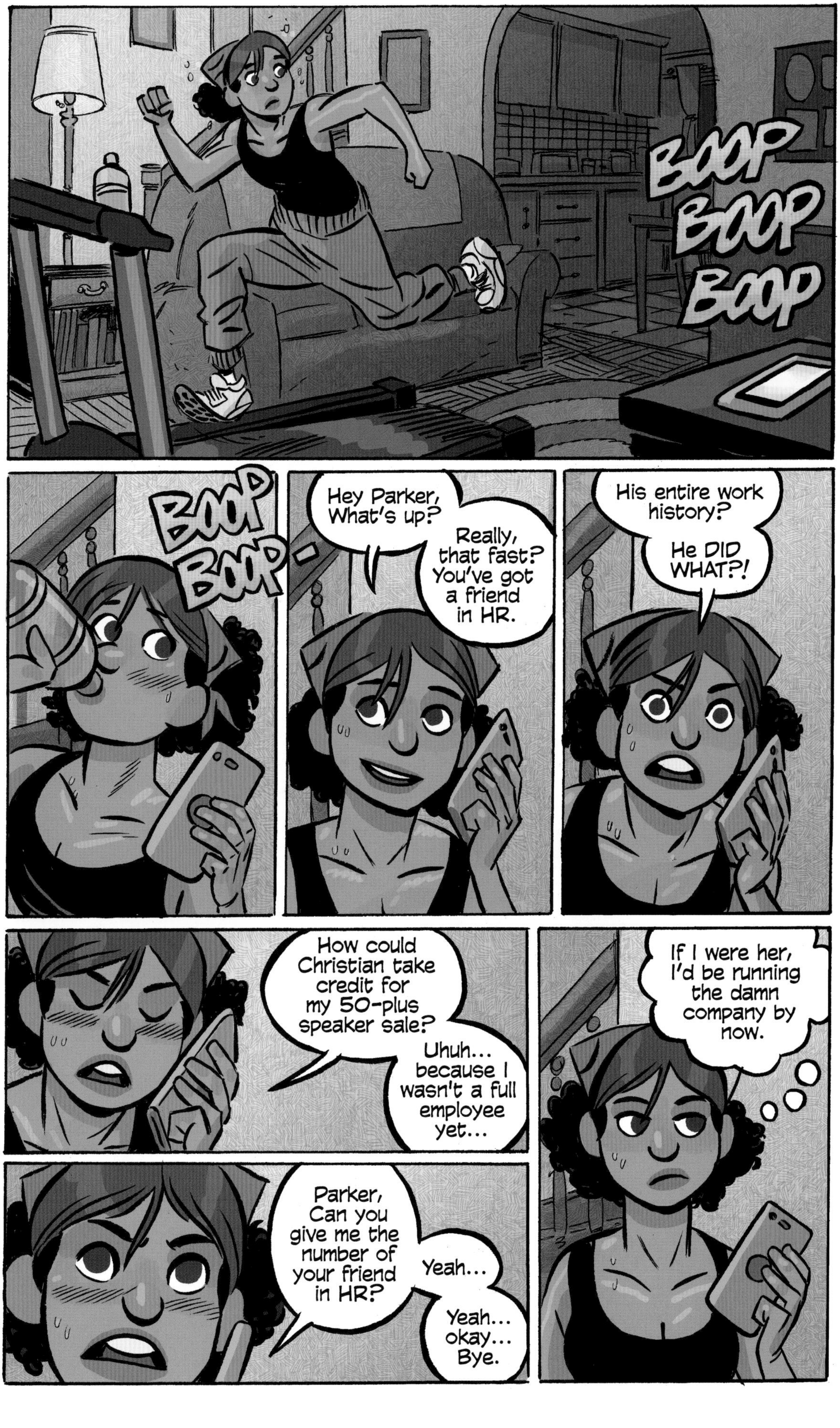
BOOP BOOP BOOP
BOOP BOOP-
Hey Parker, What's up?
Really, that fast? You've got a friend in HR.
His entire work history?
He DID WHAT?!
How could Christian take credit for my 50-plus speaker sale?
Uhuh... because I wasn't a full employee yet...
Parker, Can you give me the number of your friend in HR?
Yeah...
Yeah... okay... Bye.
If I were her, I'd be running the damn company by now.

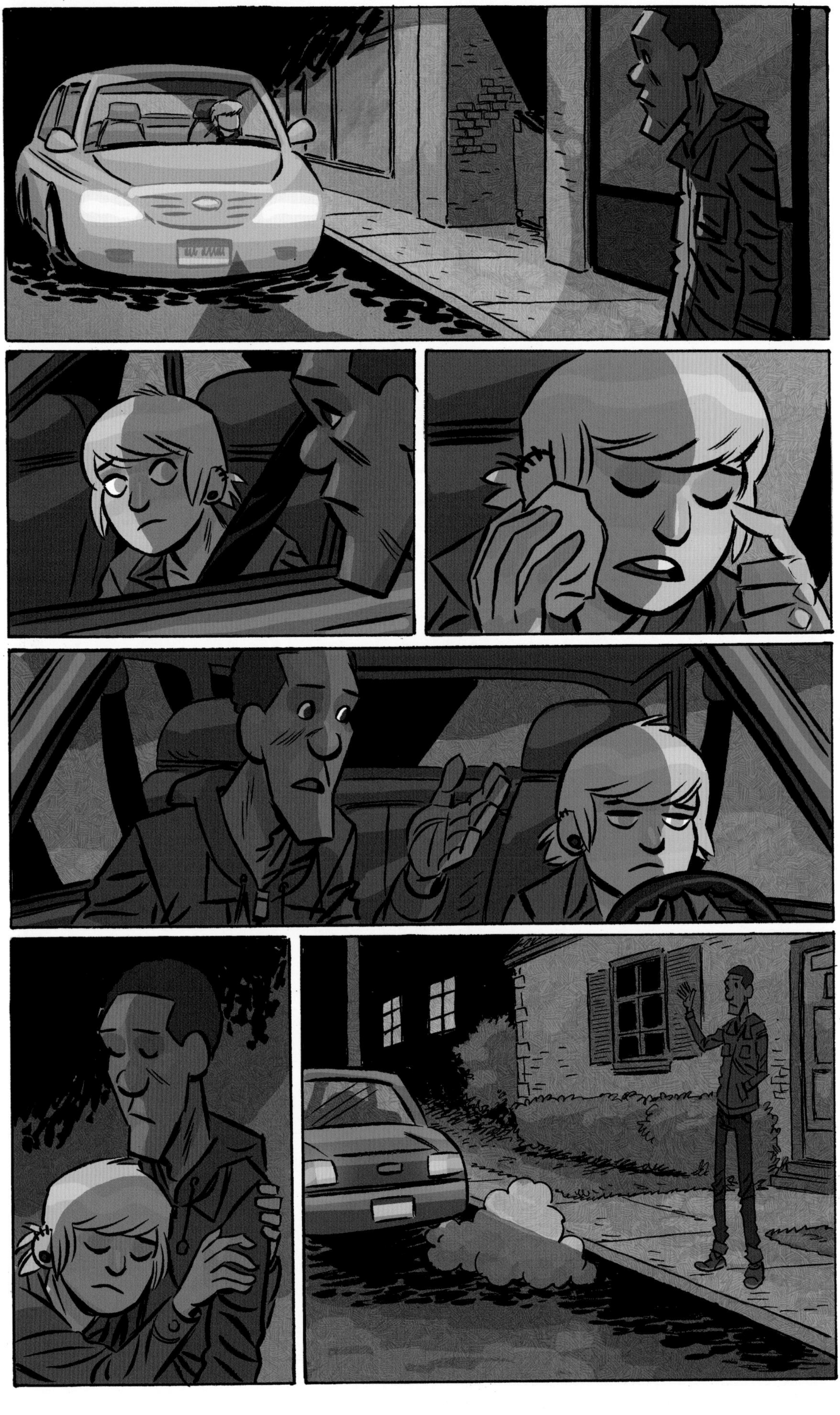

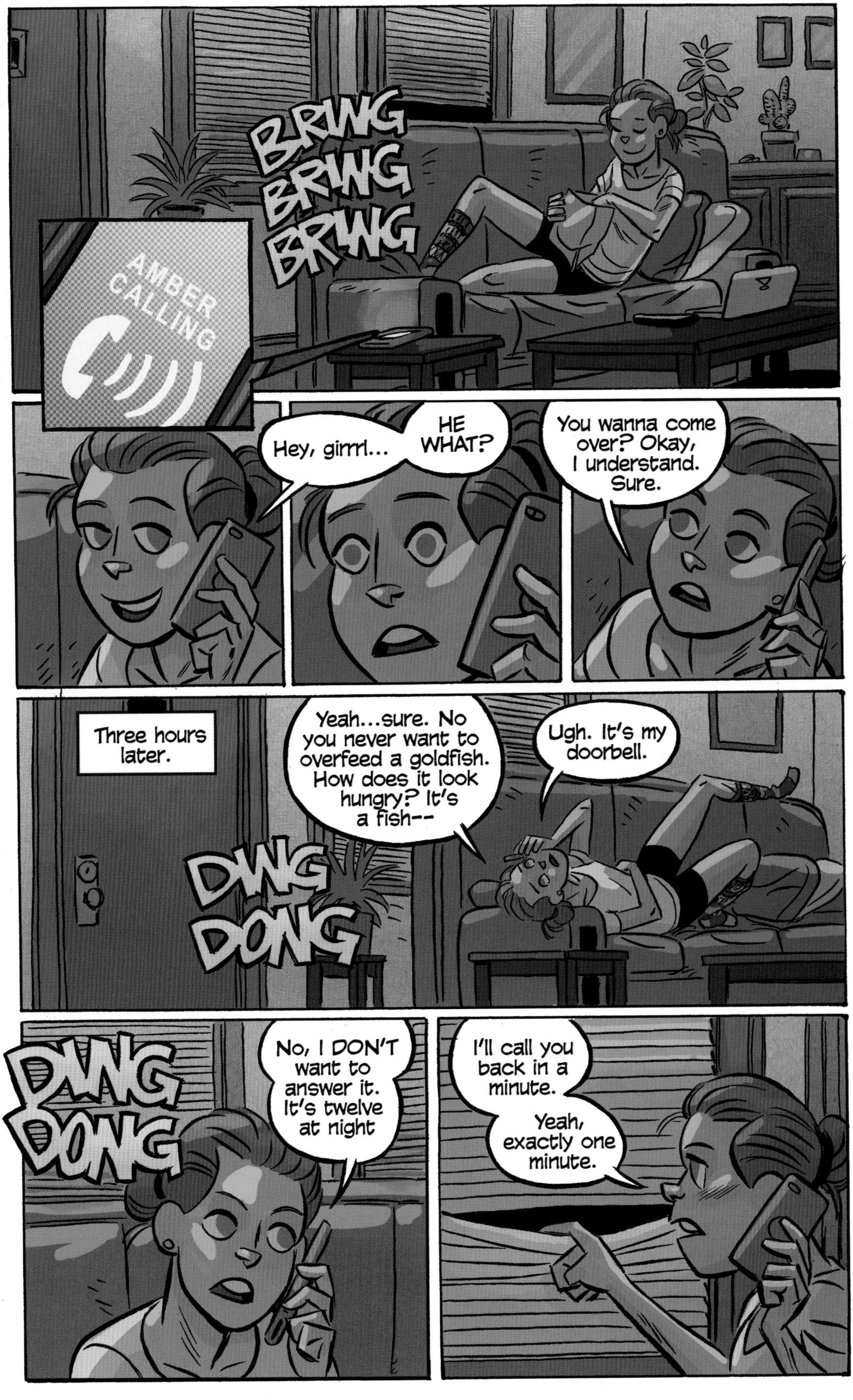
BRING
BRING
BRING
AMBER CALLING
Hey, girrrl...
HE WHAT?
You wanna come over? Okay, I understand. Sure.
Three hours later.
Yeah...sure. No you never want to overfeed a goldfish. How does it look hungry? It's a fish--
Ugh. It's my doorbell.
DING
DONG
DING
DONG
No, I DON'T want to answer it. It's twelve at night
I'll call you back in a minute.
Yeah, exactly one minute.

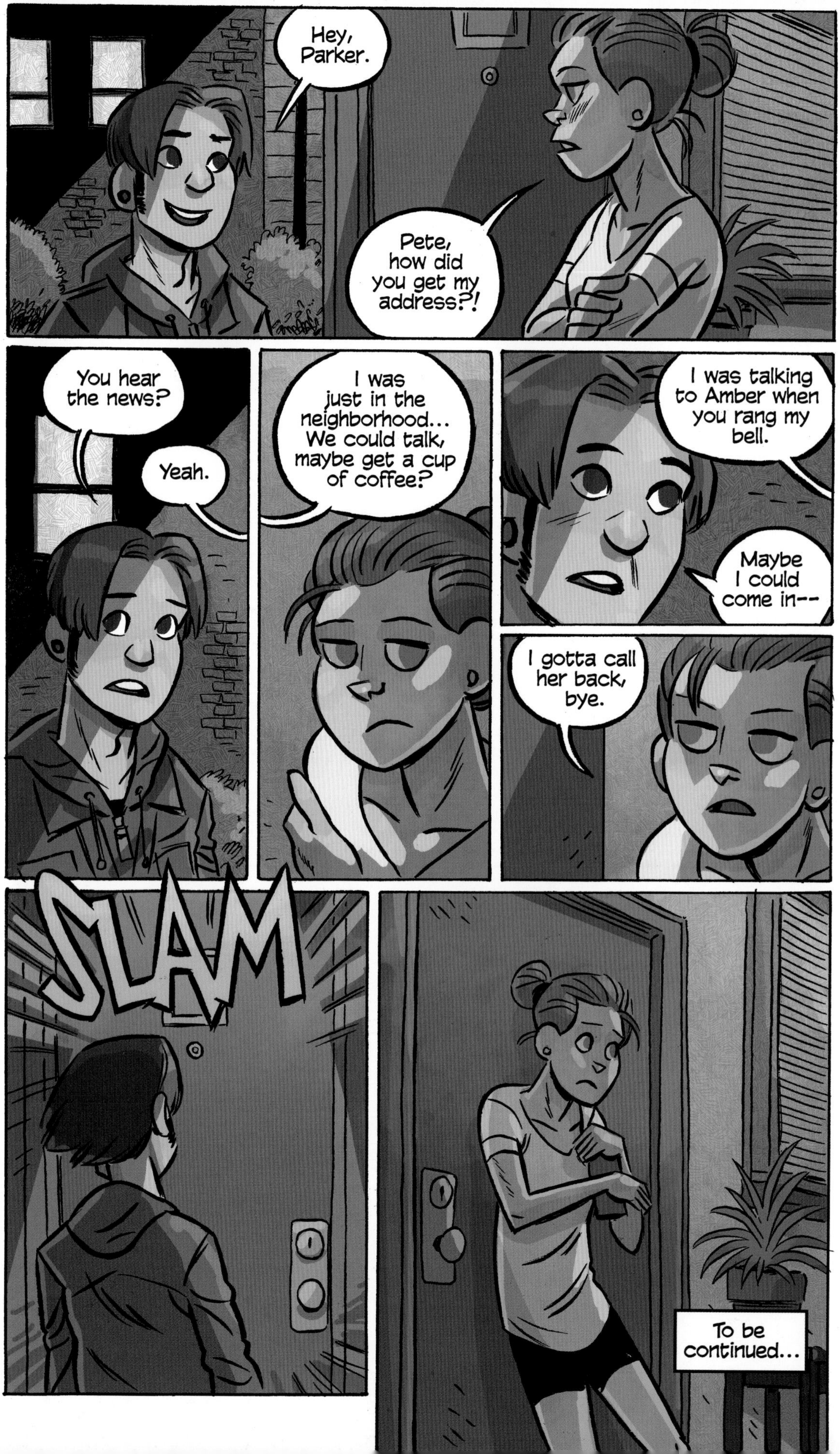
Hey, Parker.
Pete, how did you get my address?!
You hear the news?
Yeah.
I was just in the neighborhood... We could talk, maybe get a cup of coffee?
I was talking to Amber when you rang my bell.
Maybe I could come in--
I gotta call her back, bye.
SLAM
To be continued...

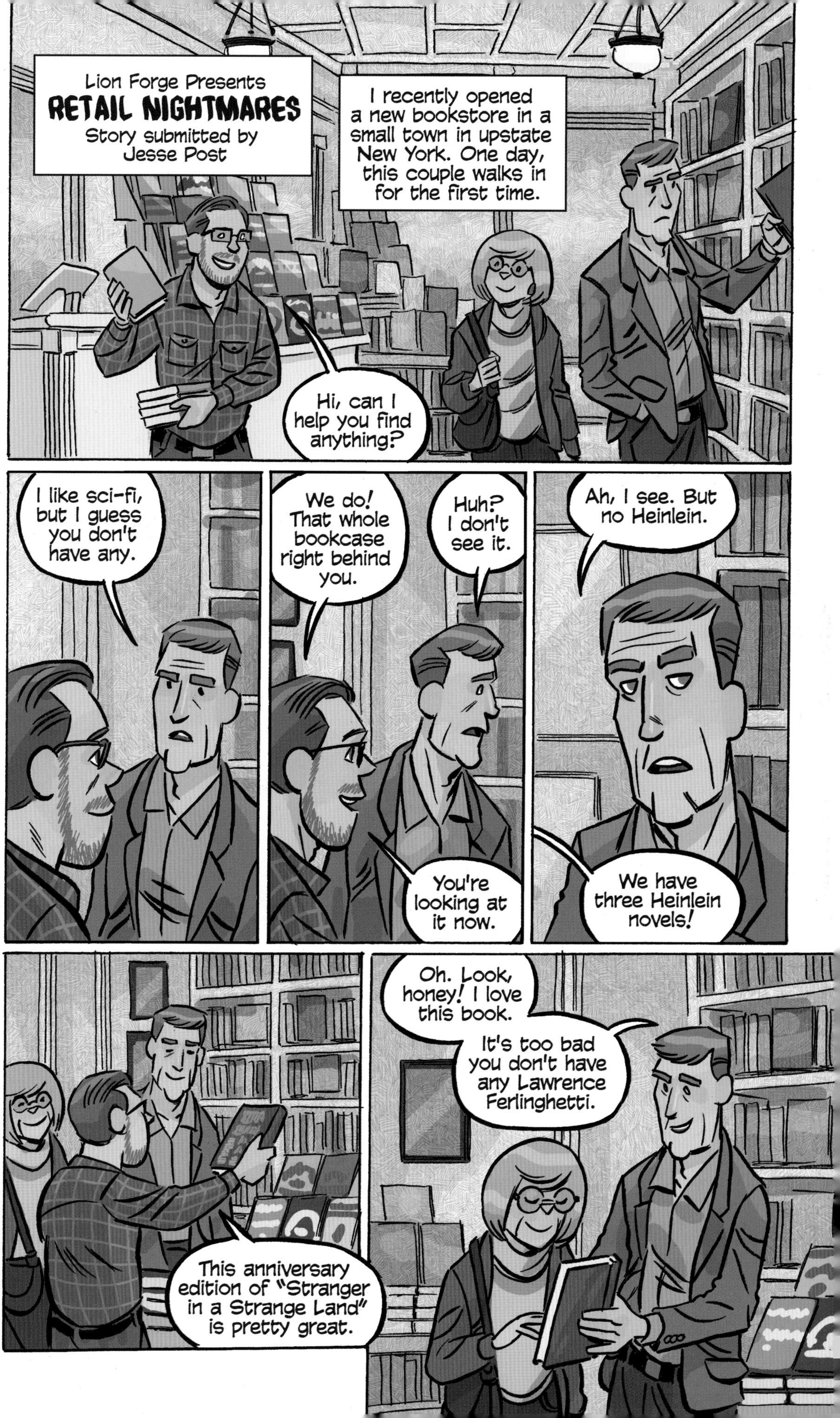
Lion Forge Presents
RETAIL NIGHTMARES
Story submitted by Jesse Post
I recently opened a new bookstore in a small town in upstate New York. One day, this couple walks in for the first time.
Hi, can I help you find anything?
I like sci-fi, but I guess you don't have any.
We do! That whole bookcase right behind you.
Huh? I don't see it.
You're looking at it now.
Ah, I see. But no Heinlein.
We have three Heinlein novels!
This anniversary edition of "Stranger in a Strange Land" is pretty great.
Oh. Look, honey! I love this book.
It's too bad you don't have any Lawrence Ferlinghetti.

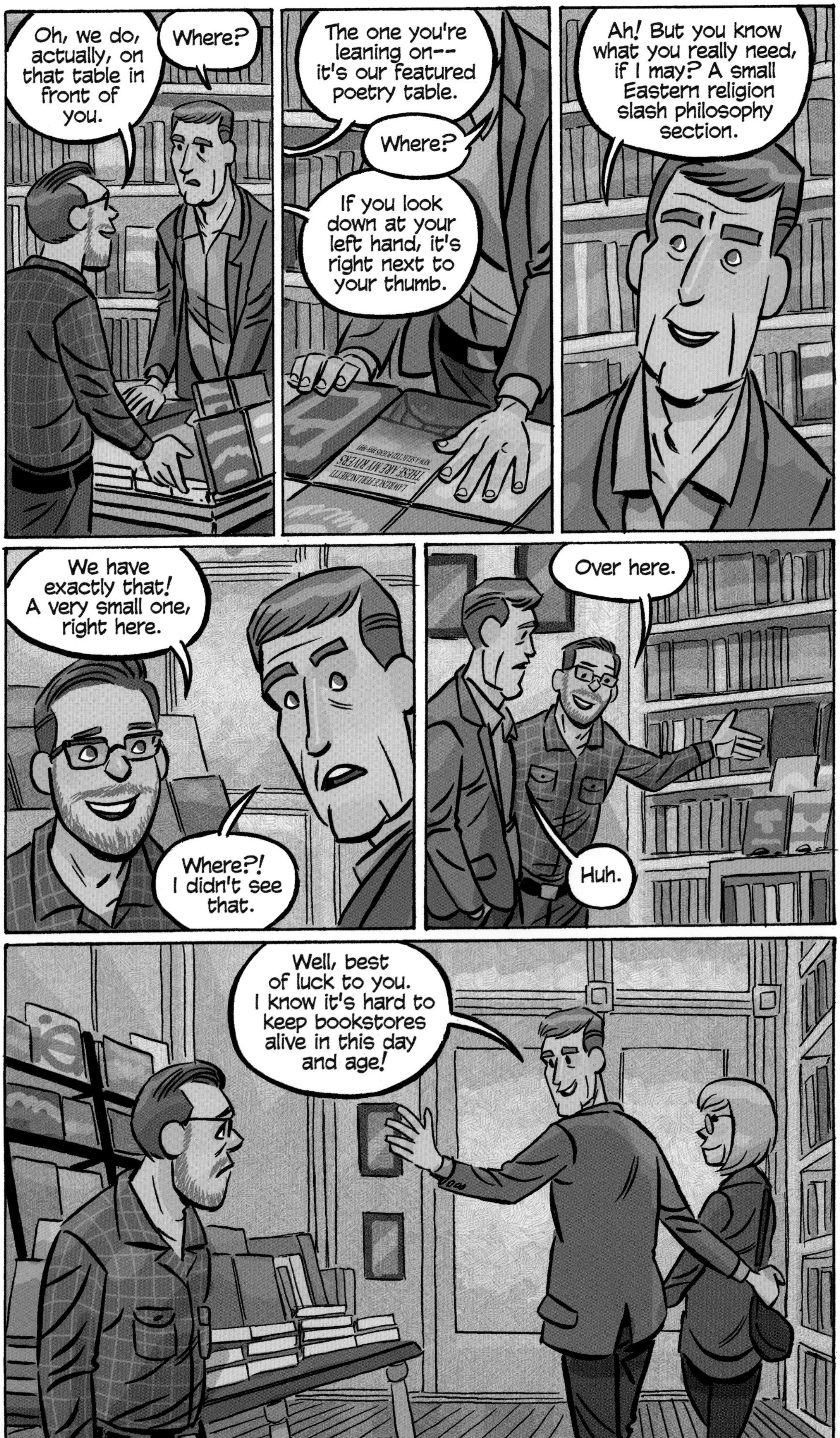

Oh, we do, actually, on that table in front of you.
Where?
The one you're leaning on-- it's our featured poetry table.
Where?
If you look down at your left hand, it's right next to your thumb.
LAWRENCE FERLINGHETTI
THESE ARE MY RIVERS
Ah! But you know what you really need, if I may? A small Eastern religion slash philosophy section.
We have exactly that! A very small one, right here.
Where?! I didn't see that.
Over here.
Huh.
Well, best of luck to you. I know it's hard to keep bookstores alive in this day and age!

# CHAPTER 5

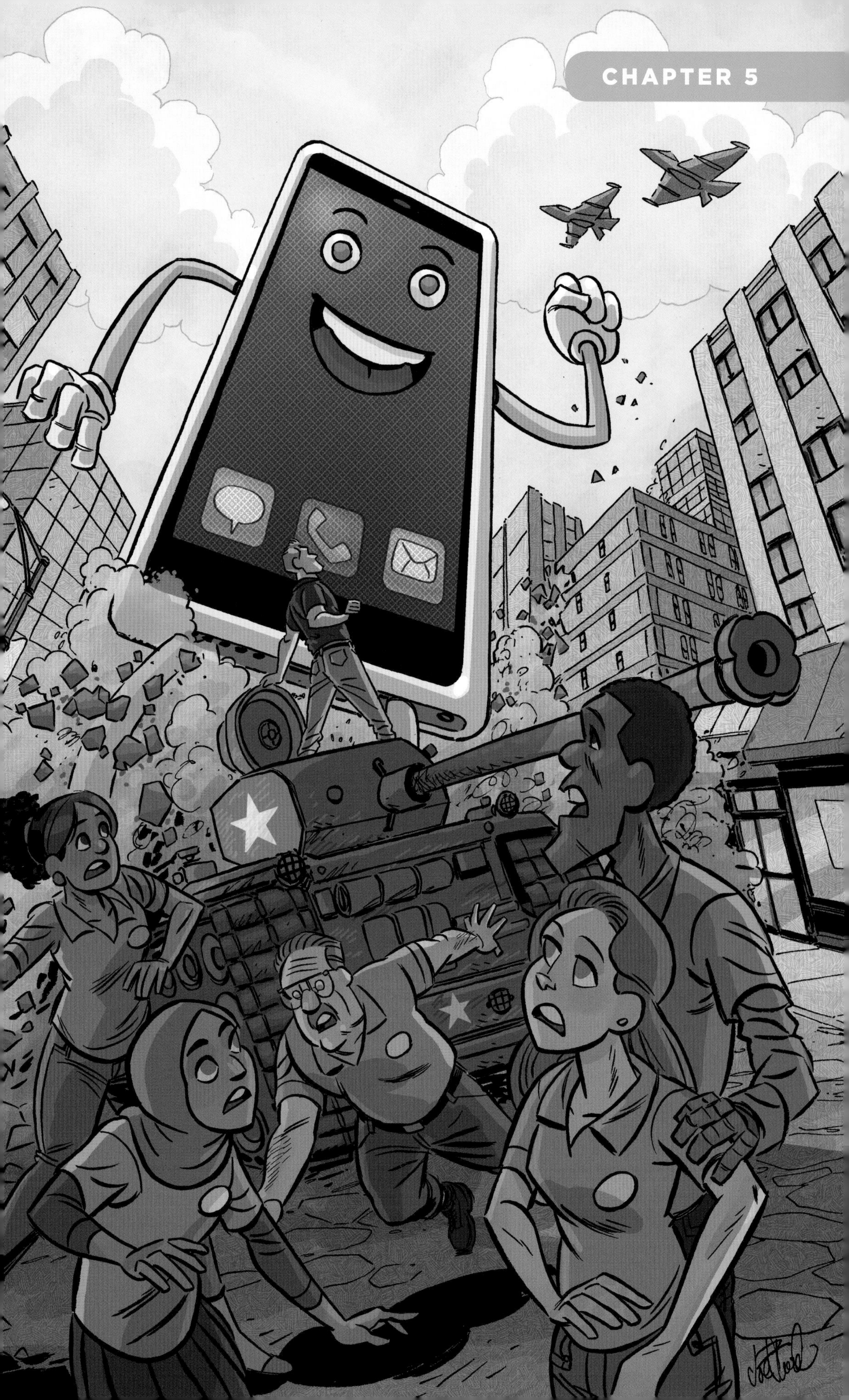

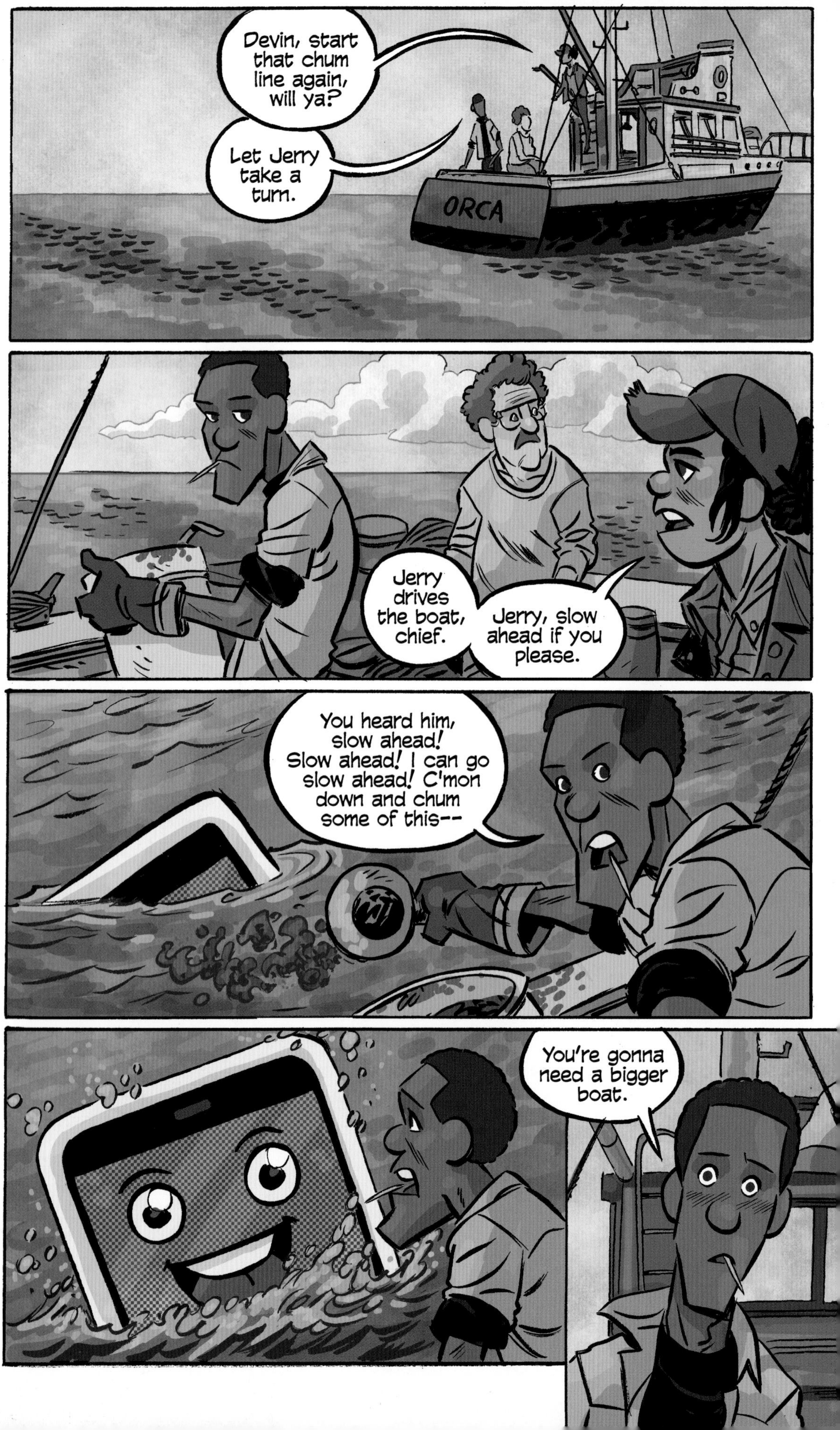
Devin, start that chum line again, will ya?
Let Jerry take a turn.
ORCA
Jerry drives the boat, chief.
Jerry, slow ahead if you please.
You heard him, slow ahead! Slow ahead! I can go slow ahead! C'mon down and chum some of this--
You're gonna need a bigger boat.

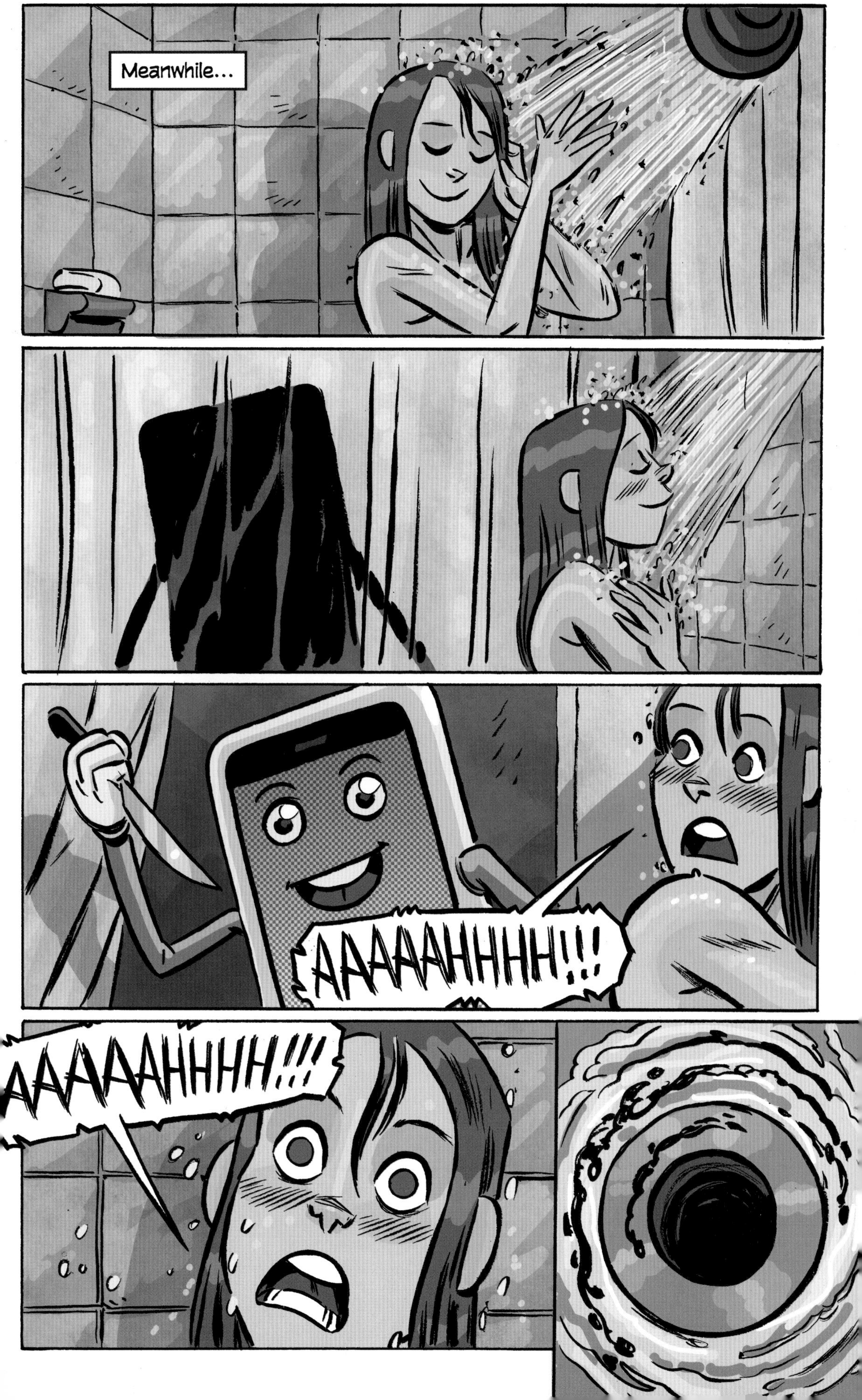
Meanwhile...
AAAAAHHHH!!!
AAAAAHHHH!!!

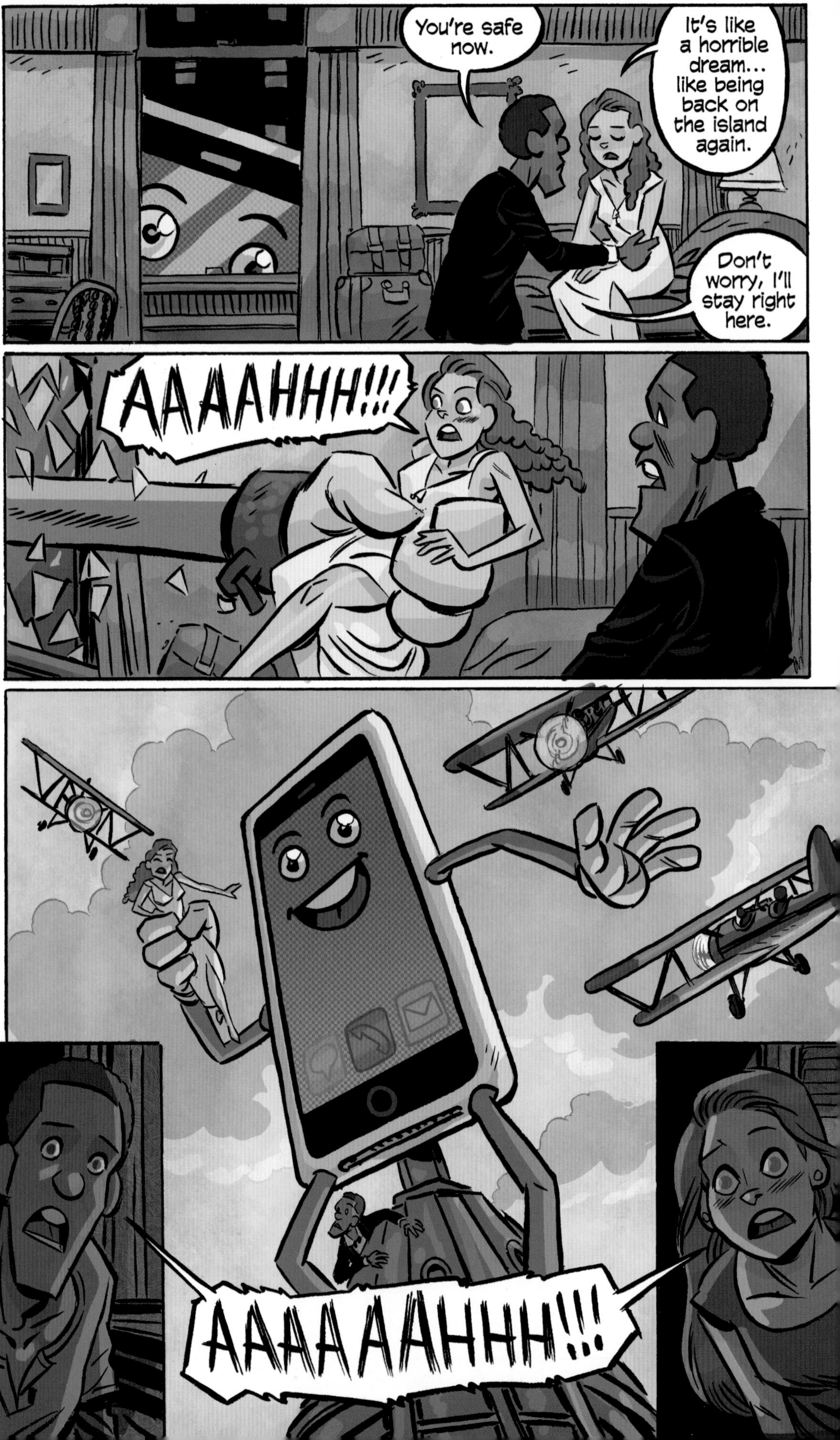
You're safe now.
It's like a horrible dream... like being back on the island again.
Don't worry, I'll stay right here.
AAAAHHH!!!
AAAAAAHHH!!!

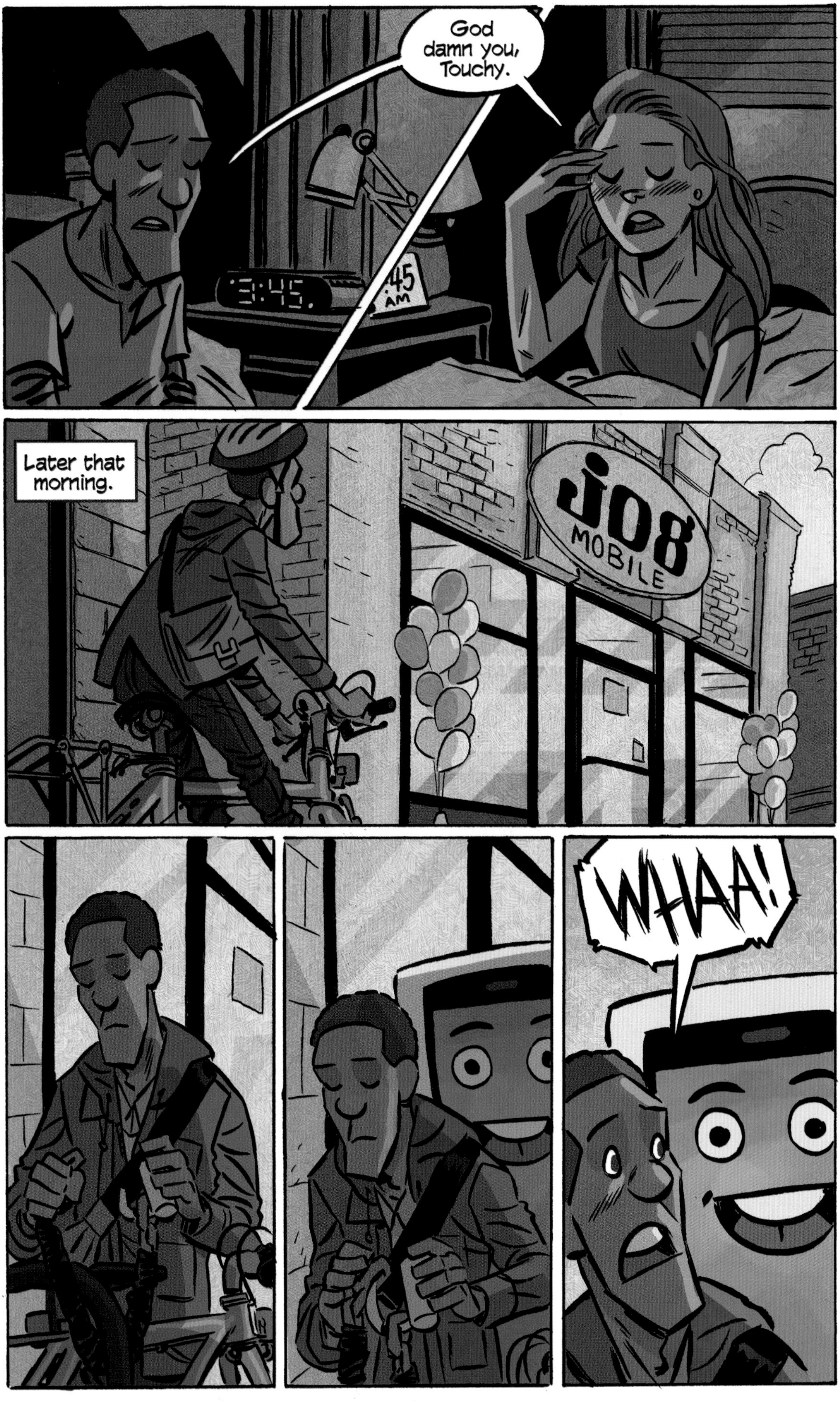
God damn you, Touchy.
3:45.
3:45 AM
Later that morning.
J08 MOBILE
WHAA!

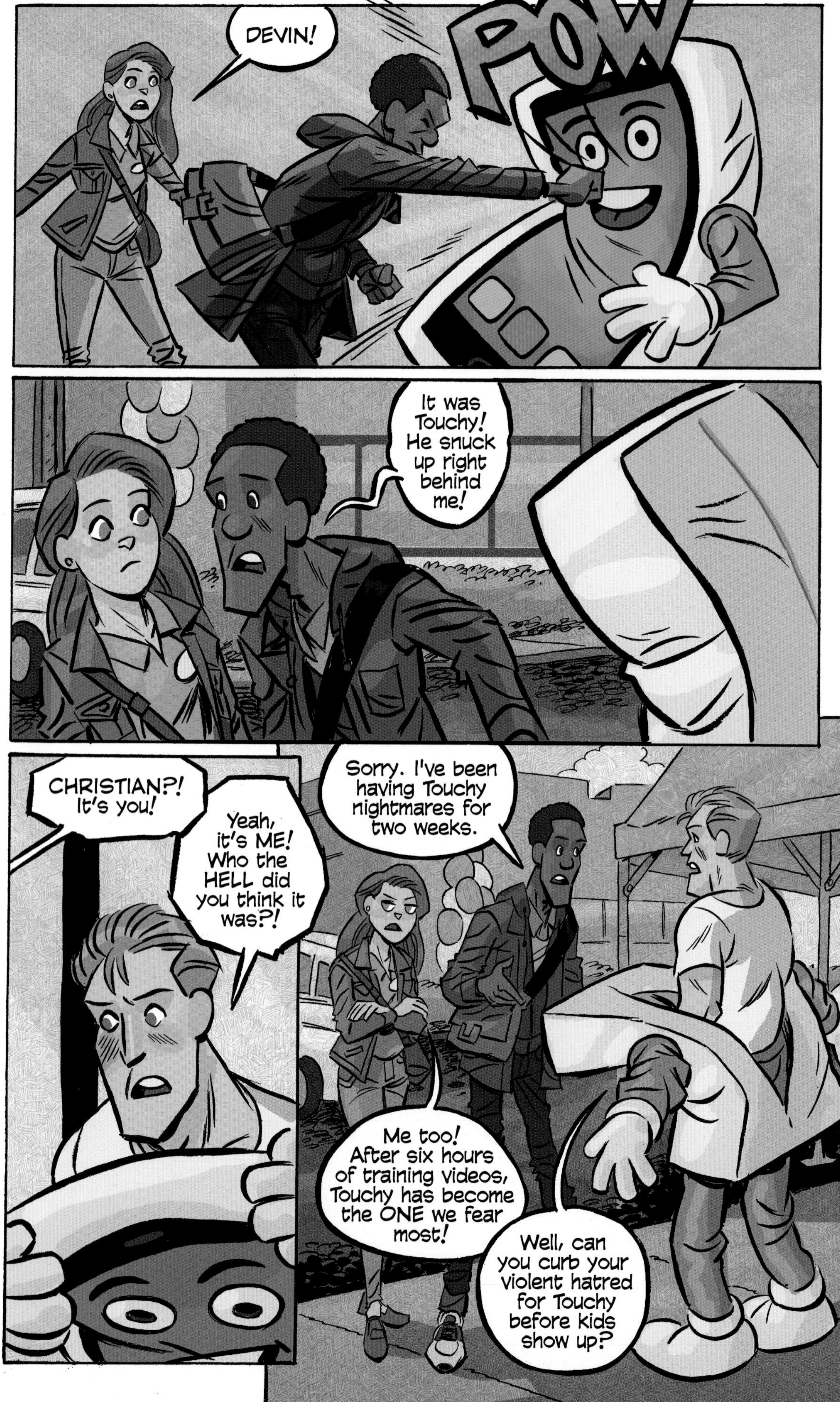
DEVIN!
POW
It was Touchy! He snuck up right behind me!
CHRISTIAN?! It's you!
Yeah, it's ME! Who the HELL did you think it was?!
Sorry. I've been having Touchy nightmares for two weeks.
Me too! After six hours of training videos, Touchy has become the ONE we fear most!
Well, can you curb your violent hatred for Touchy before kids show up?

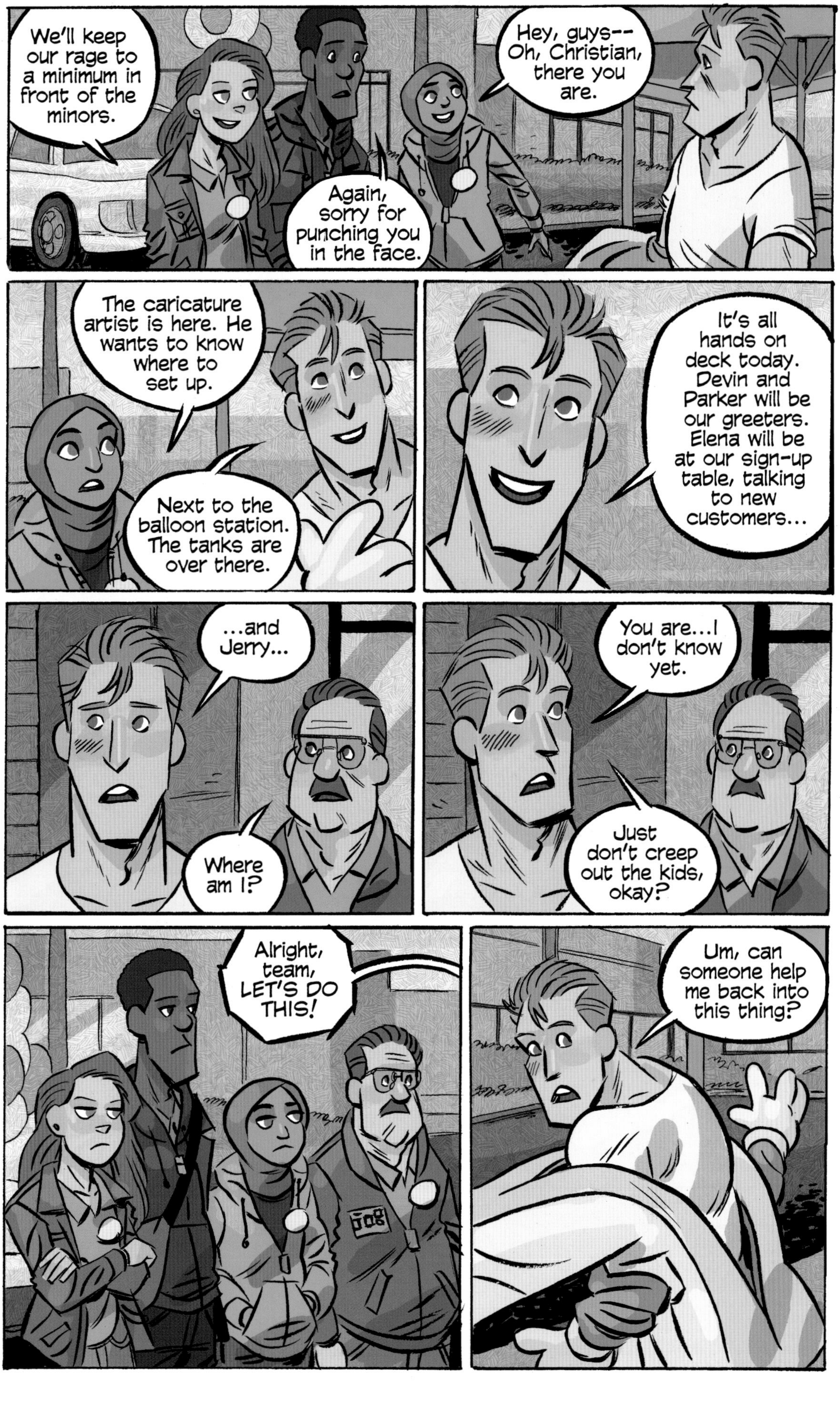
We'll keep our rage to a minimum in front of the minors.
Again, sorry for punching you in the face.
Hey, guys-- Oh, Christian, there you are.
The caricature artist is here. He wants to know where to set up.
Next to the balloon station. The tanks are over there.
It's all hands on deck today. Devin and Parker will be our greeters. Elena will be at our sign-up table, talking to new customers...
...and Jerry...
Where am I?
You are...I don't know yet.
Just don't creep out the kids, okay?
Alright, team, LET'S DO THIS!
JOE
Um, can someone help me back into this thing?

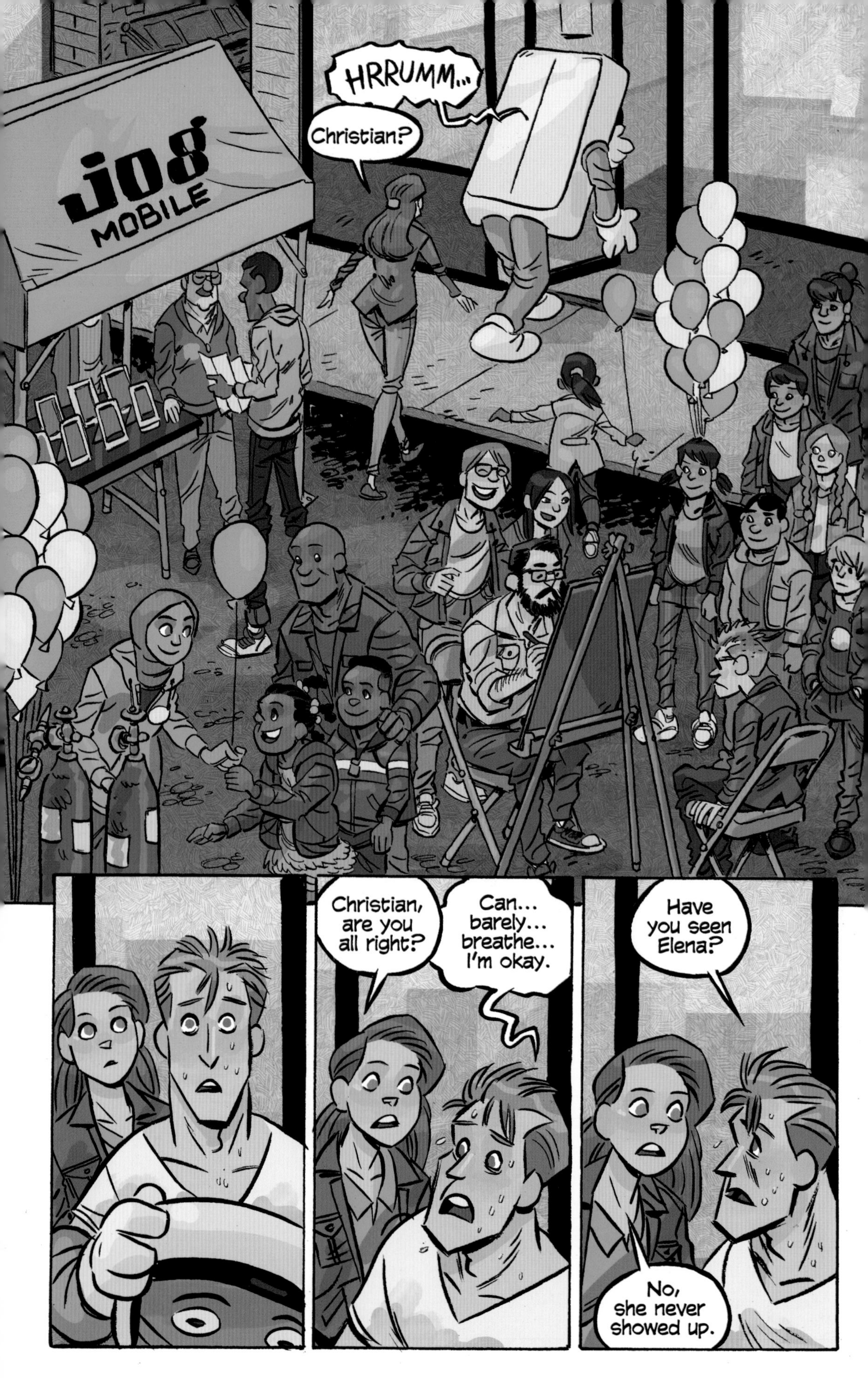
HRRUMM...
Christian?
MOBILE
Christian, are you all right?
Can... barely... breathe... I'm okay.
Have you seen Elena?
No, she never showed up.

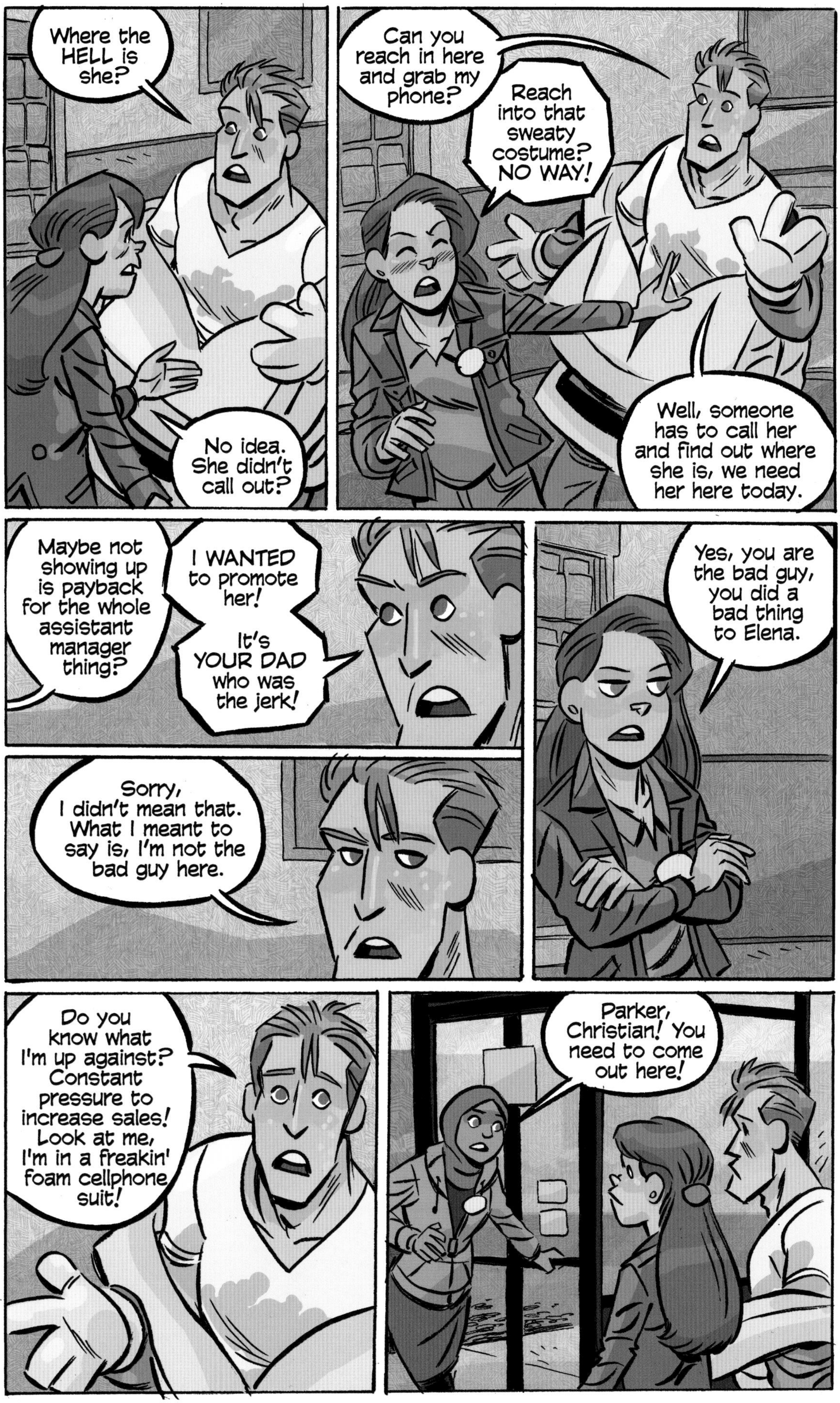
Where the HELL is she?
No idea. She didn't call out?
Can you reach in here and grab my phone?
Reach into that sweaty costume? NO WAY!
Well, someone has to call her and find out where she is, we need her here today.
Maybe not showing up is payback for the whole assistant manager thing?
I WANTED to promote her!
It's YOUR DAD who was the jerk!
Sorry, I didn't mean that. What I meant to say is, I'm not the bad guy here.
Yes, you are the bad guy, you did a bad thing to Elena.
Do you know what I'm up against? Constant pressure to increase sales! Look at me, I'm in a freakin' foam cellphone suit!
Parker, Christian! You need to come out here!

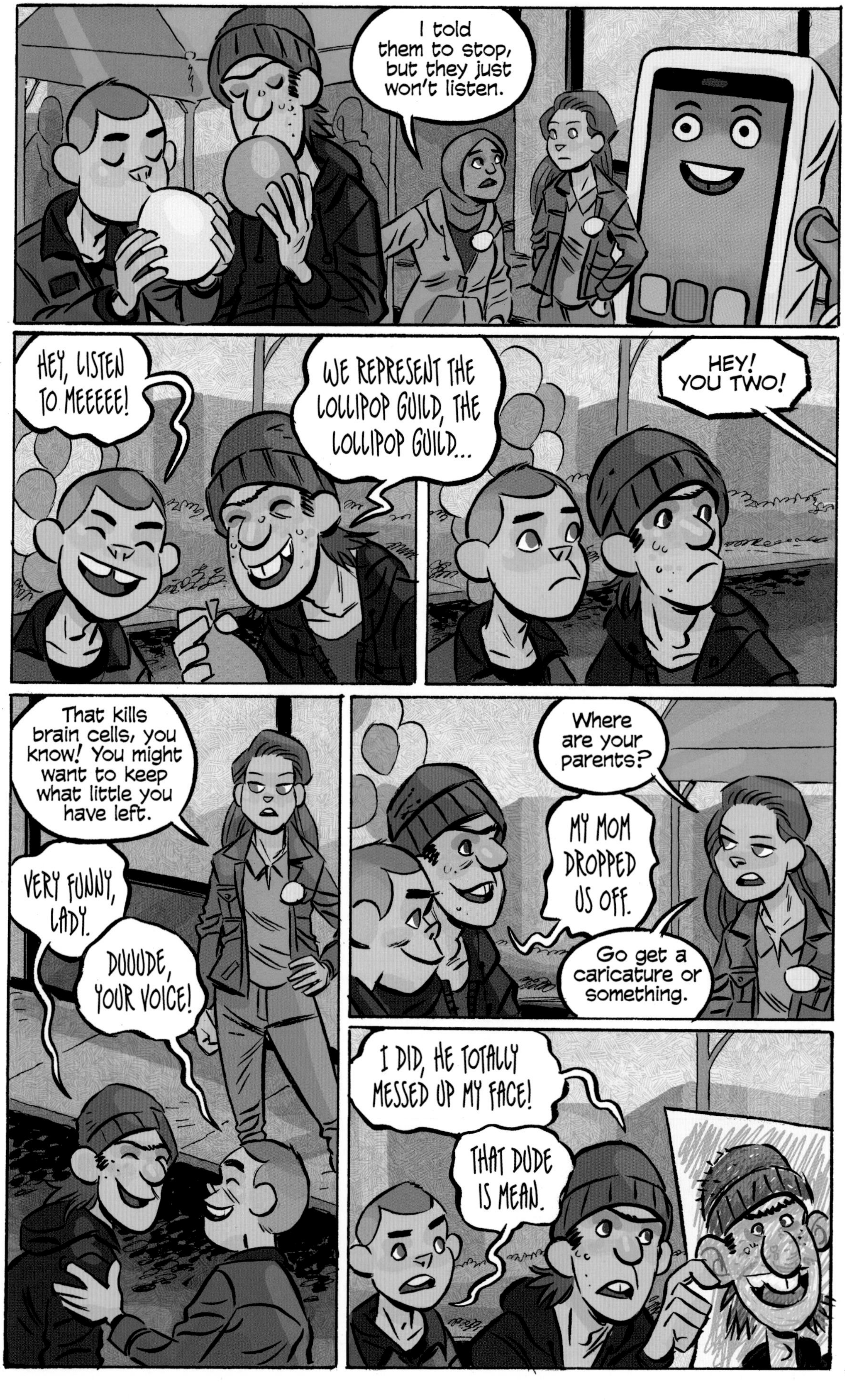
I told them to stop, but they just won't listen.
HEY, LISTEN TO MEEEEE!
WE REPRESENT THE LOLLIPOP GUILD, THE LOLLIPOP GUILD...
HEY! YOU TWO!
That kills brain cells, you know! You might want to keep what little you have left.
VERY FUNNY, LADY.
DUUUDE, YOUR VOICE!
Where are your parents?
MY MOM DROPPED US OFF.
Go get a caricature or something.
I DID, HE TOTALLY MESSED UP MY FACE!
THAT DUDE IS MEAN.

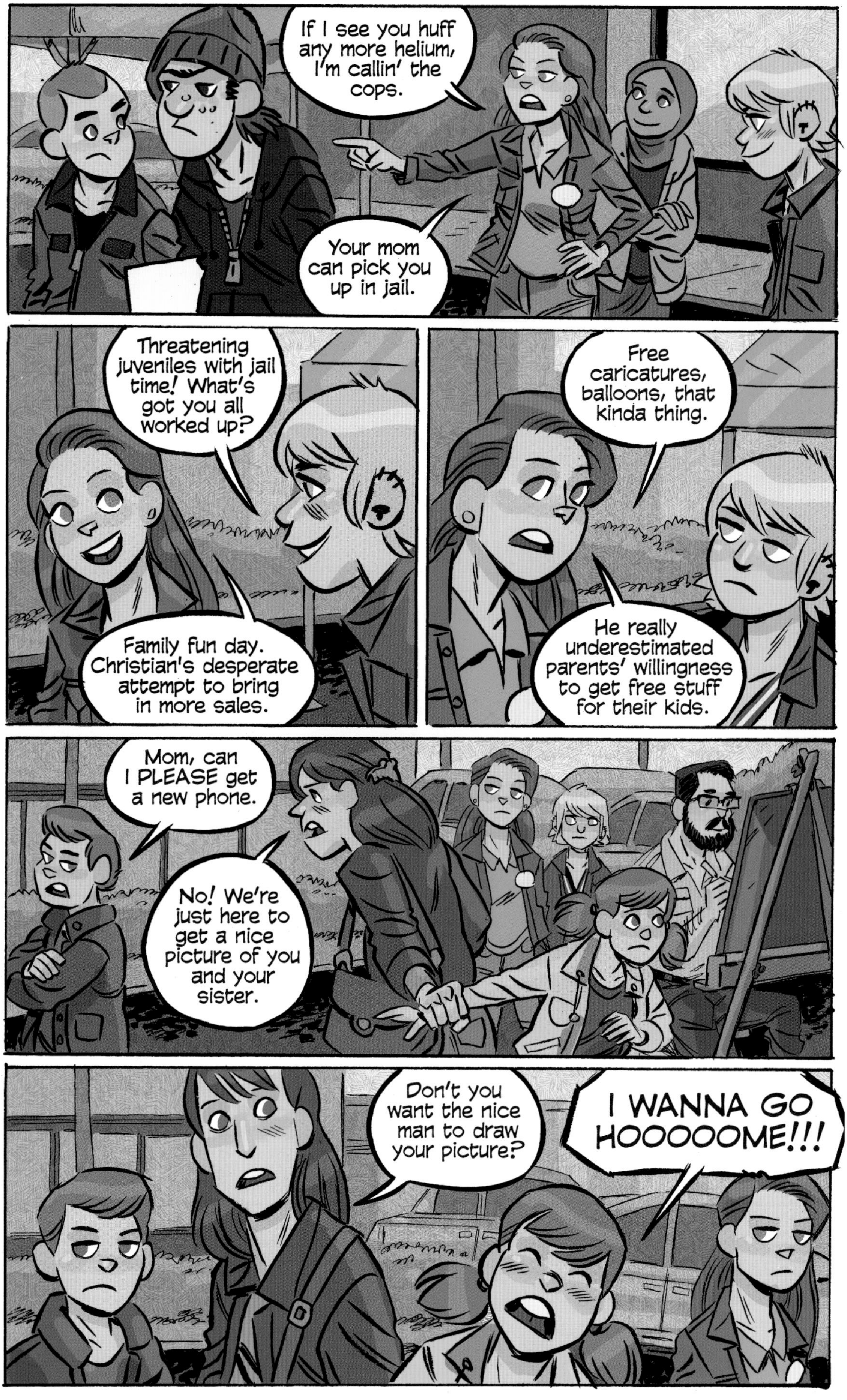
If I see you huff any more helium, I'm callin' the cops.
Your mom can pick you up in jail.
Threatening juveniles with jail time! What's got you all worked up?
Family fun day. Christian's desperate attempt to bring in more sales.
Free caricatures, balloons, that kinda thing.
He really underestimated parents' willingness to get free stuff for their kids.
Mom, can I PLEASE get a new phone.
No! We're just here to get a nice picture of you and your sister.
Don't you want the nice man to draw your picture?
I WANNA GO HOOOOOME!!!

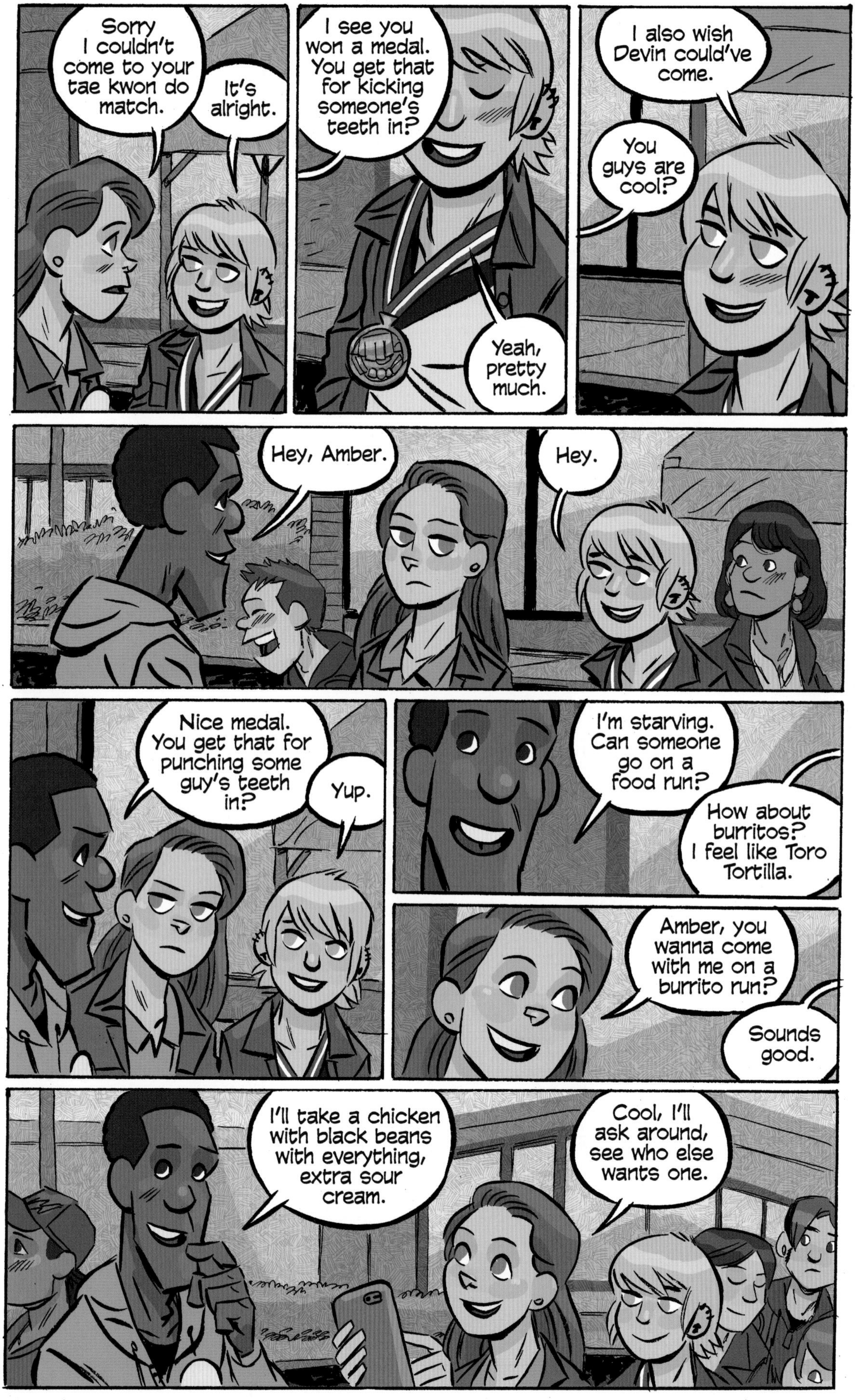
Sorry I couldn't come to your tae kwon do match.
It's alright.
I see you won a medal. You get that for kicking someone's teeth in?
Yeah, pretty much.
I also wish Devin could've come.
You guys are cool?
Hey, Amber.
Hey.
Nice medal. You get that for punching some guy's teeth in?
Yup.
I'm starving. Can someone go on a food run?
How about burritos? I feel like Toro Tortilla.
Amber, you wanna come with me on a burrito run?
Sounds good.
I'll take a chicken with black beans with everything, extra sour cream.
Cool, I'll ask around, see who else wants one.

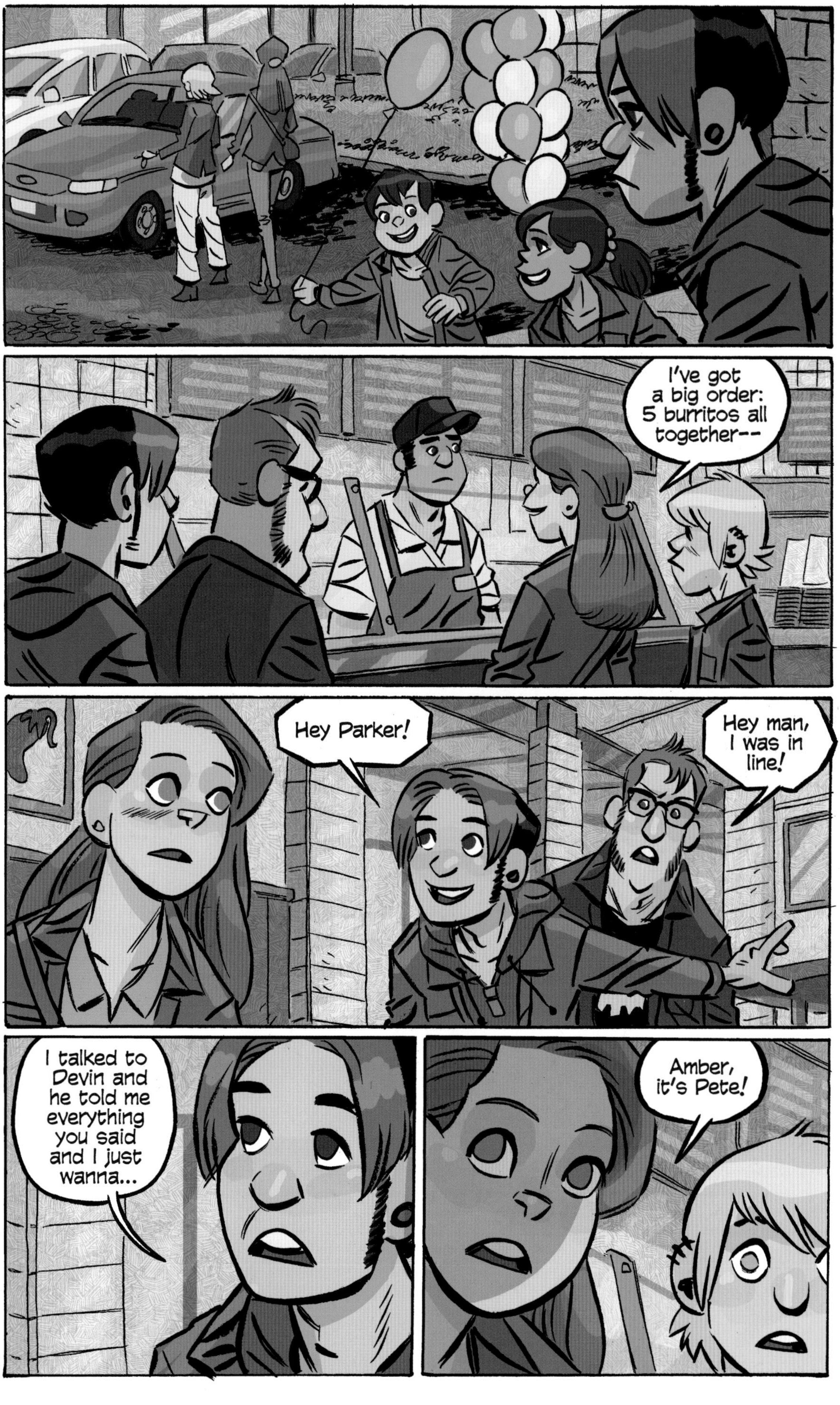
I've got a big order: 5 burritos all together--
Hey Parker!
Hey man, I was in line!
I talked to Devin and he told me everything you said and I just wanna...
Amber, it's Pete!

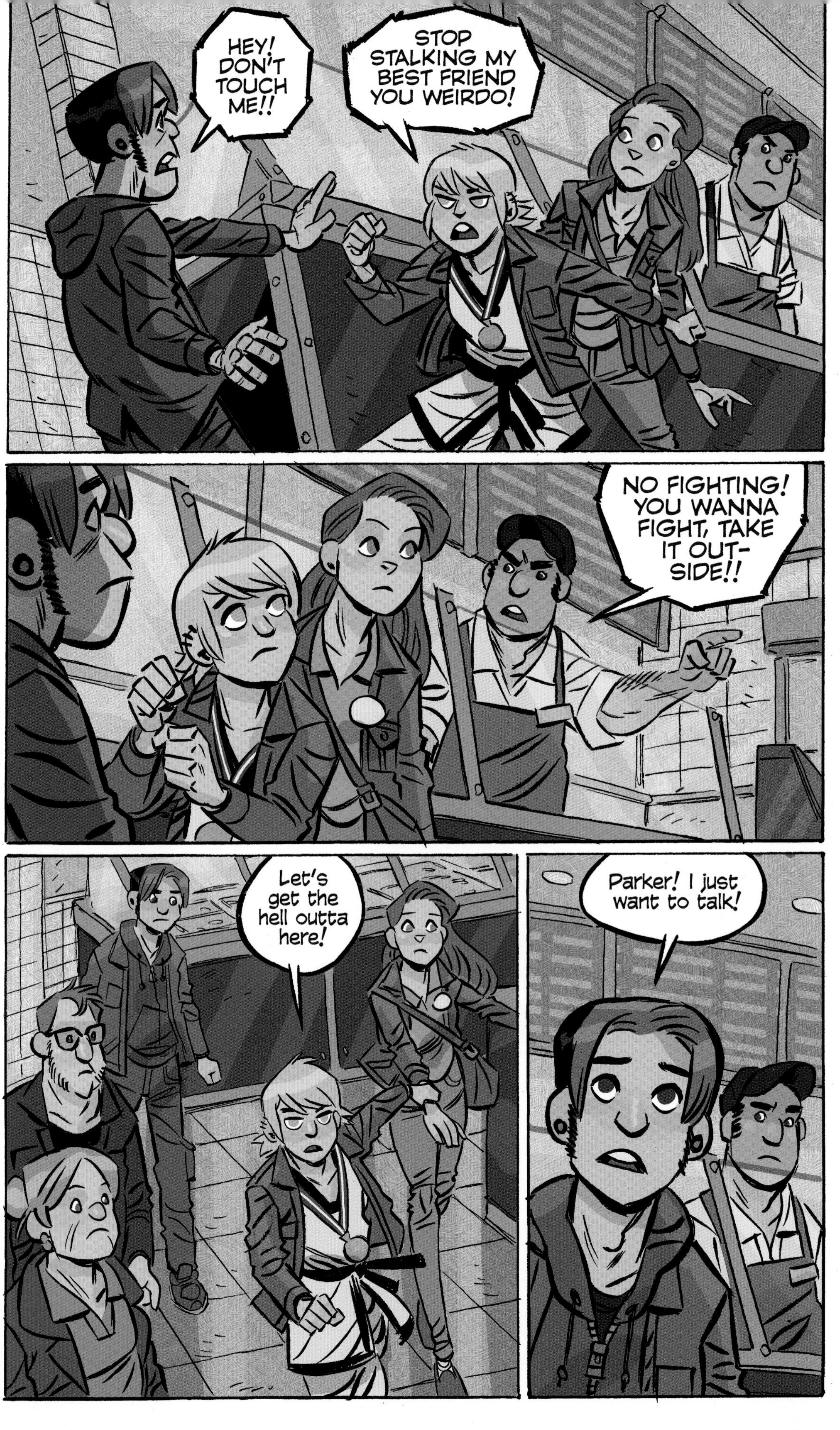
HEY! DON'T TOUCH ME!!
STOP STALKING MY BEST FRIEND YOU WEIRDO!
NO FIGHTING! YOU WANNA FIGHT, TAKE IT OUT-SIDE!!
Let's get the hell outta here!
Parker! I just want to talk!

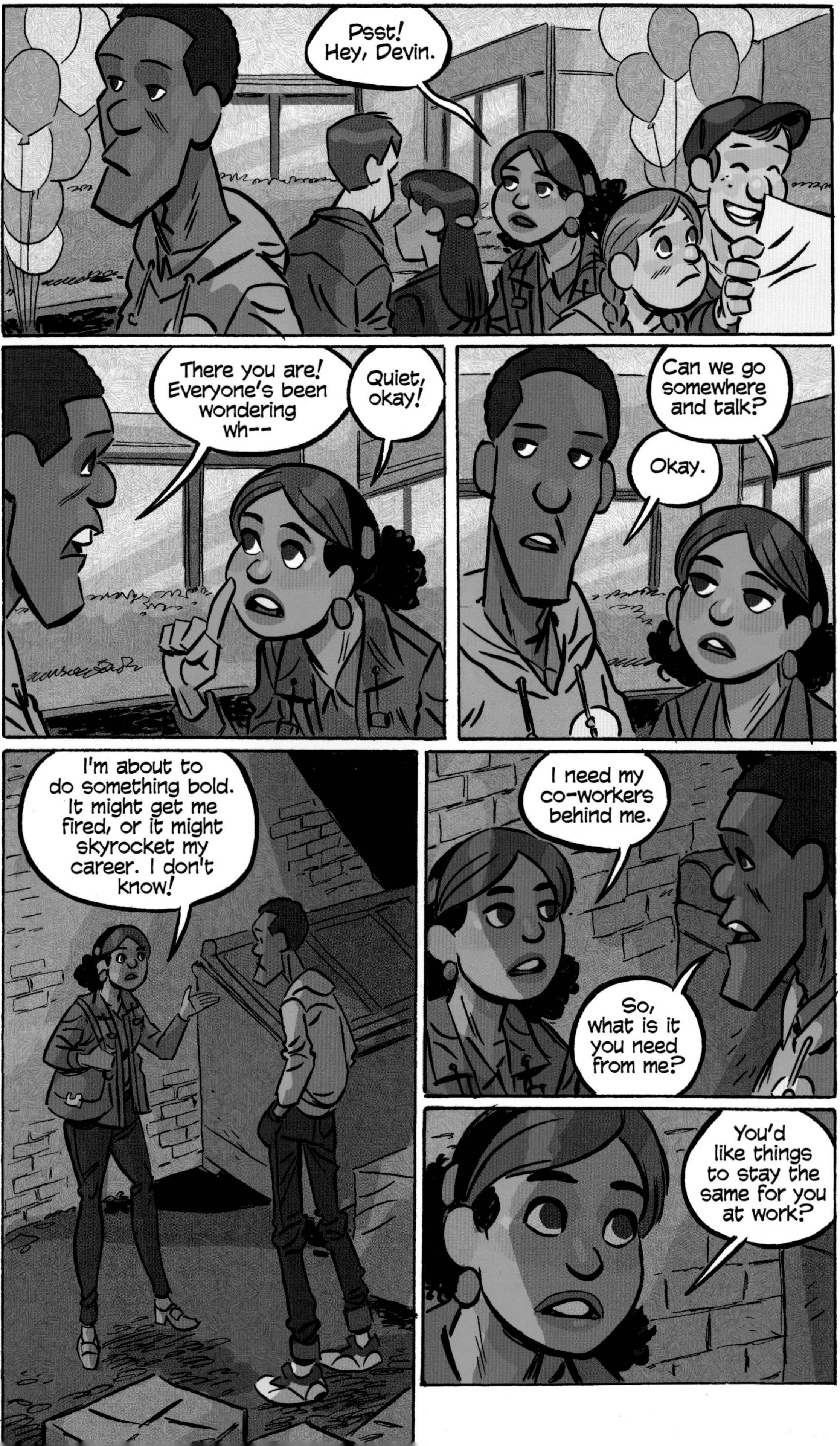
Psst! Hey, Devin.
There you are! Everyone's been wondering wh--
Quiet, okay!
Can we go somewhere and talk?
Okay.
I'm about to do something bold. It might get me fired, or it might skyrocket my career. I don't know!
I need my co-workers behind me.
So, what is it you need from me?
You'd like things to stay the same for you at work?

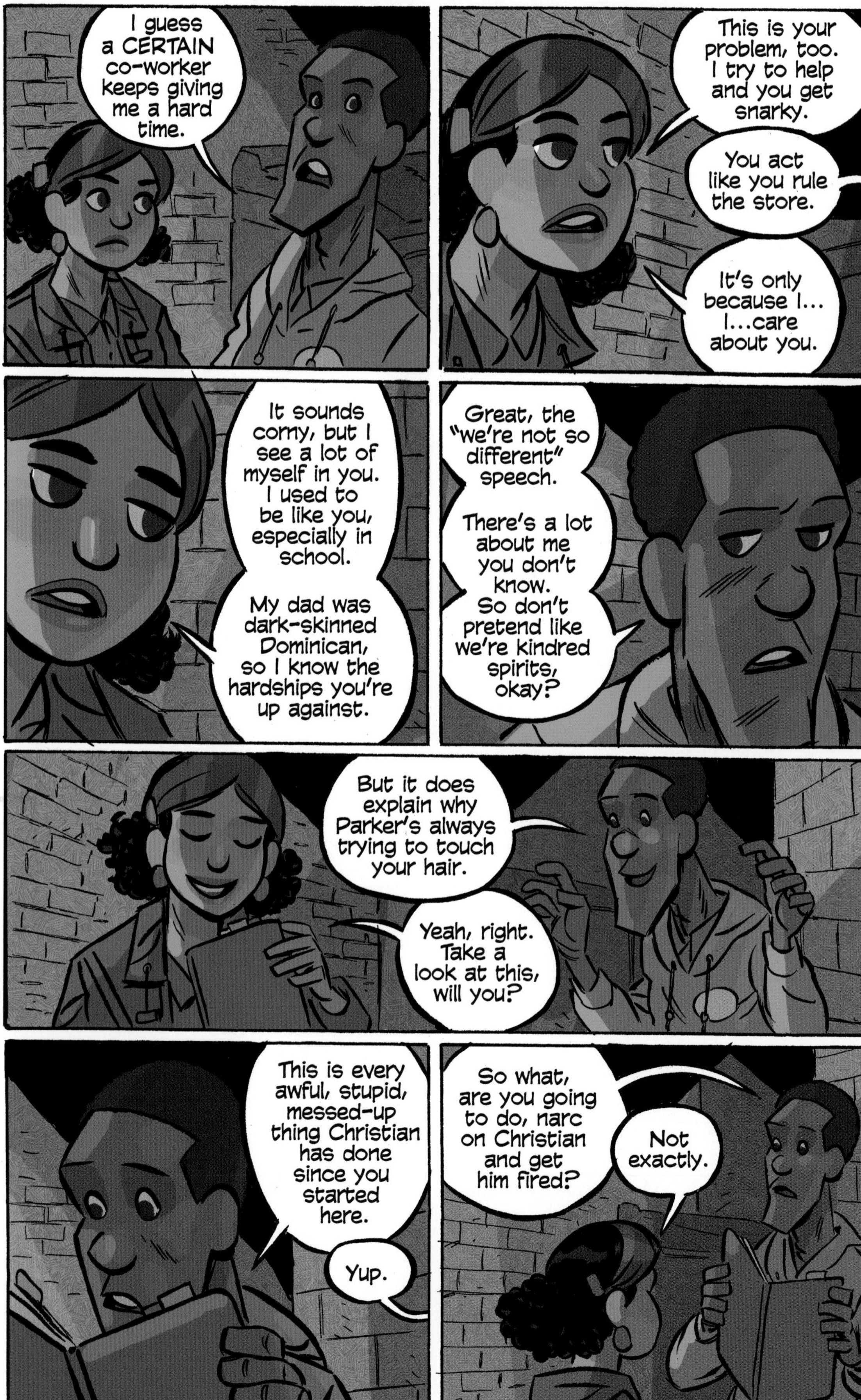
I guess a CERTAIN co-worker keeps giving me a hard time.
This is your problem, too. I try to help and you get snarky.
You act like you rule the store.
It's only because I... I...care about you.
It sounds corny, but I see a lot of myself in you. I used to be like you, especially in school.
My dad was dark-skinned Dominican, so I know the hardships you're up against.
Great, the "we're not so different" speech.
There's a lot about me you don't know. So don't pretend like we're kindred spirits, okay?
But it does explain why Parker's always trying to touch your hair.
Yeah, right. Take a look at this, will you?
This is every awful, stupid, messed-up thing Christian has done since you started here.
Yup.
So what, are you going to do, narc on Christian and get him fired?
Not exactly.

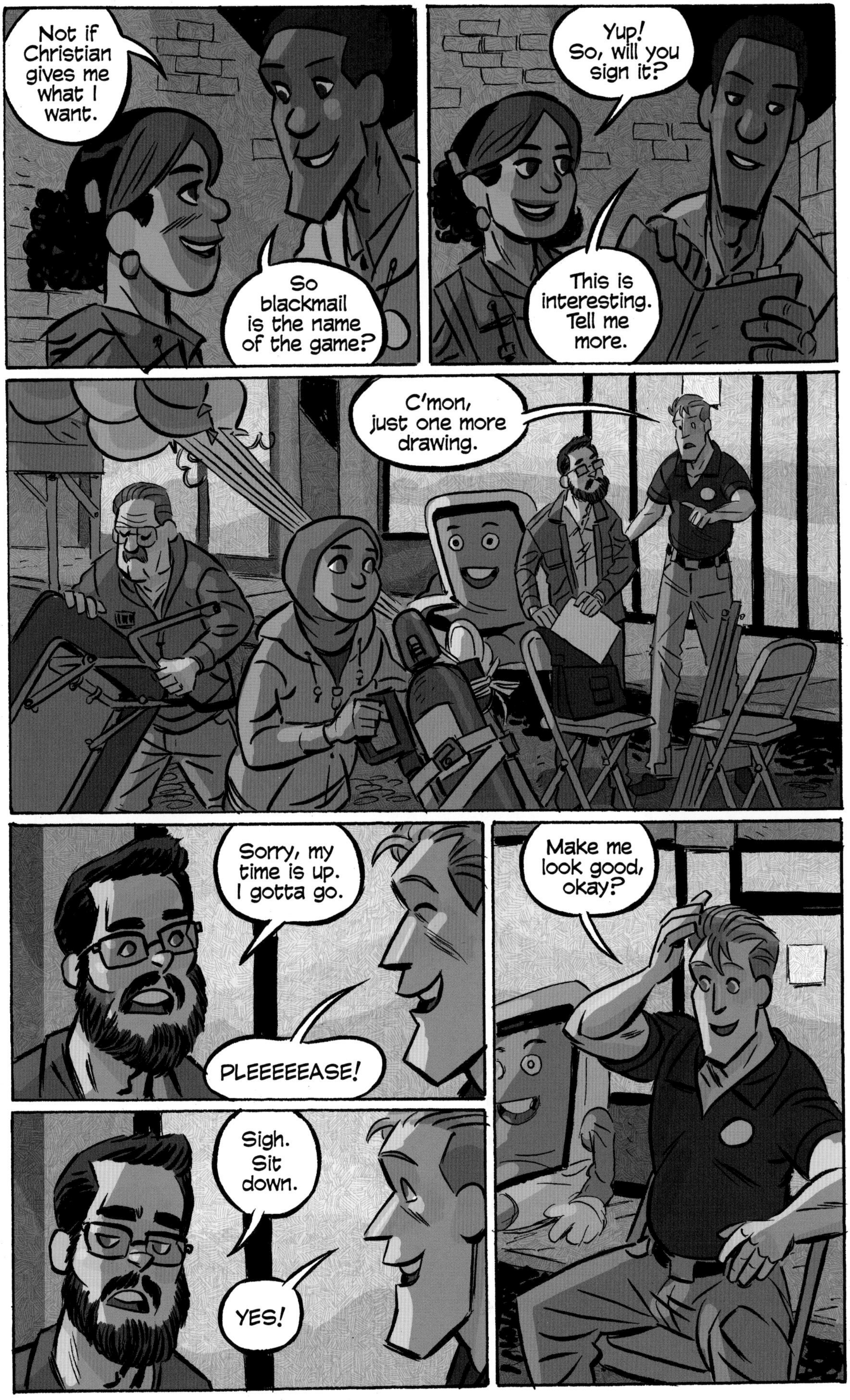
Not if Christian gives me what I want.
So blackmail is the name of the game?
Yup! So, will you sign it?
This is interesting. Tell me more.
C'mon, just one more drawing.
Sorry, my time is up. I gotta go.
PLEEEEEASE!
Sigh. Sit down.
YES!
Make me look good, okay?

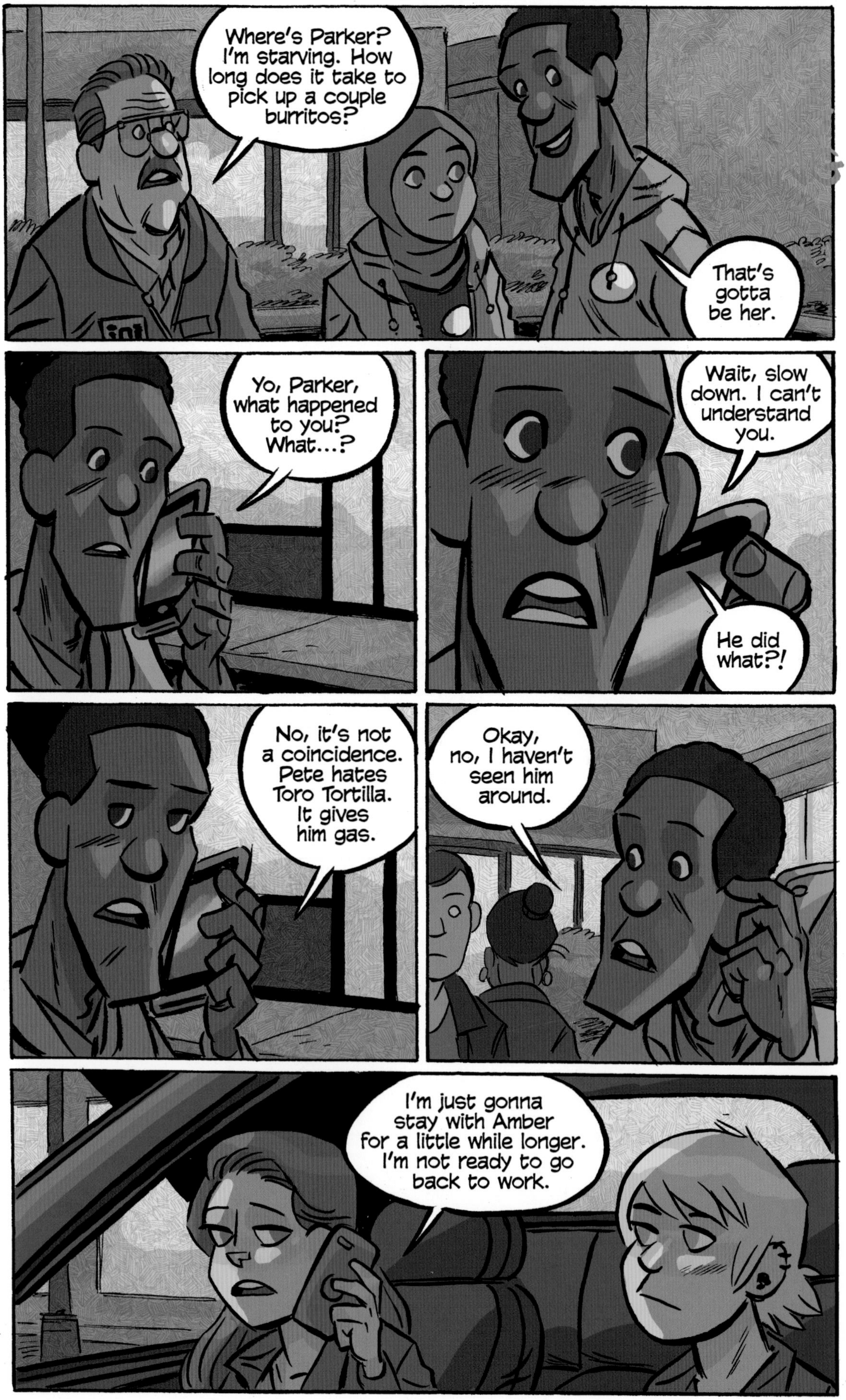
Where's Parker? I'm starving. How long does it take to pick up a couple burritos?
That's gotta be her.
Yo, Parker, what happened to you? What...?
Wait, slow down. I can't understand you.
He did what?!
No, it's not a coincidence. Pete hates Toro Tortilla. It gives him gas.
Okay, no, I haven't seen him around.
I'm just gonna stay with Amber for a little while longer. I'm not ready to go back to work.

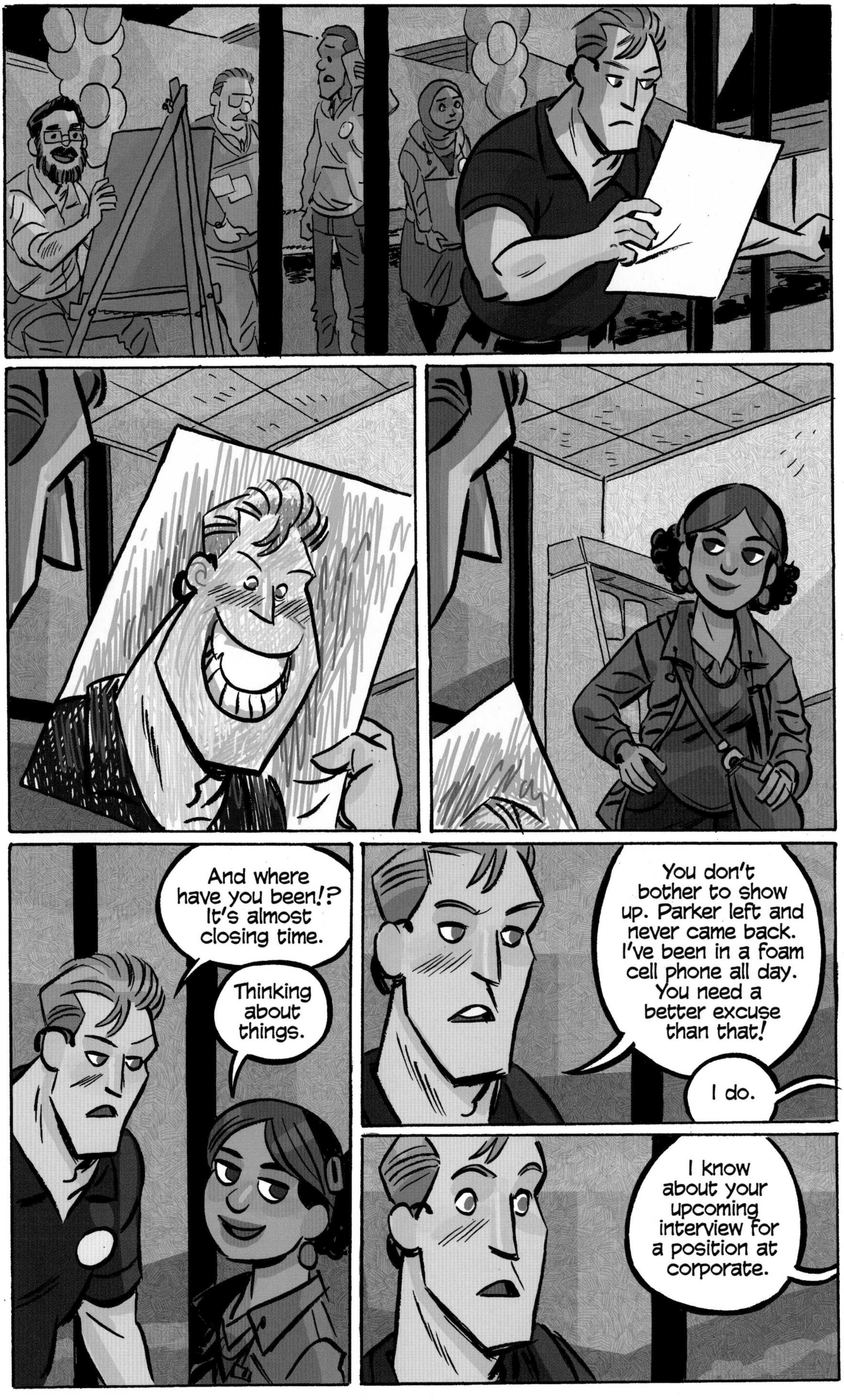
And where have you been!? It's almost closing time.
Thinking about things.
You don't bother to show up. Parker left and never came back. I've been in a foam cell phone all day. You need a better excuse than that!
I do.
I know about your upcoming interview for a position at corporate.

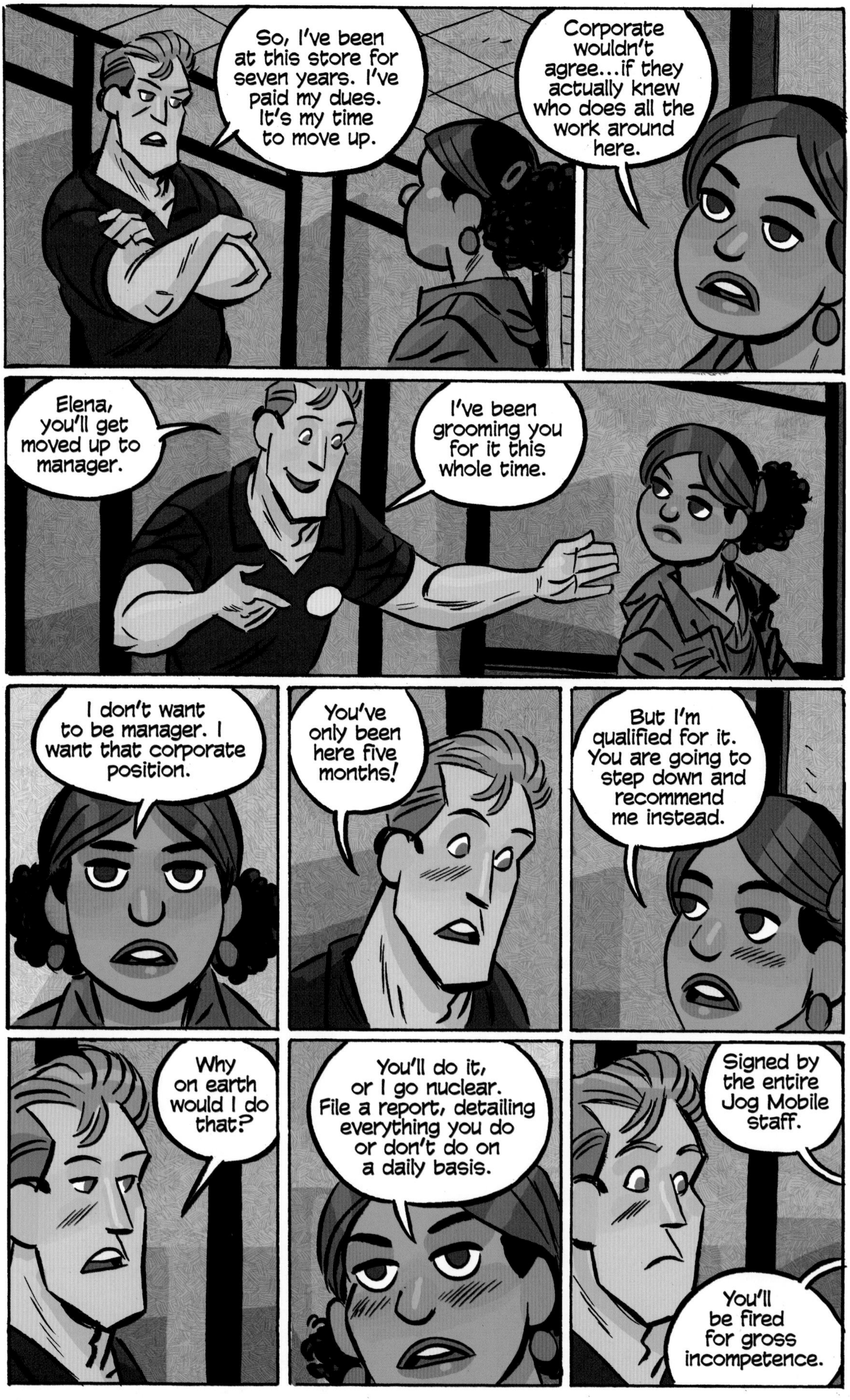
So, I've been at this store for seven years. I've paid my dues. It's my time to move up.
Corporate wouldn't agree...if they actually knew who does all the work around here.
Elena, you'll get moved up to manager.
I've been grooming you for it this whole time.
I don't want to be manager. I want that corporate position.
You've only been here five months!
But I'm qualified for it. You are going to step down and recommend me instead.
Why on earth would I do that?
You'll do it, or I go nuclear. File a report, detailing everything you do or don't do on a daily basis.
Signed by the entire Jog Mobile staff.
You'll be fired for gross incompetence.

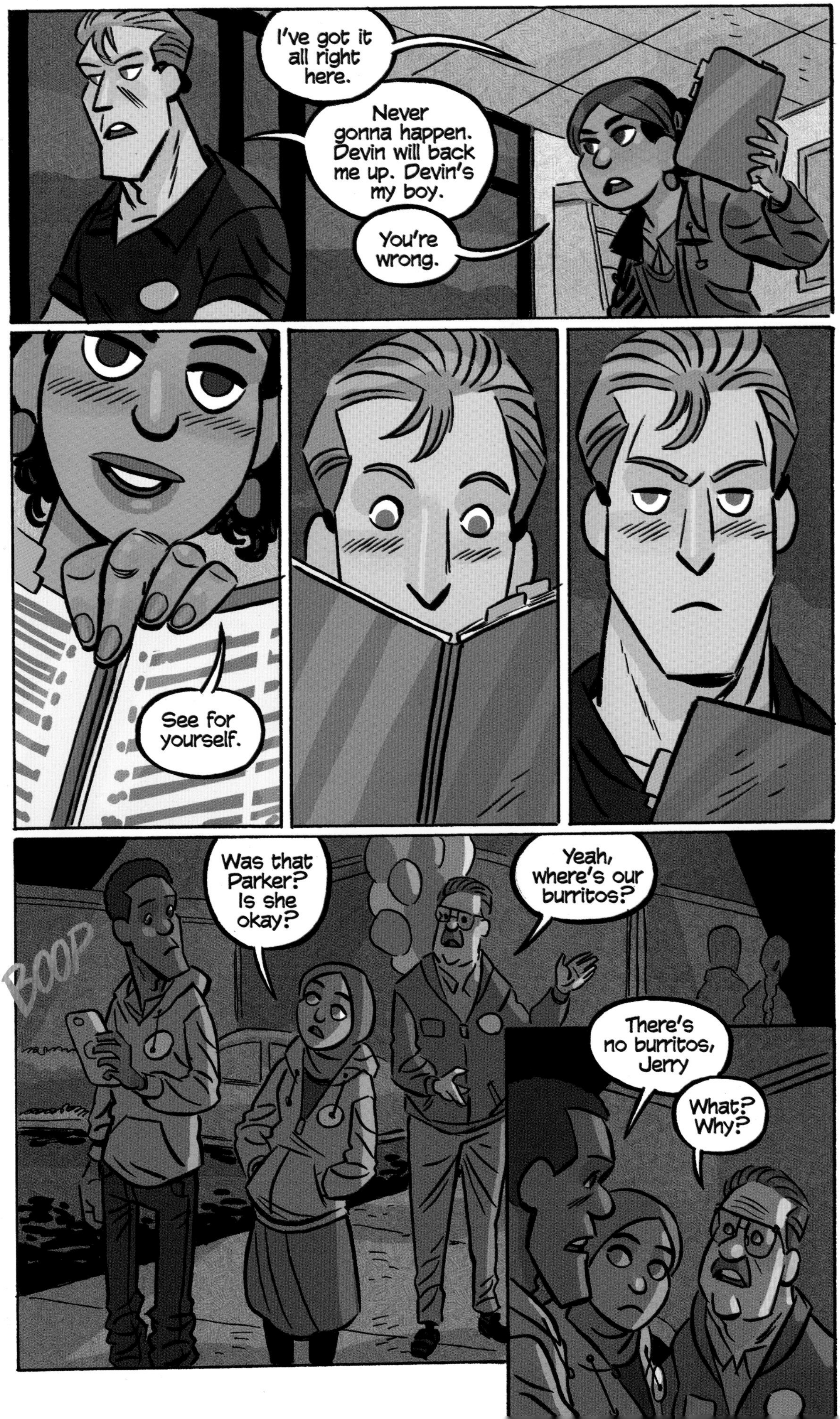
I've got it all right here.
Never gonna happen. Devin will back me up. Devin's my boy.
You're wrong.
See for yourself.
BOOP
Was that Parker? Is she okay?
Yeah, where's our burritos?
There's no burritos, Jerry
What? Why?

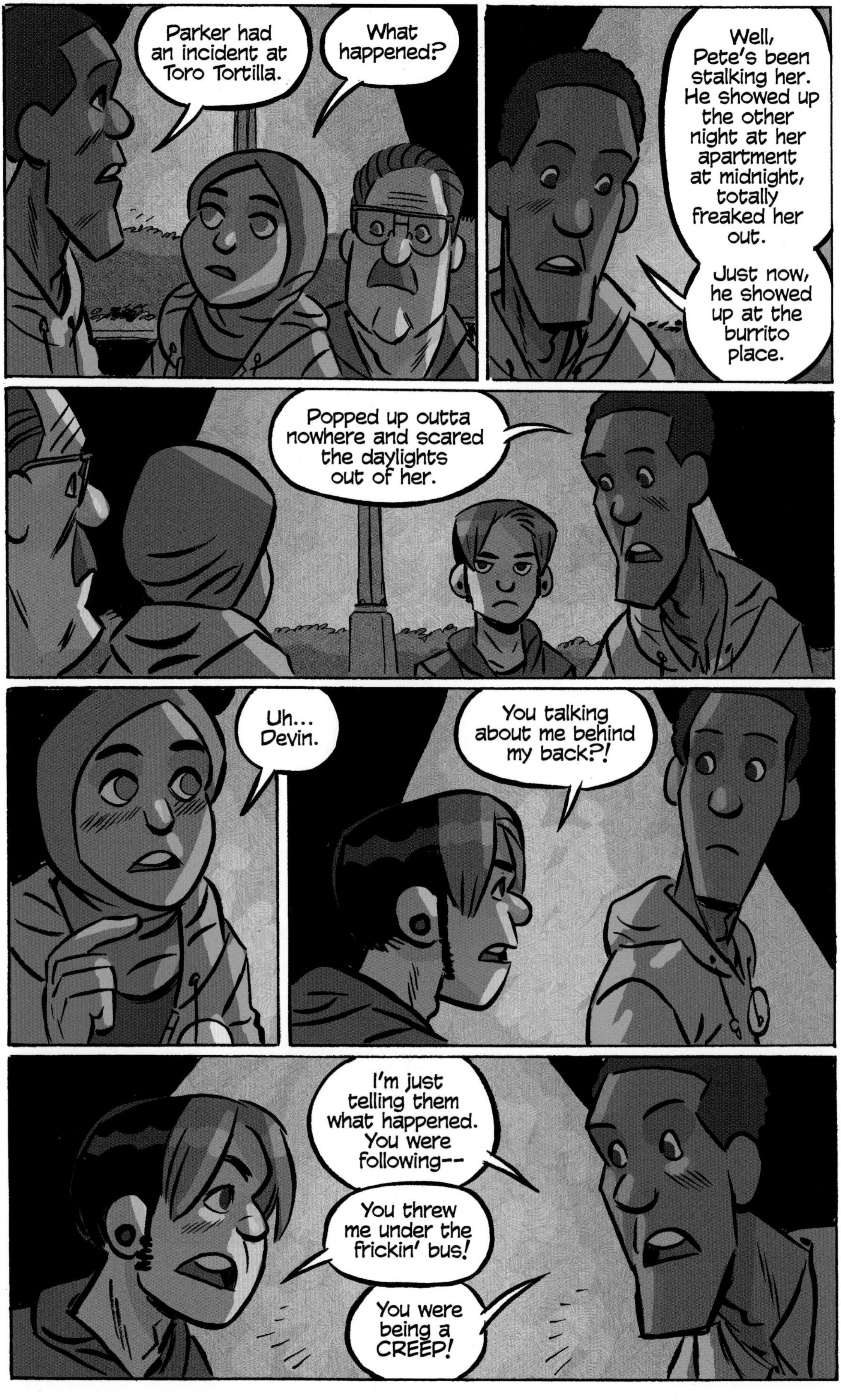
Parker had an incident at Toro Tortilla.
What happened?
Well, Pete's been stalking her. He showed up the other night at her apartment at midnight, totally freaked her out.
Just now, he showed up at the burrito place.
Popped up outta nowhere and scared the daylights out of her.
Uh... Devin.
You talking about me behind my back?!
I'm just telling them what happened. You were following--
You threw me under the frickin' bus!
You were being a CREEP!

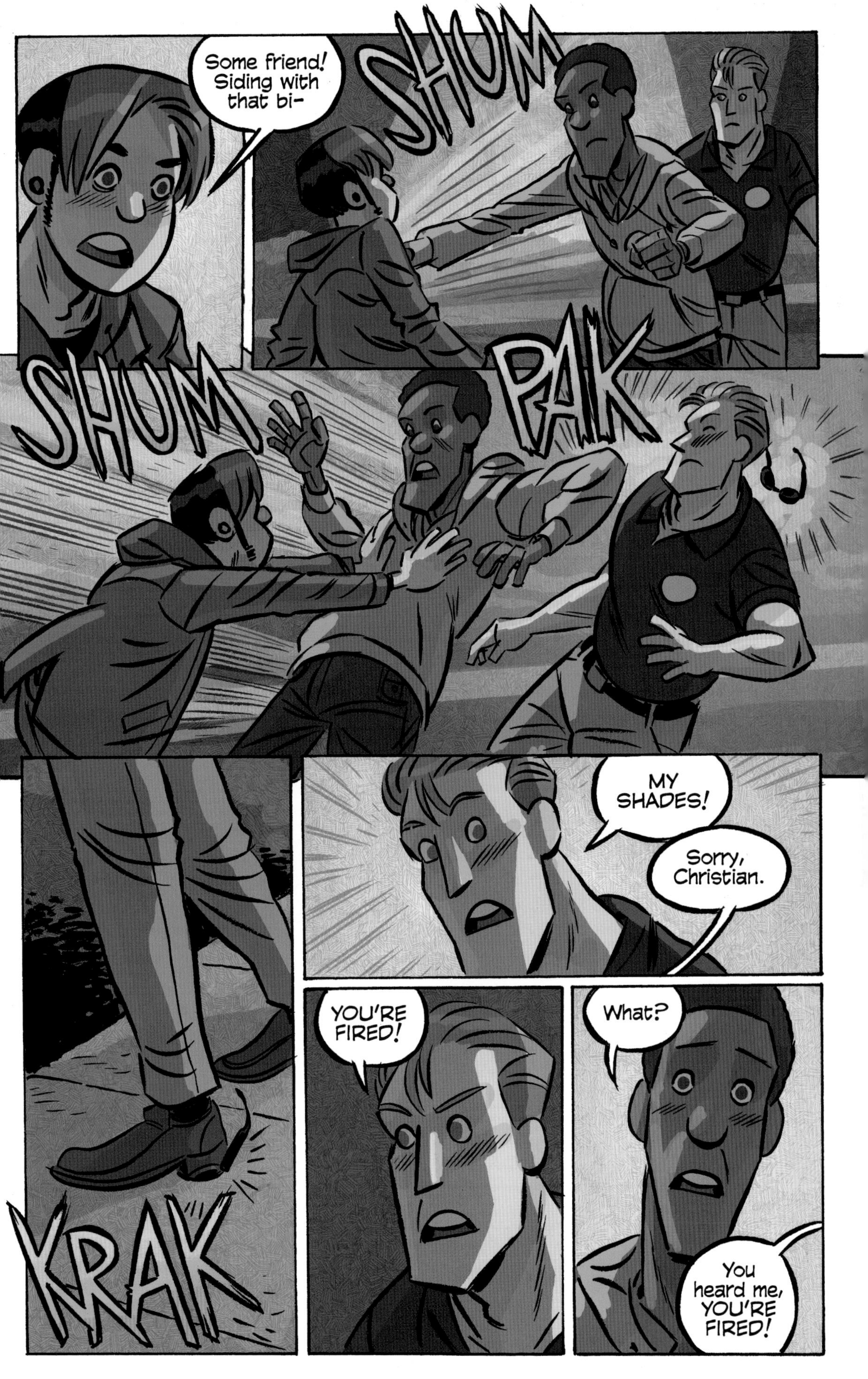
Some friend! Siding with that bi-
SHUM
SHUM
PAK
MY SHADES!
Sorry, Christian.
KRAK
YOU'RE FIRED!
What?
You heard me, YOU'RE FIRED!

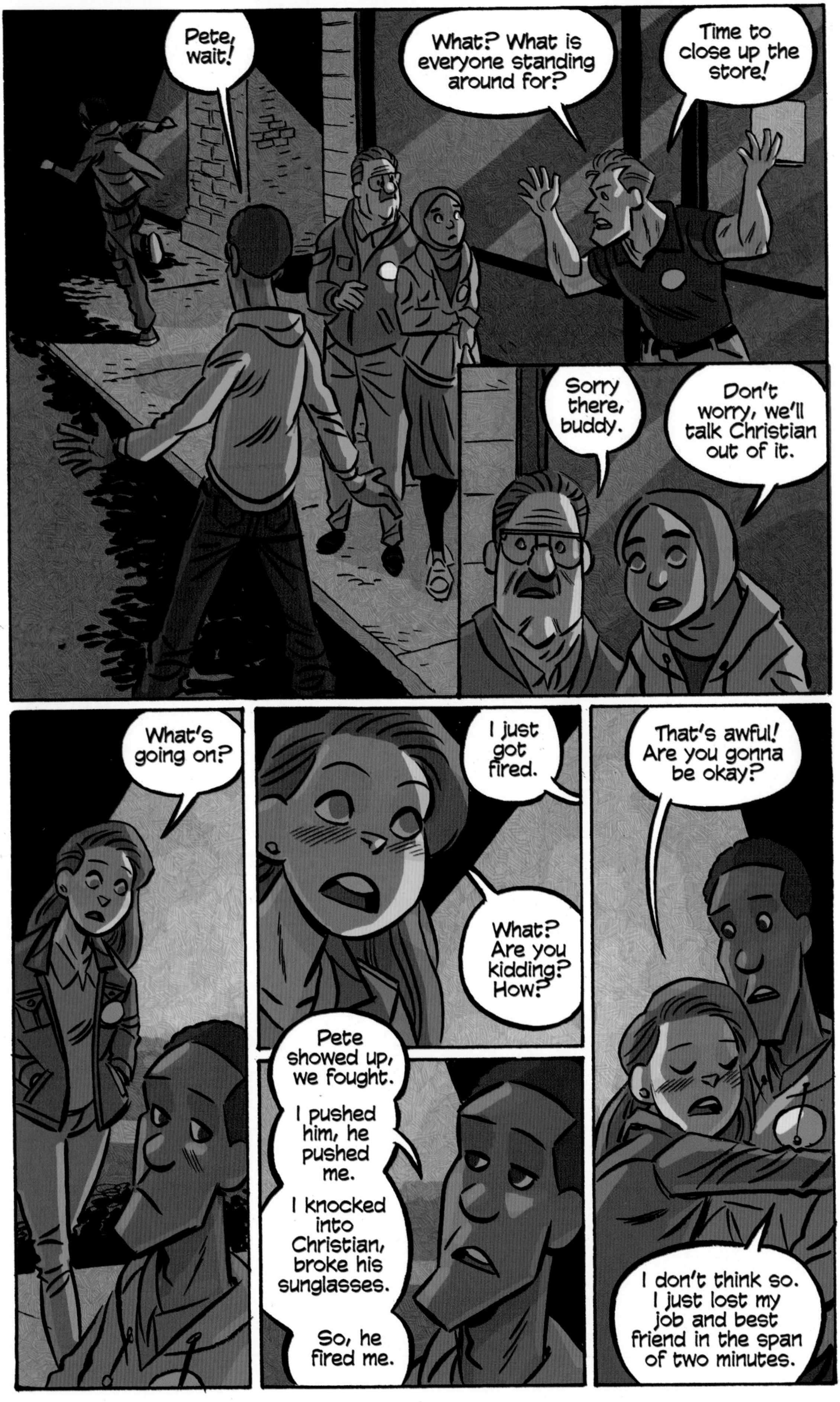
Pete, wait!
What? What is everyone standing around for?
Time to close up the store!
Sorry there, buddy.
Don't worry, we'll talk Christian out of it.
What's going on?
I just got fired.
What? Are you kidding? How?
Pete showed up, we fought.
I pushed him, he pushed me.
I knocked into Christian, broke his sunglasses.
So, he fired me.
That's awful! Are you gonna be okay?
I don't think so. I just lost my job and best friend in the span of two minutes.